I0742026

HUMMINGBIRD

Michael Tuggle

Book design by Tina Tackett

www.michaeltuggle.com

ISBN: 979-8-9994609-3-6 (paperback)

ISBN: 979-8-9994609-1-2 (ebook)

Published in the United States.

To Jackie Pope

The first who believed.

AUTHOR'S NOTE

In the last two years writing this book, a number of people I've shared my progress with have asked me, "Why human trafficking?"

It started on a Sunday morning about six years ago. I was sitting in church and instead of a sermon, we watched a 30-minute video about International Justice Mission (IJM) and their efforts to combat human trafficking around the world. I remember our congregation of 1,000 sitting stunned and silent. The content was compelling and heartbreaking. It was something I just couldn't shake.

Around the same time, one of my childhood friends named Susan Coppedge was appointed by President Obama to be the country's first Ambassador-at-Large for the Office to Monitor and Combat Trafficking in Persons. At the time, I was writing a completely different book, but the backdrop of human trafficking kept popping up and nagging at me until I couldn't ignore it any longer.

I started noticing news story after news story about human trafficking both here at home and around the world. I researched this world of modern day slavery and discovered it was far worse than I had ever imagined. I had lunch with Susan, and she confirmed that was true.

One morning about three years ago, I woke up with Jake Hardy and his sister Catherine in my head and in that moment, I felt compelled to tell their story.

You will read some harrowing scenes in *Hummingbird,* and you may read some things that make you uncomfortable. You're not alone. They make me uncomfortable. But that's because they really do happen. While *Hummingbird* and the characters in it are complete fiction, the situations it portrays are very real.

It's my hope that *Hummingbird* helps heighten an awareness about human trafficking and that by reading it, more people will be moved to support the incredible nonprofits fighting to protect the vulnerable. If even one person is so moved, this book will have served its purpose.

-MT

"The power of the Lord was upon me, and I was carried away by the Spirit of the Lord to a valley full of old, dry bones that were scattered everywhere across the ground. He led me around among them, and then he said to me:

'Son of dust, can these bones become people again?'

I replied, 'Lord, you alone know the answer to that.'

Then he told me to speak to the bones and say: 'O dry bones, listen to the words of God, for the Lord God says, 'See! I am going to make you live and breathe again! I will replace the flesh and muscles on you and cover you with skin. I will put breath into you, and you shall live and know I am the Lord.'

So, I spoke these words from God, just as he told me to; and suddenly there was a rattling noise from all across the valley, and the bones of each body came together and attached to each other as they used to be. Then, as I watched, the muscles and flesh formed over the bones, and skin covered them, but the bodies had no breath. Then he told me to call to the wind and say. 'The Lord God says: Come from the four winds, O Spirit, and breathe upon these slain bodies, that they may live again.' So, I spoke to the winds as he commanded me, and the bodies began breathing; they lived and stood up—a great army."

Ezekiel 37:1-10

PROLOGUE

I am consumed by the darkness.

For hours, I have been standing at the ocean's edge, staring out at the indigo swells of the Pacific while quiet waves break over my feet. A bank of nighttime clouds has all but blocked the moon with only the silhouette of a wayward seabird betraying the light spilling through. From where I'm standing, the deep water looks docile. I know there's a tempest raging in the places I cannot see. But somehow, that's where I am most compelled to go.

Walking down the beach, I can't see the discarded shells and seaweed in my path, but I feel them under my feet. As the sun begins to rise, I see a small cove framed by jagged faces of black rock. I slip into the ocean where the water is shallow, take one look out to sea and swim into the unknown. The frothy saltwater feels cold on my face, the swollen waves crashing over my head, trying to tug me back toward the shore.

I move through the water unafraid, even though I know I am an unwelcome guest here. I roll onto my back and watch the stars disappear one by one as the morning light bristles over the horizon. The sun rises into the sky sending pillars of light streaking down toward the ocean, piercing the surface of the water, illuminating what lies beneath. I push my way upright and bob with the current. I can no longer see the shoreline.

Breathing deep, I dive into the darkness below me. The water is 20 to 30 feet deep and halfway down I can see dappled sunlight bouncing off the waving leaves of a kelp forest spreading in all directions. I drift through a school of Painted Greenlings and bright orange Garibaldis that don't seem to notice me while bigger fish and broad winged rays glide beneath them through diminishing columns of light.

Descending into deeper, colder water, I am suddenly conscious of two things – the saltwater isn't burning my eyes, and my lungs aren't aching with a constant need for air. I am exhaling with no apparent need to replenish my oxygen. I feel at one with my surroundings, and yet, I'm acutely aware I am a stranger here.

Swimming past broadleaf tangles of kelp, the waving fronds graze my skin. With every stroke and every turn, thin, green blades reach out and caress my arms, my neck, my legs as I swim by. The sunlight penetrating the darkness is brighter now, and the kelp beds around me flutter in a translucent canvas of dark and light greens, yellows and golds. Gently, the current pushes them back and forth, back and forth, beckoning me to swim a little closer.

The leaves are smooth to the touch, a little rough around the edges. It is quiet and tranquil this far below the surface. Spreading my fingers, I sweep my right hand into a nest of kelp sending small fish darting in every direction. I look past my hand, down the colossal stalk to the ocean floor and wonder just how many of these enormous, resilient plants there are in the oceans of the world.

I move to pull my fingers through the kelp, but the leaves hold my hand tightly as though afraid to let go. The grip of the leaves feels stronger now, almost like it's grasping my hand, and I suddenly realize it's not kelp, but a woman's hand that's gripping mine. I glance from her hand, up her arm and over her shoulder. The kelp plant swaying beside me has opened up, unveiling a 20-something woman whose fingers are entangled with mine. She floats, naked, in suspended animation, her ankle shackled to a chain anchored to the seabed below.

As stronger light pours into the depths, I notice another woman, younger and Hispanic, floating to my left, also bound to a rust speckled chain disappearing below her. I reach out and gently touch her face, stroke her arm, and curl my fingers around hers, looking for a response but there isn't one.

I feel a squeeze in my other hand and looking back, the woman on my right, has now opened her eyes. They are dark brown and filled with fear. I follow her gaze to the endless forests of kelp stretching in every direction. A strong undercurrent hits me from the back and as it moves away from me, the kelp leaves fall away revealing hundreds, thousands of women of every age, every size, every shade of human pigmentation hiding in plain sight among them, each one shackled to a darkness so deep, its origin cannot be seen.

A menacing battery of barracudas silently knifes through the water below me and splinters in every direction. I now understand the fear in the eyes of the young woman holding my hand. With every whoosh beside us, every shift in the current, her eyes blink hard and anxiously dart side to side. Her body begins to shake, flooded with anxiety.

One by one, I watch each shackled woman open her eyes and immediately register the threats swimming around them. At first, the barracudas simply glide past, nudging each body as they swim closer, homing in on their targets. But then out of the darkness, another battery appears from our left with a third closing fast from behind.

I look from one panicked face to another and suddenly I am consumed by a feeling of profound guilt and permeating clarity of why I am here. Catherine is here, lost, abandoned and shackled to the darkness. I can feel her.

Yanking my hands free, I swim away. Panic washes over me as I breaststroke from one terrified face to another. Brown eyes. Green eyes. Gray eyes. Where is she?

The barracudas are now swimming in force, their torpedo shaped heads darting through the water with razor sharp teeth bared. I don't see the first strike, but I hear the muted scream of its recipient echo past me as I swim from woman to woman, face to face.

Another scream comes from a woman to my right. I turn and see her reaching for the gash on her hip, her eyes wide with pain. They are hazel. Where is Catherine?

With increasing speed, the emboldened fish take bite after bite targeting toes, breasts, backs, stomachs, and arms. One muffled scream gives way to a hundred more and as the underwater din expands, so too does the amount of blood in the water. That's when the sharks come, and the frenzy begins.

I pull and kick furiously, trying to swim away from the sanguine water as the barracudas swarm, stripping a body behind me. I seem to be of no concern to them, but I know I am running out of time. The sound, the fury, the blood will attract other predators who will keep eating until each body is just a skeleton on a chain.

Frantically, I scan the eyes of the women I can see. Where is she? I haven't seen Catherine in 20 years, but I will know her when I see her. All I have to do is look into her eyes.

In every direction, crimson blooms explode like fireworks as the barracudas and sharks attack one body after another. I swim toward the only clear water I see and thirty yards in front of me, I see her. I see her eyes. Ice blue. Open. Looking for me.

I scream her name and start to swim toward her. She sees me and screams my name, waving her arms with a panicked smile. I pull myself through the water not daring to take my eyes off her. Thirty yards. Twenty yards. Ten. I reach for her hand. The tips of our fingers touch and curl into each other. I found her.

Catherine reaches to grab my other hand, but as she does, a shark slams into me, sending me tumbling through the water. I throw out my arms and start kicking to stop my momentum, but my body won't stop. I pull with every ounce of strength I have, but the current pulls me away. I look back to Catherine through a thrashing riot of fins, tails and teeth, bubbles and blood, and I find her beautiful blue eyes. She smiles laying her head to one side with a subtle look of resignation, and in one violent, scarlet explosion, she's gone.

That's when I wake up.

1

It's 2:30 in the morning and even here in this Houston hotel room, the nightmares find me. The women chained to the bottom of the ocean. The wolves and rabbits. The perpetual pursuit of my sister Catherine and my inability to save her. The dark dreams are relentless. And like so many nights before, my failures thunder across my eyes until I give in and wake up. I will find her. But not tonight.

I can feel my heart beating through my fingers and the sheets beneath me are drenched in sweat. I throw my legs over the edge of the bed and reach for the last swallow of bourbon sitting in the glass on the nightstand. I stare at the floor, occasionally glancing up at the abstract art on the wall by the bed. Another city. Another night in another hotel room. Doesn't matter the location. I know how this will go. Catherine's eyes always find me at night. They haunt me. Shattering whatever tenuous hold I have on sleep.

The glow from the downtown buildings towering over my hotel spills through a crack in the curtains lighting a path from the window to the bed. I walk over and look down at the intersection at the crossroads of Highland Village, Houston's high-end shopping district. Even in the middle of the night, there are cars stacked two deep waiting for the light to change. The trees on both sides of the street are wrapped in white lights. It reminds me a bit of Los Angeles where I live but it could just as easily be Atlanta, or Dallas, or New Orleans, Manhattan, Boston, or Seattle.

On any given night, the vast majority of those cars will be people working the night shift. Cleaning offices. Making deliveries. Getting the city ready for the day ahead. But some of them will be driven by people who have no good reason to be where they are. Predators on the hunt. Those weak of mind and spirit who abdicated any kind of personal responsibility or control long ago. Broken men working the edges of humanity looking for a cheap release with no memory. But that's only part of the story.

People want to believe human trafficking is everywhere they're not. A big city problem that only exists in the shadows and the alleys. But that's bullshit and most people know it. The idea that teenage girls are being passed around like a bottle of whiskey is too horrible for most people to get their heads around, so they don't think about it. Human trafficking is like genocide or killing shelters or starving African orphans. Unless a late-night commercial with some haunting soundtrack starts playing, people block that shit out. I can't. I'm too close to it. Besides, it's my job to stop it.

My name is Jake Hardy. Hardy's not my given name. It's the name I chose for myself when I was 16. Long before Afghanistan. Long before I became a deep cover agent in the Department of Homeland Security. I hunt human traffickers and the people they exploit. Women. Girls. Little boys. Most are trafficked for labor. Many are forced into the commercial sex trade. Estimates put the number of people trafficked at more than four million a year worldwide, but it's more than that. Way more. Trust me, the world is full of sick fucking people.

If you know where to look, it's not hard to find the Johns and the girls being forced to satisfy their urges. Sex for money is the world's oldest profession and it goes on in every city, every town, and every suburb in America. The challenge is finding the traffickers who run the show. The men grooming runaways for a career in modeling. The animals who promise Russian teenagers and South American girls good waitressing jobs in America to support their starving families and then traffick them through the blackest circuit of rabbit holes you could imagine.

Human traffickers are the vilest of the vile. They make a fortune coercing, stealing, and selling young bodies over, and over, and over, and over again. Ten, 15 times a day. For years. Thanks to the internet, they've only gotten bolder, richer, and grown in number. Most live in the shadows. The most brazen hide in plain sight. Both are very good at what they do. But so am I.

I riffle through my bag until I find the bottle of sleeping pills hiding under my vest. Only two left. If I take them now, I might have a prayer of catching a few hours of sleep. But that's doubtful. Between the nightmares and the meeting I can't miss in eight hours, I wouldn't count on any kind of rest. I swallow the pills anyway and shove the bottle back into my bag. Two tours in Afghanistan in the Marine Raiders taught me how to function without sleep. It's not ideal. But it's doable.

At 10am, I have an operational meeting at the FBI Field Office at 1 Justice Park. Tomorrow night, there's a joint op going down at the Port of Houston. Two weeks ago, the command here received intel that a freighter arriving from Vietnam and connected to a known trafficker might be carrying more than what is listed on the manifest. Unless they've got somebody on the inside at the Port, it would be pretty brazen to ship girls in an open container knowing there's a mandatory customs search. But it's happened. Tomorrow night, we'll be there to make sure it doesn't happen here.

2

There's no missing the Houston FBI Field Office. Like a lot of government offices, it looks like a cracker box on its side covered with windows. Except in Houston, the outside walls of the FBI Office are green. A kind of withered, wind-whipped sea green with an antique patina. As an architectural design choice, it's heinous. But knowing the green exterior is actually a glass and mesh blast shield holds all cynicism in check. After Oklahoma City, new FBI buildings like this one were constructed with exterior curtain walls for protection from terrorists and Houston chose green. It's ugly, but it's safe.

Inside the front door, thick glass lines every outward facing opening and surveillance cameras are tucked in every corner. There's not a square inch of this building that can't be monitored from the massive command center upstairs. This building is strong and as good as it gets. The word from my colleagues in L.A. suggests the same can be said of the people working here.

"Jake Hardy. I'm here for a meeting at 10 with Jon Joseph," I say showing my credentials to the security officer on duty. The officer looks me in the eye, pauses, then hands me my credential. "Your meeting is on the 5th floor, conference room 521," he says opening the gate for me to walk through. "Special Agent Joseph will be waiting for you. Elevator is over there to the right."

It's been four years since I've seen Jon Joseph. Four years since the night patrols. The burn pits. The shitty food and the culture neither of us understood nor wanted any part of. Jon and I served two tours in Southern Afghanistan together. Marine Raiders charged with recon, raids, and special ops behind enemy lines. Brothers in the middle of a wasteland we were lucky to survive.

Thinking of the eternity we spent waiting for those nights to pass, I question how the years have slipped away from me so fast. But then the elevator door opens, and I'm being squeezed by a bear.

"J and J!" Jon smiles as he wraps his massive paws around me and pulls me close. I return the hug, holding him tight, then slap him on the back.

"How are you Jonny?" I ask, happy to see him after so long.

"I'm good, brother. I'm good. How you doing?" A half smile and a subtle tilt of my head tells him I'm doing as well as I can. "It's good to see you, Jake."

Jon walks me down a long hallway to a large interior conference room.

"You want anything? We've got water, soda, and moderately terrible coffee."

"I'm good," I tell him. "Just happy to see you. Heard you got married a couple years ago. How's that treating you?"

"Better than I deserve. Got a little boy now." Jon reaches for his phone, scrolls to a picture of his son, and holds it up. "He's two."

"Doesn't look anything like you," I say trying not to laugh. "Who's the father?"

"I don't know, but he's a good-looking motherfucker," Jon answers exploding into a barrel-chested laugh.

"He's beautiful, Jon."

"Thanks man," he smiles back. Then suddenly, his face changes from glowing pride to heartfelt concern.

"How are you really? You had any luck finding Catherine?" he asks.

"No," I answer simply. Jon Joseph is one of the only people in the world who knows the whole story about my sister and one look into my eyes tells him all he needs to know about my frustration, rage, and heartache. He also knows me and that I'll never stop looking for her. I start to tell him more, but as I do, Jon quickly stands as four new people enter the room.

"Jake Hardy, meet agents Bill Mitchell, Ray Dexter, and Andrew Melcher," he says as we all shake hands. "And this is…"

"Special Agent in Charge Christina Warren. Tactical command for tomorrow night's mission. Nice to have you with us Agent Hardy," she says with a response that's at once cordial, but all business. "We appreciate Homeland loaning you out to us for a night." Without breaking stride, she walks to the head of the table and opens a laptop. A wall monitor flashes to life with an image of the Port of Houston. Warren lifts her chin and looks me in the eye. "We appreciate your expertise in trafficking and we're happy you're here." I start to respond but she immediately starts into the details of the mission.

"Here's what we know. At 0600 this morning, a Vietnamese freighter called the Indigo Horizon docked at the Container Terminal on the west side of Galveston Bay carrying approximately 9,800 shipping containers. When the ship left port in Hai Phong four weeks ago, we received intel that a number of the containers may be trafficking humans, weapons and potentially other illegal substances into the United States. Of those containers, our informant listed 63 boxes we need to examine closely. Once the containers have been removed from the ship, at 2100 hours tomorrow night, we will lead a tactical team of 12 agents through a thorough tailgate exam of each container in question. That requires opening the back of the box, entering the container, and examining the contents to be sure there is nothing illegal contained within. Should you be precluded from checking the entire box, we will request it be moved to a sanctioned CBP warehouse where it will be checked more completely.

"Be aware, we will be dressed as port authority inspectors and not Federal agents so you can expect pushback from anyone who doesn't want us nosing around their cargo. Should you encounter that, or someone trying to buy you off to look the other way, consider that probable cause."

Missions like these are only as good as the intel they're based on and as much as I want to believe Warren's is solid, years of disappointment tell me it's probably dogshit. Then again, if there wasn't some credibility, I'd still be in Los Angeles.

"Mitchell," Warren barks, opening the folder in front of her to hand out assignments. "You and the Alpha team have 12 containers in the Northern sector of the port. Dexter, 14 containers in the East yard. Melcher, 19 containers in the West. Joseph, you and Hardy take the remaining 18 boxes in the South. Here are the numbers.

"The staging area is a parking lot a mile west of the container yard next to the Municipal Airport. The coordinates are on your map. We will meet at 1900 hours. Any questions?"

"Yeah, one," Dexter pipes up reading my mind. "You mentioned guns, drugs, and girls. How good is the intel on this?"

"Good enough," Warren answers. "I don't have to tell you to have your head on a swivel. Communicate. If you find something, call me. If anything goes south, we'll be there. Everyone good?"

"Yes ma'am," comes the answer. I look at the screen and the layout of the port. The endless maze of containers stacked one on the other. As happy as I am to see Jon, tomorrow promises to be an exercise in futility and another wasted trip.

So why does my gut tell me I'm wrong.

3

By the time the mission team arrives at the staging lot, the last crimson streaks of the sailor's sky over Galveston Bay are surrendering to the dark. The glow from the towers lighting the ship channel hangs on the horizon along with the anxiety about what may be buried in the containers we're cracking into.

Earlier in the afternoon, Warren received confirmation from Treasury that at least three of the containers from the Indigo Horizon were carrying something they shouldn't. Now, we just have to find them.

At 1830 hours, two black SUVs round the hangar on the north end of the Municipal Airport and pull into the empty, open building. Agents Mitchell, Dexter, Melcher, and Joseph exit the first vehicle already dressed in dark pants, navy shirts, neon yellow safety vests and caps sporting a Port logo above the brim. SAC Warren steps out of the second SUV and crosses the polished concrete floor to speak with the director of the Terminal who is standing in the corner waiting for her.

"Hey Joseph, where's your boy?" Mitchell asks looking around.

"He'll be here," Jon answers.

"Seems like a pretty angry guy," Dexter says searching for a little more detail from Joseph.

"Jake was a combat vest full of rage the day I met him," Joseph says looking toward the door. Jon wouldn't say it outside the family, but he understands why I am the way I am. Two tours in the Raiders made me tough. A childhood of beatings from my father made me hard.

"Jake's fighting some demons but trust me, when the shit goes down, there's nobody you'd rather have beside you."

"Bet you guys saw some gnarly shit in Afghanistan," Melcher says checking the mag in his pistol.

"Enough" Joseph answers and from the looks on the other men's faces, it's all that needs to be said. They never served. But they understand.

At 1850, I pull the black SUV I'm driving across the tarmac and turn toward the metal barn where we're gathering. The early reflection of the moon runs up the length of the tinted windshield as I pull in and find Jon talking to the small cluster of agents.

"You get lost?" Jon asks me, smiling.

"Just spending some time with the seagulls," I answer. After another mostly sleepless night, I spent most of the afternoon sitting next to the bay. Looking out at the water. Breathing the sea air. Trying for even a few minutes to relax and get out of my head. Back in L.A. I live two blocks from the beach for the same reason. I can't explain why but being near the water brings clarity and momentary peace that nothing else does.

"We ready to roll?" I ask, fastening the yellow safety across my chest.

"Just about," Mitchell answers. "Warren is briefing the Port Director."

Looking through the hangar door, I wonder what the night will bring. My prayers are that it brings nothing. But there's an anxious energy in the air saying I'm wrong. At least let it be guns, or drugs. As exhilarating as it is to rescue women and girls being trafficked, if they were really loaded into a shipping container that just spent 30 days at sea, the odds of them arriving alive are small. That's how little traffickers give a shit about the lives they traffic. It's all a fucking numbers game to them. If they don't make it, oh well. There are more girls where those came from. It's easy to be that callous when you're not the one finding the bloated, decomposing bodies.

"Here we go," Warren calls out, walking back toward the group. "None of the other port employees know about tonight so if anyone asks, you're new help. So many people come and go through the yard, no one should even notice you. The port director deleted our 63 boxes from the other inspection lists so you shouldn't run into any other inspectors. You all have a list of your containers. I'll set up post in the port's central office and will check in with you throughout the night. You find anything, I expect to be your first call. And if something escalates, don't be a hero. First priority is getting everyone home. Any questions?" Silence. "Good. Let's roll."

We pile into a blue sedan and a white crossover SUV for the 10-minute ride over to the yard. If we're trying to look like Houston's most boring carpool, we nailed it. Turning north up the 146-access road, the Terminal comes into view. It's not the biggest shipping yard I've ever seen, but it's big enough. A heavy-set guy with a clipboard clears us through the Pre-Check station and points us toward the front gate of the yard. A six-foot black woman greets us with a build and demeanor that screams, "nobody fucks with me, and you shouldn't either."

"Welcome to the Terminal. How can I help you?" she asks looking down at Mitchell who's driving the sedan.

"We're here for some inspections," he answers. "Us and the car behind us."

"Yeah? Don't recognize you boys. Let me see your badges."

Gathering the lanyards from Dexter and Melcher, Mitchell hands over the badges, wondering if we're already going to have an issue.

"Hang on a minute," the woman says suspiciously, glaring at Bill and then walking away from the window and into the central security hub. She picks up a tablet and scans the codes on each of the badges. A minute later, she strides back to the car with the name badges dangling from her fist. "Welcome to the Port," she says, a bit disappointed we hadn't added some excitement to her evening. Walking back to our SUV, she repeats the process with us. She punches a code into the tablet, and the massive metal gate slides open giving us entry to the yard. We pull into the parking area and double check our gear. Warren is already there and buzzing in our ears.

"Just doing a quick Comms check. Hardy?"

"I can hear you."

"Joseph?"

"Got you."

"Melcher?"

"Check."

"Mitchell?"

"Check."

"Dexter, you hear me?"

"Roger that chief."

"Good. Be safe. I'll check in at 2300 but call if anything pops before then."

The corrugated boxes painted in rust and yellow and blue and green rise in mountains of metal in every direction. Each one has the shipping company's logo stamped on the side and identification numbers on the ends and even though we have a general direction for the boxes we're checking, it's still slow going trying to find 18 containers among the thousands stacked three and four high. The Port is one of the largest ports in the country and walking through the tonnage, you realize what an incredible operation it is moving, checking, processing, and releasing every container before whatever's inside starts to rot.

We find the first four containers fairly quickly and they're clean. Boxes of cell phones. Sugar. Solar panels and soybeans. There's minimal activity in the yard around us but a distant sound of metal-on-metal floats by on the heavy sea air catching my ear.

"Jon," I call to my left, tilting my head in the direction of the clanking. "Listen." Quietly, we move toward the bay, the sound getting louder and louder the closer we get. A 777 heading to Bush Intercontinental Airport flies over drowning out the banging but giving us the cover to hurry closer. We rush past three rust and red colored boxes and stop with our backs to a newer looking blue container with the logo of a bird on the side to reacclimate. When the jet clears, we can not only hear the banging, we can feel it through the walls behind us. Jon gives me a nod and we move.

"Can we help you with something," Jon asks, startling the two lanky Asian men trying to knock the container lock loose with an industrial sized pipe wrench. "Not sure that's how you open a lock like that."

Nervously, the two start babbling in Vietnamese which neither of us understand. In tandem, we grab the two men by the shoulders and spin them toward the metal wall with their arms up. That does nothing to stop their anxious muttering, but it gives us a chance to check them for weapons. Jon reaches around and takes a pistol out of the front waistband of the man in front of him. I find a large knife in a sheath on the hip of the guy in front of me. I look at Jon and immediately, we are both on edge. After years of combat, we know chaos and confusion are one thing. Chaos and confusion mixed with armed men is something else entirely. We make short order zip-tying their hands.

"Who are you?" Jon asks loudly spinning his guy around and shoving him hard against the wall. "What do you want with this container?" Wide-eyed, the man looks toward the water and then back at Jon panicked, trying to find some explanation.

"Do you speak English?" Jon barks. The man hesitates and Jon slams him against the wall again. "Do you… speak… English?" Jon asks intently, this time leaning into the man's face.

I look into the eyes of the man I'm holding, and he too looks anxiously from me toward the water, and back to me. He cowers against the wall like a whipped dog and again looks out into the bay.

"Sit down!" Jon yells, pushing his man to the ground.

"I don't like the way they both keep looking toward the water," I say to Jon. "Hold them for a second. I want to make sure we don't have company we can't see."

Pulling my gun, I step away and creep toward the heavy concrete wall separating the container terminal from the edge of Galveston Bay. I look back to Jonny and drop to a knee, carefully peering over the bulkhead into the water. In the darkness directly below me, a 50-foot cabin cruiser sits hiding in the shadows. Two men stand at the helm talking while another stands on the bow smoking a cigarette, looking up toward the yard. It's him who sees me.

I raise my badge and before I can yell, "FBI," he pulls the machine gun he's holding to his shoulder and starts a spray of gunfire. Thanks to the angle, nothing comes close to hitting me but as I hit the asphalt, shells bounce off the container behind me and rain down in a shower of metal. The next thing I hear is the boat peeling away from the wall and accelerating into the Gulf. In the darkness, I can't make out any names or numbers on the boat, but I sure as Hell know who I'm going to question about it.

Turning back, I see Jon has pulled the first guy from the ground and now has his forearm against the man's chest. "Talk motherfucker!" he screams. "Now!" The guy looks like he's about to hyperventilate but doesn't say a word. Jon moves his forearm to the guy's throat and presses him until his eyes roll back in his head and he drops unconscious. "Fine," Joseph grunts picking up the smaller man pissing himself on the ground. "Your turn."

While Jonny tries to get anything out of the guy, I search the perimeter of some nearby containers and find a pair of bolt cutters in a box with emergency flares, safety vests, and protective goggles. My heart is beating like a fucking jackhammer. Nobody has an armed crew waiting to transport a load of batteries off the books. Whatever is inside this container isn't supposed to be seen by the United States government.

Squeezing hard, I snap the lock and open the doors. Immediately, the sickly-sweet smell of rot rolls out of the container. Front to back, wall to wall, sit stacked pallets of oranges, dragon fruit, and mangoes. Multiple pieces of the fruit sit crushed and open on the floor, certain casualties from when they were loaded. I rip open box after box. Each one contains exactly what it says on the side. I move to the back of the container and find more of the same.

"What you got?" Jon yells.

"Nothing," I yell back. "Just a bunch of fruit. I don't get it."

Pulling out my flashlight, I move the beam across the ceiling, down the walls, across the back. There's nobody hiding. There's no way even the smallest kid could fit inside one these fruit boxes. We're being played. I don't know how, but something isn't right. I storm out of the container and walk to the back of the box looking for other activity. Other people who aren't supposed to be here. In the distance about half a click away, I can see flashing lights heading in my direction. Somebody heard the bullets and called the cavalry.

I run my hand over the back of the hulking blue box, looking for something out of the ordinary but nothing looks out of place. Nothing. Except the round end of a four-inch pipe sticking an inch out of the top right quadrant of the wall.

I look at the backs of the other containers stacked around me. Only the one in front of me has a pipe coming out the back. The big blue box with the white hummingbird on the back. I grab the pipe and peer into the end but there's only darkness. I put my right ear to the pipe and cover my left. There's nothing. I step back and look again. What am I missing? The box does look brand new. Maybe it's just a different design. I start back to the front and stop. Walking back to the wall, I put my nose into the end of the pipe expecting at least the faint smell of oranges. Instead, I breathe in the dank, putrid smell of urine, sweat, and death.

"Where are they?" I yell, grabbing the man from Jon's grasp and running him back into the shipping container, slamming him into the rear metal wall bloodying his forehead. "Where!" I scream. He looks up and smiles at me. I grab my 9mm and push it into his chest. "Don't move or you will not see tomorrow."

I reach for the boxes on top of the pallet and start pulling them down. When I can no longer reach, I climb up and toss four, five, six boxes to the floor revealing a small three by three-foot door.

"Jonny, there's a door," I yell. "Do not let him out of your sight."

Crawling up to the corner, I open the hidden door and shine my flashlight inside, bile rising in my throat for what I know I'm about to see. The beam finds a small girl standing in the center of the 10 foot by 12-foot space. She's disheveled and frightened, but alive. I lean further into the hold and move my light from side to side. In all, there are 16 girls, not one older than 10. Three of them are dead. The rest, listless, terrified, and too dehydrated to cry.

"There's 16 of them Jon! Call Warren!" I scream out.

"She's coming Jake! There's an ambulance too!"

"We're gonna need 10!" I shout. "And a coroner."

Jumping down, I can feel the adrenaline pumping through my body as I grab the only person I can punish for what I've just seen. He's only one of ten thousand traffickers, but he's the one in front of me. With my forearm in his chest, I slam him against the wall gritting my teeth so hard I taste blood. "I should kill you right now," I say, growling into his face, not knowing if he can understand a word I'm saying. Suddenly, a broad, shit-eating grin spreads across this vile animal's face as he looks toward the hold, leans toward my shoulder, and whispers into my ear in perfect English.

"You haven't lived until you've been sucked off by a..."

Before he can finish, my hand goes to his throat and rage flashes through me. In the moment, all I can think about is Catherine. She was 12 when the tall, white-haired man took her away. I think of her lost. Abused. Being turned out and sold over and over. Jon couldn't hear what was said, but he saw me rack the slide of my pistol and stick it into the mouth of the man against the wall. His head tilted back, choking on the barrel of my gun. From where Jon is standing and through the darkness, I don't think he can see the muscles in my arms twitching as I weigh putting this dog down or continuing my search for the others like him. Either way, he knows I'm on the edge.

"Don't do it Jake!" Jon bellows. "He's not worth it! Come on man, lower your weapon!"

"Special Agent Hardy," SAC Warren screams from the open mouth of the container. "Listen to your partner. Put your weapon down and hold that man while we take him into custody."

Shaking, sweating, I pull my pistol out of the man's mouth, making sure to grate the barrel against his teeth on the way. Pretty sure I broke a few. Holstering my Glock, I turn and push the man to Mitchell and Melcher who are rushing in to secure him. Thankfully, the angle shielded me a bit from Warren. I step aside as the paramedics and emergency crew rush in to pull the girls from the Hell hole they've been living in for God knows how long.

I walk out the front of the box and into Jon's embrace.

"You alright?" he asks.

"No," I answer him. "I'm glad you were here."

Grabbing my shoulder, Jon looks at me with deep concern. "What did he say to you?"

I don't know why, but I don't want to tell him.

"These are fucking animals Jon. I should have dropped him where he stood."

"Not here Jake," Joseph says shaking his head. "Not where anyone else can see."

After the ass-chewing I know is coming from Warren over what she just witnessed, that may be the only option I have left. Her voice yelling "Hardy!" is all I hear as I walk away through a canyon of shadows.

4

My suspension was pending before my plane hit the ground at LAX. Warren called my boss at DHS in L.A. and voiced her serious concerns about my mental state and the fact I appeared to be dangerously on the edge of losing control. When you're deep undercover that's a perpetual state of being. It's also what makes me good at what I do. But it doesn't matter. Warren did what she had to do. Any agent would have gotten suspended for sticking a service weapon in a suspect's mouth. This is on me. But I'm still pissed. I'm grounded pending a psych eval and a review of my conduct in Houston. Forget that we saved 13 young girls from being trafficked. To the brass, I'm the fucking problem.

I grab a cab outside the airport to take me home to Santa Monica. After last night, the dark and quiet of an empty house feels good. But just for a minute. I jump in the shower, throw on a T-shirt and some jeans and walk the five blocks to Paddy's, an old Irish pub that's been here since Sunset Boulevard was the only road to the beach. I tug open the heavy wooden door and immediately start to let Houston go. I need a drink to relax. A drink to forget. At Paddy's, neither is hard to do and always welcome. There's no bullshit here. No theme nights. No dancing on the bar. Anybody ever tried to dance on Paddy's bar he'd take out their knees with the chewed up bat he keeps in the well.

"How are you boyo?" Paddy asks bringing over a napkin and a bowl of peanuts. "You look a bit knackered."

"I'm alright. You?" I answer him.

"Any better'n my Ma'd be slapping me. How was your trip?" After years of coming to this bar, Paddy is good enough to care but knows not to ask me about specifics.

"Fucked up, but satisfying."

"All you can ask for. You want the usual?" Paddy asks already reaching for the bottle.

"Please," I answer.

"You got it."

Paddy gives me a heavy pour in a rocks glass and sets it in front of me.

"You've got good taste, friend," comes a voice from my right. I look down the bar and see some schlub in a wrinkled suit with screaming pinstripes nursing something with fruit hanging off the side of it.

"Sorry?" I say, instantly regretting acknowledging his comment.

"I said you've got some good taste. That's some pretty expensive whiskey you're throwing back. What does that run, about $80 a glass?"

"What's it to you?" I say turning my shoulders to face this dumb fuck head on.

"Just an observation. You look familiar. You somebody I should know?"

And there it is. Because we're in Santa Monica, this guy wandered in here thinking he'd see some L.A. celebrity he could crow about to his cronies back at the home office. Tight shirt.

Unpolished wingtips. Loose tie. Probably a middle manager from the Midwest in town for some annual meeting. Big shit inside his office but nothing out. Same kind of gutless wiseass who runs around on his wife with the girls I'm trying to save.

"I'm nobody man," I answer. "Just having a drink after a long flight."

"Say, is that whiskey really all that? I've always wondered. It's a little rich for my blood."

"I like it. The younger version was the first scotch I ever tasted," I answer.

"The old man's scotch?"

"Something like that."

"Ah, so now you drink the aged stuff to one up him?"

"I drink the aged stuff so fuck him. And you too for bringing it up."

"Listen friend," the guy starts, getting up from his stool and moving my way. In one deft move, I pull his arm behind his back and slam his head against the bar where he can smell and taste decades of smoke, whiskey, and bad decisions. I really don't have the patience for this shit tonight. Putting my full weight against the guy's flank, I lean into his ear and articulate that the best I can.

"Look man, I don't know you and I don't want to know you. I'm here to have a drink not make new friends. That's what puppies are for. You want to trade life stories and bow up on somebody somewhere else, be my guest. But here, now, do me a favor and leave me the fuck alone. Yeah?"

Pushing away from him, I step back, sit down on my stool, and take a long pull on my drink. From the corner of my eye, I notice the sound of the guy's head hitting the bar has Paddy moving in our direction. The guy stands up slowly rubbing his shoulder where I chicken winged him.

"Real friendly place you got here," the guy mouths to Paddy now standing in front of him.

"Yeah? May the road rise to meet ya," Paddy says in his beautiful Irish lilt. "Now get the fuck out."

It's nice to know even when it's nothing, there are guys who have your back. Paddy has mine and always has. Grabbing his jacket, the guy shoots me a look. The side of his face is red and starting to swell but he's smart enough to move on. He throws a ten on the bar and walks out looking around to see who might have witnessed his quick dismantling. I'm sure by the time he gets back to Kansas City or Knoxville the story will be he whipped some Navy SEAL's ass. So be it.

"Sorry Paddy," I say lifting my chin toward him in thanks for his understanding.

"No worries Jake," Paddy says picking up the ten dollar bill for the guy's nine dollar drink. "He was a cheap bastard anyway."

I settle into my Scotch and start thinking about how to handle my suspension. I'm meeting with my supervisors at Homeland in two days and while I'm hopeful they will hear my accounting of what happened in Houston, these aren't the old days. There are some brass more concerned I might have chipped that animal's tooth pulling my gun out of his mouth than they are about me. I'm worried about shutting down sexual predators and human traffickers. They're worried about a lawsuit from some criminal.

The truth is, I don't need a gun and a badge to do what I do. I can still keep digging. Keep watching. Nothing will keep me from stalking the shadows searching for Catherine. Admittedly, when shit goes down, it's better to be official. But after years in Special Ops and undercover work, I know how to paint the edges. If they ground me for six weeks, or six months, or for good, I'll never stop. I'll just have to be more careful.

Looking around, I notice the bar has started filling up. Most of the tables are now occupied with couples and clusters of friends adding to the din in the background. I'm struck by a sudden feeling of aloneness. A playlist of Foghat, Cream, and The Who floats through the bar along with a hint of laughing and taunting from the young Angelenos at the pool tables in the back, one-upping each other like Tom Cruise in "The Color of Money."

"You ready for another, Jake?" Paddy asks, bottle in hand.

"Yeah, I'll have one more," I answer.

"How about two?" she says putting her hand on my shoulder, sliding in beside me at the bar. I turn hoping it's someone I know, or at least someone I've forgotten. It's not. I wouldn't have forgotten this woman. Long chestnut colored hair. Deep brown eyes. All natural. Just my type.

"You look kinda lonely sitting there all by yourself," she says tossing her hair over one shoulder. "I'm Nikki."

"Nikki, you're the second person who suggested that to me tonight. Not sure I'm buying it, but I'm happy to buy you a drink. What would you like?"

"You know how to make an Irish Car Bomb, Paddy?" she tosses to the bartender.

"I do lassie, but what can I make you to drink?" He laughs pouring a pint of Irish stout and grabbing three liqueurs to finish her drink.

Looking at the woman beside me, I realize how much she looks like what I imagine my sister might look like now. All but the eyes. I haven't seen Catherine since we were 12 but there's enough in my memory to connect the dots. I can only hope she still has the life in her that this woman does. You can see it. I can feel it, both when it's present and when it's gone.

It's said the eyes are the window to the soul and for a girl who's been trafficked that's painfully true. I've looked into the eyes of far too many girls and broken women to know when their spirit is gone, and their souls have been hollowed. It's one thing to suffer trauma. It's another to experience it multiple times a day, week after week, month after month, year after year. I'm not naïve. I know by the time I find Catherine there may not be much of her left. But whatever there is, I have to save it. And then spend the rest of my life punishing everyone who had anything to do with her last 20 years.

Even now pushing 33, I can still hear Catherine screaming over my father grunting, "we're even," and shoving her toward the tall man with the white hair. When I pushed between them trying to pull her back, my father and the tall man beat me bloody and threw me against the wall so hard I broke through the sheetrock. Catherine's anguished wailing and the look of terror in her ice blue eyes are the last things I remember before things went black.

Though the clarity of my memories fades with each year that passes, I can see Catherine's face as clear as day. The women beside me is not too far from that picture all grown up. Bringing Nikki's face into full focus, I have no idea how long I've been in my head. I can only hope she didn't see the hurt and the rage of the memories flashing across my face.

"So, Jake. What are we drinking to?" Nikki asks raising her drink.

"I'm betting not the same things," I answer with more than a hint of cynicism.

"I don't know. Let me guess. Broken heart? No, that wouldn't be you. Bad day in the market? Lost your dog? Oh, I know. Shitty job?"

"You're getting warmer," I answer with a smirk.

"Are there really any other kinds?" she smirks back. "What do you do?"

"I work for the government."

"Oh. Shitty and boring. Wouldn't have pegged you for a sit at your desk kind of guy," she says flipping her hair and cocking her head to the side like a golden retriever trying to understand French.

I think about parrying that the United States government is this massive machine and that not all government employees are the ones who inform the cliché. But that would only extend the conversation leading to more lies about what I don't do for a living.

"Yeah well, it's not as boring as it sounds," is all I say. "What do you do?"

"I'm an influencer," she says with a little bounce.

"An influencer?" I question her. "Who exactly are you influencing and what are you influencing them to do?"

"Well, mostly I make cool videos for social media to build my following and then companies pay me to say I like their products so the people following me will follow them and buy their stuff."

"And that works?"

"It does when you have a million people following you."

"You have a million followers on social media?" I ask, trying to hide my shock.

"No. I have a million followers on one of my channels. I have 4.6 million followers overall," she says with a smile. "The money is stupid, and I've never set foot in an office. I'm my own boss, I do what I love to do, and I don't have to get naked. Unless I want to."

Unless I want to. That's the fault line right there. The problem is there's a fundamental misunderstanding among millions of predators about who gets to draw it. From the beginning of time, there have always been prostitutes. Strippers. Women who understood they could trade money for everything from a quick peek to complete submission. But the vast majority of those women were other. Lower class. Victims of circumstance so lost and broken their bodies were the only things they had left to sell or trade to someone who turned them out. For centuries, sex for money lived in the shadows. In hidden rooms, back alleys, and seedy hotels. But at another level, it also lived in the palace. In corporate suites and Congressional limousines. Even then, sex workers were viewed as damaged. Desperate women who had no other choice. Not so now.

Thanks largely to the pandemic, in the span of 18 months, it's become de rigueur for sorority girls, bored Millennials, and frustrated housewives to start webcamming for cryptocurrency as though selling themselves in cyberspace was somehow less damaging and depraved than physical contact. That's bullshit. To a predator, it simply feeds the mindset that when it comes to sex, everything is negotiable and that when something is forbidden, that's not a no. It's a clarion call to step up. Be a man. Take what you want. And for the women and girls on camera, their bodies, their sex, every intimate secret is now recorded and online. Forever. With their consent or without it. It's sick and wrong, but it's why I have a job.

"Influencer sounds like an interesting gig," I tell her. "I don't really do the whole social media thing." A, I don't have a lot of friends. B, working deep cover, having your picture splashed all over gen pop isn't exactly the smartest move.

"That's cool," she answers coyly. "I wouldn't make you pay to see me anyway."

Good to know.

"So, what are you doing tonight once you get to the bottom of that glass?" she follows. And then leaning into my ear, she whispers, "Want to take a walk on the beach with me, or maybe, take me somewhere a little quieter?" I can feel her breath on my neck as her nose grazes the spot right under my ear. There's a part of me that would love nothing more than to take her home for everything she's suggesting. But not tonight.

One of the hazards of policing the world of the broken is not being able to separate what you do from who you are. It's especially hard when brokenness is part of your DNA. I see every girl I've ever saved and failed in my head and most nights I can't help but also feel them in my heart. Too many things to sort out. Too much to get past. Sex for recreation is too close to what I've committed my life to stopping for me to get out of my own head. From experience, it's best to leave that box closed. It never ends well for anyone.

"I appreciate the offer," I say laying my hand on top of hers. "But not tonight. It's been a long couple of days. I think I'm gonna call it. Happy to buy you another drink if you'd like."

"I'm good, Jake," Nikki says with a sweet, understanding smile. "Another night, maybe." She touches my cheek, slowly rubbing her fingers over my skin, and then walks away. The masculine animal in me instantly regrets letting her and the hips moving toward the door go. But then I'm reminded that's the difference between me and the prey I'm chasing. I know how to keep the animal in the cage.

5

The call comes at 7:02am. My suspension is official. Twelve weeks paid leave and no contact with any ongoing investigations. I wasn't determined unfit, but no one argued an extended vacation wasn't warranted. I'm not surprised. Pissed, but not surprised. Just more bureaucratic bullshit getting in the way of the real work.

I roll into the bathroom and look at my haggard mug in the mirror. For the first time in a decade, I have nowhere I have to be. No mission in front of me except the one I secretly harbor to find my sister. I won't have my regular arsenal to lean on, but this break could be good. The chance to search without interruption, unencumbered by obligation is an unexpected gift. It's an opening I intend to exploit to its fullest.

I open the cabinet under the bathroom sink and rummage through years of discarded toiletries until I find a half-filled can of shaving gel and a razor. I've barely touched my beard in two years, but for some reason I'm moved to shave it off. I look old for 32. A clean look wouldn't be the worst thing. Besides, when I find my sister I want her to see the face she remembers. The one I hope she remembers.

Column by column, I cut the coarse black hair from my jaw. The air moving from the ceiling fan in the bedroom feels cool on my cheeks. The skin on my face is red and tender from the strokes of my razor, but it still evokes a familiar recognition of a past incarnation. A younger me. Naively optimistic and somewhat unjaded, devoid of any wisdom for how the world works. Knowledge that can only be purchased with scars and the forfeiture of small parts of your soul.

I look at the clock and it's after 10. Father Charles should be at the church by now. I have been an irregular guest at St. Matthew's since my last tour ended in Afghanistan and I moved to L.A. but right now, I'm feeling moved to visit.

The first time I met Father Charles Fordham there was an instant connection. He wasn't stiff and scary like the priests I remember from going to Mass with my Mother. He was pious, but real. A genuine, nonjudgmental confidante who always shot me straight. The voice of accountability when I needed to hear it. Between the war, and spending my life chasing human traffickers, there is a lot to unpack. Humanity doesn't get uglier than the foul shit I see and the soulless predators I pursue. Father Charles is my counterweight to that.

Grabbing my helmet, I mount the Ducati parked against the wall of my garage and make a full frontal assault on the asphalt between my house and the church. In what is otherwise a fairly pedestrian neighborhood, St. Matthew's stands out as a stunning testament to the faith and talent of the men who built it in the 1930s. The gothic front looks out of place both for the neighborhood and Los Angeles. But the fact that it's been iconic for nearly a century renders that point completely irrelevant.

Entering the front doors in the morning, one is immediately bathed in a wash of color from the sun pouring through the stained glass window of the resurrection behind the altar. The effect of the hanging Christ with His abstract rising behind it is always moving.

Dipping my fingers into the marble font holding the holy water, I genuflect and make the sign of the cross. I walk to the front of the church and sit in the second pew. I close my eyes and pray for the souls of my mother and my sister. Smelling the incense burning at the prayer tables, I am taken back to many of the early Masses we attended together. We were happy once.

Opening my eyes, I rise to seek out the arbiter of my contrition, but there's no need. He's seen me and is walking down the pew to sit beside me.

"Hello Jake," Father Charles says extending his hand as he sits.

"Father," I respond taking his hand. "How are you?"

"Blessed. And you? It took me a minute to recognize you without the beard."

"Yeah, I thought it was time to change things up a little," I respond.

"How's work? More importantly, how are you?" Father Charles asks looking me straight in the eye, searching for any flicker of variation from the truth.

"The book of Job comes to mind," I say with half a smile.

"Mmmm," he says nodding in response.

"A mission in Houston got a little hairy and because of something that went down there, I got suspended for a few months. Nothing serious but I will be floating unmoored for a bit."

"How do you feel about that?" Charles asks.

"Not sure, really. I'd rather be on the job, but it does open up a window. Thought I might spend some time poking around in the shadows."

"Catherine," he says. I nod in acknowledgement.

"Any new information about your sister? Last we talked you were looking through the Federal and state databases to see if you recognized her anywhere."

"That was an exercise in frustration."

"I would imagine 40,000 women a year arrested for prostitution in the U.S. generates a lot of mug shots."

"Fifty. And those are just the ones who get caught," I answer. "This will take more than looking at mug shots and walking the streets hoping to find something. The only logical option that makes sense to me is going back to the beginning and working out from there."

"You mean Georgia?" he asks. I nod. "How long's it been?"

"Twenty years."

"Any chance Catherine is still there?"

"No, but I'm hopeful that maybe she was there long enough to have crossed paths with someone who is. You know how it is Father. Part of the trafficking game is to keep the girls moving. Truck to truck. Hotel to hotel. City to city. I just wish there were more people like you willing to help."

Three years ago, I knocked on the door of Father Charles's private quarters at 2:30 in the morning in the middle of a freak L.A. rainstorm. Beside me was a soaking wet, 12-year-old Hispanic girl in a short, sequined dress, smeared mascara, and heels so high she could barely walk in them. A pedestrian brain might have questioned the two of us standing there, or maybe, why a little girl playing in her mother's closet had gotten caught outside in the rain in the middle of the night. Father Charles immediately saw the truth and never flinched. Without a word, he opened the door and provided refuge from the storm.

Earlier that night before the rain came, I had pulled into a dark parking lot littered with discarded trash, cracked bottles, broken concrete, and the aged remains of hundreds of cigarette butts. An online ad promising something "beautiful and exotic" for $200 had brought me to the Palm Breeze Motel in West Hollywood and the sting was on. My instructions were to go to the front desk and ask for the key to room 106. Once in the room, I was to call and order dinner from Room Service.

I followed what the raspy female smoker's voice on the phone instructed me to do and 20 minutes later, there was knock at the door. Touching the Glock on my hip, I looked through the peephole and saw a bony, twitchy 20-something with a face full of acne scars standing there with a dining cart that looked more out of place than he did. I opened the door and without word, the young punk wheeled the cart into the room and pulled the metal cover off a hamburger so shitty a high school cafeteria wouldn't serve it.

"Dinner is served. That'll be $400," the kid blurted holding out a dirty hand palm up. A tattoo of a skull with blood dripping from its eye sockets peeked out from the sleeve covering his forearm. He wanted so badly to be hard.

"$400? Your ad said $200. What the fuck?" I punched back taking a step in his direction. Shaking, this wannabe gangster swung a cheap pistol up and pointed it between my eyes. It was small, but totally capable of getting the job done.

"Delivery fee man! Everybody gotta eat. You want your dinner, or not motherfucker?"

I wanted to beat the shit out of this kid on principle, but more than that, I wanted to see who he brought through the door next. I had partners with eyes in both corners of the parking lot, so I let it ride. Once he brought the woman into the room, we'd move in and nail this son of bitch.

Throwing my hands up in feigned supplication, I slowly took a step back, reached for my wallet, and handed the kid $400 in fifties. Nervously looking back and forth between the money and me, he counted the cash twice, stuffed it into the front of his jeans and backed out the door. I stood, waiting for two minutes. Three minutes. Five minutes waiting for him to return with the woman I paid for. Impatient and thinking I'd been scammed, I cursed under my breath, and moved toward the door. That's when I heard her crawling out from beneath the dinner cart.

I turned and found a prepubescent Hispanic girl standing in front of me wearing a reddish pink dress with a single strap over her left shoulder. I could tell it had been torn and hastily repaired numerous times. Her hair was pulled up and the makeup on her face looked way too subtle and natural to have been done by a girl this young. Someone made her up to look sultry, as sick and out of place as that felt. She was wobbly in the heels that were a size too big for her feet and holding her arms out for balance, she started to walk toward me.

"Qué Quiere?" she asked in a tiny voice. "What do you want? I give."

"Come here sweetheart," I told her reaching out my hand. "What's your name? Nombre?"

"Gabriela," she answered quietly.

As I moved closer, I felt her reach for my zipper. I grabbed her hand and pulling it away, I leaned in so I could whisper in her ear. "You are safe. Estas segura," I said. "I'm here to save you. Rescatarte!"

Immediately, her eyes filled with tears, and she grabbed onto my leg with every ounce of strength she possessed. Now I had to figure out how to get her out of the room and into a car without both of us getting shot. Traffickers even as young as the guy shaking me down weren't stupid. In for a dime, they were in for a dollar and capping some John and a runaway in a shitty motel was still better than going down for trafficking.

Patting her head with one hand, I tilted her chin up to look into her eyes. "Chica, confía en mí," I pleaded. "Trust me," I repeated hoping it somehow sounded different from the other times she'd heard the same from predators who betrayed her. Putting my index finger to my lips, I walked over to the skirt covering the bottom of the dinner cart and motioned for her to crawl back under. I had expected her to resist. But timidly, she nodded and crawled back onto the cold metal shelf between the wheels. I walked to the door and looked through the cheap, threadbare curtains covering the window. I could see Twitchy leaning against the wall outside, staring out at the surprising rain that had started to fall. I could smell the smoke from his cigarette snaking its way through the warped frame of the door. He didn't know it, but he was exactly where I wanted him to be.

Pulling my phone out, I texted "Code 3 on my mark" to the uniformed agents standing by in the parking lot. We had one shot to get this right, and as with everything, it all came down to timing. Returning to the cart, I knelt down and pulled back the curtain. "Lista?" I asked ready to get this little girl somewhere safe. With wet eyes and a quivering chin, her precious face nodded at me and smiled. I pulled the curtain back in place, grabbed the back of the cart, and to make sure and sell this, I bit my wrist with just enough force to draw blood. With a loud crack, I threw open the door and blew through it pushing the cart hard into the parking lot.

"What the fuck man?" I shouted at the kid against the wall. "Your little bitch bit me!"

This is the last thing he was expecting and when the door crashed open, he almost bit his cigarette in half.

"She fucking bit me man," I yelled grabbing the front of his shirt, shoving the bleeding bite mark on my wrist toward his face. "She bit me and locked herself in the bathroom!" I turned my head and spit before pulling my Glock and putting it to his head. "Give me my money you asshole, or I swear to God…"

Now panicked and not about to give me the money back, the guy bolted through the door and started screaming and pounding on the bathroom door I locked and pulled shut. Just like I knew he would.

The second my team saw me grab the girl and start running to my car, they descended on Room 106 like a swarm of locusts, blue lights flashing, guns drawn. By the time my ignition turned over, the trafficker was on the ground with a knee in his back, cuffed and inhaling the foulness of 30-year-old motel carpet that had never been cleaned. I heard later when he turned and found eight DHS agents with their guns drawn he literally shit himself. Good thing my $400 was in his front pocket.

An hour later, I knocked on the Rectory door at St. Matthew's and delivered another lost lamb to the bosom of the Good Shepherd. It was not the last time Father Charles would prove to be a rescuer of children. Or of me.

"Jake, I pray God's blessings on you for your protection and your peace. You know that God works for the good of those called according to His purpose."

"I do," I mutter.

"Just be safe," Father Charles stressed, squeezing my shoulder. "Your mission is noble, but nobility has never been much protection against evil."

"Thank you Father," I say, rising to search out the evil of which he spoke.

6

At 4:20am, I am jolted awake by my sister's terrified cries for help. This time, it's the nightmare I have where she's chained to the bottom of the Pacific, screaming for me as predators tear her apart a bite at a time until there's nothing left but a skeleton on a chain. Our family has a long history of chains. At the beginning of Anna Karenina, Tolstoy wrote "happy families are all alike; every unhappy family is unhappy in its own way." I can't imagine families finding more ways to be unhappy than ours did.

My mother was a stunning woman with sapphire eyes and a pedigree equally as brilliant. I got her cunning and independence. My sister inherited her eyes. Born on the coast of Sea Island, Georgia, Julia Grace was the only child of wealthy parents who gave her everything she could want except the permission to make her own choices. My grandfather was a smart, staid man with a bristly mustache and a distinctive laugh. He had taken over my great grandfather's textile business at 30 and, under his guidance, it flourished into one of the largest companies of its kind in the world. Though my grandmother had come from a modest upbringing in Iowa, she too was quite erudite with a penchant for entertaining and playing the piano.

My grandparents treated my mother like a princess. Private school. Parties. Horses. Cotillion. But my mother was no doe-eyed debutante. She was smart and she didn't suffer fools. She was a writer, she could paint, and by 16, she had her heart set on attending the new Savannah College of Art and Design. That, or the University of Georgia if Savannah just seemed too close. My mother always knew what she wanted and for the most part, my grandparents indulged her in everything that entailed. With one exception.

Miller Clark was born to the servant class that waited on the wealthy on Sea Island. Despite an alcoholic mother and an abusive father, Miller picked his way through the darkness to become an adequate student and one hell of a linebacker for the high school out in Brunswick. His junior year, Miller had 11 interceptions and led the team in tackles beating both Cairo and Thomasville in the same year. There was a buzz building about Miller Clark. A rumor of scouts in the stands from Clemson, Auburn, and Tennessee. Miller was a strapping young kid with big dreams of doing something more than fixing boat motors and serving Bloody Marys to the rich like his father. Unfortunately, he also liked to drink whiskey like his mother. It was over a fifth of Jack Daniels that Miller Clark met my mother.

When the football team finally did lose to Valdosta in the State semis, there was disappointment but also a fierce sense of pride. Only one high school from Glynn County had ever made it that far and it was Miller's. Tonight, there was much to celebrate.

By 11:30pm, the afterparty was roaring under the Avenue of Oaks on St. Simons Island. The ancient grove of Southern live oaks with the thick canopy of Spanish moss was sacred ground and not just because John and Charles Wesley had once sat under the trees discussing the tenets of Methodism, the Christian denomination they founded there. To the teenagers who lived in the south Georgia islands, the Oaks were a sanctuary and parties like this were a rite of passage. For Julia Grace, it was more than a window into another world. It was a door.

It could have been her dress, or the way she had her hair pulled up that caught Miller's attention. But the second he laid eyes on my mother, the world stopped for him. He would forever think of his life as time before that night and time after. He could tell by the way she carried herself she was a better than. On most nights, Miller would acknowledge how unattainable a young woman like Julia Grace was for someone like him. But on this particular night, Jack Daniels called out that weak bullshit for what it was and pushed Miller off the hood of the truck he was sitting on and over to where my mother was standing alone. Shivering.

"You looking for somebody?" Miller asked her smiling.

"The two girls I came with," Julia answered. "One is in a blue dress and the other is in jeans and a pink sweater."

"Haven't seen 'em. But I'm happy to help you look if you want," he offered.

"That's ok. They'll turn up," Julia said now looking into the brown eyes in front of her. "I'm Julia Grace."

"Miller. Clark. You look cold. Here, take my jacket." And that was how it started. My mother's rebellion. My father's obsession. A year later, my sister and I arrived along with a shotgun wedding and generations of familial regret. Nine years after that, my mother was gone.

I only know this story because after my mother died, my father recounted it almost nightly as he killed another fifth of Scotch. Pining for the only woman he ever loved in one breath and in the other, wailing that my mother was a "greedy, heartless cunt" for not including him in her trust when she got sick. That was usually the point he passed out in his recliner, an empty bottle in one hand, a lit cigarette in the other. Most nights I remembered to check and put any lit butts in the bottle. Looking back, I should have taken Catherine to my grandparents and let the motherfucker burn.

I get up, throw on a T-shirt, and head to the beach for a quick run. Even in L.A., the air is crisp this early in the morning. I can see my shadow bouncing in front of me as the sun rises to my back. Not many people out yet. I like mornings like that. Nothing to ruin my solitude.

Running is a drug for me and equally dangerous. As hard as I try, I find it impossible to run and not think. Not remember. Not get consumed with how it is I got from losing my sister to the Marines and Special Ops, to now suspended for doing my job. I'm still so fucking pissed at Warren no matter how justified she was in urging my suspension.

I take off and sprint down the beach, my arms pumping. I run as hard and as fast and as long as my body will allow, churning through the sand until my legs and lungs are burning. Gritting my teeth, I bite the inside of my cheek and slow my pace as I start to taste blood in my mouth. I look up and see the new day now fully dawning behind the silhouette of the carousel at the Santa Monica Pier. I look out to the water, red glints of the sunrise tipping from the tops of breaking waves, and I say a silent prayer for Catherine. For my search for her. Enough of the defeatist, negative bullshit. The world is a big place, and I have to believe my sister is still somewhere in it. In my heart, I know I'm the only one looking for her. I turn and run back to my house. There's work to do.

7

Whatever authenticity Los Angeles has in the daylight, it fades into dark façade when the sun crosses the Pacific horizon. In L.A. everyone hugs you to say hello, but only so you can't see them looking behind you to see if there's someone more famous in the room. Hollywood is the grand illusion. Forced perspective. Paint on plywood. All American stories frosted on top of lies and somebody without power getting fucked by someone who has it. Los Angeles has built a billion dollar industry on creating an illusion of real when in truth, there's nothing there. It might be shocking to know human trafficking in the U.S. generates twice the revenue Hollywood does. But it shouldn't. They're built on the same bones. Same lies. Just like too many families.

I spend the afternoon roaming the corners of the dark web looking for anything familiar. Working undercover, I've spent months at a time down the rabbit hole. It's a dark, heartbreaking tour of human depravity I wouldn't wish on anyone. But someone has to keep evil in check, and I signed up a long time ago.

Today, there was only so much I could do. As pissed as I am about being suspended, if someone at Homeland notices my login is somewhere it's not supposed to be, that won't help. I scan the solicitation menus online. This for sale. That for the taking. Most listings are at least a little dressed up, but many do nothing to hide how sick and twisted they really are. Amazing, the effect the supposition of anonymity has on what one human being will do to another. Drugs. Weapons. Children. They are all here in every form, every age, every quantity. The only question is price.

I shut my computer, a familiar nauseous feeling swirling in my stomach. As long as I've been hunting traffickers with the DHS, I still feel sick when my brain fully engages the implications of what I'm seeing. I didn't see anyone I think could be my sister today. But it's somebody's sister. Somebody's daughter. Somebody's son. I look up and four hours have passed since I started searching.

I throw on some clothes and head to Paddy's for a liquid dinner. The walk feels good. I breathe in the night breeze and try to let the afternoon go. I learned a long time ago if I can't separate what I do from who I am, it will eat me alive from the inside. Tonight, I need to will myself to be open to something good. Something positive. Jokes from Paddy. An engaging conversation. Anything on the lighter side. I just pray to God we can skip the assbags like the one I put down the last time I was here.

I open the door and U2's "Sunday Bloody Sunday" hits me in the face. Paddy is unapologetically rocking his Irish playlist and it's turned up. I love it. It's not my era of music, but as much as I'm here, the music has grown on me. Any night with a steady stream of U2, The Pogues, Horslips, and The Boomtown Rats is good by me. I fucking hate Mondays.

"Anam cara," Paddy says, extending his hand. When he leads with Gaelic, I know he's already had a few. He's clearly missing somebody. "The regular? Time to feel better boyo!"

"Sure Paddy," I answer. "I'm liking the music."

"It warms the heart, lad," he says. "Lost my ma 27 years ago today." And there it is.

"She'd be proud of you," I tell him.

"Oh, she is," he says grabbing a bottle of amber Irish Whiskey and pouring two shots. Paddy isn't fucking around. That bottle costs $350. "Sláinte!" We slam the shots and as always Paddy is right. I do feel better. Paddy pours three more ounces into a rocks glass and leaves the bottle in front of me on the back of the bar. He winks at me and dances down the bar as the Edge and the dull snare of Larry Mullen Jr. fill the room.

The bar isn't bursting at the seams, but it's full. A few of the day drinkers are still tucked in the corners, either too drunk to leave, or just enjoying Paddy's playlist. A young couple dances by the pool table while others sit at high tops along the walls, leaning into each other trying to talk over the music. There's a good vibe in the air tonight. People are happy. Social. I kill the rest of my drink and walk toward the back of the bar to hit the head.

Paddy's bathrooms always make me smile. The signs on the doors aren't "Men" and "Women." They're "Shillelagh" and "No Shillelagh." For a bar, the bathrooms are immaculate. The walls are adorned with pictures of Dublin and Irish fields filled with sheep Just inside the door, there is a sign that says, "May the Lord keep you in His hand and never close His fist too tight." The Gospel according to Paddy O'Shea.

As I round the corner from the bathroom, I realize my seat at the bar is still empty but the one next to it is not. A woman is sitting there talking with Paddy and from the side, I can already see she has the kind of body that silhouettes were made for. She has a long neck, strong shoulders, and medium length blonde hair that's pulled over to the right side of her face. I take a breath and walk to my seat trying to summon any semblance of optimism.

"Jake, meet Rachel," Paddy says, smiling at me and raising his eyebrows like "Get a load of her!" "Rachel, this is Jake. Give me a second Love. I'll be back with your drink."

I smile at the gorgeous woman sitting in front of me. Now that I can see her whole face, she's even prettier than I thought. "Thanks for keeping my seat," I quip starting to sit.

"Oh, I'm sorry," Rachel says suddenly taken aback. "My… date is outside parking the car. He'll be here in a minute. I thought…"

"No. Sorry," I say looking around for another seat to escape to. "I made a… sorry… it's not MY seat. I mean…"

"Jake," she says reaching out and grabbing my hand. "I'm fucking with you. I don't have a date." Rachel tilts her head, and with eyes that soften everything hard within me, she hits me with a smile that immediately makes me want to know everything about her.

"Nicely played," I smile, straddling my stool and turning toward her. "Actress?" I ask.

"Oh, God no," she responds. "Way too artificial for me. It's hard enough living in this skin. I'm not interested in jumping into anyone else's."

I smile as Paddy comes back with Rachel's cocktail. "Here's your drink love." He drops a few chunks of ice into my glass and pours another couple ounces of whiskey over the top. He smiles and leaves us to get acquainted.

"I saw you and Paddy getting on," I say. "Do you know each other from somewhere? I haven't seen you here before."

"No, we just met," Rachel answers. Good sign. Paddy's a solid judge of character. If he took an instant liking to this woman, that's saying something.

"I'm in town for business and when I Googled 'great bars near the beach,' this one popped up. It looked like my speed and here I am," she says, coyly sipping her Manhattan. "I clearly got here at the right time," she adds.

I smile, staring at the glass against her lips and take a pull from my drink. "No arguments from me."

"You live here?" Rachel asks.

"At the bar? Only part time," I answer. She laughs. "I live about a mile from here. Less than. Close enough to walk on a pretty night."

"Are you from L.A.?"

"Georgia, originally. South Georgia down around Sea Island. You?"

"Born in Baltimore but I've moved around a lot. I love Sea Island. It's beautiful," she says.

"It can be," I answer.

"Sounds like a story there," she says leaning toward me.

"Oh, there is," I agree. "A long one I won't bore you with. But yes, the Golden Isles can be beautiful."

"So, what was so fantastic that it drew you away from home?"

"The Marines."

"The Marines?" Rachel questions, immediately lighting up.

"Marine Raiders, actually."

"Well, Semper Fi," she says, leaning forward and hugging me tightly. Her cheek feels warm against my ear and for the first time, I am close enough to smell her perfume. It stirs me ten times harder than the Scotch.

"A hug for your service, sir," she says sitting back as though this is common practice. My expression betrays my surprise. "My father was a Marine," she says. "I have a soft spot for you boys."

"That certainly beats the free college tuition," I joke. She smiles.

"Did you like it?"

"The Corps was great for me. Coming out of high school, I didn't have a whole lot of direction. Lot of misplaced anger and frustration. Serving gave me the structure and discipline I desperately needed at the time. It wasn't all roses, but I came out whole and healthy on the other side. For the most part."

"How long were you in?" Rachel asks.

"Eight years," I answer. "Two tours in Afghanistan."

"That had to have been rough," she says. "Was it as bad as I imagine?"

"Probably worse. We were actually pretty lucky. Our unit lost nine men during our two tours. A Kiowa crashed on a training mission during the first tour, and we had three IED casualties during the second. Looking back, that's a miracle considering some of the shit that went down."

"I would imagine," Rachel answers. "What's the worst thing you saw while you were there?"

This is normally where I would shut things down. Make a quick joke about having to live on chickpeas and goat for eight years, but

I find myself wanting to talk to this woman. Not to spill secrets, but to get to know her. Looking into Rachel's eyes, there seems to be a depth to her that I don't usually see in the women I meet at Paddy's or any other bar for that matter. Rachel feels like an old soul and maybe someone who's lived through her own version of the desert. I finish my drink, grab the bottle, and pour another. I haven't told this story before and I'm not entirely sure how this will go.

"One night my partner Jon and I were part of a small unit patrolling a village about three miles from our base. We had walked through the same village half a dozen times before during the day and even then, it seemed pretty quiet. Shepherds herding goats. Women cooking and doing laundry. Little girls hidden away. The boys playing in the street or running behind the men whacking the goats with sticks to keep them moving.

"The night of our patrol, the village was dark and dead. There was no air moving and other than the near full moon, there was no real light. We had gotten some intel earlier in the day that a cache of weapons was being stockpiled in a building on the north end of the village closest to the mountains. Word was a new shipment was coming and we were sent to intercept the new exchange and destroy what we found.

"We moved quickly across the open desert and at the edge of the village, we split into three groups. One approached the building from the left, one approached from the right, and one came straight down the main street, moving through the shadows, trying not to be seen. Jonny and I were in the last group and even though things were quiet, it just felt wrong. On one corner, we passed a weathered old man with wrinkled skin like burlap, just pointing, and laughing as we passed. He was most likely a senile, crazy old drunk but I remember circling out away from him, praying he wasn't sitting on a grenade, deciding whether that was the night he wanted to meet Allah.

"Looking down the alleys left and right, we could see the other groups tracking with us as we moved closer to the target. Then two blocks away, we stopped, consumed by some putrid smell. Just off the street, a pack of feral dogs were snout deep in the carcass of a dead sheep that had clearly been there for days. It turned out to be our one saving grace as the dogs were too engaged with the sheep to start barking.

"We held about a block from the target to confirm intel from all three teams. From our vantage point, there were no guards. Nobody outside at all. The front windows were lit up behind the heavy windscreens hanging from above. From inside, we could hear the muffled sound of music playing. A lute, some drums, and the wailing voices of some old men. Confirming ready positions from the left and right flanks, we moved toward the building and stopped again, backs to the walls.

"Next to the building, the music poured through the slivers of open space around the windscreens giving the feel of some party going on inside. With a breach team poised at the front door in case things went to shit in a hurry, we peered inside and realized our intel was solid. On one side of the room, there were probably 100 rifles lined against the wall along with stacked wooden boxes filled with ammunition and grenades on the floor.

"Sitting around the perimeter of the room, there were a dozen Afghan men from their 30s to their 60s, clapping and chanting as four young boys danced for them in the middle of the room. Each of the boys was wearing a dress and a veil, and even in the limited light, we could see the boys were wearing crude makeup. Lipstick, eye shadow, rouge. The boys looked petrified, and their dancing was as stilted and uncoordinated as you'd expect from a 12 year old but they didn't dare stop.

"While we were checking the front, the team on the right flank had moved to the back of the building where there was a door and two additional windows. They radioed that they couldn't see any weapons but thought they could hear the sound of goats or sheep screaming inside. We asked for confirmation but all we got back was a long silence. Then, in a frenzied burst we heard, 'the screams aren't fucking goats! Breach now!'

"Jonny was the first one through the front door and threw a flash grenade into a small cluster of the rebels. The next three of us grabbed the boys and pulled them to the floor, getting them out of the line of fire. The rest of the team drew a bead on anybody that looked like bin Laden and never flinched. The traffickers were dead before they could get off a shot. The front was clear, but we had it easy. When the team at the back crashed through the rear door, they found themselves in a long hallway with four small rooms off to one side. Heavy fabric curtains hung in the doorways, but they couldn't mask the painful screaming coming from inside each of the rooms. At each door, our team ripped the curtain away from the entrance, revealing an old man raping a young boy on a dirty, dusty mattress tossed on the floor."

I reach for my drink and kill what's left already set on burying the memories I just recalled. I look at Rachel and there's a stunned look of horror on her face.

"Oh my God," Rachel breathes, finally exhaling, letting what I'd said wash over her. Then, seeing some semblance of recognition in her eyes, she says the last thing I expected her to say. "You stumbled on a Bacha bazi ritual."

"How do you know about Bacha bazi?" I ask. "Most people here have never even heard of it and those who have wish they hadn't."

"Monitoring sexual slavery and human trafficking is part of what I do. I haven't been to the Middle East, but I understand the heartbreaking child abuse going on there."

"You deal with human trafficking?" I ask, dumbfounded at what this woman does and the emotional common ground we will immediately have.

"I do," she answers.

"Who do you work for?"

Rachel hesitates. She looks into my eyes and chooses to trust me. "The people I primarily work for are no one you would know," she says suddenly looking a bit more serious. "Let's just say they fly under the RADAR and the less the world knows of them, the better."

"The first rule of Fight Club," I say knowingly.

She nods. "I do some work for the DOJ, but all in service of shutting down traffickers in the U.S.."

"You're an operative," I surmise.

"More of a journalist," she responds.

Fuck me. A journalist? I can count the number of not completely shitty experiences I've had with journalists on my dick and have one too many. Most journalists pretend they're doing some noble job but there are no Morrows and Cronkites left. Most writers now are in it for click bait and sound bites. They're not interested in telling the real story. They're in it to justify some obtuse agenda or to make some personal, political point. I've spent the last six years digging in the muck with the vilest motherfuckers on the planet. The last thing I need is some wannabe freelancer making promises and then burning me, fucking up half a decade of undercover work. I don't care how beautiful she is.

"Journalist. Right." I say standing up and feeling the full effect of drinking half a fifth of Scotch. "And you just happen to cover human trafficking. What a huge fucking coincidence that is."

Shifting back onto her stool, Rachel stares at me with a look of confusion and hurt. "I'm sorry," she says. "You want to fill me in?"

The volume of my discontent draws Paddy to our end of the bar. "Jake? Rachel? We ok?" he asks.

"Did you tell her?" I say to Paddy angrily.

"Tell her what?" he answers.

"About me. About who I am. What I do."

"About?... No," he pushes back. "I would never, and you know it."

"Sure," I spit back at him.

"Boyo! I think it's time you gave that bottle back to me," Paddy answers grabbing the nearly empty bottle of whiskey. It's not the first time he's seen me angry and overserved.

"Jake," Rachel says reaching out her hand, her eyes starting to fill, "I don't know what I said that upset you but I'm sorry. Can we talk about this?"

Looking at her face, I have clearly overreacted to what she's said to me, but it's too late to unravel my reaction. Once again, I have taken a promising connection and let the darkness of my life blow it all to Hell.

"We all have demons we can't outrun," I say swallowing the last of the Scotch in my glass. "I just try to stay as far away from mine as possible." I open my wallet, throw two Benjamins on the bar, and take Rachel's hand. "You are stunning," I say and walk out into the evening chill convinced I am forever destined to walk my path alone.

8

Two weeks into my suspension, I call the brass about an early release for good behavior. The answer is an unequivocal no. "Consider it a gift," they say. "Rest. Go for a run. Get in a better head space and we'll see you in 10 weeks." As much as I want to get back, it isn't happening. I'm strictly forbidden from officially engaging with anything falling under the DHS purview for the next two months. It should be easy to lean into a three month paid vacation, but I can't. It's just not how I'm wired.

I hang up and call Jon to check in. We haven't talked since the fallout from Houston. I didn't want any of the stink on me rubbing off on him. Jonny knows the drill and that I'll call him when the time is right. I punch the contact info for his cell and before it even rings, I hear it click.

"How's your tan?" he asks, the sound of his office door shutting in the background.

"Ghostly," I reply. "Yours?"

"It got a little toasty but it's all good now. You alright?"

"It is what it is. I called this morning about cutting my suspension short. No go.

"I figured. How long?"

"Ten more weeks. Fucking eternity."

If anyone knows how hard this is for me, it's Jon Joseph. I don't sit. When there's a job to do, I'm the guy they send to do it and right now, there are more than a few jobs that need doing.

"Seriously man, you ok?" Jon asks.

"I'm fine. I just… you know what it does to me to be out of the game."

"Guess you're locked out of the system too," he asks.

"All of it. Can't search. Can't track. I'm dead to them."

"I'd say enjoy it if I was talking to anyone but you."

"Any news on the two we took down in Houston?"

"The one you gave the oral exam to with your pistol definitely needed some dental work. But other than bitching about that, he isn't talking. The taller one isn't giving up much now, but when we were taking him from the shipping container to the cell, the agents said he kept mumbling something about talking to Soma Yay, or a Suma Ye. We ran it through the system but didn't get a hit on anything like that. We asked him to repeat the name later, but so far, we got nothing. They're taking another run at both of them today."

I had my shot, but I'd sure like another.

"Thanks for the intel Jon," I say, putting on my shoes and grabbing my keys. I've got to get out of here.

"I got you," he replies. "I'll call you when I know something. Go have a Mai Tai for God's sake."

I click off, jump in my car, and start driving up Sunset, into the hills toward West Hollywood. At Highland, I drive a block north to Hollywood Boulevard and check both sides of the street for Big

Alice. On any given day, the stretch of Hollywood Boulevard between La Brea and Highland is one giant tourist trap. A colorful mix of street performers, T-shirt shops, Starbucks, and the homeless, all pandering to the out of towners who've come looking for a Hollywood that's not really there. It's the perfect place for working girls to blend in. At least most.

Big Alice has been working this stretch of Hollywood for damn near 43 years. The first time I met her, she told me all about how her father turned her out at 13 to support his drinking and gambling habit. When she turned 19, he sold her for $1,000 to a cruel wannabe hustler named Winston James who fashioned himself a pimp on the rise. According to Alice, Winston James loved three things in the world – drinking brandy, throwing dice, and "teaching lessons" when his girls got out of line. Most of the lessons were delivered with a belt. Some with a fist. On one really bad night, Winston put a loaded .44 between Alice's legs and made her beg him not to kill her. She told me there were more than a few days she wished he had.

By 1978, Winston James was running 15 to 20 girls a night in L.A. Some up in Hollywood, a few by the strip club on the way to LAX, and a big group who did porn during the day and worked the Valley at night. He was never the gold pimp businessman he thought he was, but in the L.A. underground, Winston James wasn't a nobody.

One morning in October 1979, a cleaning woman at the Roll-In Motel found James dead in a bathtub full of tepid, bloody water. A needle with the remnants of pure heroin was still stuck in his arm and his eyes were wide open. Someone had also sliced off his junk and shoved it down his throat. It was clearly a message, but the police weren't too concerned with the death of some junkie pimp.

The case was closed never knowing who killed Winston James. But Alice knew. Turns out the last lesson was for Winston James.

I asked Alice why she didn't walk away after Winston died, finally free of someone else's control. She said, "Baby, when you ain't been to school and your body is the only valuable thing you got, it's not that simple." Alice was in no way formally educated. But with what she learned from life, she could play a man like a concertmaster plays a Stradivarius. That is, beautifully, completely, and with virtuosic command. Alice's life – selling herself six days a week – wasn't Mayberry. But she was in control. She kept every dollar she made, she didn't get hit, and here in the land of make believe, she created her own legend.

As years turned into decades, Big Alice as she came to be known, started spending more time looking after the other girls instead of turning tricks herself. Then again, a three hundred pound ebony queen with gold teeth is a pretty specific ask for most Johns. And yet, in West Hollywood, Alice is a presence. In the movie *Chinatown*, there's a great scene where John Huston tells a young Jack Nicholson, "politicians, ugly buildings, and whores all get respectable if they last long enough." Big Alice has lasted long enough.

I turn left on Hollywood Boulevard and see Alice on the corner just to the west of the old Mann's Chinese Theater. You can't miss her. She's spilling out of a purple dress, surrounded by five girls who look half her age and a third her size. A full head of platinum hair is piled high on top of her head. I pull into the closest parking lot and walk over to where she's holding court. She sees me coming half a block away.

"Look at this fine piece of man coming here!" she wails. "What you say sweetheart? You ready to tell Big Mama all your troubles?"

"Hello Alice," I answer, smiling quietly. It takes her a minute, but she finally recognizes me.

"Jake? Where's your beard, honey? I ain't seen you all cleaned up. Look at you!" she says spinning me around for a look. "My God child, are you eating? You are wasting A-WAY!"

"I'm fine," I tell her. "You look beautiful as always."

"Aww, Jake. You know what that kinda talk and a hundred dollars does to Big Alice."

Just to be safe, I scan the intersection and don't see any patrol cars sitting around that could cause any headaches. We're only talking, but without my badge, some overzealous cop is some bullshit I don't need right now.

"Yeah, speaking of that, you think we could go somewhere and talk for 10 or 15 minutes."

"Honey, if the price is right we can talk for 20!"

Alice grabs my arm and pulls me toward an alleyway behind the pharmacy. Just for effect, she turns back to the other girls and says, "Um-hmm! You see who's walking away with the white prize!"

Down the alleyway out of sight of the others, I grab Alice's hand and pull her toward me. For five years, she's been an invaluable source of information giving me the pulse from the street and tipping me to trafficked girls who need help. I wrap my arms around Alice and for a moment, I feel the tension release from her shoulders in what for her is a rare moment of real safety and genuine affection.

"How are you Alice," I ask taking a step back.

"Everything hurts baby. Course you know, Big Alice ain't so young no more."

"Anything new I need to handle?"

"Naw, it's been quiet and pretty normal since I saw you last. I did have one little white dude ask me if I had a sister for a three way. You believe that shit? Where he gonna go in a three way with two of me? I was a little worried about his skinny ass, not gonna lie."

"But no new girls. No teenagers you think might be in trouble?'"

"I know what you asking baby. Far as I know, at least up in here, ain't nothing new."

"Any chance you've ever heard the name Soma Yay, or Suma Ye?"

"Who dat? Some Asian pimp?"

"We don't know who he is and don't have record of anyone by that name. We think he might be higher up. We're wondering if it's a new pseudonym someone's using. We heard it from two traffickers we busted in Houston about a month ago."

"Houston? That's a long way from L.A., Jake."

"I know but it was worth the ask."

"I got a cousin in Houston," Alice laughs. "But she ain't as pretty as me."

"Nobody's as pretty as you Alice," I say looking into her eyes. What a life this woman has led. Looking around one more time for any voyeurs in blue, I hand Alice $100 which she promptly puts into the front of her bra. "Thank you baby," she says with a wink. "You know there's always a little comfort on the house when you ready."

"I'm not sure I could handle you Alice," I grin as I walk out of the alley back toward Hollywood Boulevard. From behind me, in a hushed, loving voice, I hear, "That's for damn sure." I turn back to Alice laughing. She looks at me and says, "You be careful Jake. You know Mama loves you too much to get hurt now."

Back in my car, I drive my normal route through Hollywood checking out the shadowed streets I know girls tend to work. Alice is right. Nothing looks out of the ordinary to me. I recognize many of the faces and no one appears to be younger than their 20s. That's not a great thing, but it's better than seeing girls in cocktail dresses that should be in middle school.

I wind my way across Sunset past the Roxy and the Whiskey and head south on La Brea to catch the 10 back to Santa Monica. Everything south of Sunset seems quiet and pretty normal. Until it doesn't.

At the corner of Melrose and La Brea, I see a girl about 14, standing by herself outside doublewide hotdog stand. She's hugging a weathered streetlight with one arm and talking on her cell phone with the other. I pull into the lot behind the restaurant to check on her, but before I can get out, a couple comes running out the front door, scolding the girl for running off by herself and pulling her back inside with them. They're right to be anxious. If they knew how quickly a trafficker could lure their daughter away, they'd never let her out of their sight again.

I hit the 10, thankful traffic is light. I flip through a couple of radio stations, but all the music is shit. Even in L.A., some nights are like that. I grab my phone to punch up a playlist and it buzzes in my hand. It's Jon.

"What's the word, Bear?" I ask hoping Jonny's got something.

"The word, Jake, is "sommelier.""

"Sommelier? You mean like a wine steward?"

"I mean exactly like a wine steward. We thought those chucklefucks we collared were saying "Soma Yay" or somebody's name. Turns out they were just butchering the language."

"So, what the fuck does Sommelier mean?"

"No idea. We ran it through the computers and nothing with that name or pseudonym popped."

"Hey, it's more than we had six hours ago."

"And get this, when we pressed them, they said the girls we recovered would have been on a truck to Vegas the next day if we hadn't found them."

"Vegas? Damn Jon, that could be 100 different groups."

"I know," he answers. "It's just a piece, but it's still a piece. I'm on it. Just wanted to let you know what we've got. I'll keep you posted."

"Thanks buddy."

One word. Sometimes that's all it takes, but I'm betting we'll need more than just this. It's generic and it's random but it's gotta mean something. As I reach the exit to Santa Monica, I realize I've traveled 10 miles with no conscious memory of actually looking at the road. My mind is swirling and grinding playing one giant game of connect the dots. I just picked up a new bottle of Valium yesterday. It's time to go to sleep and let my subconscious go to work on this puzzle.

9

I woke up again at 5:30am, but I'm thankful for the six hours I got. After my call with Jon, I spent most of the night stuck in some dream loop. I drifted in and out of consciousness and every time I stirred, the dream would restart. It happens a lot when I'm deep undercover and in pursuit of someone. It means waking up tired, but it's nothing coffee and exercise can't fix.

Running by the Pacific is beautiful this early in the morning, especially when the wind is blowing out. On days when it's blowing in, the marine layer traps the smog, and you can feel it. You can almost taste it. But on days like this when everything is blowing out, you can see Catalina once the sun peeks over the horizon.

As I run down the shoreline, I roll "sommelier" over and over in my head trying to make some connection with trafficking little girls. Are we dealing with a company? Someone French? Maybe shipping is the connection. I need to go back and look at the Vietnamese manifests and the shipping container where we found the girls. It could just be some pretentious shitbag with expensive tastes. Impossible to know at this point. Until we have another piece of the puzzle, it will be tough to know where else to look.

I change direction to run back up the beach and ten minutes later, the sun breaks from behind the lone cloud in the sky spilling sunlight across the beach like it's showing me the way home. I'm almost to the path where I turn back onto the street when I see Rachel moving toward me, front lit from the rising sun. She's wearing jeans, a gray-blue sweater, and a cautious smile, happy she found me, but unsure how warm my reception may be.

"Well, this is a nice surprise," I say trying to put her at ease. "How'd you know I'd be here?"

"Oh, a good journalist never gives up her sources," she responds, noticeably relieved that the raving asshole from the other night seems to be somewhere else.

"Uh huh," I say with a big smirk, "Well when you see your source, tell him he owes me the rest of that bottle of Scotch for ratting me out."

"He knows. I have the bottle in my car to give you."

Like I said, Paddy is an excellent judge of character.

"Listen, Jake, the truth is, I didn't like how the other night ended, and I wanted to come apologize for whatever I said that offended you."

"It wasn't you," I stop her. "I was three or four shots in before you even got to Paddy's. I was liking you and I let my guard down. When you told me you were a reporter covering human trafficking, it felt like an ambush. Not because of anything you did, but that's how it felt. I've been burnt badly by journalists Rachel, more than once, and I've gotten really good at throwing the walls up pretty quick. With my dear friend Scotch calling the shots the other night, I reacted very poorly, and I'm sorry."

"Apology accepted," she smiles. "You think we might try this again?"

"Sure," I answer. I'm willing to take another run at this dance. "Hi" I say extending my hand. "My name is Jake Hardy."

"Rachel Meredith," she answers. "I'm a sneaky journalist. And what is it that you do, Mr. Hardy?"

"Off the record?" I ask with a casual, but serious smirk that says don't fuck me.

She cocks her head and confirms, "off the record."

"I do undercover work for the Department of Homeland Security hunting human traffickers moving underage girls into the United States."

"That's what you do?" she asks, the lights starting to come on.

"It's what I do." It's who I am.

"Well, now I know why you lost it the other night. In your shoes, I would have reacted the same way."

"You'll find this hard to believe Rachel, but I'm not everybody's cup of tea."

"I like tea," she says coyly. "Which speaking of, any chance you're hungry for some breakfast? I had to get up really early to find your ass and I haven't eaten anything."

"Always hungry for breakfast," I answer, "but you're gonna have to spot me. My wallet is back at the house and seeing as you're all ravenous and all."

"I think I can cover a few eggs and some coffee," she grins.

"No bacon?" I ask. "Oh God, you're not Vegan are you?"

"Not in this or any other lifetime!"

I'm starting to like this girl again.

"Come on," I say pointing back down the beach. "They serve a great breakfast at a restaurant in this five-star hotel down the way."

This early, we're one of only a few couples in the restaurant. The hostess sits us in a booth over in the corner which is fine by me. True to form, Rachel orders some hot tea, and I get a large coffee, black. Looking across the table with unbuzzed eyes, I realize she's more stunning than I remember. I really hope she's who I'm wanting her to be. As though she's sensing my caution, Rachel leans into the center of the table, moves the salt and pepper shakers to the side, and taps the table to focus my attention.

"Jake, I want to make something really clear to put you at ease and so there's no confusion. For as long as you know me, unless I tell you I'm talking to you as a journalist, everything we talk about is off the record. I had no idea who you were when we met. I wasn't there to get a story. And frankly, while I'm obviously intrigued by this connection we share, I would far rather keep my private and professional lives separate. That work for you?"

"Very much."

"Good."

"So, tell me about Rachel Meredith's private and professional lives. You said you work for the DOJ and others who shall remain nameless. What did you do before that? Where did you grow up? How did you end up here?"

"Well, how much time do you have?"

In this moment, I have all the time in the world.

10

When the waitress comes over with new menus and asks if Rachel and I would like to order lunch, we look at our watches and realize we've been sitting there for nearly four hours. And yet somehow, neither of us wants to stop our conversation. I don't know why, but I feel more connected to this woman than people I've known for 20 years.

"I can't believe it's time to eat again," Rachel says making a writing motion in the air to signal the waitress we're finally ready for the check. "I hope I'm not keeping you from something,"

"I'm actually on a bit of a vacation," I admit smugly. "Some would call it a suspension. I pretty much just call it bullshit."

"A suspension? Wow! What'd you do?"

"I stuck my pistol in a bad guy's mouth and threatened to add a window to the back of his skull. The thing was, I did it in front of the wrong person and she didn't quite have the stomach for it."

"Some dogs just need to be put down," she says wide-eyed and serious.

"I couldn't agree more," I agree. "Hey, listen, I don't know what you have going on tonight, but I'd love to cook you dinner if you're interested."

"Dinner would be wonderful. I've got to run around some this afternoon. Would six work for you?"

"Six o'clock is great. How about filets? You good with steaks?"

"Love steaks."

"Cab or Merlot?"

"Cab. Can I bring anything?"

"Why don't you bring something sweet for dessert?"

"Done."

"You have time to run me back to my house so I can show you where it is?"

"Sure. Let's go."

We walk up the sidewalk winding through the palm trees and the beach to Rachel's car parked in the lot. She climbs into a white European sportscar and unlocks the doors. Whoever this woman is working for they clearly pay her well.

Rachel starts the car and pulls out onto Pico. I have her take a quick left on Ocean Avenue and we follow Ocean along the coast past The Ivy and the Farmer's Market. At Idaho, I have her turn right in front of the Oceanside Santa Monica, a cool retro resort with swanky revamped apartment suites. My house is just up Idaho off of 4th.

"Thanks for the ride," I say, painfully aware that I have no idea what to do next. Do I shake her hand? Give her a wave? If it was Jon he'd punch me in the shoulder and say, "Later Fucker!" but that's wrong. I pause, but clearly Rachel has no anxiety about how this should end. Without hesitation, she leans over and kisses me on the cheek.

"Thanks for breakfast," she says.

"Hey, you bought," I answer.

"You know what I mean," she smiles.

I do. And I fully intend on returning the favor tonight.

"See you at six," I say closing the door.

"Bye Jake," she says before pulling away from the curb. I stand and watch until I can no longer see her brake lights disappearing in the distance.

I spend the afternoon cleaning up the house making sure the den, the kitchen, my bedroom, and bathroom are presentable and wondering what it will feel like to have a woman in the house again. It's been a long time. Two years. Three? I've been so focused on the job at hand and finding Catherine on top of that, that I haven't taken much time to breathe.

Even after our morning together, I still can't put my finger on what it is about Rachel Meredith that intrigues me so much. There's definitely something familiar about her. It's like we've met before though I know we haven't. Maybe it's the common ground we share. Human trafficking is a Vulcan flame most people don't want to get anywhere near. Rachel understands it. She understands what I do and that dealing with the shadow side of the world is hard. It's dark, it's lonely, and it's heartbreaking. Because of that, there's a prickly, cynical side to me that dominates who most people get to see. I'm hopeful that guy will take the night off.

I run over to Flurry's, Santa Monica's best meat market, for the filets, some Brussels sprouts, and sweet potatoes, two bottles of nice Cabernet, some roses for the table in the den, and some charcoal for the smoker. No one will ever mistake me for one of the world's great chefs, but I can grill a better steak than you can buy in a restaurant.

That paired with a rich Cab? There are worse ways to spend an evening.

Around 5:45, I start the fire in the grill, and light the logs in the fireplace, pull up a music channel on the TV and open the wine to let it breathe, trying to remember to do the same. The Brussels are cut, the oven is preheated, the flowers are on the table, the steaks are rubbed and at room temperature and I'm showered and shaved.

Right at six, I hear a knock at the door and when I come out of the kitchen, Rachel is walking through the door carrying a handled bag with, I'm guessing, dessert. She hugs me and puts the bag on the bar by the kitchen.

"This is nice!" she says looking around the house. "The fireplace is super cozy."

"I like it," I answer.

"How long have you lived here?"

"Four or five years?" I say trying to remember how long it's been. "It's not huge, but it's all I need. And I love being running distance from the beach."

"I would be there every day."

"I am when I can be," I agree. "You hungry? Thought we'd eat around 6:30. You good with that?"

"I'm great with that. I am in your hands."

"In that case, here's your wine, change the music to whatever you'd like, and I'll be right back."

"Something already smells good," Rachel calls after me.

"The Brussels sprouts and the sweet potatoes are in the oven," I yell running to the kitchen to make sure they aren't burning. "Another 10 minutes or so and we'll throw the steaks on and be ready to go."

Rachel slips off her shoes and curls up on the sofa with her feet pulled up under her. She takes the remote and starts flipping through the music channels. I go outside to check the fire and when I come back, she's settled on the "Coffeehouse" channel. Some mid-tempo pop song fills the house from speakers in every room. She's holding the pad I left on the table last night after talking to Jon.

"Who is the Sommelier?" she asks. "It's got three exclamation points and a box around it. You must really want to know," she teases.

"It's just a lead in a case I'm following. It's nothing."

"I thought you tracked people, not wine."

"Me too," I answer. Thirty minutes later, I hand her a plate with one of the top three dinners I've ever prepared. The crust on the filet is perfect. The Brussels have a little crunch topped with a pineapple habanero chutney and the sweet potatoes are perfect. Rachel raises her eyebrows impressed and smiles, patting the sofa beside her. This feels good.

For about an hour, we talk about L.A., how long Rachel will be in town, and her impressions of the city. We touch on politics, the books we love, and that our favorite way to relax is to turn on a great movie, no matter how old. Hitchcock to Tarantino, great is great no matter when it was made. Oh, and we discuss how much I really do need a dog. Dinner could not have been better. When our plates are empty, I take them to the kitchen and refill our wine glasses, now into the second bottle of Cabernet. I set it on the coffee table and sit back down.

"So, tell me more about growing up," Rachel says sipping her wine.

"You mean the island?" I ask.

"I mean growing up. What is it that made Jake Hardy, Jake Hardy?" she asks. Deep breath.

"I guess it all starts with my mother. Her name was Julia Grace. She was a beautiful woman from a somewhat wealthy family that had lived on Sea Island for three generations before her. She was creative, she was smart, and fiercely independent. My mother literally had the world in front of her, but she fell for a boy who didn't. From the day he was born, I think Miller Clark was really angry about that. For his size, he was apparently a hell of a football player which gave him some hope for something better. But then he met my mother and suddenly his road to prosperity was made clear. I don't know what it was about my father that fascinated my mother enough to defy her birthright. I don't know how she didn't see him for what he was, but she was entranced.

"A year later when my mother was 17, she got pregnant. You can imagine how well that was received. She and my father married quietly and seven months later my sister Catherine and I arrived. Apparently, my mother was very excited about having twins. My grandparents bought her a modest house where we could live and always gave her a bit more money than we needed. But always to her. Just to her.

"I think my grandparents were civil to my father, but they saw him for the climber he was. He was the nightmare scenario and cautionary tale for every wealthy family with a daughter. Had he made any real effort to go to college, to learn a trade, to do anything to replace his rage about his status with anything productive or supportive, things might have been different. But he didn't. He drank and gambled and constantly disappointed my mother, failing to fulfill whatever promise she saw in him. For years, she never wavered that there was good in him. But by the end, I think even she knew the truth. There's a fine line between charisma and entitlement and my father thought the universe owed him. That's about the time the universe jumped up and showed him otherwise."

I'm not sure I've ever told anyone this story so completely, even Jon. The beginning of the story is easy. It's the finish that's difficult, but Rachel seems completely engaged and I'm not going to stop now. I refill both our glasses with the Cabernet on the table and take a giant swallow of mine. I take a deep breath and let myself remember.

"One day in May when Catherine and I were nine, we were out on the porch swinging with my mother. Catherine would always sit as close to my mother as possible, cuddled up right next to her. My mother would put her arm around my sister's shoulder pulling her closer and Catherine would lean into her and giggle as she scooted closer and closer, pressing her cheek against my mother's side. Always secure that my mother would never let go of her. After a few minutes, I remember Catherine sitting up on her knees and looking into my mother's eyes. Catherine asked her why her eyes were yellow. My mother teased back that her eyes were blue. Very serious, Catherine reached up and touched the side of my mother's face and insisted again that her eyes were yellow. Mom shrugged and said she was tired. Maybe that's why her eyes were a funny color. It wasn't. A few weeks later, we found out my mother had Stage 4 pancreatic cancer. Six months later she was gone."

"Oh Jake," Rachel says, seeming to breathe for the first time in minutes. "That breaks my heart. How did your father respond?"

"Not well. When my mother told my grandparents about the cancer, it destroyed them, but at the same time, they were extremely mindful of what needed to happen and happen quickly before my mother's death. Financially, my grandfather formalized a trust for my mother with Catherine and myself as the secondary beneficiaries. In the event of her death, her full inheritance would pass to us in Trust that we could access at 21. Miller received the same monthly stipend we had been getting to help take care of us, but long term, he didn't get a dime more. He hated my grandparents for that and the more he drank, the more that hatred festered."

"So, your father ended up raising you," Rachel wonders.

"Raising suggests some modicum of care," I answer coldly. "The only things Miller Clark ever raised were a glass and the pot in any poker game he was invariably losing. At best, my father made sure we went to school and didn't die because he knew my grandparents would be further up his ass the second anything bad happened. And he was right. But a few years after Mom died, we lost our grandparents too. My grandmother never really got over losing my mother and once my grandmother passed, my grandfather was just lost. He died about three months after her."

It's been a long time since I really thought about my grandparents, but even now, I can feel myself choking on the emotion. Our lives would have been so much different had they lived, but I'm beyond thankful for the trust they left behind for us. I'm not exactly making a mint at Homeland, and my grandparents' gift has always given me the means I needed to search for my sister.

"My recollection is that Miller was undone by my grandfather dying, but looking back, I think it's because it meant he had lost any chance he had to have my grandfather change his mind about the Trust. The day we buried my grandfather, any delusions my father had about getting his hands on my mother's money died too. Catherine and I were 11 when my grandfather died, and I can still remember the night we got home from the funeral. My father didn't even change out of the cheap black suit he wore to the burial. He walked in the door, grabbed a bottle of Scotch, and sat down in his recliner. When we asked about dinner, Miller screamed back we were, 'old enough to make our own goddamned dinner and if we didn't like that, we could go to our fucking rooms and not eat.' I don't remember what we ended up eating, but I do remember the more Miller drank that night, the louder he got. Cursing my grandparents. Cursing my mother. Cursing God. Screaming that if it wasn't for the two of us, he could leave all this behind and maybe be happy.

"This became my father's ritual. Go to work. Come home. Drink, smoke, curse, pass out. Catherine and I became very efficient latchkey kids and quickly learned that being invisible was the path of least resistance."

"And it never got better?"

"No. The real darkness was just beginning."

I take a breath and unexpectedly feel it catch in the back of my throat. My head feels thick, and my chest feels heavy. I can feel sweat starting to form on the back of my neck and down my back. If I didn't know better, I'd worry I was having a heart attack. But this isn't that. It's a panic attack being choked down. It's the energy my body is producing to keep my rage from blistering up and consuming me. I know this feeling well. I've only spoken about what happened to Catherine once and that was to Jon in Afghanistan. That night, I leaned against Bear and sobbed for hours in the dark. No idea if tonight will be any better, but for some reason, I want to tell Rachel the rest of this story.

"Being twins, my sister and I were alike in every way possible other than gender. We were extroverts, we were smart, we had the same sense of humor, and despite our situation, we were happy kids most of the time. We just knew we had to steer clear of Miller, especially when he was drinking.

"On our 12th birthday, my father bought Catherine a really pretty dress with flowers all over it. She loved it. I can remember her putting it on and twirling around so she could see all the flowers. It was the first dress Catherine had ever worn that didn't look like kids clothes and since she had started developing early, she filled it out a bit. It looked like something my mother would have worn and as much as my sister looked like my mother, if you squinted your eyes, you could pretend you were seeing my mother reborn.

"I didn't know it until Catherine told me much later, but that was the first night Miller went and crawled in bed with her. He told her how pretty she was, as if that justified his betrayal, and that with her mother gone, it was now her responsibility to take care of him."

When I hear Rachel gasp and see her close her eyes, I consider stopping. But I don't.

"Catherine said that first night, Miller put his hand over her mouth and stinking of whiskey and cigarettes, whispered in her ear that if she ever said anything or let on to me in any way that anything was wrong, that he'd kill me in my sleep and bury me where 100 dogs would never find me. This became my father's new ritual the four or five nights a week when he didn't just pass out in his recliner.

"It didn't take long for me to realize something wasn't right with Catherine. She got very quiet and stayed very close to me whenever we were at home. She lost any real sense of fun, or joy and I had the feeling every smile I saw from her looked forced. From school, I knew teenage girls were moody, but this felt like more than that. Catherine started spending a lot of time in her room just lying in the dark. She'd say she had a headache, or she'd blame it on her period, but I was worried. She wasn't alright, but at 12, I didn't know enough to see the signs of abuse that were right in front of me.

"Three or four months after our birthday, Catherine sat me down one morning after Miller left for work and told me what had been happening to her. When she saw the horror and the fury on my face, she threw her arms around me and started crying. She told me about Miller's threat to hurt me and made me promise I'd never let on that I knew what he was doing to her. I promised her. But I knew it was a promise I'd never keep."

I'm sure Rachel can see the rage and the emotion building in me. I can feel my face getting warm and when she reaches over and takes my hand, I smile. I lean over to the table and take another big swallow of wine.

"Without saying anything about what was happening to Catherine, I started provoking Miller to draw his attention away from my sister. It would start with some innocuous question like "why do you drink so much?" or "why can't we live in a nice house like other people?" always hitting him where he was most insecure. I was relentless. I'd poke him, and poke him, and poke him, and poke him until he went after me with a belt, or his fists. One night, he beat me with the cord to the vacuum cleaner until I had bloody welts across my back and legs. Once he beat me with an empty whiskey bottle. It was never easy, but by the end he was too worn out to go after Catherine, so fuck him."

I look at Rachel to see if she is ready to bolt out the door. Most people can't handle this kind of darkness. It's just too much. But Rachel is sitting quietly, looking at me with a genuine gaze of what feels like empathy, sympathy, and love. I get the feeling this is not an unfamiliar story to her and remembering what it is she does for a living, I'm sure it's not. And yet, I'm also sure that none of her stories end the way ours does. I breathe deep through my nose and exhale through my mouth. Rachel squeezes my hand.

"It was no secret to us that Miller was a gambler. There were many nights when we got sent to our rooms early when six to eight guys Miller knew from somewhere showed up to smoke, drink, and play poker around our kitchen table. The next morning, the house was always rancid and there was nothing left to eat, but part of me liked those nights because they went so late, Miller was always too tired and drunk to bother with Catherine. I would sleep in her room those nights and I remember we would stuff towels under the door to keep the smoke and some of the noise from seeping into her room. Miller rarely finished a night ahead, but that summer, after months of losing, he found himself where no addict ever wants to be.

"One night, I think it was July, there was a knock at the door and when Miller opened it, there were two huge men standing there. I still remember one of the guys because he had big gold rings squeezed onto all five of his fat fingers. Miller told us to go to our rooms and we assumed these were just the first two guys to show for that night's game. That's not why there were there.

"As these guys pushed their way into our house, Catherine and I ran to her room. She jumped onto her bed, but I crouched down and watched the scene unfolding in the den through a skinny crack in the door. I have no idea how big these guys really were, but they towered over my father by six inches at least and had to outweigh him 60 pounds. While the smaller of the two started talking, the bigger one circled behind Miller and put his arm around his throat. Had he wanted to, I have no doubt he could have snapped my father's neck like a dried branch. Instead, he just held him in check, intermittently cutting off his air supply when Miller gave the wrong answer to whatever the smaller man was asking.

"I couldn't hear much of the conversation, but I could see Miller was terrified of what he was being told. He pleaded, shaking his head and his hands but that only drew punches from the man in front of him and then from the man in back. By the time they left, Miller was already bruising with blood dripping from the cuts on his face. We didn't dare come out of Catherine's room, but I sat by the door for an hour or more just watching. Miller was frantic. Pacing back and forth. Talking to himself. He opened a new bottle of Scotch and filled up a rocks glass. But when he drank it, the alcohol must have burned his bleeding lips because he immediately bellowed like a wounded animal and threw his drink against the kitchen wall sending shards of glass everywhere. Still cursing, he grabbed the bottle and collapsed into one of the kitchen chairs. For all I know, he stayed there for the rest of the night. When we woke up the next morning, he was gone.

"We did our best to clean up the house and about five o'clock, Miller breezed through the door as though nothing had happened. His face looked like a finger painting of red, black, and blue smudges, accented by a couple of butterfly bandages, but he seemed lighter. Confident. He even brought home dinner which he never did. We ate, we watched TV, and we went to sleep. The next sound I remember was my sister screaming, "No! No! No!"

"From the tone of her scream, I expected to run out and find Miller on top of her on the sofa. What I found was much worse than that. Standing at the front door were the two men from the night before flanking a third even taller man with snow white hair, slicked back. His beard and mustache were the same bright white and I remember thinking there was something really fucking evil about the smirk in his smile."

Rachel drops my hand and stiffens in her chair. The gravity of our story is finally landing on her.

"My father and sister were standing in front of him, Catherine still in her pajamas. She kept screaming "No!" trying to squirm out of Miller's grasp but his grip on her was too strong. With a violent shove, he pushed Catherine toward the man with white hair and said, "We're even." When Catherine turned and screamed my name, everything became distorted. Sounds were muffled. Time slowed down. Faces were exaggerated. I ran to the door and pushed my way between my father and the tall man, grabbing Catherine and trying to pull her away. My father grabbed my arm and tried to sling me away. When that didn't work, the white haired man picked me up and threw me against the wall so hard, it left an indentation. The hit broke my arm all the way through just below my shoulder and my throbbing head felt like I was under water. I could still hear Catherine screaming, but I couldn't move. The last thing I remember seeing was the white haired man pulling my sister through the door and my father slamming it shut. Then, everything went black."

"Oh, Jake," Rachel says again, this time wiping tears from her eyes. "Where is Catherine now?"

"I don't know."

"You don't know what happened to her?"

"No."

"Who was the man who took her?"

"I don't know," I answer, just, empty. "I don't know anything."

"What about your father? He never said anything to you?"

"A month after Miller Clark sold his daughter to settle a gambling debt he chose a bottle of whiskey and the barrel end of a shotgun for his last meal. Anything that would have helped me find my sister died with him. But I've never stopped looking. That's why I do what I do. The world is a big place, but I still believe my sister is somewhere in it."

Rachel finishes the last of her wine and moves closer to me on the sofa, looking at me in a way that suggests she would gladly take the pain away if she could. She reaches up and cups the side of my face with her hand, her little finger resting just behind my ear. Her palm feels soft and warm.

"Nothing has been easy for you, has it," she whispers. There is no need to answer. It was a statement, not a question. Rachel leans into me and gently brushes my lips with hers. For some reason, I hesitate to respond but then run my fingers through her hair and press my mouth into her kiss. I feel her knee move between my legs as her tongue pushes between my lips. She is now straddling me with her arms wrapped around the back of my head pulling me into her. There is something fearless and a little ferocious in her kisses. There is often a fine line between anger and passion, and I'm suddenly aware it's been too long since I balanced the former with the latter.

With a final tug of my bottom lip, Rachel rises up from my lap grabbing her wine in one hand and the bag off the bar in the other.

"Is that our dessert," I ask her.

"I am dessert," she flirts back. "Where is your bathroom?"

"Right through there," I say, drinking her in as she moves away from me.

"I like your bedroom," she says getting to the door.

"I cleaned it up," I joke. "I even changed the sheets,"

"Good," she says looking at me over her shoulder. "I like fucking on clean sheets."

For most of the night, Rachel and I explore each other with abandon. It is clearly something that both of us need. She feels good. She smells good. Our bodies fit together and move as though we've done this dance a thousand times. We are exhausted but neither of us wants to stop. We go and we go and then just lie back, curled into each other, breathing. Rachel flips onto her stomach and tells me to move behind her. She grabs the headboard and as I move up onto my knees behind her, she reaches up and pushes her hair up off the back of her neck. Underneath, there's a small, colorful tattoo at the base of her hairline. A tiny bird with its wings unfurled. This woman is full of surprises. And she saves her most surprising move for last.

Around 6:45 the next morning, a flash of sunlight crests the bottom of my bedroom window and hits my eyelids waking me up. I reach over to pull Rachel into me, but all I grab is air. The other side of my bed is empty. I look up and see the bathroom door is open and the inside is dark. The shower quiet. I go to the kitchen to see if maybe she's there. The house is still with the exception of the slight hum of the dishwasher cleaning the wine glasses and plates from last night. Rachel's clothes are gone. Her purse. Her keys. Her car. I look for a note on my nightstand, on the fridge, on the bar, on the coffee table. But there's nothing. She's gone. As is the top page of the notepad sitting on the end table where I had written, "Who Is The Sommelier?"

That missing page and the faint smell of perfume in my bed are the only signs that Rachel Meredith was ever here.

11

It's not the first time I've gone to sleep next to someone and woken up alone. It's just not what I was expecting. I've spent more than a few nights that ended in meaningless sex with someone I met at Paddy's a few hours before. But that's not what this was. I connected with Rachel Meredith in a way I haven't connected with a woman in a very long time. Maybe ever. And yet she's gone. Part of me hopes she just ran out to get us breakfast. But I know that's not what's happening. Rachel is a ghost and I'm here wondering what happened.

Maybe the truth about my family was too much for her to handle when she stopped to think about what I'd said. Violent alcoholic pedophile for a father. Childhood trauma. Suicide. I know that genetically on paper, I'm no fucking picnic. But I really thought this woman got me. Maybe she did and it's just too hard. I am who I am. Nothing I can do about it.

I go back to bed and try to sleep, but I can still smell her perfume in the sheets and on my pillow. I can still smell her on my skin. What did I miss? I'm not stoned. I wasn't hammered. Did I do something to offend her? Did I say something? Once we left the den, there wasn't a whole lot of talking and it wasn't just good. We moved the same. We anticipated what the other wanted and when one shifted positions, the other was there to receive them. We were in total sync. Then I woke up to an empty bed. No goodbye. No note. Nothing. And why in the Hell would she take my note about the case?

After 45 minutes of staring at the ceiling and replaying the last eight hours in my head, I walk to the kitchen and find my phone. No calls. No texts. I move to the table in the den and check my laptop. Just a bunch of random emails from websites I should have unsubscribed to long ago. I try to log into my DHS email hoping there might be some new intel from Jon. The denial reminds me I'm suspended and off the network.

I slam my computer and walk back to the bathroom. I look into the mirror and see the face of annoyance. Hurt. Disappointment. Anxiety. Where did you go Rachel?

I start the shower and climb in under the hot spray. I breathe through the hot water beating on my face until I feel it starting to cool. I soap up quickly and rinse off, sending any last remnants of last night down the drain. I get dressed, turn on the coffee, and try to focus on the one thing I can control – figuring out who this Sommelier is and why he's smuggling 12-year-old girls in shipping containers.

What was it Jonny said on the phone? Had we not found the girls in Houston, they would have been trucked to Las Vegas. What better place to hide trafficked girls in plain sight than America's adult playground? If we're going to find this guy, that's as good a place to start as any. Vegas is a big town, but if he's connected to cargo that precious, somebody there knows who this guy is. If I can find them, I can get a bead on finding him.

I pack a quick bag, grab my coffee, and head out for the 270 mile trip through the desert from Santa Monica to Las Vegas. Four hours is a long drive with just my thoughts to keep me company, especially today. But vast nothingness can also give way to clarity if channeled well. Worst case I'll turn on a good playlist and try to relax.

Traffic is heavy coming out of Santa Monica, but it lightens up the closer I get to Barstow. As the cities give way to the Mojave and its sprawling vista of asphalt, mountains, and sand, I try to focus on the task ahead and not let my thoughts wander back to Rachel. Wondering where she is. Wondering if I'll see her again. Maybe nights like last night are destined to be fleeting. Maybe I should just appreciate it for what it was. No. Fuck that. That's not how I'm wired. That's not how any of us are wired. Good and bad, we're built to want to experience the things that pleasure us again and again and again. It's our blessing and our curse.

About 1:30, the façade of the Vegas Strip rises on the horizon. At night, the view coming into Vegas is spectacular, a beacon of Capitalism all lit up in neon. But in the middle of the day, coming for work, sober, not in Vegas to play, there's very little that's magical. With the tall rectangular hotels, a towering pyramid and now a sphere, it just looks like a landscape of geometric shapes blinking an anxious welcome. Daytime is actually quite ordinary in Vegas.

The nights are a different story.

There are few cities in the world as lit as Las Vegas. But for every bright light, there are two dark corners. From the casinos and hotels to the bars and alleys off the strip, there is no shortage of places where girls can be run. Purchased. Exploited. Hurt. Abused. Ruined. Broken. The Vegas that draws most of the world is nothing but a veneer. The themed casinos. The dancing fountains. The acrobatic shows and the rock star residencies. It's fantasyland for grownups. But punch through that candy coating and there's a dark underbelly where bodies are sold, souls are squeezed, and evil is embraced by thousands of people a day, all pretending that it's somehow normal. It's what you'd expect in a town called Sin City with a tagline like, "What happens in Vegas, Stays in Vegas." The real heartbreak is that the same evil is happening right now in every city in America.

12

Around 3pm, I check into my room in a tower off the Southern end of the strip and lay down to take a nap. After being up most of the night and making the long drive across the desert, I can feel myself fading. I crash and crash hard.

Around 8pm, I wake up to a rainbow of colored lights flashing outside my window. From my balcony I can see all the way up the back side of the strip. The streets are packed. Couples walking hand in hand on the way to dinner. Loud groups of women in town for bachelorette parties wearing short skirts, low cut tops and carrying brightly lit schooners of frozen drinks. Grifters on the hunt and drunk homeless asleep in the corners.

I walk out the front door of the tower and turn right onto Las Vegas Boulevard heading up the street toward the Venetian. Immediately, a large man brushes up against me slapping a brochure against his palm. "Strip club tonight? Titties and beer brother! Titties and beer." I push past him and see he's one of a dozen of these guys all pushing different bars and strip joints. I cut left to take the walking bridge over the traffic to the opposite side of the street and halfway across the bridge, I'm assaulted by the worst singing voice I have ever heard coming out of a skinny, black kid holding a blunt in one hand and a cheap microphone in the other. He's drunk and beyond tone deaf, but the lyrics make me laugh. As melodically as he's capable, he sings, "Put a dollar in my cup, and I'll shut the fuck up!" By the money in his cup, I know two things are true. Others find his schtick funny and, he's a liar. I give him a dollar.

From the street, I walk up a long ramp and into the front entrance of a palatial casino. The lobby is full of people standing with suitcases, looking up, mesmerized by glass flowers covering the ceiling. All enjoying their last quiet moments before the madness. Even this early at night, there's a crackling energy on the floor. There must be a thousand people moving through the casino, in and out of restaurants, on the way to check in for a show or the spa. A thousand people with a dollar and a dream. Each with a fantasy of going home richer than they came.

I head into the casino, instinctively scanning the bars and tables for working girls that may actually be girls. I don't see any but that's not surprising. Even in Vegas, a pimp running young girls isn't brazen enough to have them working the floor of a $600 dollar a night hotel. At least not tonight.

A steady soundtrack of calliope horns and plinking coins fills the air around the slot machines along with the faint, lingering pall of stale cigarettes. A chorus of yells repeatedly erupts from a craps table to my right. Somebody's on a heater and apparently everybody's winning. I make my way to the cage and exchange $800 for chips. The blackjack tables are just past the high limit slots and tonight, winning is all about information. I just need to find the right person to spill it.

I make a lap around the Blackjack area of the floor, scoping out the people sitting at the tables. Most of them look completely normal, like people who flew in this morning from Des Moines, or Sarasota, or Peoria to put everything they learned in "'Vegas for Dummies" to the test. I stop, scanning the floor again and see a guy I completely missed the first time around. Some balding cheesedick in his late 50s wearing a silk shirt with cufflinks, holding court with a woman at his side who's way too built and beautiful to be with a guy like him. Either she's a pro, or he's loaded. Whichever is true, guys like him think they know everything and aren't the least bit bashful trying to prove it. That I can work with.

As if on cue, the couple sitting next to this guy pick up their chips and move to a new table as I'm moving his way. There are six seats at the table, and he's camped on the far left. I sit down two seats away from him and put my chips on the table in front of me. I greet the dealer and nod to the three players to my right. Even before I turn to the left, I can feel the gaze of the guy in the silk shirt boring into me. He's clearly a bit annoyed I didn't acknowledge him first. Perfect.

"How you doing? I'm Jake," I say to him extending my arm. He pauses and then reaches out and shakes my hand. Weakly.

"Harold," he says with a distinct sense of arrogance.

"I'm Happy" the woman next to him smiles extending her hand across his chest to greet me. She giggles and puts her hand back on Harold's shoulder. Pro or sugar baby. Nailed it.

"Happy and Harold," I say, purposefully putting her first. I need to get under this guy's skin a little. "Good cards tonight? Looks like you're building up a small fortune over there."

"It's alright," Harold says sizing me up. "Can always be better."

"My Harold's a shark!" Happy says with a giggly growl, bearing her teeth in her best Great White impression. "We're going for lobster later."

"Honey, why don't you get us another round of drinks, huh?" Harold says nudging her away.

"The drink girl should be…"

"Happy!" Harold snaps. "Go get the drinks. I don't need to tell you a third time."

And in that statement, I know exactly who I'm dealing with. Harold is your basic Scorsese disciple. He's seen "Casino" and "Goodfellas" a few too many times and fancies himself as someone important. My father was the same way. Miller watched those movies on a loop, and I can see him in Harold. When life and the people around him don't give him the respect he thinks he deserves, he manufactures it. Comes to Vegas where money talks. Hires an escort like Happy who's more than willing to play into his charade for $500, free drinks, and a 10 minute lay with a guy who's quick on the trigger. With Happy gone, Harold leans over to show the new lion who's in charge of this particular watering hole.

"You play a lot of cards?" he asks pulling out a cigarette and lighting it with the gold torch lighter from his shirt pocket. "The couple that just left were fucking morons. Been taking my cards for the last hour and a half. Let's hope you're a little smarter than they were."

"Yeah, let's hope," I say.

For about twenty minutes, we just play cards, and everything goes according to Hoyle. I'm basically even. Harold is up a few hundred and offers tacit approval of my playing style by offering me a cigarette.

"Smoke?" he asks waving the pack in my direction.

"I'm good, thanks," I say waving him off. "Appreciate the offer. That's one vice I don't have."

With a pop, a blue flame arcs out of Harold's lighter igniting the end of another smoke. "Yeah," he answers. "So, what vices do you have?"

"Oh, you know, wine and women," I say starting to frame the conversation for where I need it to go.

"Grape Juice and pussy. You and your goddamn generation," Harold mumbles under his breath. "Why don't you let me order you a Scotch or a tequila shot. Put some hair on your balls."

"I'm good with cocktails," I say. "I just like a glass of Cabernet given the choice."

"I didn't say cocktails son," Harold answers getting more amped up. "I said a Scotch or tequila. Whiskey. Gin. Vodka. I don't give a shit. Just pour it in rocks glass and drink it neat like God intended. Be a man, Jake. You and your fucking wine club generation need to grow up."

"So, I guess you don't know any good sommeliers in Vegas?" I say poking him back.

"Some what?" he asks. I can tell from his eyes he's completely lost. Harold has never heard the word sommelier in his life. Harold may know all the back pages and strip clubs where I can find a girl like Happy, but he's not smart or sophisticated enough to be trusted with the kind of deep web intel I'm chasing. It's a needle in a haystack but somebody knows something. It's just not this guy.

I play one final hand and the dealer hits me with a blackjack. I know Happy is back when I hear the squeal go up to my left.

"You won!" she chirps putting Harold's drink down in front of him and sipping on something blue.

I gather my chips to leave and Happy purses her lips in a pout. "I'm gonna take that as my sign to quit for evening. Harold, Happy, it was a pleasure," I say walking away from the table, thinking about where I should head to next. Behind me I hear Happy say, "I liked him."

I turn to take one last look at Harold. He has one hand cupped tightly around Happy's ass and the other is holding another cigarette and throwing back three fingers of Scotch. "Fucking quitter," he mumbles shaking his head.

I head down the ramp between the Bellagio and Caesars and walk up the driveway past the fountains Evil Knievel tried to jump in '67. He wasn't the first person to come to Vegas and end up broken. Or the last.

I do a lap through the casino and end up staying for three hours playing at different tables trying to engage guys who look like they might be in the know. Some more blackjack. Craps. Roulette. A little poker. I have a number of interesting conversations but every one turns out to be with someone who's visiting Vegas from somewhere else. I've got to find out where Vegas people play. And I'm betting it's somewhere without a 40-story hotel attached and a $300 show down the hall.

Around 1:30am, I head to the men's room and run into a croupier leaving for a break. I ask him where the Vegas locals go for some serious action, and he runs down five or six back rooms or specialty areas at hotels I recognize. In my gut, I don't think that's what I'm looking for. I thank him and turn to leave, but then he throws out one more place he says might be interesting. It's a private club called Alistair's that's tucked away about half a mile off the strip. According to the croupier, they have stiff drinks, big antes, and the hottest women in Vegas. I ask him why it's not the most popular spot in Vegas. He surmises the $500 cover at the door might have something to do with it. This is the place I've been looking for. Rich, expensive, and exclusive enough to attract men on a mission. I flip the croupier a $100 chip and walk out to Las Vegas Boulevard.

If you didn't know exactly where Alistair's was, you'd never find it. There are no flashing lights. No marquee. No posters with sultry sirens beckoning you inside. It's just a massive red door with the number 221 over the top. I open the door and walk into an entry that looks more like a sparse Wall Street board room than the entryway to a club. A moderate gentleman who appears to be a young 60 rises from a mahogany desk. He's wearing a trim, tailored suit and from his mustache and goatee to his shoes, he's impeccably put together.

"Good evening sir," he says greeting me. "How may I help you?"

"I'm looking for a club with a little action and a friend of mine said I might enjoy it here. Is this Alistair's. Are you Alistair?"

"It is and I am not," the man answers. "May I ask what kind of action you're looking for?"

"Sorry?" I say, a bit taken aback by the question.

"Action," he answers. "Which persuasion of action are you seeking. Cards? Mixology? Female companionship?"

"How about all three," I smile. He looks me up and down and begins a rapid-fire battery of questions.

"Are you carrying any weapons?"

"No."

"Are you carrying any illegal substances on your person?"

"No."

"Are you an active member of law enforcement?"

"No," I answer. I'm on suspension. That's close enough to the truth.

"Identification please," he says holding his hand out. I pull my I.D. out of my wallet and hand it to him. He turns, walks back to his desk, and lifts the hinged lid of a large wooden box sitting to one side. Inside sits a small machine with a heavy glass window on top. He places my license on the glass and pushes a button. A bright light streaks from one side to the other beneath my license, copying it. I can see a green light illuminate the inside front of the box. The man hands me my license and snaps the box shut.

"Welcome to Alistair's," he says now smiling politely. "We are delighted to have you. As a private establishment, we do require a membership fee for entry into the club. The cost of entry this evening is $1,000."

"$1,000?" I echo, my eyes popped open. "I was told the cover was $500."

Without blinking, he answers, "Inflation. You know." Sneaky fuck. I know $500 is going right in his pocket.

There's no question $1,000 is extreme, but this feels as close as I've been to some kind of truth. Thank God the trust will save my ass when the bill comes. He taps my credit card against another electronic reader and escorts me to a second heavy door toward the corner of the room. He keys in a ten-digit code, and I hear a deadbolt unlock. The door opens inward and extending his arm toward the club, he says, "Enjoy your evening."

I step through the door into a long, dimly lit hallway adorned with large prints of Frank Sinatra, Dean Martin, and Sammy Davis Jr. in mid-performance during their prime. I walk toward the pulse of live jazz coming from the other end of the hallway and I'm met with an enormous, two-story club that could best be described as discreet cool. The backlit bar towers on the right wall with 300 bottles of high-end booze. Next to it is a glass door looking into a wine chiller bigger than my first apartment that holds what has to be 1,500 bottles of wine. A jazz trio worthy of Columbia Records sits in the front corner on the other side of the room providing a vibe so heavy you could step on it.

Throughout, there are dark, leathered seating areas with adjustable lighting where people can sit and talk or choose to sink back into shadows to enjoy each other. There are no poles here. No lighted stages. That's far too gauche for this place. But everywhere I look, stunning women are ever present and I'm betting with the right questions and enticements, they are most certainly in play.

I sit down at the bar and start to order my regular whiskey neat, but then I stop myself and order a glass of $65 Cabernet instead. If I'm going to find a sommelier, I need to get in the mindset. The bartender puts a crystal wine glass in front of me and gives me a nice heavy pour of the Cab. This is, indeed, not a typical club.

I'm thanking the bartender when I feel a small hand touch the inside of my knee. A subtle and pleasing waft of perfume pulls me toward a sultry voice on my left saying, "Welcome to Alistair's."

The woman moves her hand from my knee to my arm and smiles with invitation. Her curled, brown tresses and green eyes suggest Madrid, but her light Italian accent betrays her.

"I don't believe I've seen you here before," she says. "My name is Alistair."

"Jake," I answer looking into her eyes. "Your club is exceptional."

"Thank you," Alistair answers looking at the room. "It's not for everyone. I built this to cater to richer, more discerning tastes. People with the means and the will to embrace their appetites and consume life. So, tell me Jake, what is it you are hungry for?"

"Oh, I'm hungry for a lot of things," I say raising my glass to her. "A good bottle of wine. A well-cooked meal. Financial success. Intimate companionship. Happiness."

"Happiness is an illusion. It's a mirage that only becomes real when accompanied by blinders and lies. If that is truly you're pursuit, the question, Jake, is how far are you willing to go to be happy?"

"I guess it depends on the lies."

"Are you married?"

"No."

"Involved with someone?"

"No."

"When was the last time you were truly loved by someone?" she asks. I want to say last night, but I don't know if that's true anymore.

"It's been a long time."

"But it doesn't have to be. Look around Jake. Take a breath. What does pleasure look like?"

I scan the room and see more than a dozen stunning women of varying ages, heights, and hair colors engaging men in the sitting areas, at the bar, and simply passing through the room. Some stand transfixed in conversation. Some are sitting on the laps of their marks, and one is leading an older gentleman by the hand toward a private area at the back of the club. Each woman is dressed in heels and lingerie that are tasteful, and yet, leave very little to the imagination.

"Do you see her Jake?" Alistair asks standing up and putting her hand to my cheek.

"I do," I say, giving the room one last look. Then I raise my chin looking Alistair straight in the eye. "But not here. Your girls are stunning. But I prefer someone a bit younger."

"Younger," she echoes looking for her youngest escort. "What about…'"

"A lot… younger," I interrupt.

I can literally feel Alistair's hand chill on the side of my face. She pulls her hand back and sits back down next to me.

"It's not often we can't accommodate the pleasures our guests dream about, but I'm afraid we do not have what you are looking for. Assuming I am understanding you correctly."

"I believe you are," I answer still looking Alistair in the eye. Her gaze is caring and a little heartbroken. She moves forward in her seat and leans toward me speaking quietly.

"I like you Jake. And because of that I will tell you this. Be very careful with the pleasures you seek. You can find anything in Las Vegas but the more forbidden, the greater the risk. There are real devils here to whom you do not want to be in debt. For the fulfillment you seek, this can end very badly, very quickly for you."

"I'm aware. Thank you," I answer. Her genuine honesty and discretion move me to put what cards I can on the table. "I have heard there's a sommelier in town who might have what I'm looking for."

"There are dozens of excellent sommeliers in Vegas. All of the super high-end restaurants have them and many of them have more than one." Alistair rattles off the names of the five or six most exclusive restaurants in town. It's entirely possible this guy isn't a wine expert or in the restaurant business at all, but I've got to start somewhere.

"I'm sorry you didn't find who you were looking for here," Alistair says standing up.

"Well, I just assumed you weren't on the menu," I answer coyly.

Smiling, she leans into my ear and whispers, "You should have asked." She squeezes my wrist, and pulls away, her perfume lingering. I reach to pay for my Cabernet, and she waves off the bartender.

"I've got this one," she says signing her name across the receipt. "Take good care of yourself Jake."

Alistair points me toward the exit in the back and as I walk away, I hear her call, "Jake!" behind me.

"I just remembered, there's a new restaurant called Violetear that opened about four months ago. From everything I've heard the food, and the wine list are other worldly. It's pricey and impossible to get into but you might put it on your list."

"Thank you Alistair," I answer raising my hand.

Violetear just went to the top of my list.

13

By the time I leave Alistair's, it's already 3:15 in the morning and certainly too late to try to visit the restaurant. That will have to wait until tomorrow. I go back to my room, pull up Violetear's website on my computer and check out the gallery of spectacular images.

In Las Vegas, there are two kinds of extravagant. There's the excessive, over the top extreme of a roller coaster on top of a high-rise hotel, black Beluga on top of a full lobster tail on top of a Wagyu filet, and a penthouse suite with a private pool for $100,000 a night. Then there's the exceptional, full realization of a concept that's so incredible you can't imagine it ever being done any better. U2 at Sphere. "O" at the Bellagio. Dinner at Joël Robuchon. Violetear is most certainly in that category.

The outside of the restaurant is a swirl of vibrant blues and greens framing massive two-story windows. Around the perimeter, giant kettles with blue flames illuminate the walls while a brighter orange flame fills the negative space in the copper Violetear sign above the door. The cuisine is Mexican/South American fusion made from organic, often exotic ingredients and the menu looks exceptional. What's unexpected are the two massive bars on either side of the restaurant.

On one side of the dining room sits a massive Tequila bar offering what has to be 500 brands of Tequila and Mezcal along with tapas, a full dessert menu and a Cuban cigar porch on the second level. On the other side, there's an even bigger wine bar. If Violetear is half as good as the pictures on the website, it's no wonder it's the hottest restaurant in Vegas.

I crank the air down and look in my bag for the bottle of Valium I travel with. I take one hoping I can crash hard for a few hours. Thankfully, the nightmares stay away, and I sleep until two. I want to hit Violetear as they are opening for prep so I can avoid the crowds and hopefully get the chance to chat with their sommelier. Maybe today is finally my day to get lucky.

My car drops me in front of Violetear just after three, still more than two hours ahead of the open. Even in broad daylight without the dramatic lighting from the fire kettles, the building is impressive and for a restaurant, massive. I walk into the lobby and am immediately greeted with the sweet aromas from various desserts being made in the kitchen, mixed with the faint smell of burning wood. It wouldn't surprise me to find out they are crafting their own signature Mezcal out back.

The inside of the restaurant is stunning with the same blue and green swirl motif from the outside mixed with copper, heavy oaks, and glass. The kitchen is open and from the door I can see more than a dozen people moving with purpose in the orchestrated yet improvisational dance that makes restaurants like this special. I walk over and peek into the Tequila bar. Paddy could learn a thing or two from this place. I reverse course and make my way to the wine bar. This is the reason I'm here. Behind the main bar in the center, I see a door leading to a crystal walled wine room that must have 1,000 bottles racked. Reds, whites, champagnes. Cabs, Merlots, Chardonnays, Malbecs, Ports. Whatever you like. The room is visible from the entire bar and is a very cool touch. There's no doubt this room is the vision of a world-class sommelier. Whether it's my sommelier remains to be seen.

"Can I help you sir?" a man asks approaching from my right with purpose. "We don't open until 5:30 and I'm afraid we are completely booked for this evening."

"Yeah, I heard this place was pretty popular," I answer.

"Popular. Yes." he says smugly. I'm guessing this guy is Violetear's maître d'. He's wearing a sharp suit minus the tie, and he just has that kind of air about him. "Our first open reservation is in about four months but if you'd like to leave your name and contact information we can put you on our waiting list."

"Actually, I was hoping to speak to your sommelier. I'm a wine distributor and I was hoping to introduce myself. Any chance he or she's around and has a few minutes?"

"He, and the answer is no," he says. "I'm sorry sir, but our sommelier is presently out of town visiting our restaurant in Washington, D.C. He should be back in two to three weeks. Perhaps you can come back then," he adds, again with a dismissive tone. Clearly he doesn't like the fact that I took it upon myself to explore his restaurant without asking.

"Actually, that doesn't work for me. I'm visiting Las Vegas from Maryland," I lie, "but I do go to Washington from time to time on business. Maybe I can catch him there while he's out east. What's the name of the restaurant there?"

"The restaurant is called Anna's," he answers. "It's near the Beltway but I cannot recall the exact address."

"Thank you for that," I say picking up one of the menus lying on the end of the bar. "You mind if I take a copy of your wine list? I always love to know what the best restaurants are serving." To grease the skids a bit, I take out my wallet and pull out a crisp hundred dollar bill.

Trying not to completely implode, the guy reaches over, grabs the menu, and puts it neatly back in the stack on the bar. "Actually, I do mind," he smirks. "We don't give out our wine lists to anyone outside the restaurant. I'm sure you understand. Now if you'll excuse me, I have to get the restaurant ready to open. If you'll please follow me."

"No worries. I've taken up enough of your time," I say putting the hundred back in my wallet. "One last question – any chance you have a business card for Anna's or something with the address on it? I would really like to visit it."

He looks at me annoyed, pauses, and then says, "I may have one in the back." With a pronounced sigh, he walks around the end of the bar, through the door to the crystal wine room and out the back toward the kitchen. I pick up the Violetear wine menu for the second time and quickly make my way to the door. If my money isn't good enough for him, fuck him and his lack of hospitality. I've got a case to solve.

14

Back in my room, I pore over the menu searching for any clues I can find. Any information at all that might give me some direction. Like the restaurant, the menu is impeccably designed down to the color, the weight of the paper, the font, and the embossed leather cover. But those pale in comparison to the actual menu.

The top of the menu is dated with today's date. Not surprising. Fine restaurants rotate their menus all the time or have inspired chefs who constantly change what they're serving. It adds to the exclusivity of the restaurant and for regulars, it leverages the fear of missing something exceptional before it's gone. It also allows the restaurant to hike their prices which Violetear certainly has.

◊   Fresh quail, flash fried in cornbread flour and brushed with a mango, ghost pepper glaze, served with a jicama and corn salsa, and pickled dragon fruit – $47

o   Catch of the day Ceviche served with poached lobster and melted organic butter - $63

o   Rare Marinated Wagyu medallions, flash seared and served with a spicy Korean dipping sauce, and wasabi mashed potatoes - $57

And those are just the appetizers. Unless you plan to nibble on a salad, dinner at Violetear is two bills a person easy. If it tastes half as good as it sounds, it's probably worth it. Reviewing the back of the menu, the wine is no less spectacular.

For the specific menu items on the front, there are a dozen different wines to choose from including Reds and Whites both domestic and European, a French Rosé from Provence and two sparkling wines from Italy and Portugal priced from $65 to $300 a bottle. These are the specials. But according to a note at the bottom of the menu, patrons can request Violetear's comprehensive wine Bible and choose from any of their 7,000 bottles of wine including wines north of $25,000 a bottle. Mother of God. That is an entirely different league.

I read the entire menu again, front to back, but still nothing jumps out at me. No names. No information about the sommelier or the company that owns the restaurant. Just a ridiculous menu I would happily consume from top to bottom.

Seven thousand bottles of wine is a massive investment. I can't imagine there are thousands of people, sommelier trained or not, you could trust to guide that kind of collection. And how much time would it take to care for it, know enough about each brand to explain the nuances to customers, and replace whatever it was that got purchased? And for multiple restaurants across the country? No way someone's got time to do all that and mastermind a trafficking ring. This sommelier isn't who we're chasing. But damn, I would love to talk to him. This guy is clearly a Master at the highest level and at the very least, he might be able to shed some light on the mindset of the guy we're chasing. I'm curious.

I flip open my laptop and Google "requirements to become a sommelier." There are varying degrees of expertise, but to be legit at even a basic level requires training, field experience, formal education, and multiple exams. According to Forbes, preparing for a Master Sommelier certification is akin to getting a medical degree. With a pass rate of only 10 percent, it might be harder to get an MS than an MD.

Clearly, we're dealing with someone who is smart and disciplined. Someone patient. Someone measured. Selfishly, I like my criminals on the stupid side. It makes them a lot easier to catch. This guy will be neither. The predator we're chasing – the real Sommelier – understands the stakes of what he's doing and I'm betting he'll be smart enough to insulate himself from any kind of immediate threat. Then again.

It occurs to me this guy may not be a sommelier at all. It may just be some nickname he heard and thought it sounded impressive. Some thug who can't even pronounce the word but thinks it makes running girls sound cool. Either way, there has to be some significance to the name, and I'm convinced talking to the guy who set up Violetear is a worthwhile conversation to have. I just have to find him.

I Google "Anna's" in DC and a set of links pop up for an HVAC company, a taco joint, an accounting firm and a fascinating animated short about an enslaved woman who jumped out the 3rd story window of a tavern on F Street seeking freedom in 1815. But none for any restaurant the caliber of Violetear. I start wondering if the maître de was completely full of shit and just trying to get rid of me when I see it halfway down the second page. "Anna's. Fine dining for discerning tastes. Reservations required."

I click the link for the restaurant and from the look of the pics on the website, I know it's familial to Violetear. Though smaller than the Vegas restaurant, the outer façade of Anna's is a similar swirl of greens and grays with huge windows. But unlike its sister restaurant, Anna's has a bright pink front door that would be shocking were it not the perfect accent to the rest of the design. A smallish nameplate hangs on the wall to the right of the door under the gas fed flames of the carriage lamps lighting the approach. If this is where Violetear's sommelier has gone, I can be in Washington by tomorrow morning. I just hope he's still in DC when I get there.

15

I've flown into Washington Reagan National Airport in DC a dozen times, and it always fascinates me flying in at night with the monuments, White House, and Capitol all lit up. It all looks so peaceful even though I know this town is anything but. The people in this city have the power to render my job almost pointless, but for them, there's no money in the cure. With a modicum of imagination and commitment, they could solve all kinds of problems. But why do that? What would they do then? The answer is rejoin the regular people. But that's something very few politicians have ever done willingly.

I check into my hotel near the National Mall about a mile from Anna's and head up to my room on the seventh floor. Even at one in the morning, I can hear TVs, music, and talking coming through the doors as I walk down the hallway. My room is as far from the elevator as it can be, but from the balcony I can see the Jefferson Memorial off to my left and the Lincoln Memorial in the distance. After five hours in the air, I think about taking a shower, but I'm already beat. I dig in my bag for the Valium, take two and pray for sleep. Five minutes later, prayers are answered. It's a good sleep.

At 8:47am, my eyes pop open and I realize I never set my alarm. No one will be at the restaurant before midday so no big thing. I throw on a light sweatshirt, some shorts and my running shoes and head out for a run around the Mall. I haven't gone running since the morning I saw Rachel again and the burn in my legs and lungs feels really good.

Just past the Washington Monument, I take a quick right on Constitution Avenue and a left on 15th to run up past the White House. When I get to Lafayette Square Park to the north of the Presidential residence, I stop for a stretch and a quick breather. Every few feet or so, I feel uneven bricks pushing up under my feet, displaced by the knotty roots of the 70-foot oaks giving shade to the park. To think what all this park has seen. It's a chilly morning and still half the benches are occupied by the homeless, curled up under newspapers or worn military jackets trying to get warm. From the insignia on the jackets, many of them are veterans from the Vietnam War and even Korea. From the smell, this is not the first night they've been here.

Fucking sacrilege.

As I'm about to head back toward the hotel, I notice a young girl sitting alone on one of the benches. She's small and wearing a threadbare T-shirt with a pink and purple unicorn on the front. One of her braids is completely unraveled. The little girl is wrapped up in what looks like an old sleeping bag and drawing in a coloring book. She doesn't look a day over 10. Not seeing any adults nearby, I approach her cautiously, trying not to scare her.

"Hey sweetheart," I say gently. "Are you O.K.?"

"I'm fine," she says looking up at me without an ounce of fear. This is clearly not the first time a strange man has approached her.

"What's your name?" I ask.

"Mia," she says smiling.

"That's beautiful," I smile back. "Where are your parents, Mia?

"Mama's doing business," she answers switching crayons, continuing in her coloring book.

"Business? Does your mother work in one of those buildings across the street?"

"Naw," she says. "She pretty much works in that building over there." She points to the public toilets in the corner of the park.

"Where's your daddy?" I ask, pretty sure I know the answer.

"Ain't got no daddy," she says.

"How long have you been sitting here?" I ask her, looking around again for an adult.

"About two pictures. Mama said she'd be back in 20 minutes."

"Well, do you mind if I wait with you until she comes back?"

"I don't mind," she answers with a smile for even a random kindness.

"What are you coloring?" I ask sitting down on the other side of the bench from her.

"Alice. She just went down in the rabbit hole. It's kinda weird."

All I could think was it's no weirder than the life you are currently living. I don't know this child or her mother at all, but I bet I know the narrative. No education for the mother, probably for the third or fourth generation in a row. Got pregnant with no alternative other than having the baby. The father bailed long ago if he ever stayed around at all and now Mom is hooking trying to stay alive in one of the most expensive cities in the world using the only asset she has. What's most sad is there's a good chance this little girl will end up in the same situation if not something worse. If a trafficker saw Mia sitting here, he'd lure her away before her mother ever knew what happened.

"Hey mutha fucka!" I hear from a voice behind me closing fast. "Get away from that goddamn bench!"

I stand up quickly and turn toward the little girl's mother running toward us. She's wearing a puffy white coat that's flopped open revealing a cropped tank top and a tight skirt underneath. She's carrying a big floppy purse in one hand and a lit cigarette in the other. Her eyes are wide open and frantic with a mixed look of fear and guilt.

"Mia, you ok, baby?" she asks panting from the 30-yard run from the toilets.

"I'm fine," Mia says giving her favorite, programmed response.

"What you doing with my baby?" the woman accuses, moving around the end of the bench putting herself between Mia and me. She tosses her purse onto the metal seat and reaches behind her back to touch her daughter.

"I'm not doing anything," I answer calmly. "I was running through the park and noticed your daughter sitting here all alone. I just stopped to see if she was alright."

"Mia just fine. That true what he say, baby? This man hurt you?"

"No, mama. He's nice."

"Alright then," she says started to catch her breath. "You ain't no CPS or anything like that is ya?"

"No ma'am," I say. "Just wanted to make sure your daughter was ok. She's very sweet."

"Very sweet," her mother repeats with half a smile. "Alright. You go on with your run now. We fine."

I look into Mia's mother's tired eyes and like with so many women before her, I see a lifetime of pain and poor decisions. There is little I can do for her in this moment, but I can do what I can do. I pull my wallet out of my pocket and take out $300. I take a step toward Mia's mother, put the cash into her hand, and holding her bewildered gaze, curl her fingers around it tightly.

"You take care of this precious girl," I tell her. "Go somewhere safe today. Eat something hot. Color a picture with your daughter." Looking past her, I say, "Bye Mia," and I start the run back to my hotel. I will never know what happens to them from here.

The entire run back, all I can think about are the millions of Mias being forgotten, ignored, and neglected. Then there are the ones being trafficked. Too many look like Mia, but there are countless others like Catherine who have been stuck in a tragic circle of Hell for years and even decades. Catherine was about Mia's age when I lost her, and I can feel the emotion starting to well up in my chest. I choke it down. Tears are fucking worthless. But my search for Catherine isn't and neither is finding this guy who calls himself "the Sommelier."

On the way back to the hotel, I divert a few blocks, so my run takes me past Anna's. As expected at 10:30 in the morning, the parking lot is empty, and the inside is dark. But actually, standing in front of the restaurant, I am struck again by how similar Anna's feels to Violetear. The exterior swirls of green and gray. The front staircase leading to the door. And that door. In full daylight, the pink is even more shocking than at night.

I walk around the building, stopping to peer into the windows I can reach. From what I can see, it's every bit as upper crust as Violetear, but it's tough to really tell without the full effect. That, I got when I returned for dinner at five o'clock.

Like Violetear, Anna's is completely booked for the night but if there was ever a town where money talks, Washington is it. I learned long ago if you show up to a restaurant when it opens with the right cash incentive, they'll often squeeze you in before a reservation 30 minutes later. At Anna's, the number is $200.

Pocketing my gratuity, the host walks me back to a two-top near the kitchen and hands me a menu and a wine list that's even more robust than the one from Violetear. I recognize about half the names on the list. The others are out of my league. $200, $300, $400 a bottle with one French Cab listed for $1,500. I check the front and back of the wine list and again, no mention of the sommelier overseeing the wines being served. Many menus include that information. Anna's, like Violetear, does not.

I switch to the food menu and am immediately intrigued by the creativity of the dishes. I could make a full meal out of the appetizer specials alone. A spicy buffalo chicken wedge salad topped with fresh bleu cheese and thick cut maple bacon. Grilled street tacos with sautéed scallops, water chestnuts and greens with a light Schezuan sauce. Quail eggs Benedict made with Italian prosciutto, fresh baked English muffins, and made from scratch hollandaise. I'm about to look over the entrees when a tall, lanky kid in a starched white shirt and blue apron walks up to the far side of the table.

"Good evening, sir. My name is Ryan. Welcome to Anna's!" he says gesturing to the restaurant behind him. "Have you dined with us before?"

"I haven't," I answer.

"We are an all-organic, farm to table restaurant for discerning palates who appreciate elevated cuisine, fine wines, and craft cocktails, and we pride ourselves on delivering experiences you will not find anywhere else. What questions can I answer for you?"

Quickly reviewing the menus, I order a nice Napa Cab and the quail eggs Benedict. They squeezed me in, but I have no intention of rushing. There's something different about this place and I'm here to soak it all in. It's hard to pinpoint but the vibe is different. There's an air of expectation and from the people I see filling up the dining room, there's a professional elegance and sophistication to both the restaurant and its patrons. These people have money and whatever their "discerning palates" are hungry for, they expect Anna's to deliver it.

In short order, Ryan returns with my wine and the quail eggs. I wouldn't have thought the pairing would be perfect, but it is. Befitting the smaller size of the quail eggs, the English muffins are half their regular size presenting four single bites of the Benedict which are incredible. Before I can lick the plate, Ryan returns to take my dinner order.

"How was the Benedict?" he asks.

"Incredible," I answer, gesturing to the empty plate.

"That seems to be the usual response. I've never tasted Hollandaise that good anywhere."

"Please let the chef know it was exceptional," I smile. "As is the wine. Would your sommelier be around by chance? I'd love to chat with him if he has a minute."

"Ahh," Ryan says, "a fellow connoisseur?"

"Actually, I'm a meat and wine distributor," I lie for the second time in a week. "I'm wondering how I might get into a restaurant like Anna's. I see from your menu that your patrons have refined tastes."

"Yes, many of them do. Some bordering on the exotic I'd say. As I mentioned before, we like delivering people delicious things and experiences they can't find anywhere else."

"Interesting. Does that ever extend beyond the menu?" I ask, fishing a bit.

"Well, we're a restaurant so… I'm not sure what you mean." Either there's nothing going on here, or Ryan has no idea about any extracurriculars in the background.

"I just mean if I had something exotic that might satisfy a palate craving something fresh, how would I get it on the menu?"

"Well, for that you'd have to talk to the chef and the sommelier."

"Perfect. Is the sommelier here tonight?"

"No. I'm sorry, he's not," Ryan answers. "Do you have a card? I'd be happy to give it to him when he comes in."

"Do you expect him tonight?" I ask hoping I might be in luck.

"No, I'm afraid he left this morning to go out of town."

"Oh, is he visiting another Anna's?" I ask.

"No, this is the only Anna's there is," he says picking up my appetizer plate. "But the group that owns us does have restaurants in other cities." Ryan reaches into his apron and hands me a thick, rounded business card embossed with his name and "Epicurean Sherpa" on the front. I flip it over and there on the back is another potential piece of the puzzle. The top of the card reads, "JM Restaurant Group - For the discerning palate," followed by foiled logos for a group of seven restaurants. Calliope in Atlanta, GA, Marvelous in Dallas, TX. Costa's in Miami, FL, Violetear in Las Vegas, NV, Anna's in Washington DC and coming soon, two new restaurants in Los Angeles, CA and Houston, TX.

There is no phone number or address for the JM Restaurant Group but it's more information than I had when I walked in. Looking over the names and cities again, Houston immediately jumps off the card to me. That could just be a coincidence. You can't throw a rock and not hit a world-class restaurant in Houston. But what if that's not the case. What if the girls we saved from the shipping container weren't going any further than Houston and the Vegas intel was some bullshit bluff? What if? What if I'm connecting dots that shouldn't be connected? That will send the case in the wrong direction quicker than anything.

"Are you ready to order your entrée, sir?" Ryan asks refilling my water glass.

"Uh, sure," I answer. "Actually Ryan, I'm stuck between the Japanese Wagyu Filet with the mustard and vinegar new potatoes, and the Grilled Salmon with fried crawfish and gouda grits. What would you recommend?"

"Honestly, I like the filet. But if you're truly stuck, for a bit of an upcharge, I can bring you half portions of the filet and the salmon so you can enjoy both dishes."

"Done," I smile handing Ryan the menu. "I'm hungry and that sounds fantastic."

"I like your style sir," he answers. "I'll be right back with another glass of your Cabernet."

I'm disappointed the sommelier isn't here, but at least I now know where to look next. Making sure no one is looking my way, I tuck the wine menu into the back of my pants and pull my shirt back into place. I finish the last swallow of the wine in my glass and open the American Airlines app on my phone. I'm going to enjoy the Hell out of this dinner and then head back to the hotel to pack. Tomorrow morning, I intend to be on the first flight to Atlanta.

16

On the final glidepath into Atlanta, thoughts of my mother flood my mind. Her smile. Her hugs. The last time I ever felt really loved. It's been a long time since I set foot in the state of Georgia, and though we're five hours from Sea Island, the tragic events that punctuated my childhood come bubbling up, peppered with anger, hatred, and sadness. What would our lives look like now if my mother hadn't gotten sick? Had my father not paid his gambling debts with his 12-year-old daughter? What if he had eaten that fucking shotgun a few years earlier? How often have I wished we could have been a normal, boring family where nothing ever really happened? I'm not alone in that.

Walking through the mass of humanity in the terminal at Hartsfield-Jackson, I look at all the people in a hurry to be somewhere else. I wonder how many times Catherine has flown through this airport. More than 100 million people a year fly through Atlanta and of those, tens of thousands are being trafficked. If only it was easier to tell which ones.

Flying here from DC, I went online to check the JM Restaurant Group but there was nothing there. Twenty, thirty pages deep in the search listings, there was no mention of it anywhere. No website. No articles. No ads. Like Violetear and Anna's, there were websites for the other three restaurants, but the holding company is a ghost. That's odd. What business venture wouldn't want to be found, especially one building exceptional restaurants where the average tab is $600? I grab my phone and send myself a note to check the dark web for the JM Restaurant Group when I get to the hotel.

Last night, when I realized I was coming to Atlanta, I reached out to Oxford Wood who works on the DHS trafficking team here in Georgia. Ox and I went through Basic together at Parris Island and I was hoping we might be able to catch up. When I take my phone out of airplane mode, he's answered my invitation with an address for some place called The Worx in Midtown at 7pm and a note. "Best burgers and beer in Atlanta!" I'm in.

I pull up to the restaurant at 6:45 and Ox is already sitting on the patio waiting for me putting the hurt on a massive pitcher of beer. One thing about Marines, we're never late. Ox rises from the table pointing at me and then opens his arms wide.

"What do you say brother?" he says wrapping his arms around me.

"I'm good Ox," I half lie. "You look good! How are you?"

"Fighting the bad guys. You know how it is. Heard about your rescue in Houston. That was some ugly shit."

"I'm sure it's no worse than what you see here."

"True that. What do you want to drink?"

"Beer's good," I say pointing to the frozen mug in front of him.

"Got it," he says squeezing my shoulder. "Be right back. It's good to see you Jake."

While Ox is grabbing me a mug, I take a look at the menu, and he wasn't kidding about the burgers. I'm sure we'll get to those but first, I want to hear about Ox and his family, and then see if he's heard anything about this guy we're chasing. Ox knows about my suspension. But like Jon, he knows there are more important things at play. He'll tell me what he knows.

"Here you go, buddy," Ox says setting down a frosted 36-ounce schooner filling it with his favorite IPA from Athens. "Cheers."

"Thanks man," I say clinking my mug against Ox's. "So, how's the family?"

"We're blessed, man. Allie's selling houses like they're candy. William is four and into everything. Caroline is two and already can't get enough of her brother. She follows him everywhere and so far, he's being pretty sweet to her."

"That's fantastic. Good for you Ox," I smile, inwardly envious of his happy, normal-sounding life. "How's the office?"

"Brutal," Ox says without hesitation. "You know what we're up against. I'll tell you, having kids has made it a lot harder. Every time I see a report or come in contact with a kid in the field, all I can see is Will and Caroline and the rage I feel for the people we're arresting just goes through the roof.

"Last month, we closed a case we'd been working for two years going after a group of teachers trafficking girls through the foreign exchange programs at a dozen high schools. These assholes would serve as the ambassadors for the 16-year-olds coming through their programs from Japan, Korea, Chile, Kenya – girls from all over the world, already struggling with their English – and they'd push them to join one of the high school sports teams so they could make friends, get involved. For the away games, the girls would ride the bus with the team, but after the game, as the foreign exchange rep for the school, these guys would arrange to take the girls home. But they didn't take them home. They took them to doctor's offices for a "postgame health check" they somehow made these girls believe was part of being on the team. Once they got there, the doctors were sedating the girls with Ketamine and abusing them while they were under. By the time we got a tip, this shit had been going on for five years."

"Jesus."

"We ended up arresting 27 people in six counties and I'm still not sure we got 'em all."

"You got 27 Ox. That's a lot," I assure him, even though we both know 27 is a drop in the ocean. "How'd you crack it?"

"One of the girls studying here from Monterrey, Mexico had a super high tolerance for sedation so when they gave her what should have been enough Ketamine to knock her out, it didn't. And she remembered everything. She'd been manhandled for sex by the cartel back in Mexico and beaten up pretty badly when she resisted, so when shit started to go down at the doctor's office, she said she played possum for fear they'd beat her. Every time they took her to a new doctor's office, she pretended to be out of it but was making mental notes the whole time."

"Smart girl."

"Very. The last night they took her to one of the offices, she said there were two men who raped her, instead of just the doctor. Apparently the second guy didn't pull out in time because when the girl went back to Mexico she was four months pregnant. Her father went ballistic as you would imagine, and she ended up telling him everything. As fate would have it – I fucking love the universe – one of her uncles was in North Georgia working in the carpet mills. Her father got on the horn to his brother and the uncle called in the tip. Two hours later we went straight to the doctor's office with a dozen agents and a search warrant, and it took him all of 10 seconds to flip on everyone else. We did a DNA match to the second rapist the doc said was there that night and when it was a match, we landed the plane."

"Nice work buddy," I say clinking his mug again.

"You know, they're like roaches. You kill three and seven more come crawling out of the dark."

"Speaking of roaches, any chance you've heard anything in your office about a guy who calls himself 'the sommelier?'"

"You mean like a wine expert?"

"Yeah."

"I haven't. But I've only been back in the office for a few weeks and haven't studied up on other cases around the country. Who is he?"

"Not sure. The name popped up after we found the girls in Houston, and I've been trying to birddog it since. There's something to this guy, but it's been tough to run any real leads being suspended and not being able to use any of the Homeland databases or resources."

"Yeah, that was bullshit what they did to you. I've heard from more than a few people that Warren's tough."

"I still think she overreacted, but if I'm honest, she wasn't wrong. Had Jon yelled my name a minute later, the lowlife choking on my gun might have been missing the back of his head."

"Nobody likes predators, brother, and these are the worst."

I spend the next 30 minutes filling Ox in about my trip to Vegas and DC. About my evening at Alistair's and my interesting conversation with the waiter at Anna's. I pull the business card he gave me out of my wallet and hand it to Ox, showing him the back with the names of the restaurants.

"What do you know about a restaurant here called "Calliope?"

"I know it's the hottest restaurant in Atlanta. Impossible to get in."

"So, super high-end I'm guessing?"

"Very. I think it's French fusion. Bright colors, super expensive, and it's tiny. The whole place holds like 60 people, but it's packed for two seatings every night. It's right up Peachtree near Piedmont."

"Sounds a lot like Violetear and Anna's, the other two restaurants I visited. I don't know if their sommelier is the guy I'm chasing, but my gut tells me he's involved with all of these places somehow."

"Running great restaurants is a far cry from running girls, don't you think?"

"Yeah, but there's something gnawing at me that I won't be able to put to bed until I actually meet him. The name 'JM Restaurant Group' mean anything to you?"

"No."

"Anything else you've heard about Calliope, good or bad?"

"There is one other thing. Calliope is closed one night every week."

"That doesn't seem super strange for a restaurant."

"They're closed on Fridays to host private dinners for specially invited guests."

"They shut down on the busiest night of the week? How do you get invited to one of these private dinners?"

"For starters you have a shit ton more money than I have."

"What are we talking?"

"I heard Allie gabbing about it one night with one of her girlfriends. Apparently the dinners go from $2,500 to $10,000 a person depending on what wines are being served."

"Fucking rich people," I mumble finishing my beer. Ox smiles at my cynicism and raises his mug.

"May we one day join the ranks," he says, putting a shred of optimism back into the universe.

I give Ox a hug and head up Peachtree following his directions to Calliope. I see it lit up three blocks away. Same green and pink façade as Anna's but framing a building that looks like it could have once been a colonial house. Large black shutters accent the sides of the windows somehow balancing the outer swirls of green on the walls and the bright pink front door. A circular brick drive curls around in front with a small cadre of valets waiting to take my car.

I hand over my keys and head up the walk to the front door. Up close, it seems darker than the pink at Anna's, but it's still in the family. I pull the door open and am met by a delightful maître de at a tall oak desk. He regretfully informs me they are booked for the night and for the next few months, but that he can place my name on a waiting list. I've seen this movie before. I thank him and ask if there's a bar where I could at least enjoy a cocktail.

"Of course, sir," he answers. "Right this way."

Together, we walk toward the back of the restaurant. The look inside is a lot like Anna's, but smaller. The open kitchen is centered in the middle with people seated on both sides of the dining room. The walls are a much darker version of the pink color on the door with golden accents of trim at the chair rail and in the crown molding at the top of the walls. An enormous, crystal chandelier that must have cost $50,000 hangs from the ceiling over the room. I'm not entirely sure what French fusion looks like on a plate, but it smells divine. Gazing over the dining room, everyone is dressed well, sophisticated, and seems light and jovial. No one in this room is a stuffed shirt. This is status at its highest and they intend to enjoy it.

"The bar, sir," the maître de points, shaking my hand. "Enjoy your evening."

Outside, at the end of the walkway leading from the main dining room, sits a bar area that must be twice the size of the dining room inside. While not as full as the restaurant, there are more than 100 people enjoying the cool Atlanta evening with cocktails I'm sure are setting them back $20 or $30 a pop. I spy an empty seat near the end of the bar and sit down, catching the eye of one of the bartenders who moves in my direction. A pretty, natural-looking blonde about my age with a perfect smile and I'll bet my life, no penchant for bullshit.

"Welcome to the Calliope Bar," she says grabbing the back rail of the bar and leaning toward me. "My name is Noelle and I'm happy to serve you however I can."

"Thank you Noelle. I'm Jake."

"Nice to meet you," she answers with a bit of a twinkle. "What can I get you to drink?"

"How about a whiskey, neat?"

"Done," she says, her gaze lingering on mine. "Be right back… Jake."

I've never considered myself any kind of looker, but by comparison to the uber-wealthy, aging patriarchs you know are throwing bad sex jokes and ham-handed passes at her every night, I'm not the worst alternative. Bartenders and waitresses are always a tough read. While the cynic in me screams she's just being flirty, angling for a better tip, with a woman like Noelle, the man in me wants to believe there's something attractive and enticing about me that could draw legit attention. This is the dance I go through when rationally, I should just enjoy the moment for what it is. It's a fucking drink, not a proposal. But watching Noelle walk back to me with her blue-eyed smile and a rocks glass full of whiskey, the male side of my brain is beating the cynic's ass to a pulp.

"Whiskey, double, neat. What else can I get for you?"

"You have anything to eat? There's not exactly a seat inside."

"Sure," she answers handing me an elegant appetizer menu. "What sounds good to you?"

"What do you like?" I ask looking over the dozen options on the menu.

"I think the Kobe sliders with Gruyére are the best thing on the menu. If you like olives, the tapenade is good. The onion tarte is tasty if you like onions and the chicken liver pate with the raspberry jelly is fantastic if you like that kind of thing."

"Let's go with the sliders," I say handing her the menu.

"You won't be disappointed," she promises. "Probably take 15-20 minutes. Let me tell the kitchen and I'll be right back."

"Hey, when you come back, could I please see the menu and the wine list from inside? I'm curious to see what I'm missing in there."

"Sure," she answers, walking to the other end of the bar to put my order in. I shift in my chair to face away from the bar and for the first time, I see the full layout. The bar area's got to be 1,000 square feet with 10-15 feet of grass stretching out on every side. On the other side of the yard stands a 15-foot concrete wall that connects at the front corners of the restaurant and wraps all the way around the back bar area. The only passageway from the bar to the front goes through the restaurant the way I came with the maître de. It's not that odd, I guess. Lots of restaurants build thick walls to act as sound barriers. But this is certainly private.

I start trying to connect the dots and the cynic in my head starts in again about the fool's errand I'm on. Assuming the architect of these exquisite restaurants is even remotely the guy we're looking for. Jesus, Jake. You want so badly to make a case, you're swiping at shadows in the hope of hitting anything relevant. It's Catherine all over again. You've had one job for six years. To find her. And you've failed at it miserably. Yes, you've saved others. By one count 247 girls and women are no longer being trafficked because of the work you've done. But locked away, deep in your heart, there's one horrible secret you would never tell another soul. And that's given the chance, you'd trade every one of those victims and more to have Catherine back. She's the nightmare that can't be unseen. The guilty ache that won't go away.

"Here you go," Noelle smiles setting the sliders and another glass of whiskey down in front of me. "I took the liberty," she says. "That ones on me."

"Thank you," I respond, sipping from the new glass. "Much appreciated."

"You mind if I keep you company?" she asks. "It's starting to slow down a little."

"Of course," I answer. "I wish you could sit down. You hungry? You want one of these?"

"No, I had some earlier. Thanks," she says. "So, are you from around here? I don't think I've seen you before."

"I live in L.A. I'm just here for a quick business trip."

"What do you think of Calliope?"

"It's stunning," I answer looking back toward the main restaurant.

"It's certainly that. The owners put $9 million into this place. You've been through the restaurant, and you've seen the bar out here. What you don't see is a complete subterranean wine cellar that houses every kind of liquor you can imagine and about 50,000 bottles of wine. If you want a cocktail that's not on our menu with even the most exotic ingredients, we can make it. If you're a wine enthusiast, there is literally nowhere in the Southeast like this place. You want the most remote bottles of wine in the world, I'll bet you we have them."

"So, what's with the private dinners on Friday night? Are they really $2,500?"

"That's the starting price. The most I've heard was $22,000 a head one night, but yeah, it's a whole different level. CEOs, investment bankers, real estate moguls, professional athletes. Basically, all the guys who really know and love the wines that only they can afford."

"What's the dinner like?"

"I don't know. I've never worked one. It's invitation only and exclusively all male."

"No women?"

"Nope. Not a one."

"That seem odd to you?"

"It's the Old South darlin'. The patriarchy isn't just alive and well here. It's working out, ripped, and benching 350. It's not always out in the open, but trust me, men are running the show. And you know what? Let 'em. If they want to pay a fortune for some hoity toity French food, a couple bottles of fancy wine, and some smelly cigars, why should I care? It's not hurting me. A lot of those same guys will be back on Saturday night tipping me $200 for overpouring their Scotch, leaning over, and laughing at their jokes. Now who's in charge?"

"Touché," I answer raising my eyebrows and my glass.

"Oui, oui," she answers, flashing me a mischievous smile. "So, what's your business in Atlanta?"

"Actually, I was trying to get a meeting with your sommelier, but it sounds like he's out of town."

"Jean-Michel? Yeah, he's gone. I think he's in Miami until late next week or the week after."

"Jean-Michel? He's who put all this together?"

"Yep. Jean-Michel Baptiste."

"What do you know about him?"

"Not a lot, but he's an impressive guy. There are only 273 Master Sommeliers in the entire world and he's one of them. There's literally nothing this guy doesn't know about wine."

"So, I'm guessing he's the JM in JM Restaurant Group."

"He is. Calliope was his first, but he's building fine restaurants like this all over the country. He takes the whole 'discerning taste' thing super seriously. Food, wine, cocktails. He's all about his friends indulging in the things that make life worth living. For a price."

That bell in my head that says there's something here, suddenly sounds like Quasimodo is ringing it. Not surprisingly, the cynic has suddenly shut the fuck up.

"I would love to meet this guy. What's he like?"

"Charismatic is a good way to describe him. He's charming but that sounds calculated and that's not how it feels with him. When Jean-Michel is talking to you, it feels like you are the only person in the world he cares about. He listens intensely, he asks questions. And he's just, kind. A few years ago, I was late for my shift because my piece of shit car broke down. The next night, he handed me an envelope with $5,000 to help buy a new one. I don't know. He just has this aura about him that sucks you in. He's tall. He's like 6'5". I'm betting early 60s. Just a really impressive, accomplished guy. Can I get you another drink?"

"No, I'm good," I say waving off another whiskey. "But thanks for the awesome dinner and conversation."

"I enjoyed it. Please come back and see me when you're in Atlanta.," she says putting her hand on top of mine. "Maybe next time you can take me to dinner."

"It's a date," I smile back.

"One second sugar, I'll get your check."

The sliders and whiskey are $112 not counting Noelle's drink on the house. I add $100 for her and call it a night. I start to stand up and see Noelle hurrying toward me from the door to the restaurant.

"I'm so sorry," she says reaching out to me. "You said you wanted to see the menu and the wine list from inside, and I completely forgot to bring them to you. Here they are if you still want to see them."

"Thanks. I think I'm good on the menu, but I would love to see the wine list." I take a quick look around and lean into Noelle. "You think I could keep it?"

"It didn't come from me," she says moving close to me and turning around to give me some cover. I slip the menu into the back of my waistband and drop my jacket down over the top of it. "You are a sweetheart. Thank you!" I say.

"Don't forget me," she smiles moving back behind the bar.

My trip to Calliope has turned out to be well worth the effort thanks to Noelle. An hour ago, I was sure my logic was flawed, and my intentions misplaced. Now, I'm surer than ever that I need to find this Jean-Michel. The cost and the exclusively male dinners scream to me there's more going on here than meets the eye. Misogynistic good old boy bullshit? Possible. It's the Deep South, so more than possible. But I've seen male control too many times to dismiss this as nothing out of hand. It takes way more than time and hard work to become one of 273 of anything in the world. It takes ego and drive. And at the summit, the reward is a fierce sense of elitism and entitlement. Those are part and parcel to anyone you would describe as "charismatic."

Back at the hotel, I pull out the Calliope wine menu and start looking over the exceptional list of wines. With each $400, $500, $700 bottle of wine, I wonder what a $2,500 dinner must taste like? Wait. The dinners. I'm struck by a sudden thought and quickly make two phone calls – one to Violetear in Vegas and one to Anna's in Washington. Whether I completely missed it, or it was being withheld, there's one thing uniting these three restaurants I didn't realize until this moment. They are all closed on Friday nights for private dinners that are invitation only. Today is Thursday. I'll bet $1,000 Costa's in Miami will be closed tomorrow night.

There's only one way to find out.

17

I don't always like being right. But pulling up to Costa's restaurant in Miami, I know that I am. Even at dusk, the intricate swirls of mint green and plum purple bring the walls to life giving them a motion and an energy that portend whatever is going on inside. Despite the activity of the valets in the driveway, the lights inside the restaurant seem low as though everything is on a dimmer switch that's been turned down by half. Strictly seeking information, I pull into the drive and roll down my window.

"Can I help you sir?" asks a young, Latinx 20-something in an embroidered, white Guayabera shirt and khaki slacks.

"Yeah, I'm in from Atlanta and I heard this was THE place in Miami to have dinner," I say. "Where should I park?"

"I'm sorry sir, but Costa's is closed this evening for a private event. Perhaps another night."

"Well, that's shitty luck," I tell him. "Must be some real bigwig to shut down the whole damn restaurant."

"It's a private dinner being hosted by our owner," the kid answers.

"Oh," I say. "Sorry I missed that."

"Actually sir, we hold these events every Friday night."

"Wow!" I exclaim feigning my surprise. "How do you get on the list for that?"

"I'm afraid I don't know sir," he answers, clearly tiring of my questions. "Thank you for coming to Costa's. We hope to see you again another evening."

I've probably gotten as much out of him as he knows, and this isn't the time or place to push this anyway. I pull out of the driveway and turn onto a side street in a neighborhood two blocks away. Walking back toward Costa's, there's little between me and the restaurant other than streetlights and palm trees, and yet I can't see it. When I get to a block away, I can see why.

The back side of Costa's is surrounded by a huge concrete wall just like the one at Calliope in Atlanta, only this one has 50-foot Magnolias around the entire perimeter adding a whole other layer of protection. So much for getting a look inside. I keep walking until I'm past the edge of the wall, but now I'm in the eyeline of the valets in the driveway. I'm on a public street so there's nothing they can do really, but after the conversation I just had, I don't want to draw any additional attention to my curiosity.

From the sidewalk, there's nothing much to see. Like in the front, the lights are dimmed on this side of the restaurant, and I can't see any people or any motion inside. I wonder how many people attend these things. And what did the kid say? It's a private dinner being hosted by our owner. Is Jean-Michel inside Costa's right now? If I wasn't on probation, I might push the issue and see if there was a way to get inside. But getting caught now would be bad and keep me out of the game way longer than the time I've got left. It kills me, but far better to wait to fight another day. Besides, there are always other ways to get information.

Walking back to my car, I enter Ocean Drive into the GPS on my phone and pull out of the neighborhood driving toward South

Beach. This city has some of the hottest clubs in the world and I'm banking that as the alcohol flows, so too will the intel.

Unlike Ocean Avenue in Santa Monica, you can feel Ocean Drive in Miami long before you reach it. Even in the car, I can feel the percussive bass from the clubs thumping in my chest. I pull up to the valet stand outside a club called "Hevven," lit up in neon pinks and greens like the party version of one of JM's restaurants. I'm not sure if the name is a play on "Heaven" or "Heaving," but I'm pretty sure there will be plenty of both inside. For a $50 cover, I would hope so.

The anteroom connecting the street with the club is filled with rainbow colored chaser lights and a mist that smells like grapefruit. This is the stopping point for anyone with epilepsy or the least hint of claustrophobia. I pull open the heavy wooden door to Hevven and am immediately consumed by a sea of people, flashing lights, and music throbbing with an infectious tempo. The club is packed wall to wall with young beautifuls drinking and dancing. Like a giant python, the throng pulls me in and moves me through with no consciousness of doing so.

The downstairs is one giant dancefloor with a ring of neon bars around the sides and a massive, elevated DJ booth in the front. Shafts of bright light explode through my eyeline as the entire club vibrates. Above me, hundreds of people hover and dance at the railings guarding the edges of the upstairs balconies. Behind them, there are most certainly tables where those who are connected will sit. That is where I need to be.

Moving through the sea of sweaty, transfixed dancers, I find one of the staircases that lead upstairs but it's roped off. A guy who is easily twice my size stands there guarding the entrance to the VIP area. This is not going to be cheap.

"I guess this isn't a please and thank you type situation," I say, trying to crack his icy demeanor stuck somewhere between annoyed and assassin. I get nothing. "Sorry. I'm just fucking with you. What's it gonna take to get upstairs?" I pull out my wallet and peel off two hundred dollar bills. He doesn't blink. I add a third. And then a fourth. Four hundred dollars and the guy is a fucking monolith. As I peel off a fifth, he reaches for the velvet rope and unhooks it from the mooring with his left hand as his right closes over my hand like a catcher's mitt taking the $500. "Enjoy your evening," is all I get. That, and access.

At the top of the stairs, I scan the seating area looking for an open table and spot a young girl clearing a space against the back wall. No sooner do I thank her and sit down than one of the Hevvenly bottle girls starts moving my way. Even from across the room, there is nothing left to the imagination. Plunging neckline. Short hem. Plumped lips. Her blonde hair is pulled back into a playful ponytail revealing a beautiful face that any model would covet. I'd bet my house this woman is pulling down six figures if she's making a dime.

"Hi," she mouths, waving at me. Without hesitation, she sits down next to me, in case her standing was skewing my view in any way. "My name is Aria and I'll be your angel here in Hevven."

"Thank you Aria," I say smiling. "I'm Jake,"

"Hi Jake," Aria says in a flirty, drawn out purr, putting her arm around me and squeezing my hip. "What can I bring you?"

"How about a nice bottle of whiskey, a cold bottle of Vodka, and a bunch of glasses?"

"You got it," she says, not so subtly grazing my side as she stands up. "Any particular brands?"

"Surprise me."

Aria looks at me over her shoulder and winks as she walks away to pick up my bottles. Two minutes later, she's back with three other women in tow.

"I ran into some friends on the way to the bar and I thought you might like to meet them," she fawns with a little pout. "You looked a little lonely."

"Hey, the more the merrier," I say as Aria sets $700 of booze on the table and hands out the glasses I just bought. She's not stupid. She also brought four two-ounce shot glasses. It turns out the Miami mating call is the same as everywhere else. One by one, the girls sit down next to me. Angela and Isabella, the two beside me, are Latin with big brown eyes and their hair pulled back. They bounce in their little cotton dresses and smell a bit like chai. With every sentence, they move closer and closer, touching me as they talk. The third girl, Carmen, sits across from me in a white leather bustier and a bright red skirt with nothing underneath. They look to be in their early to mid-20s. Pretty. Fit. Put together. I start running the traps in my head. Are they pros? Doubtful. Hookers don't hunt in packs and certainly not at a place like this. They could be college girls out for a free night on somebody else's dime. Hell, they could be high school girls and you'd never know without checking IDs. I'm always on high alert for girls being run, but that's not what's happening here.

I look up and Aria is back to see if I'm ready for another bottle of vodka. In the span of 20 minutes, these three have killed an entire fifth and show no signs of stopping. I question whether this investment is getting me anywhere.

"One more bottle, por favor," begs the girl to my left, holding my bicep with one hand and patting my chest with the other. I look up at Aria to order another bottle and from behind her, I hear a husky male voice order for me.

"Bring our friend here another bottle," he says looking at me with a wry smile on his face.

Aria recognizes this guy as one of the VIP managers and steps back. My investment may pay off after all.

"I think maybe it's time to share, huh Papi?" he says moving closer. "Another bottle for the ladies," he says pulling the girl with no underwear out of her chair and taking her place. "I'll just share this one here," grabbing my bottle of whiskey by the neck and filling one of the rocks glasses on the table.

"I'm sorry," I answer him, moving the bottle back in front of me. "Exactly who the fuck are you?"

"You know," he says with a cocky shrug. "Just one of the proletariat looking to share the wealth." Fuck me if this guy could define proletariat on a bet.

"Yeah, well it's my wealth, motherfucker." I sit up, stiffening my back and looking dead into his eyes meeting his bullshit with strength. He tries not to flinch, but I can see the resolve melt in his eyes a bit. He may be a bigshot here, but he's smart enough to know guys like me make his existence possible. Doesn't matter. I can work with this asshole no matter what he drinks. "Lucky for you, I'm not ungenerous."

I'm not actually pissed. This guy is the whole reason I let the girls sit down in the first place. I need information and I'm betting a guy with balls this big knows something about the scene in Miami.

"No offense, Papi. You know how it is." He grins knowing he got away with one. This could have gone very differently, and I imagine it has before. "Just taking inventory of who's joining us in Hevven tonight." All I can think is this is probably the only Hevven this guy will ever get into. "Thank you for the drink," he says.

"I'm Jake," I say extending my hand.

"Luis," he answers. "Come here baby," he says pulling the girl in the bustier onto his lap. She looks annoyed but grabs her glass off the table and sits.

"So, Jake, what do you think of our little club, here? Nice, no?"

Aria is already back with another chilled bottle of Chopin and more ice and glasses.

"This place is hot, no doubt. And the service is spectacular," I say winking at Aria. She smiles.

"Aria's the best," Luis says topping off his glass. "Do you live here in Miami?"

"No, I'm in town scouting new locations. I work with a big director in L.A. and I'm looking for cool places to shoot and for some young, undiscovered talent."

"Carmen is undiscovered," one of the girls next to me says pointing at the girl in the white bustier. "At least that's what she tells all the boys."

"That's a better story than the played out pussy you're passing around," Carmen fires back jumping up and reaching toward her friend. I put my arm around Isabella while Luis curls his arm around Carmen's waist pulling her back down.

"Come on now," Luis says giving all three of them the eye to let it go. "That's enough of that. Have a drink."

"I need to go to the bathroom first," Isabella answers pulling away from me.

"Me too," Angela says following after her friend. "Come on Carmen."

Carmen downs the rest of her drink and sets her glass on the table. In a huff, she turns and walks after the other two girls toward the bathroom. I'm actually glad they're gone so I can talk to Luis alone. He's more likely to share information just between the two of us than with three nosy sets of ears sitting nearby.

"Gotta love the fire, no?" Luis smiles.

"Always," I answer, moving over a seat to sit a little closer to Luis. I lean into him to give the impression I want to talk to him in confidence. "So, if I needed to find some smoking hot girls in this town, where should I go?"

"You mean for your movies, or you just want to get laid?" he pauses. "Or are those the same thing?"

For a second, I consider playing this above board, but the information I need is in the gutter not on the sidewalk. Besides, I'm betting Luis has spent a lot of time playing in the street.

"Just to be clear, I'm not the talent. But yeah, I'm looking for girls who aren't afraid to play dirty."

Immediately, I can see the wheels starting to spin in Luis's head. This is not a world with which he is unfamiliar.

"I might know a few places I could send you," he answers looking around and then filling his glass with whiskey. He looks at me but says nothing.

I grab my wallet, pull out two crisp hundreds and put them on the table under his glass. "I would love to hear any suggestions you have."

Luis takes the money and puts it in his pocket. He takes another drink from his glass and leans toward me.

"What kinds of girls are you looking for, Jake? Black? White? Hispanic? Asian? I gotta know what section of town to send you to."

"Actually, I'm more concerned with age."

"What you want? 20s? 30s?" I shake my head. "Older? Oh shit, you're not shooting abuelita porn, are you?"

"No," I answer curtly. "The other end of the spectrum. Legal. But younger."

"Oh," he says wide-eyed, I think relieved I wasn't walking him into any illegal territory. I could let this play out longer, but I'm running out of time before the girls get back from the bathroom. I decide to tip my hand and see if Luis knows anything that could help me track down this Jean-Michel.

"I hear there's a restaurant here called Costa's that might be a good place to start."

"I know that place," he says. "It's fucking white hot jefe. Even if you can afford it, you can't get in. And on Fridays, they close the whole damn thing for some private dinner. It's crazy. But yeah, I've heard the rumors."

"The rumors?"

"Word is that place is a front. Expensive motherfucking front, but from what I hear, food and booze aren't the only things running through that place."

"Like drugs?"

"Like young girls. Not really sure how that even works, but I think there's some dark shit going down over there. I'd stay away from there if I was you. I can give you a dozen names of some serious pieces who'd shoot with you tonight. And trust me, they all know what they're doing."

Luis could be completely full of shit on every front, but if he's half right, this if the first solid connection I've gotten between the restaurants and the girls we saved in Houston. It gives me just enough confidence to believe I may not be chasing an outright phantom. I've got one more lead to chase down and then it's back home to reassess.

"Luis," I say extending my hand, "It's been a pleasure. Enjoy the rest of my whiskey."

Luis stands, grips my hand strongly and thanks me for the drink. "Buena suerte, jefe!"

I feel my stomach growl and I look at my watch. It's after 10 and I haven't eaten since breakfast.

"Hey man, you know any good places to eat," I ask.

"You want the best food on South Beach, go see my cousin Hector at the Tito's Taco truck at 12th and Ocean. Tell him I sent you."

"Will do. That gonna get me some discount?"

"Fuck no. Hector hates me," Luis laughs. "But it's the best Mexican food you've ever had."

He wasn't kidding.

18

After waking up super early to catch my flight, a four hour delay reminds me again why I hate the Miami airport. Last time I was here, a woman on a flight to South America tried to bring a fucking chicken as her carry on. Swear to God. I don't like the layout. You walk forever and there's always an issue. Besides that, I'm tired and frustrated to be chasing this dickhead across the country. At this point, I know he won't be in Dallas, but hopefully seeing the other restaurant will be another piece of the puzzle. Right now, my one saving grace is the beer at the bar is cold and the cheeseburger is better than expected, even if the bill is ridiculous.

Being a Saturday morning, the flight isn't full and there's no one else in my row. Thank God for small mercies. Once we're in the air, I pull out my notebook. What do I know other than not enough? I know there is a master sommelier behind this restaurant group. I know his name is Jean-Michel Baptiste. I know he's holding private, invitation-only parties on Friday nights and I know he's on the move. I also know – well, I've been told by an unvetted source with an unconfirmed story – that JM may be running young girls through at least one of his restaurants. That's not a ton of probable cause but it's enough to fly to Dallas for a night.

According to the pilot, the strength of the Jetstream will cost us another 20 minutes in the air. I've got nowhere to be, but it still adds to my piss poor mood. I haven't been on a run in four days, and I can feel it. I should have some time to hit the gym when I get to the hotel. I need to park this aggression somewhere or it will just get worse, and I hate feeling this amped up.

Around 2pm, we finally reach the southern edge of Dallas and looking down from my window seat, I'm struck by the massive suburban sprawl of the Metroplex. I read somewhere that by 2100, Dallas-Fort Worth will be the largest city in the country with more than 34 million people. God knows they have the room. DFW airport alone is bigger than Manhattan.

I grab a taxi at the airport and 30 minutes later, it drops me off in front of a towering high rise luxury hotel and spa in downtown Dallas. It's pricey but I booked a room for tonight because Marvelous is here on the 47th floor, just below the three penthouses at the top. I've already called to get on the waiting list for dinner, but this afternoon, I'll go up and at least try to get into the bar for a glass of wine.

I check in at the main desk and they tell me my room is ready early. Finally, something good. I get in the elevator and punch 43 to go up to my room. At the last minute, an older couple moves into the elevator and asks if I would please push 22 for them. They're dressed like they just got off the golf course and both smell like sunscreen. When the doors open, they tell me to have a good day and head to their room hand in hand. As the doors close, I look down at the 43 lit up on the elevator keypad. Four rows above it, I notice Marvelous listed next to the 47.

For the moment, the 43rd floor is quiet and deserted except for the low hum of an icemaker hidden behind one of the doors near the elevator. Halfway down the hall, I hold my phone up to the keyless entry for Room 4312 and a few seconds later the tumblers click inside letting me into my room. Even for a luxury hotel, the room is posh, and the view from my window is spectacular. The hotel overlooks the 6,000 acres of the Trinity River Forest on the south side of Dallas. It's the largest urban forest in the United States and they say in the spring, from the upper floors, you can follow the flow of the Trinity by watching the mist drift up between the trees from where the warmer air is hitting the winter water. I imagine the forest is beautiful when everything is in full bloom.

It's such a dichotomy, the world. So much beauty offset by so much darkness. I struggle on days like today when what I do seems so futile and the hope of saving Catherine, or any girls for that matter, seems fleeting. Last year, my doctor tried to put me on an anti-depressant to help but I refused it. As painful as all of this is, I don't want to cover it up. Dulling the pain only keeps it from doing what it's meant to do. Cause discomfort. Keep me focused. Force me to find the ultimate source of the pain and kill it.

Some days, I worry the pain may overwhelm me and with a father who found solace in swallowing the barrel of a shotgun, that won't be good for me. But for now, I've mastered the art of consolidating my pain and only letting myself feel what and when I choose. I think that's why it hurt so badly to wake up and find Rachel and my case notes gone after the night we spent together. For the first time in a long time, I made the conscious decision to let myself feel something. It fucked me. But I don't regret it.

Were it not for my sister, I think I could navigate this job better than most. Call it constitution, or learned behavior, but I've always been able to shoulder hard things. When I was younger, I never made an intentional choice to be the rock in everyone's storm, but somehow the winds always found me. Eventually I learned a burden can also be a blessing and that there's only one way to reconcile it. The day I enlisted in the Marines, I swallowed that burden and yoked myself to enduring hard things. To feeling the pain and looking evil square in the eye with a ramrod countenance and the iron resolution to outlast it. Whatever heartache and anguish I'm feeling, it pales in comparison to the millions of women being abused and broken. With fists. With cocks. With governments committed to turning a blind eye to the truth staring them right in the eye. Sexual tourism. Enslaved teenagers being passed around. Little girls still years before their first period, being sold to the highest bidder. The world can be a dark fucking place. I'm just not willing to accept that as the dominant, inevitable orientation.

I hit the treadmill in the gym for 45 minutes and take a long hot shower, my thoughts fleeting between Catherine and the sommelier. Two disparate ends of my universe, and yet presently, the two greatest focal points in my life. I towel off and shave for the first time in a week. I iron a shirt, throw on some slacks and slip on a blazer. Looking in the mirror, I'm pleased enough with what I see. People dress in Dallas and like every occasion undercover, rule one is looking like you belong.

I walk down the hall and punch the elevator call button. Almost immediately, I hear a ding, and one of the four elevator doors opens. Three of the five people already in the elevator greet me with a smile. The other two, a couple in the back, are engrossed in some whispered conversation. I reach for the 47 button, but it's already pushed. It's the only circle illuminated. From the doors, I can see the muted reflection of the others around me, and my assumptions were correct. They are all dressed impeccably for whatever it is Marvelous has to offer.

At floor 47, the doors open to an enormous foyer with a heavy, dark wooden floor that looks as though it was made from the sides of an old English ship. The walls share a complementary wainscoting with the top halves of the walls painted in purples and greens. Of the dozen people waiting in the lobby, I am the only one who understands whose work this is. All I know for sure is this guy likes a similar décor in all of the restaurants he's built. But there's more. I just have to connect the dots.

It's still early in the evening but the bar is already filling up. I imagine most of these people have been on the waiting list for dinner for months and they're early, not about to miss out on the full experience now that their turn has finally come around.

I'm in no hurry to chat it up with the masses so I pass on the two open seats at the bar. Instead, I take a seat at a small two-top at the back of the bar where I can watch the people coming and going. I know it's not a Friday night, but I wonder if some of these people are the same ones who have attended one of the private events. Looking around the bar, the men look to be from their 40s to their 60s, and all seem to exude the confidence that comes with money. That in itself doesn't make them degenerates but how they spend their money might.

Even here in the bar, the table is draped with starched white linen. A white cylindrical votive burns inside an azure sconce on the wall casting a blue glow onto the menu sitting on the table. I pick it up and find it weighty and impeccably designed like the menus I took from Vegas, Washington, and Atlanta. The food here has a southwestern flair but to be sure, it's the same high-end cuisine found at the others. Looking at the back of the menu, the wines are equally exclusive and even more expensive. A few of the wineries sound familiar, but most I've never heard of.

"Good evening sir. Welcome to Marvelous," says the young waiter at my right. "My name is Charles. What can I bring you to drink?"

I decide to change things up and order a Pinot Noir from Oregon. It's $27 a glass but according to the drivel on the menu, this one is supposed to have a blackberry nose with notes of pear and a slight chocolate finish. It's pretention at its finest. At least when the waiter comes back I see the bar gave me a healthy pour.

"Thank you," I say taking a taste of the Pinot. The kid stands patiently waiting to make sure the wine is to my liking. It's actually very good and I tell him so, bringing a big smile to his face.

"Hey Charles, any chance the sommelier is here tonight?" I ask already knowing the answer to the question. I figure worst case he might cough up some new details about this Jean-Michel.

"Actually, I just saw the sommelier back in the kitchen. Give me a second and I'll go check."

Before the kid takes the first step away from the table my heart starts to race. I feel sharp pricks of anxiety rising in my chest and I consciously try to slow my breathing. For more than two weeks, I've been chasing this motherfucker across the country when he was nothing but a ghost. Could I really, finally be in a position to see him face to face? Hear his voice? Ask him questions? The resolution for every speculation I've had since the word sommelier tumbled out of the trafficker's mouth in Houston is 100 feet away and quite possibly heading my direction. I won't make any kind of scene here in the bar, but the second I see him, I'll know. I'll feel him one way or the other, and I'll do what I need to do.

I look over the room again, game filming what that might look like. Seven men, five women at the bar. Another four couples at other tables. A group of loud, 30-something women having an early girls night. From the lobby adjoining the dining room, a smallish man in a trim cut suit enters the bar and starts walking toward my table. He must feel me looking at him because he finds my eyeline and smiles. When I consider standing to meet him, his eyes break from mine and he walks past me, disappearing around the corner by the brass sign that says "Restrooms." I follow him with my eyes until he's gone and then turn my head back toward the bar. I see Charles eyeing me from across the room, pointing at the fit, stylish woman approaching my table. She looks to be in her 40s, blue glasses, hair pulled back, and despite her black dinner jacket, is not at all what I was expecting.

"Can I help you sir?" she asks. "I was told you asked to see the sommelier."

"I did. You're the sommelier here?" I ask, sure she's seeing the surprise and disappointment written on my face.

"I am. My name is Harper Yale. Do you have a question for me?"

"I'm sorry. I was expecting someone else," I say, still a bit flustered.

"That's alright," she smiles. "How can I help you? Is there something wrong with your wine?"

"No, no. It's very good," I answer gathering myself. The young sommelier looks relieved and leans toward me with bright eyes and what I sense is a very helpful spirit. It's time to dance a little. "This is my first visit to Marvelous and I've heard your wine menu is exceptional. I was hoping to try something I can't easily find other places."

To my surprise, Harper sits down in the chair next to me. She clasps her hands together and rests them on the table. It's clear this is the part of her job she enjoys.

"I would love to help you, um…"

"Jake."

"Jake. Nice to meet you," she says extending her hand. "Welcome in. Do you live here in Dallas?"

"No, I live in L.A."

"Nice. I love L.A. So, what do you normally like to drink? Charles mentioned you started with the Oregon Pinot. I like that wine a lot."

"I do like Pinots, and I haven't found many Cabs I didn't like."

"Perfect," Harper says picking up the menu. "Is there a price range you're trying to stay within?"

"No," I answer mustering a little swagger. "Exclusivity has a price tag. If I can find something that few others have tasted, I'm happy to pay more. Perhaps there is something off menu that you think I should try."

I watch Harper's eyes to see if my innuendo is registering and it's not. She looks up and toward the bar as if she's trying to conjure the names of the expensive wines she's seen sitting in storage that are so expensive the restaurant might serve them once or twice a year. She looks back at me, resigned to find something I'll like.

"If you want a really full-bodied red we have a 40-year-old French Bordeaux that's pretty exceptional. I think it's about $2,500. I know we have a few bottles of an Italian red from Tuscany that's fantastic. Those are about $900 a bottle. There's a 50-year-old Portuguese Port that's $400 a glass. I haven't tasted it, but I've been told it's life changing. Any of those sound intriguing to you?"

What's intriguing to me is whether this woman can be of any help at all. I doubt it. But with my next question, I immediately realize how wrong I am.

"I was hoping to maybe sample something off one of the Friday menus," I say, slightly cocking my head to one side and looking Harper straight in the eye. She tries to hold my gaze, but her body language betrays what she knows. She pulls back slightly, and I notice her breathing pick up. Subtly, she pulls her hands into her lap and her eyes shift toward the kitchen and back.

"The Friday menu?" she says trying to mask some surprise. "I'm sorry. I'm not sure what you mean."

"Oh, I think you do," I push. "Some very close acquaintances told me the private Friday night dinners at Marvelous are the experience of a lifetime and worth every penny. They told me to come up to the bar and to ask the sommelier about getting an invitation."

"Well sir, I am the sommelier here," she answers trying to recover.

"Actually," I interrupt her, "I was told to speak to a sommelier named Jean-Michel."

As I start to speak, a well-to-do gentleman happens to be walking through the bar and past our table, but at the mention of Jean-Michel, he stops on a dime.

"I'm sorry, who did you say you're looking for?" he asks looking me up and down.

"You know, I'm not sure that concerns you pal," I answer standing up.

"I assure you sir, as the manager of Marvelous, it's very much my concern. Now, exactly what is it you would like to discuss with Mr. Baptiste?"

Clearly I've hit a nerve about something. Maybe this guy is part of the charade. Maybe he just doesn't like me. But either way, I decide to escalate the tension to see what I can find out.

"I was told by a friend that some Jean-Michel, I'm guessing this Mr. Baptiste you mentioned, runs some private dinner for discerning tastes on Friday nights at Marvelous that isn't to be missed, and I want a taste. What's it gonna take Garcon," I ask pulling out my wallet and knowing the insult will cut this guy to the quick. "$200? $300? Come on man, what's it gonna take to get on the list? I'm dying to see what's behind the closed door."

From the plum color in his face, and the slight tremble of his mouth, I can see this guy is seething. He spins on an axis of status and respect, and I haven't given him an inch of either.

"I'm afraid you were given bad information, sir. Any events held at Marvelous are indeed invitation only, but they are at the discretion of our owners and their personal friends."

"I can be a personal friend. How personal are we talking?"

I pull 10 hundred dollar bills out of my wallet and count them right under his nose. "I've got $1,000 right here and it's yours if you can hook me up with this Jean-Michel. Come on man, $1,000 cash. Right now." The manager doesn't even look down at the money.

"I'm sorry sir," he says shaking off his disdain and shifting back into manager mode. "It's my profound regret that I cannot satisfy your request. But I cannot. Perhaps it's time to pay your bill and call it a night. Thank you for visiting us here at Marvelous." And with that, he turns and walks back toward the dining room.

I sit down and peer over at Harper who looks a bit more shaken by the conversation than she should. I don't know what all she knows, but her eyes and the way she's looking at me tell me it's something. She rises and walks over to my waiter. He reaches into his apron and hands her a small leather binder that she brings back to the table.

"Your bill sir," she says a bit sadly, laying it gently in front of me. As she does, I reach up and clasp my hand around her wrist. This is a moment of truth and though I don't know this woman from Eve, my gut says I can trust her enough to show a little transparency.

"Harper," I say quietly, "I want you to know that I'm not a bad guy. I'm not some rich, entitled prick. I'm just trying to figure out what's going on here."

She looks at me with a hesitant smile and lets out a long sigh. "I wish…" she starts but then stops as the manager reappears beside the table, standing over me like some overimportant schoolmaster.

"Perhaps I wasn't clear before," he starts gripping my arm, pulling me up. "It is time for you to go."

"Jesus man, I'm signing the bill," I say ripping my arm away from him. I open the binder, leave Charles a hefty tip and sign my name. "Get your fucking hands off of me."

I smile at Harper knowing the intense grilling she is sure to get from this asshole when I'm gone. I push past the manager and walk to the lobby to call the elevator. Looking back to the bar, I see him watching to make sure I'm leaving and then he disappears into the kitchen. Probably to call his boss to say some unexpected guest was asking questions about him.

Above my head I hear a ding, and the elevator door opens in front of me. I walk in, punch the button for my floor and when I turn back toward the restaurant, I see Harper moving quickly toward the elevator. I grab the closing door, pushing it open. At the elevator, Harper reaches out as though she intends to shake my hand. I reach up but instead of shaking, she hands me a printed menu and puts a piece of paper in my hand, curling her fingers into mine.

"Your receipt sir," she says looking at me intensely. I could certainly have done without my receipt, but her hand and her eyes hold me transfixed. I feel her strengthen the grip of her fingers curled with mine as though she's trying to press the paper more securely into my hand. Harper steps into the elevator and pulls me closer. She leans into my ear and with a single breath, she whispers the word "Hummingbird." Harper pulls away and with a clap, the doors close. The elevator starts to move, and I look at the receipt she put in my hand. It's a copy of what I just signed. But then I turn it over. On the back it reads, "8147 Sunset Boulevard, L.A."

I sprint down the hall to my room, grab my laptop and pull up Google Maps to see what's at 8147 Sunset. According to every map I can find and a crosscheck of Google Earth, 8147 Sunset Boulevard is a parking garage. Twelve floors of open concrete. It seems an odd piece to the puzzle and with the comings and goings of parking garages, endlessly variable. I double check the receipt to make sure I have the address right and I do. Harper's handwriting is impeccably clear. I've never been more thankful to be heading home to L.A. than I am right now. If I hurried, I could probably catch the redeye out of DFW, but tomorrow will be fine. I think there are a few more sleeping pills in my bag and the parking garage isn't going anywhere. A decent night's sleep wouldn't be the worst thing.

No sooner has that thought occurred to me than I feel my phone vibrating in my pocket. I pull it out and my breath catches when I see the screen. It's Rachel Meredith.

"Rachel?" I answer, not really believing she'd be on the other end of the line.

"Hi Jake," comes the warm voice I wasn't sure I'd ever hear again. "Where are you?"

"I'm in Dallas. But I'm coming home tomorrow."

"Good. Listen, there's something important I need to tell you, but I want to talk to you in person. I thought it could wait, but it can't." I immediately flash back to our night together and hold my breath, anxious for whatever it is she's about to say. "I know who your sommelier is."

"Yeah? That makes two of us," I answer coarsely. "I know who the son of a bitch is, but I can't seem to find him."

"I know where Jean-Michel will be this Friday night. That's part of what I want to talk to you about. Listen, I can't talk about this right now, but I promise, I'll explain everything to you when I see you. You have a pen? Write down this address and meet me there Friday night at 11:30. Do not be late. And Jake? I'm sorry about how I left. I've missed you and I'll explain that too."

Rachel gives me the address and I ask her to repeat it just to make sure I heard what she said. She confirms it and with a curt "Bye," she's gone. I put my phone on the nightstand and put my hand to my chest. My heart is pounding and the hairs on the back of my neck are literally standing up. I breathe deeply and look at the address I just wrote on the pad next to my bed.

It's the same address Harper gave me in the elevator. 8147 Sunset Boulevard, Los Angeles.

19

I've been gone for a week and walking in my front door I wonder how I ever made it being gone for eight years in Afghanistan. I drop my suitcase next to the bedroom and prop open the front door and the door to the patio to let the Pacific breeze air out the house. Everything seems frozen in suspended animation with just the memories of the past lending any motion to the scene. I look from the kitchen to the fireplace to the sofa and imagine Rachel sitting there.

All I could think about for the full three hour flight from Dallas was her surprise phone call last night. Over and over, I replayed our conversation trying to remember exactly what she said. Her tone of voice. "I've missed you and I'll explain that too." Isn't that what she said? Part of me wants to believe that. But the practical, cynical side of me wants to know how this random woman who dropped into my life for two days not only knows this man I'm chasing but knows about his comings and goings. Is she working with him? Am I being played in some way? If I am, I can't see her angle, but this can't be coincidence. Until our last night together, she didn't even know I was looking for any kind of sommelier. Now, she suddenly knows where he'll be in five days. I need to talk to her again. But she isn't answering her phone. Three calls straight to voicemail.

Frustrated, I grab my phone and call Jon Joseph. If Rachel isn't going to tell me more about this guy, maybe Bear knows more than the last time we talked. And while he's at it, maybe he can tell me something about Rachel Meredith too. I call his personal cell and it barely rings twice before he picks up.

"What's up my brother?" Hearing Jon's voice always puts me at ease. It reminds me there is at least one person in the world I can truly count on.

"You know, just enjoying suspension," I answer.

"Yeah? How's that going?" he asks laughing.

"Well, let's see. I just spent a week traveling across the country trying to find this sommelier we're chasing and now the woman I spent the night with before I left has resurfaced and claims to know where he'll be this Friday night. I think that's everything."

Bear pauses while he registers everything I just said. "You spent the night with a woman?" he says.

"Shocking, I know." I answer back. "But that's part of the reason I'm calling you. Can you run this woman through the system and see if you find anything? When we met, I really liked her and at the time, it felt like a random meet at the bar. But now, even suggesting she has some connection to this guy just feels a little too perfect and I don't like it."

"Sure, what's her name?"

"Rachel Meredith. Or at least, that's what she told me. She wants to meet me Friday night to tell me or show me where this guy is."

"Do you know anything else about her?"

"She said she was a journalist covering trafficking for the DOJ."

"Fuck man, she works at Justice?"

"Not AT Justice. She said she worked with Justice writing articles about trafficking. She's a reporter. I don't know. It could all be bullshit."

"OK. I'll run her name and see what I can find out. Might take a day or two."

"All good," I assure him.

"You know what's *not* good Jake? Chasing after a suspect when you're suspended. What do you mean you've been traveling across the country looking for this motherfucker?"

"You know I'm not just gonna sit at home. When you told me the girls from Houston were bound for Vegas I decided to take a little road trip out to the desert. Play a little blackjack. Drink a few cocktails. See a show."

"I know that's bullshit but keep going."

For the next 30 minutes, I tell Bear everything I uncovered on my trips to Vegas, Washington, Atlanta, Miami, and Dallas. I tell him about the restaurants, the menus, the wine, the people I met, and the conversations that have convinced me this Sommelier, this Jean-Michel Baptiste, is an evil, connected guy we needed to find yesterday. From what Jon knows, he concurs.

"This Baptiste definitely sounds like a bad guy Jake. Let me run the lead and see what I can find because right now he's a ghost." I can hear the stress in Jon's voice. It's the level of anxiety that comes with a case that's on the RADAR of everyone two and three levels above you. "Nice work finding a name. I'll run it through the system, but I need to think of a plausible way to get it into the case file without it coming from you. Don't want you to get any bonus weeks tacked onto your suspension for bad behavior."

"I appreciate that. Any more intel on your end?"

"No, but in the past month Homeland Security has intercepted three other shipping containers like the one we found in Houston. Forty-seven girls in all. Every one under 15."

"Jesus, Jon. How many of them were alive?"

"Thirty-four." I can hear the defeated resignation in his voice. "We have five guys in custody but like the others, they're not saying much. We did find out some of the girls were being trafficked to L.A. but we're not sure they're connected to the ones we rescued in Houston."

"I don't know how this is all connected yet Jon, but it is. I'm telling you."

"I feel it too. Listen, I'm heading to the office now. I'll get to work connecting the dots and you keep your head down. I need you officially back in the game Jake and going rogue has a bad habit of fucking that up. You know what I'm saying?"

"I hear you Bear."

"I don't suppose I can talk you out of the meet and greet with the mystery woman Friday night?" My silence answers what he already knows. "You want any backup?"

"Thanks, but no. I don't want to spook her. Let me see if she's legit or completely full of shit and I'll let you know what I find out."

"Alright. Be careful."

"Thanks man," I say ending the call. Turning my phone over, I see Rachel listed second, third, and fourth on the Recent Calls list. I press her name and number and hold my breath. It clicks and then rolls to voicemail yet again.

Rachel Meredith is determined to meet me on Friday as scheduled, and on her terms. For the next five days, all I can do is pray that she's real. Pray that she's on the right side of whatever this is. Pray that she's not trying to fuck me.

I let her do that once. And here we are.

20

If I needed a reminder why meeting Rachel Friday night and unraveling this evil is so important, I didn't have to wait long.

Wednesday morning before I even wake up, my phone pings with a story from *The Washington Post* about a pedophile caught in a sting up in New England. Apparently three months ago, DHS flipped another predator in Florida who was conversing with the guy in Boston on the dark web, and the Feds made a deal to start talking to him through the guy's account. It wasn't enough that the guy in Boston bragged about abusing his sister's kids when they were on vacation. In two months, he and his partner were adopting a baby through a surrogate, and he was already pining about how he intended to abuse the new baby. He even picked out a special onesie for the occasion. What the fuck is wrong with people? There's a special place in Hell for people who abuse babies and toddlers. But that was just the beginning. In the same paper, there were three other stories about trafficking and abuse.

In Arizona, local officers rescued nine teenage girls from a truck stop in Flagstaff who had been groomed and trafficked in a ring running "lot lizards" from San Antonio to Santa Fe, up to Denver, over to Salt Lake and then down to Flagstaff and Phoenix. The girls said they were forced to work truck stops in groups of eight to 10 for a week at a time. Then on Sundays, certain trucks would show up and take them to the next stop in the ring. But only after a free hour in the back of the rig to pay for the transportation. Officers suspect there could be as many as 200 girls making the circuit, but they don't have any leads yet as to who could be running an operation that size.

In California, authorities arrested an Indian couple running a labor trafficking ring supplying servants to families all over Southern California. The couple were promising girls from Mumbai a shot at the American Dream, but then once they got them here, they were selling the girls to families that were subjecting them to coerced labor, false imprisonment, sleep deprivation, starvation, and assault. On more than one occasion the girls were disciplined by holding their hands to a blazing stovetop.

On the next to back page of the News section, there was a small story from southern Kentucky about a daycare taking money to let predators in the back door of the facility to spend some alone time with the kids. The scheme was diabolical. The abuse always took place in a dark room, so the kids had no idea who was molesting them or what was happening. When the kids said something, and made what sounded like outrageous claims, the teachers and parents wrote it off to kids making up stories or just being afraid of the dark. The calculating logic of the dark room was fucking insidious, but it worked. The only reason they got caught is one of predators left the back door of the preschool open when he snuck in and one of the kids got out and walked to a shopping area a few blocks over. A beat cop found her sobbing on a park bench and when she told him about the monsters who touched her in the dark, he actually listened to her and investigated. They busted the couple that ran the daycare and discovered they had warrants for child abuse under different names in three other states.

By Friday morning, I am chomping at the bit to meet Rachel and hear what she knows. The second I wake up, I'm already anxious so I go for a long run along the beach. For a second, I expect Rachel to walk out of the palm trees like she did before, but she doesn't. I'm not sure what to expect tonight, but one way or the other, I will find out what she knows. I hate days like this. All the waiting. Every day leading up to a night op is stressful and I don't know what to do with myself. I don't really want to eat or watch anything. I'm too amped up to read and I can only run so much. Rachel said she knows where Baptiste will be. Does that mean she's going to take me there? Just give me the address and let me find this guy on my own? I still don't know what he looks like.

Rachel said to meet her at 11:30pm sharp but I leave my house at 9:00. L.A. traffic has a bad habit of biting you in the ass when you can least afford it and this way, I've got plenty of cushion should I need it. Turns out, there's next to no traffic on the 10, Sepulveda, or Wilshire, and I'm early. At 9:45, I pull off Sunset into a lot across from the address and confirm that indeed, 8147 Sunset is nothing but a parking garage.

For 30 minutes, I sit, watching the comings and goings of the people zipping up and down Sunset on the way to nightclubs and restaurants. I check the address again and nothing has changed. Ultimately, my curiosity gets the better of me. I drive across the street and enter the bottom floor of the parking garage winding my way to the top to find out what this structure is attached to. An office building? A restaurant? There's gotta be something. But there's not. Slowly, I wind my way back down, looking for doors, entrances, bridges that might connect to something nearby, but there's nothing. It's just a garage, albeit one filled with a number of extremely nice rides. I'm not sure there's a car in this lot that costs less than $80,000. I'm also not sure where all the owners have gone. I guess it's possible it's general parking. This is Sunset and we're only blocks from luxury hotels, and a dozen clubs and restaurants. But still.

On the ground floor of the garage, I pull back into a shadowed space where I can still see the entrance. The bottom level is still empty by half and from here, whether Rachel parks or drives past me, I'm where I can see her. Our meeting is still an hour away and I'm not sure when she'll arrive, but other cars are starting to pull in.

One by one, $90,000 luxury sedans, special edition SUVs, and sleek convertibles pull into the garage and park. People dressed for some clearly hip affair emerge and make their way to the elevator in the front corner of the garage. There must be some event on the roof of the garage that's only accessible from the elevator. The view from up that high will be spectacular with the Hollywood Hills behind us and the Pacific in the distance. I wonder if that's where Jean-Michel will be or where Rachel is planning to take me.

About 10 minutes later, I see her white sportscar pull into the lot and park in a space not too far from the front. I haven't seen Rachel since the night at my house, but the second she steps out of the car, I recognize her shape. She's dressed in a tight silver dress and her hair is pulled back like I last remember it. Even though she's 45 minutes early, I expect her to pause and look over the parking lot looking for me. But she doesn't. Not for a second. Immediately, Rachel turns, walks to the elevator, and presses the call button, I open my door but before I can even call her name, the elevator doors shut behind her. Tonight, it appears, will begin with a game of pursuit.

As I'm locking the car, my phone rings. It's Jon calling me back. I get in the car and shut the door. I can only hope he's found some information on this woman who never is who she seems to be. I hate going into any mission blind and right now, I'm completely in the dark where Rachel Meredith is concerned. I hit answer and hope he knows something that will turn the next few hours in my favor.

"Tell me something good Bear," I say putting Jonny on speaker.

"I wish I could Jake," he says. "You're not gonna like this."

21

Jon's right. There's nothing I like about what he tells me.

"I can't find her." The disappointment of Jon's words takes me out of the moment, my brain scrambling to make sense of this woman who parachuted into my life and continues to be a complete enigma. From the second I talked to Jon about Rachel and asked him to check the intel on her, I was convinced he'd find her. Find something. But she's as much of a ghost as this sommelier we're hunting. The only difference is at the moment, I know generally where she is.

"I checked every database we have Jake and there wasn't a Rachel Meredith to be found. At least not the woman you described. You said she mentioned working with Justice. I checked the DOJ records specifically and they've never heard of her. She's not a listed contact. She's never been part of any task force. She certainly doesn't work for the DOJ directly and they don't even have notes on her as any kind of suspect. I'm sorry buddy. I know you wanted to know more about the shadow you're slow dancing with, but I've got nothing for you."

"It's alright. Thanks for checking Jonny," I say disappointed but already shifting my attention back to the moment at hand. Bear couldn't find Rachel Meredith in the system, but you can be damn sure I'm about to find her now. "I've gotta go. I'll call you tomorrow."

Jon sighs. "Be careful with her."

I click off the call and run to the elevator. Rachel can't be more than 10 minutes ahead of me and besides, the top of the parking garage and whatever setup they have up there can't be that big. I'll find her.

I hit the call button and wait impatiently while the elevator makes its way back to the ground floor. I'm anxious about other people joining me, but no one else drives in while I'm waiting. The door finally opens, and I hit the seven button to take me to the roof of the garage. I don't remember seeing a staircase from the seventh floor up to the roof but there has to be one. I'm sure I just missed it driving by in the car.

With a loud hum, the elevator rises toward the seventh floor. The faint remnants of expensive perfume linger in the air. I tuck my shirt tails flat, and smooth out the front of my jacket. I look up at the digital display above the door. Four. Five. Six. Here we go.

When the door opens, I step out and expect to hear the overflow of a party above me but all I hear is the sound of the wind whipping down from the hills through the empty garage. It's dark and it's cold and there is nothing here. I walk to the four corners of the garage, looking for the staircase, or the door or bridge I missed on my first trip, but they don't exist. In every direction, it's just concrete walls, oil slicks, scuffed walls, and parking lines overdue for a fresh coat of paint. Where the fuck are all these people going?

Confused and frustrated, I get back in the elevator and take it down to the sixth floor. I get out and walk the perimeter of the garage and it's just the same as it was on seven. Five is the same. Four is the same. At three, I get out and just follow the flow of the garage around and down to the next floor and the next. Top to bottom, this parking garage is just a parking garage. I'm missing something.

At the bottom floor, I get back in the elevator and look at the number panel. There is a silver circle next to the button for the seventh floor that would have been used had there been an eighth floor. I press it hoping for a light, a sound. Some connection. But it's just a circle. I look up at the ceiling and there are small cameras in every corner. Beneath the floor buttons, there are standard buttons for closing the door, opening the door, and calling in the case of emergency. I look at the walls, the floor, and back to the ceiling and nothing seems out of the ordinary. Except that I saw 100 people get into this elevator and take it to nowhere.

For the first time, I notice the panel that says "Phone" on the front. I open the door and take out the receiver. I put it to my ear and immediately it starts ringing. I hear a click and what sounds like a sophisticated voice fills my ear.

"Good evening sir, how may I help you?" The cameras. The voice can see me.

"Uh, yeah, Hi… umm, I'm here to meet some friends for a party but I can't seem to find them. I've gone to each floor of the garage but I'm not seeing anyone. Any chance you can point me in the right direction?" In truth, I don't really expect any help and the voice does not disappoint.

"I'm sorry sir, this is a line for emergencies. I wouldn't know about any social events going on at or around your location. If this is an emergency I can dispatch an EMT or the police to your location. Would you like me to do that now?" the voice asks politely.

"No," I answer. "I'll figure something out. Thank you."

"You're very welcome sir. Have a good evening."

I hang up the phone, completely flustered by the situation. Either this elevator is the coolest speakeasy in L.A. that I can't access, or we have ventured into some Dr. Who fantasy world. Either way, I have lost Rachel and cannot see the path that leads to her. I look at my watch and it's 11:25. I'm supposed to meet her in five minutes. It's entirely possible that wherever she is, she's heading back to meet me here as scheduled. But I'm betting not.

I walk back to my car to wait for her, but she doesn't magically materialize at 11:30. Or at 11:45, or at midnight. She's gone. Again.

Grabbing my keys to go home, I look down at the cupholder and in it, I see the Marvelous receipt sitting there with the address written on it. I look out the front window at the elevator I just got out of and my mind flashes back to Dallas to the moment Harper curled that receipt into my hand. It was the same moment she whispered something into my ear.

At a full sprint, I race back to the elevator, take a deep breath, and pick up the phone. The same sophisticated voice as before comes on the line.

"Good evening sir, how may I help you?" he asks.

I close my eyes and squeezing the receipt in my hand, I utter the word, "Hummingbird," into the receiver. There is a long pause. And then I hear the voice again.

"Thank you sir," he says. Enjoy your evening."

I hang up the phone and immediately, the elevator goes completely black. With a start, I feel the box begin to descend. There are no illuminated buttons for this. There is no way to access wherever I'm going from the street. I'm just moving, down. I can sense my pulse and breathing starting to pick up and I feel the need to touch one of the walls for stability. Moving in total darkness, I am completely disoriented. Two hours ago, I had envisioned some massive party on the roof of this garage. Never in a million years did I think this night would take me half a mile beneath West Hollywood into a pit of depravity so vast even I couldn't imagine it.

We're not descending all the way to Hell, but we're damn close.

22

The elevator doors open, and I step into a small metal room about four times the size of the elevator, lit only by the pale blue light bouncing off the ceiling. To say the room is stark is a gross understatement. The only thing in it is the gargantuan man standing in front of me. He's every bit of 6' 8" and pushing 350. The thing is, he's not heavy. He's ripped and perfectly manicured, dressed in all black. This guy could rip a phone book in half and not breathe hard. I need to play this as straight up as possible.

"Good evening sir. Can I have your name please?" Jesus, the guy is polite, too. I give him my I.D. and he punches it into the small electronic tablet dwarfed by his hands.

"I'm sorry sir, but I don't see your name on tonight's guest list."

That's not good but I do have one card to play.

"Could I trouble you to check under the name Rachel Meredith? I was supposed to meet her upstairs at 11:30 but I was running late, and I think she might have already come down looking for me." It occurs to me Rachel could also be using a different name. If that's the case I'm done.

"Did you say the last name was Meredith?" the guy asks unconsciously shaking his head. My stomach drops but then I see his eyebrows arch up and his eyes open wider. "Rachel Meredith and her guest… yes. Here it is. My apologies for the wait."

I take a step forward and the guy takes hold of my arms and pulls them out to the side. Very meticulously he pats me down from top to bottom and I am thankful for once that I'm suspended and not carrying. With a pat to my shoulder, the guy steps aside and motions to the back wall of the room behind him.

"Thank you for your patience sir. Enjoy your evening."

I'm not sure how to describe what happens next except to say the entire wall recesses into itself. Mechanically, I can't explain it. It's like looking at an Escher painting and feeling amazed but confused when reality defies perception. What's even more difficult to understand is that where moments before, the sterile room I'm standing in was completely silent, with the door open, it's now filled with flashing light and the deafening pulse of club music with a bass I can feel in my chest. With no idea of where I am, or what I'm stepping into, I walk through the door and by the time I look back, it's already shut. From this side, it's like it's not even there.

I turn back and move toward the enormous circular bar dominating the center of the room. On both sides of me, the club rises three stories with long observation overhangs looking down on the bar and the people below. It feels like Costa's did in Miami only bigger and more advanced somehow. In front of me, past the bar, the room drops off dramatically, to the extent I can't see it from where I'm standing. All I can see is the far wall covered in massive video screens you'd sooner see in a professional sports arena than a club this size. Looking around, the space is full of the same high-toned half percenters I saw in the garage and there is an expectant energy crackling between them. I scan the crowd looking for Rachel and see a little bit of everything. Old couples. Young couples. Women with women. Old men with young girls. But no silver dress.

I walk around the left side of the bar and see there's a large dancefloor full of people dancing, drinking, and grinding. Again, I stand looking for Rachel, but I can't see her in the mass of people. I need to move higher up so I can look down on the floor. I reverse course to the right side of the bar to find a staircase that leads upstairs and as I do, I look into the space under the overhangs. It's a dimly lit seating area with plush chairs and sofas where people are paired off in twos, threes, and fours, most having carnal knowledge of each other. Very quickly, I realize where I am and why Rachel wanted to meet me here.

I race up the staircase and move to the railing for a better look at the room below. With the various colored lights flashing, it's difficult to make out distinct dress colors, but nothing flashes silver. From the second floor, I can see the space beyond the bar that drops off a good 10 feet below the dancefloor. The back of the club is a tall, rounded wall with large seating areas in front of what appears to be a bank of windows. From here, it's hard to tell with so many people gathered around them.

I look over the top of the bar to the elevated balcony across from where I'm standing and through the strobes, the people crowding the rail vibrate like a nest of snakes. Pants down. Skirts up. Blouses open. Bodies absorbing bodies as they push against the edge and each other. From my right, I feel a hand move across my chest and into my shirt. I turn and see a blonde, middle-aged woman with a wanton look of lust in her eyes. She runs her fingers through the hair on my chest, scratching harder with each stroke. Unquestionably high, she smiles seductively as I feel a second hand reach between my legs from behind, groping me. I take a step back and nearly stumble over the second woman grabbing me. She sits up on her knees, reaching for my zipper.

Pushing her away, I'm suddenly aware of the strong scent of sweat and sex around me. Both second floor balconies have turned into a Roman free for all and I can only assume the same is true in the lofted balconies above us. Weaving through bodies, I move down the stairs and around the back side of the bar to the edge of the dancefloor. At the top of the stairs leading to the lower area, a flash draws my eyes upward to the images on the video boards above my head and for the first time I see their actual content. The collages of half-naked girls on the screens aren't music videos as I assumed. They're auction boards. Every 10 seconds, each screen cascades from one GIF to the next. Images of girls from their early teens to their twenties. Every ethnicity. Every hair color, eye color, and body type. Some try to look seductive. Others just try not to look scared. The screens are sparse. Just images, first names, and a running bid total at the bottom of each frame. A second, smaller countdown clock sits in the bottom right corner counting down to the end of the auction at 2am. I feel a pit in my stomach when I realize the highest bid totals match the youngest girls.

I descend the stairs to the lower viewing area in the hope of finding Rachel somewhere among the throng of people entranced by the windows they're staring at along the back wall of the club. I'm struck by the couples gathered. Each is impeccably dressed, drinking cocktails and champagne, and whispering, pointing, laughing, smelling of expensive perfume and money. You would be forgiven for thinking you were at some high-toned gala or the opening of L.A.'s newest billion dollar art museum. But this isn't a museum. It's an aquarium.

Pushing through the curious but reserved crowd watching from the back of the lower basin, I move to where I can get a full view of the first window. Behind the glass, there's a set dressed to look like the loft bedroom of a Manhattan apartment. Floor to ceiling bookcases filled with succulents and the world's great novels frame the sides of the room and arch above the queen sized bed in the center. Small lamps on the bookended nightstands provide the only light in the room. But it's more than enough to illuminate the naked couple grinding with abandon behind the glass. The crowd around me seems to hang on every movement not daring to look away or even blink. A woman next to me gasps quietly. She's transfixed, gently rubbing the older man beside her.

Looking to the right, I see thick clusters of people sitting on sets of flat benches in front of each of the windows. At each bench, larger groups are gathered tightly behind those sitting. Each of the windows is a living, breathing display of people's darkest fantasies. Lesbians dressed like schoolgirls entangled behind the second window. Two ripped ebony men with hoses for cocks standing over some demure housewife behind window number four. Multiple couples switching and swapping on a blue leather sectional behind window five. A leather clad Dominatrix with a spiked riding crop whipping three guys wearing dog collars behind window seven. A middle-aged woman lying on a small bed in the center of the room behind window nine servicing an endless stream of men. It's painfully clear she's been there for hours.

I shouldn't be shocked at people's fascination with sex and depravity. But I am. I always am. We are all hardwired for curiosity. But for too many, the expressly forbidden and taboo are siren calls that can't be ignored. Demons that cannot be shouted down. If there's one saving grace in front of me, it's that there are no kids behind these windows. That doesn't mean there aren't any somewhere else, or that the acts behind the glass are all consensual. I'd bet my house they're not. But at least there are no children.

Just past the last window, I see an additional staircase I hadn't seen before matching the one I came down on the other side. I move quickly up the steps and into the seating area under the balcony that I first noticed when I came in. The space is fuller now with nearly every sofa and chair occupied with exhibitionists tangled in every position possible. But it's not the sex that catches my eye. It's the silver dress I see moving away from me across the room. I scream Rachel's name but there's no chance she can hear me over the music. She's walking behind a tall man having an argument with the petite woman beside him. He has a firm grip on her arm and seems to be pulling her toward wherever it is he wants her to go. I have no idea why Rachel is following him, but she's 30 feet behind him and closing fast.

Sprinting to catch her, I see Rachel reach behind her head and pull out the two thick needles holding up her hair. Shifting them to her palms, she tightens her grip on the heavy, wooden needles and raises them toward the man in front of her as though she's about to stab him through the neck. I speed up and before Rachel can make a descending blow, I grab the needles from her hands, throwing them to the side. She turns to me stunned and before she can take even a step, I put my hand over her mouth and drag her toward the bar, away from the tall man and woman now disappearing through an open door.

Even side by side, I can't hear Rachel screaming because of the music, but her, "What the Fuck Jake!" comes through loud and clear. She starts blistering me with a string of expletives and spit, but suddenly stops, thinking twice about causing a scene here or simply wasting her breath when I can't hear a word she's saying. She punches me in the chest, and then grabs my hand pulling me toward the wall where the door was. Rachel punches an eight-digit code into a keypad and once again the walls shift revealing the door to the small metallic room. We move through the room's dim blue glow and Rachel punches the call button on the elevator. The hulk who checked me in steps toward us and reaches out his hand to Rachel.

"Always a pleasure to see you Ms. Meredith," he says politely.

"Thank you Bruno," she answers.

"You know each other?" I say, more than a bit shocked.

"Not here," Rachel answers quietly turning toward the opening elevator doors.

"Seriously," I say following her into the elevator. "You've been here before?"

Rachel hits the button for the Ground Floor and says again, "Not here," putting extra emphasis on the word "here." We get in the elevator and as the doors are shutting, she tilts her chin up, motioning to the cameras in the four corners of the elevator. I can only assume they also contain microphones.

Darkness swallows us as we make the long ascent toward Sunset. I reach to find Rachel in the dark, but she's moved as far away from me as she can get. After what feels like an eternity rising, the elevator opens, and we walk out into the solemn glow of the garage. At 2:30 in the morning, most of Hollywood is winding down and thankfully, there is no one else around us. Without a word, Rachel walks away from me still seething from the scene downstairs.

"You want to explain all this?" I say, yelling in her direction. "The cloak and dagger bullshit? The sex auction going on downstairs? How about all the lies?"

Irate, Rachel whips back in my direction and gets so close to my face, I can feel the heat in her breath.

"Yes, Jake, I'll tell you everything. I'll explain it all. But before I do, know this – you, are a fucking idiot."

23

I walk over to Rachel's car and tell her to drive to my house. We can talk there. It'll be an $80 cab ride to come back for my car but now that she's in front of me, there's no way in Hell I'm letting Rachel out of my sight. At least not until she explains to me the evils we just escaped.

From the passenger seat, I can see Rachel's face flash in and out of shadow with every streetlight we pass. I can see her moving through an emotional progression of rage, frustration, and finally resignation. The expressions on her face and the eventual heavy sigh tell an explicit story. But not once in the entire 30-minute trip does she utter a word or look in my direction.

At the curb in front of my house, she quietly turns off the ignition, steps out of her car and walks to my front door. I unlock the door and she strides across the threshold like it's her house. I punch in the code to kill the alarm and when I turn back, she's gone. I feel momentary panic rising, until I hear the door of the refrigerator close. The cabinet doors open and shut. The sound of liquid pouring. Rachel rounds the corner from the kitchen holding two full glasses of orange juice. I wonder if 3:00 in the morning is too late to add vodka.

"Where would you like to start," she asks dropping onto the sofa. "We have a lot to talk about."

"You think?" I bark at her sarcastically, pacing between Rachel and the fireplace. "I'd love to know why you disappeared after what

I thought was a pretty nice evening a few weeks ago. But before that, let's tackle tonight. No, wait. Fuck that. Before we deal with any of it, what I really want to know is who you are, Rachel. And don't give me the journalist bullshit or tell me you work for Justice. We both know that's a lie. I want to know who you are. I want to know how you're involved in all this and why of all places, you wanted me to meet you at, literally, an underground sex club. You claimed to know this sommelier I'm chasing and said you'd tell me where he is, but at this point, I'm thinking that's just bullshit too. Is there anything about you that's honest? Because I'm not seeing it."

"I've never lied to you Jake. When we met and I came over here, you saw what you wanted to see and heard what you wanted to hear."

"That's bullshit."

"It's not. With the exception of saying I'm a journalist, the rest is absolutely the truth."

"I ran you through the system Rachel. You're not there. You're not anywhere."

"You ran a background check on me?"

"You're goddamned right I did. I work for the Department of Homeland Security, Rachel. You drop into my life, seemingly out of nowhere, connect with me, eat with me, fuck me, and then disappear without a trace – stealing my case notes on the way out the door by the way – and yeah, I'm gonna check to see who you really are. But that's the thing. You're nobody. You're a ghost. I checked everywhere I could, and your name didn't come up once. There's no way you've worked at Justice, or for Justice, or even walked past the fucking building. There would be some record of it. So do not sit there and tell me you're being honest with me."

"I never said I worked for Justice, Jake. I said I work with the DOJ."

"Semantics."

"Actually, it's not. I've never worked for the Department of Justice. I work with an anti-trafficking organization called the Daughters of Jacob. DOJ."

"Never heard of them."

"You wouldn't have. But I assure you we are very real."

"Come on Rachel. This is what I do for a living. If there was an anti-trafficking group of any significance, I would have heard of them."

"The fact that you've never heard of the Daughters of Jacob tells me we're doing everything right."

"Fine," I say with a skeptical, sarcastic tone. "If I'm so uninformed, enlighten me." I drop into a chair and give Rachel an incredulous look like, "let's go. Give it to me."

"Do you know the story of Jacob?"

"Jacob? In the Bible, Jacob?" Rachel nods. "Sure. We read the stories in Sunday School when we were kids. Son of Isaac. Stole his brother's birthright. Had a bunch of sons including Joseph and the brothers who sold him into slavery. Sure. I've heard of Jacob."

"Most people know about Joseph and his brothers. Nobody remembers their sister Dinah."

"I didn't know they had a sister."

"My point exactly. In addition to his sons, Jacob had one daughter named Dinah. In the 34th chapter of Genesis, Dinah visits a neighboring kingdom where she's raped by the son of the prince. Some asshole named Shechem. When her brothers find out their sister has been raped, they are enraged. The king comes to Jacob and his sons and tries to smooth things over for his rapist son by convincing them to basically trade their daughters for his. He figures, my son already defiled one of your daughters. He likes her. Let's just finish the drill. With some deception, Jacob's sons agree to the plan, but only after convincing Shechem's people to become circumcised like they are. The Hivites agree and circumcise every male in the kingdom. But while they are recovering, Jacob's sons sneak into the kingdom and kill them all. They put a sword through the father, then Shechem, then every living male. They rescue their sister and take everything of value back to their camp. The flocks, the herds, the donkeys, the wealth. All of it."

"That's an ugly story, Rachel. But what's it got to do with you?"

"I don't like men who trade women like chattel. I don't like entitled predators who think raping women and just taking what they want is ok."

"That was 4,000 years ago."

"I'm not talking about the pricks in Genesis, Jake. I'm talking about the ones doing the same thing right now. The ones trafficking 12-year-old girls. The ones taking sexual tourism vacations to Thailand, and Vietnam, and Europe. I'm talking about the same assholes you've spent your life chasing. I was Dinah, Jake. I had some narcissistic fuck steal from me what wasn't his to take. And when it happened to me, I swore I wouldn't be one of those women who just sit there and take it. My trust, my confidence, my life gets destroyed and the motherfucker who raped me gets to walk free because we had a "miscommunication about consent?" Fuck that and fuck him! Real toxic masculinity has no place in this world, and I decided to do something about it."

"So, it's just you?"

"No. There are six of us," Rachel says proudly. "For now. Think of us as an underground personal demolitions team."

"What? You're some vigilante?" I ask cynically.

"That's not inaccurate. Trafficking aside, do you know what the numbers are on rape convictions in this country?"

"I know they're not good."

"They're fucking anemic Jake. For every 1,000 rapes reported, seven rapists are convicted and six go to jail. Six, out of a thousand! And don't get me wrong. I'm not saying every man accused is guilty. But what I am saying, is out of the 994 who don't go to prison, there are a lot of predators out there walking around living their lives who aren't being held accountable."

"And that's what you're doing? Holding rapists accountable."

"In our own way, yes. But it's not just rapists. There's a bigger picture here."

"You want to explain that to me?"

"No, because you won't understand it. Let's just say to do what we do requires getting close enough to the fire that going up in flames is a very real risk."

I contemplate what Rachel is saying to me, but it's like hearing calculus or philosophy for the first time. It's just way too complex to instantly understand. She's intentionally embedding herself with sexual predators so she can take them out? I'm not sure what that really looks like, how long that would take to pull off, or what kind of resources it would take. Plus, if I really understand what she's saying, it's illegal. And if she's going after some bigger picture, she's not trying to take out one guy. She's trying to take down a network. That's the same thing we're trying to do at Homeland, but if I believe what she's saying, she's more on the inside than we are. She must see the confusion on my face because she takes a deep breath and continues with more than I think she intended.

"What do you want to know Jake?"

"How did you know where the sommelier… where Baptiste would be tonight? I'm assuming they are one in the same, yes?"

"They are," she answers. "I knew where Baptiste would be because I work for him. I wasn't sure where he'd be when I met you a month ago, but now I know."

"You work for Jean-Michel Baptiste the restaurateur?"

"I work for Jean-Michel Baptiste the human trafficker. I have for seven years."

"You what?"

"I have nothing to do with Baptiste's trafficking, but I'm close enough to him and what he's doing to get intel I can pass along to those who can do something about it.'"

"What, are you his girlfriend?"

"I'm an escort Jake. Baptiste sends me out to his high-end clientele at $3,500, $4,500, $5,000 a night and in exchange I get close to the men with the kind of money and power that buys little girls. I know you can't possibly understand that but trust me there's a greater good."

"There's no greater good worth that price."

"No? You know the girls you saved in Houston? The anonymous intel that led your team to the shipping container?"

"That was you?" I whisper, shaken.

"Yes, Jake. That was me."

"Jesus, Rachel, the position you're putting yourself in to get information? You're completely sacrificing yourself."

"When you were in Afghanistan, how many men never came home?"

"That's different," I interrupt her. "That was war."

"And this isn't? It's no different Jake. Look at history. Jesus? D-Day? The only thing that has ever beaten back evil was sacrifice. I was dead inside a long time ago. At least I can use my pain to help save someone else."

"You didn't seem dead in there," I argue pointing toward the bedroom.

"Men expect a lot when they're paying $3,500 for something that personal, Jake. I'm very good at what I do."

Whatever warmth I felt from Rachel before is gone. The frigid, pointed tone of her comments is painful and a sober reminder I can't always read people like I think I can. Even hyper-alert, I have my blind spots and this woman knew exactly how to slide into a space I couldn't see. My heart aches for whatever happened to Rachel and the path she's chosen since, but I'll have to reconcile that later. Right now, she has information I need, and I have no idea whether she intends to give it to me. I move from the hearth in front of the fireplace to the sofa and sit down next to Rachel. She doesn't flinch or try to move away.

"What can you tell me about Baptiste?" I ask, squaring myself and looking into her eyes. This is the closest I've been to her since the morning she left.

"There's a lot I don't know, but I can tell you with certainty he's trafficking girls all over the country. Some he grooms domestically. Most he brings in from other countries. Thailand. Russia. Mexico. The Congo. He's got a pipeline to a dozen countries and processes in place to get them through Customs."

"If it's that widespread, how is he not on our RADAR?"

"He's really good at what he does Jake and he's insulated himself with layers and layers of lieutenants who protect him and give him plausible deniability on anything serious. He pays them well and gives them access. But trust me, Baptiste is the one running the show."

"So where is he? You asked me to meet you on Sunset tonight to tell me, but then you disappeared. Where is he, Rachel?"

"Did you see the guy in front of me when you grabbed my arms at the bar?"

"The tall guy you were following back at the club. That was Baptiste?"

"Yes."

"The guy you've worked with for seven years?"

"Yes."

"So why were you about to stab him with two giant needles?"

"Because it's time for that motherfucker to die. That's why. Another 20 steps and this would have been over."

"You can't kill a man in the middle of a crowded club, Rachel. People tend to notice that shit. Tell me everything you know, and I swear to you, we'll take him down."

"I don't want him in jail, Jake," she says with an urgent desperation in her voice. "I want him dead. There are things he knows. Things I've had to do, and things the other girls have had to do that would all come out at trial. Good prosecutors would put us in prison. Those things can never see the light of day, Jake. It's one thing to do what we do in the shadows. It's quite another to be forced to share that information with the world and spend the rest of our lives in a cell for the privilege."

"What if we could keep you out of it?"

"You know that would never happen," Rachel answers with profound resignation. "I'm witness number one, and you know it so stop blowing smoke up my ass. The only way we can disappear is for Baptiste to die. I know you want this guy and I'm sorry I lied to you. I needed to know what you and the Feds had on Baptiste so I knew what kind of time I had. Once I knew you were on the trail, I decided I had to end things quickly. Tonight, would have been perfect. You could have landed a jet in there and nobody would have heard a thing. But you fucked that up royally and now, I'm not sure when I'll get another shot like that."

I've seen plenty of angry women and Rachel is livid. She's trying not to cry but her eyes have welled up and I can see they're about to spill over. That will only make her madder. I know she's pissed but I've got to find a way to bring her back. I reach out to touch her arm and she jumps up and pushes past me. She grabs her purse and pulls out something to dab her eyes. She won't look at me. But she starts to talk.

"I know you don't trust me, but if you ever hope to see your sister again, you have to let me handle this."

It takes me a minute to register what Rachel says, but when I do, it feels like someone punching me in the gut. I can't feel any air in my lungs and when I try to speak, my words are choked.

"My sister? What does my sister have to do with this? Wait… do you know where Catherine is?" I rise and close the gap between us reaching for Rachel's arm to spin her toward me. "Damnit Rachel, where is Catherine? WHERE IS MY SISTER?"

I'm a step away when Rachel spins and throws her arms around me. She holds me so tight I can feel the warmth of her body. Her right arm curls around my back hugging me close while she cradles the back of my head with her left, pulling my face against her cheek. I can feel the wet tears still running down her face.

"I know where she is Jake. I've seen Catherine with my own eyes and she's alive."

With both arms I pull Rachel into me as uncontrollable sobs explode out of my chest. For a decade I wasn't sure I'd ever hear that sentence. Catherine is alive. And the woman holding me can take me to her. I try to breathe but the sobs keep coming. I feel Rachel's face turn and her lips kiss the side of my neck behind my ear. Her lips linger, filling me with the warmth of a hope I had long abandoned.

"I promise I'll tell you everything," she whispers kissing me again. "But right now, I'm too close."

I wish I could say I processed the betrayal a little quicker. I wish I could say I hadn't let my guard down in her embrace. I wish I could say I felt Rachel move her hand from my back to her purse and back again. But I didn't. By the time I registered any kind of threat whatsoever, Rachel had already put the TASER to my neck.

"I'm sorry, Jake," was the last thing I heard. And the world went black.

24

It's disconcerting to wake up in the dark and not know where you are. Especially when your head is throbbing. My body is twisted in a heap between two hard pieces of furniture and from the scant moonlight peeking in, I can see a ceiling fan spinning above me. I try to raise up, but my head feels like a stone weight. I'm also suddenly aware of a burning pain below my right ear and an ache on the side of my head that seems to expand and contract with every breath I take. My vision is blurry. But with every blink, the room comes a little more into focus. Slowly, my thoughts grow more lucid, and I remember how I got here.

Rachel was here. We were talking and then she grabbed me and said something about Catherine. She said Catherine was alive. She said… oh my God. Rachel knows where my sister is. She kissed me. But then she said, "I'm sorry" and shocked me. I must have hit my head falling to the floor. The shock from a TASER wouldn't have lasted more than 30 seconds and it shouldn't have knocked me out. I check my watch and it's 4:37am. I've been out for a while.

I grab the edge of the coffee table and pull myself up. For an instant, I feel an emotional swell from the realization Catherine is alive. But then I realize the one person who can tell me where she is, has disappeared. The one person who can identify Baptiste and tell me where to find him is now God knows where and not coming back.

My head feels swimmy and immediately I feel nauseous. I don't know if it's a concussion or being so close to breaking this case and having it yanked away that's making me sick, but either way, all I want to do is throw up and sleep. Fucking Rachel. I don't have time for this shit.

I stumble to my bedroom, set an alarm for 7:30 and lay back onto my pillow. I probably shouldn't sleep, but I don't think I'm gonna die from a three hour nap. I'm hoping most of this headache will be gone when I wake up. It's not. But at least when the alarm rings, my symptoms are better than they were. The nausea is gone, and a warm shower relieves most of the ache in my head. A jolt of black coffee brings me back to the living.

Over breakfast, I replay the events that led to me unconscious on the floor. Late last night, we were at some underground sex club on Sunset. Hummingbird. Highly exclusive. Security was tight. Women and girls were being auctioned on giant video screens. There were exhibitionists having sex in every corner of the club and there was some sordid peep show going on that was particularly disturbing. Then I saw Rachel. She was grabbing the long wooden needles holding her hair up. I stopped her from stabbing some guy she was following. Some… the man she was following was Baptiste. I try to picture the moment, but there are no details. It was dark and I was so focused on Rachel, I didn't register anything about the man in front of her. Except that he was tall. Probably five or six inches taller than Rachel which would put him at 6'3" or 6'4". Other than that, he was dressed in black and wearing a hat which offers no help.

Rachel said she worked for him. That she… it's all coming back to me. She's an escort… who slept here two weeks ago. Jesus, I hope she's been tested. And she's seen my sister. If she's seen Catherine, there's a better than even chance my sister is being trafficked as well.

It's a certainty I've long assumed, and while there's no proof that's what's happening, in my soul, I know it's a confirmation of my worst fears. What did Rachel say? She's seen Catherine and she's alive. Not well. Not thriving. Not safe. She's alive. For some, there are worse things than being dead.

For three days, I spiral between anger, disappointment, and grief. I drive back to the parking garage on Sunset and try the phone, but it's dead. I call Rachel's cell repeatedly. I cruise up and down the streets desperately looking for her. Once again, I'm in the dark. Whatever elation I felt from Rachel's revelation about Catherine is gone and now all I feel is rage. At Rachel. At my father for giving my sister away. At myself for not finding Catherine sooner. I call Jon and ask him to run the Daughters of Jacob through the system, but I know before I hang up it's not going to be there. I go out on the Dark Web to look but there's nothing there either. Rachel's DOJ runs silent and deep. I only know what I know because she told me. She's in control. And I hate it.

By late afternoon, I'm restless and growing increasingly more irate at my lack of progress. I haven't eaten since breakfast, but I'm not hungry. I'm just anxious and pissed. I throw on a jacket and walk to Paddy's for a drink. Four hours and more than half of a fifth of whiskey later, I find myself stumbling back in the opposite direction, repeating the same thought I've had for days – find Rachel, and you find Catherine. It's really that simple, but I don't even know where to look. Rachel found me. Not the other way around. I have her cell number but she's not answering. I don't have an address. I don't know any acquaintances. Who am I kidding? I'm not gonna find either one of them.

I walk to the kitchen and grab a rocks glass and a bottle of Scotch from the cabinet over the refrigerator. I pour three fingers into the glass and take that and the bottle back to the sofa. I lift the glass and kill half the whiskey in one slug as the imposter voice in my head continues the evening's refrain. Not good enough. Not smart enough. You're fucking worthless, Jake. Give up already. Your sister made it this long without you and you won't find her anyway. Let it go. Hell, for all you know, she's dead.

I down the other two ounces in my glass and add three more. I sit back, falling hard against the back of the sofa. My head is heavy but through the soup, I can still hear the muffled echoes of my inner voice whispering. Give up Jake. You're not going to find her. Some fat, sweaty fuck has her bent over right now and there's not a damn thing you can do about it. You failed. You failed. You failed. You failed. You failed.

I get up and walk back to my bedroom. I raise the lid of the wooden box on top of my dresser and slide my fingers around the 9mm inside. I lift it out, pop a full clip in the bottom, and carry it back to the den. I place the pistol on the table in front of me next to the whiskey bottle. This scene certainly feels familiar. It's not a shotgun, but the nut doesn't fall far from the Goddamn tree.

I drink what's left in my glass and grab the butt of my pistol. I've always liked the weight of this gun. The balance and how it feels in my hand. Instinctively, I point my finger down the barrel. You never curl your finger around the trigger until you're ready to pull it. Killing this pain would be so easy. I've lived with this failure for so long. Eight years in Afghanistan, I never once thought of eating a bullet. But here we are. Listen to the voices. Catherine won't miss you. It's been 20 years. She's long forgotten you exist. Other than Jon, nobody would even come to your funeral. Decorated agent for Homeland Fucking Security. You're a dickless piece of shit who's completely failed the one person you've loved more than any other in your life. Punch your ticket Jake. It's over.

I sit back into the sofa and lay the pistol on my chest, my hand still around the grip. I close my eyes and imagine the Catherine I grew up with. The sweet laugh. The long brown hair. The piercing blue eyes that always brightened the second she saw me. How it felt to have her arms around me knowing I was the one person in the world she trusted to protect her. I can feel tears welling up in my eyes but there's no wiping them away. Let them come. I want to feel this pain. I need to feel it. I have failed to rescue my sister from whatever Hell she's been living in and there's no measure of the anguish I deserve for that. "I'm sorry, Catherine," I say lifting the pistol from my chest, gripping it tightly. "I'm so sorry." The barrel feels cool against my ear. But then I remember, when push comes to shove, fear is a coward.

Yes, I failed her. But tomorrow morning, Catherine will still be lost. And I am still the last, best hope to find her. As long as I have breath, I cannot give up. Not once in my life have I ever taken the easy path and fuck me if I'm about to start now. Dropping the pistol to my side, I stand up and walk it back to its home on my dresser. I pop the clip, eject the shell in the chamber, and lay the gun inside the wooden box and close the lid, tapping it in thanks for just enough lucidity. After damn near a whole bottle of whiskey, I'm going to have one Hell of a headache in the morning. But at least the back of my head will still be intact.

Looking into the bathroom mirror, I am shocked by my bloodshot eyes and the exhausted face staring back at me. Two empty sleeping pill bottles sit on the counter as a testament to how poorly I've been sleeping. I look in the medicine cabinet and find a third bottle, also empty. I thought the two on the counter were brand new but what do I know? I'll have to remember to get those refilled. For tonight, the whiskey will have to suffice.

I strip down and crawl into my sheets. I pray for my sister. I pray for those being trafficked. I pray for a night without horrific dreams.

Mercifully, sleep comes quickly.

25

When I wake up, it feels like two angry dogs are fighting each other inside my head. I have very little recognition of the night before, but the near empty whiskey bottle in the den tells me all I really need to know. It's nothing water, Advil, and time can't fix, but for now, it hurts. A shower and some breakfast wouldn't be the worst thing.

I start the coffee and walk into the den to clear off the coffee table. Rachel is gone. The sommelier is still a ghost. I can't change either of those things. All I can do is go back to where I was before I got Rachel's call a week ago.

I grab my travel bag and pull out the physical evidence I've collected. The menus from the restaurants. The receipt from Dallas. They're not much. But they are what I have. I've looked over these menus half a dozen times and see no real distinction. They are what they are. Super high-end cuisine. Exclusive, expensive wine lists.

Side by side, I lay the menus from Vegas, Washington, and Atlanta across the table. There are a few of the same dishes listed on each of the menus and there's certainly a lot of overlap on the wines as expensive as they are. It makes complete sense for a restaurant group. But wait. Something is missing. The Dallas menu.

I unzip the side pocket of my bag and pull out the menu Harper shoved into my hands with the receipt. I lay it next to the menu from Calliope and nothing jumps. I stand up to take in all four menus together and once again, they're just menus. I pick them up one by one, examining the edges. Holding them at an angle to see if there is something in the paper. I grab some water from the kitchen and sprinkle drops across the open spaces of the menus. Maybe there is some special watermark with information you can only see when it's wet. There's not. I grab a black light and run it up and down the menus. Nothing.

I lay the receipt from Marvelous to the side of the menus. There is nothing special about the paper it's printed on either. Like the menus that are just menus, it's just a receipt. With one exception. On the back, written in a woman's handwriting, is the word Hummingbird. It was the password that got me into the club in Hollywood. Is it possible that it has more significance than that? When in doubt, start at the beginning.

I grab my laptop and type "Violetear" into the search bar. Based on my search history, the first thing that comes up is a listing for the restaurant in Las Vegas. Pictures. The Menu. A link to make a reservation. I start to click the images of the restaurant to see what I missed before, but I stop as my eye catches the second listing for Violetear just below the restaurant. My breath catches as I feel one strand of this Gordian Knot start to pull free.

"Violetear – Wikipedia – The violetears are hummingbirds of the genus Colibri. They are medium to large species found in Mexico, and Central and South America. The Mexican violetear occasionally wanders as far north as the United States and even Canada."

I click the link and an image of a beautiful blue, green, and gray hummingbird fills the screen. I can't help but smile. They're the same exact colors as the décor of the Las Vegas restaurant that shares the name. With every assurance I'm right, I type "Anna's Hummingbird" into Google and hit return. A stunning yellow and green hummingbird with a shock of pink around its head fills the screen. Son of a bitch.

I search "species of hummingbirds" and with the click of a button, they are all there on a single screen. Violetear. Anna's. Calliope. Costa's. Marvelous. Every restaurant in the group is named for a species of hummingbird. A naming scheme's not completely out of the ordinary in and of itself. But the fact that the word hummingbird also picked the lock at the sex club tells me there's more to it. There could easily have been pictures of hummingbirds on the menus or in the restaurants but there aren't. I only know it because Harper whispered it in my ear back in Dallas. This connection isn't common knowledge. Baptiste has been a step ahead of me for weeks. Maybe hummingbird is what finally allows me to catch up.

I grab my wallet and pull out the business card I got from the waiter in DC. I completely missed it before but there's a tiny image of a hummingbird on the top of the card above "JM Restaurant Group – For the discerning palate. Restaurants in Atlanta, Dallas, Las Vegas, Miami, Washington – coming soon to L.A. and Houston." That's it. Coming soon to L.A. If I can figure out what the restaurant here is called, I might have a prayer of finding this guy.

I scan the names of the other hummingbird species searching for one that would best fit a high-end restaurant in Los Angeles. Berylline? No. Black-chinned? No. Blue-throated, Broad-billed, Broad-tailed? No, no, no. Buff-bellied? No. Green-breasted Mango sounds like a dancer in Miami. And then there it is. A small, brown, and white bird with a long black beak, a gray-brown speckled head, and an iridescent lavender throat – the Lucifer hummingbird.

A quick Google search for "Lucifer" returns multiple listings for the popular Netflix show, a few links related to all things satanic and at the bottom of the first page, a link to "one of L.A.'s newest and hottest restaurants and wine bars." Looking at the address, I can't help but laugh at the irony. Lucifer is 15 minutes from my house.

26

On Friday night, I wind my way into Beverly Hills and find Lucifer north of Sunset, tucked into a hillside just past Rodeo Drive. From the approach, the exterior is a surprisingly subtle mix of brown, white, and black, but getting closer, the lavender front door shimmers into view. After my experience at the club, I'm struck wondering if there's much more to this restaurant than is visible to the eye. I was never privy to one of the invitation-only gatherings at the other locations and I wonder if they too have rooms tucked away in some speakeasy hideaway safe from prying eyes, law enforcement, and accidental witnesses.

I park and by the time I get to the front door, I'm ready for the drill. I'm dressed in tan slacks, a light blue dress shirt open at the collar and a sapphire blue linen jacket with a subtle purple windowpane. A slight man with what seems like a German accent opens the door smiling and welcomes me to Lucifer. He's well put together and extremely articulate, much like the gatekeepers at the other restaurants.

"Good evening sir. My name is Claus. What is the name for your reservation please," he asks politely.

"Oh," I answer feigning surprise. "I don't have a reservation. Do I need one?"

"Yes, I'm afraid you do," he answers, now sounding a bit annoyed and condescending. "We are completely booked for this evening and every night for the foreseeable future." Moving behind the host stand, he picks up a leather binder and starts crisply flipping page after page after page as though my showing up without a reservation is somehow an insult to the sanctity of his position here. Finally landing on a page with an opening, he runs his finger left to right and taps on the right side of the book. "If you would like, I have an opening in April, and we'd be happy to serve you then."

"How about the wine bar?" I ask, looking him directly in the eye. "My understanding is the wine bar is spectacular, especially on Friday nights."

He smiles. "Yes, well, the wine bar is just for special tastings. It's extremely exclusive, very expensive, and like the restaurant, requires a prior reservation." Then, just to be prickly, he adds, "I'm not sure you would care for it. It caters to people with more… exotic tastes."

"You mean people with a *discerning palate*," I throw back, taking a large step forward closing the distance between us. The German stares at me, still skeptical, but with a new sense of recognition. This is the moment to take my shot. If I'm ever going to get in, it's now. I pull out my wallet and lay 10 hundred dollar bills on the desk in front of him. "I'm here for the hummingbird. Is that exotic enough?"

Never breaking eye contact, the host pockets the quick grand and asks for my identification. I hand him my ID and he moves to a space behind the bar where he raises the lid of a wooden box just like the one I saw at Alistair's in Las Vegas. He scans my license, looking back at me as it processes. A green light illuminates the inside of the box. I'm in. Claus makes his way back to where I'm standing and hands me my license. For the second time tonight he smiles and says, "Welcome to Lucifer," only this time, it feels like there is something more sinister in his delivery than in the initial greeting.

"You are in luck, Mr. Hardy. It seems we had a cancellation tonight and there is a seat available. Right this way sir." He leads me to the wine bar on the left side of the restaurant. By my count, there are 11 other men seated in the bar. Most are sitting alone, engaged in their phones. A few by the window seem locked in conversation, while the remaining smattering at the bar sit talking with the three bartenders holding court. I order a Pinot Noir and grab an open chair where I can survey the entire bar.

The men in the room look to be between 40 and 65. Most of them are dressed for cocktails in casual designer blazers with open collars and no ties. One man in his 60s wears a cardigan and a bow tie like some wayward college professor or crazy inventor. He is sitting alone, nervously bouncing one knee as though he's second guessing his decision to be here and considering a hasty retreat. The Scandinavian to my right has opted for a monochromatic look with black slacks and a cashmere half-zip that would look right at home in Vail. Two trust fund fucks in their 30s are holding up the bar, laughing about something I'm sure would gall my ass to no end. Everyone seems rich, extremely clean cut, with short hair, and no visible ink. Old school.

At 8:30 sharp, a stunning woman emerges from a door next to the bar wearing a tight electric blue dress that leaves nothing to the imagination. The confidence in her approach does nothing but accentuate that. Part of me wonders if she is the proverbial devil from the song. I have long been convinced that if I ever do meet the devil face to face, he'll look like the woman approaching me now. Then again, he may look exactly like Jean-Michel Baptiste, whatever he looks like.

"Gentlemen, if you'll follow me please," she says leading us back through the door she came from. There's not a man in this room who wouldn't follow her off a cliff if she asked. Once through the door, she takes us down a long passage that seems to decline as we walk. About 100 feet in, the hallway switches back and the downward slope increases as we move further underground. At the same interval, it switches back again and then levels out. The temperature has dropped a good 15 to 20 degrees since we left the restaurant and a sudden break in the wall tells me why.

On the left side of the passageway, we walk past a pair of massive iron gates that mark the entrance to the Lucifer wine cellar. From the gate, it appears the cave has been cut back at least 40 or 50 yards. The lighting is so subtle, it's hard to tell. There must be 10,000 cases of wine down here. I can only imagine what that must have cost, but I'm pretty sure I know how it was paid for.

Stealing one last glance at the wine enclosure, we continue to the end of the hall where we are met by two massive wooden doors, each at least eight feet tall and four feet wide. The flicker of large sconces housing orange and blue flames light the hand-carved doors, angled to illuminate the mirrored images of the Lucifer hummingbirds in mid-flight just above the door handles. I don't see our hostess punch the security code into the keypad by the door, but I hear the massive tumblers move in the locks as the doors slowly open inward. What greets us is the full manifestation of every mancave fantasy there's ever been.

The massive club is framed by dark, mahogany walls stretching in every direction lit by sconces matching the ones by the door every six to eight feet. The floors are a polished marble softened by a collection of fine oriental rugs. Inside the door about 20 feet to the right, we're met by a crisp bartender fronting a dozen shelves holding every kind of high-end liquor and wine you can imagine. Crystal wine and rocks glasses sit in front of him, each with an elegant "L" engraved on the front. There are tall, handcrafted barstools made of rich leather, cowhide, and oak lining the front of the bar, but no one would dare stop here. To our left, we're greeted by the scent of Spanish Cedar and the sweet, earthy aroma of fresh, unburnt tobacco. The doors to Lucifer's walk-in humidor have been opened for us to peruse what must be 2,500 of the world's finest cigars. Humans are not the only thing Baptiste is smuggling into the country.

Past the bar and the humidor, the club opens up into a huge sitting area fronted by a colossal stone fireplace. A ten-log blaze is roaring in the fireplace casting a warm glow on the oversized Art Deco, whiskey brown club chairs that sit in a semicircle in front of it. This isn't a room for chit chat, at least as presently configured. It's a place for someone to hold court with a fraternal brotherhood, no matter how warped its connective tissue.

One by one, we take our seats in one of the 12 chairs and as we do, the beauty in the blue dress brings each of us a full glass of a Cabernet so rich it almost hugs the inside of the glass.

"Gentlemen, welcome to Hummingbird. In your hands is a glass of a '98 Bordeaux. At $7,500 a bottle, may it be the least delicious thing you taste tonight. Enjoy." And with that, she was gone.

I swirl the wine in my glass and take a sip, letting it run across my tongue into the back of my throat. I am by no means an expert, but there is a body and flavor to this wine like nothing I've ever tasted. Beyond the status and wealth it confirms, I can understand why the filthy rich drink this wine like I drink a $50 Cab. It's not simply the arrogance I had always expected. This is truly exceptional.

I stare into the fire, thinking about how I got here. Thinking about Rachel and Catherine. I look around the room at the opulence, at the privilege, at the secure passage we took to get here, and I know I am no longer just close, but sitting in the devil's lair. Baptiste is here. I can feel him. There is a heaviness to the air. A thickness to the anticipation we are all feeling for what comes next. I take another swallow of wine and register my heart beating in my chest and a faint pulse in my fingers. I shift in my chair and take a deep breath, suddenly aware of an anxiety spreading through my body. I sense him before I see him. But when I hear the deep, resonant bass of the voice behind me, the hairs on the back of my neck stand straight up and my blood runs cold.

"You don't know it yet," the voice booms, "but this is the beginning of the greatest night of your life."

It's been an eternity, but I would recognize that voice anywhere. I turn and watch the tall, muscular, well-tailored man circle around the edge of the chairs and pass in front of me, appropriately backlit by a wall of flames. I didn't know it until this moment, but I already know Jean-Michel Baptiste, the sommelier and human trafficker. I've known him all along. He's older, but the image seared in my consciousness leaves absolutely no doubt. The man standing in front of me is the same white-haired motherfucker who took my sister 20 years ago. I know it like I know with complete certainty that I will kill him, and not quickly.

Just not before I find Catherine and save whatever is left of her.

27

It's all I can do not to erupt and end this right here. But then I'd never find my sister and that cannot be the way this story ends. It will take everything in me to play this out, but it's the only way I can bring Catherine home. Whoever said "beware, the devil is charming" had clearly made his acquaintance. Like any great carnival barker, Baptiste understands how to own the room and make each person feel as though they are the only one he's talking to. As he moves his gaze around the circle, I try to lock eyes with him when he makes eye contact with me. But he just keeps moving. The one advantage I have is that while I know who he is, to him, I'm just another mark. The last time he met me, I was a 12-year-old boy he was throwing against a wall. I cannot wait to fully introduce Jean-Michel Baptiste to Jake Hardy the adult.

"Let me say again gentlemen," he says opening his arms wide, gesturing to everything around us, "welcome to what promises to be one of the greatest nights of your life. But before we get to that, I have a question for you. Why are you here?" Baptiste asks.

"Because we have discerning tastes," the Swede smirks, completely missing that the question was rhetorical.

"That is certainly the case," Baptiste smiles. "But that is not why you are here. You are here because you hunger for something the world tells you you cannot have. And that, you find unacceptable. As you should. At the risk of being blunt – you are here to take what is yours. Gentlemen, you are the very definition of the alpha male.

You are smart. You are rich. You are successful. And you understand the world runs not with your blessing, but with your permission. You are the engine that drives this country. You are the builders. You are the conquerors! And you are entitled to enjoy the spoils that come with that victory. It's not just what you want. It's what you deserve. There will always be those who are threatened by you. By your success and your desires. Those who are angry that you have, while they do not. There will be those who try to criticize and tear you down and keep you from satisfying the pleasures you deserve because they are too afraid to embrace the truth. You are the kings of the jungle. You were destined to be an apex predator. You are who they wish they could be."

Sitting in the second chair from the right, I can see the rest of the men in the semi-circle. I do not know their backgrounds, their professions, their political leanings, or the status of their relationships, but they are consumed by the elitist, animalistic bullshit Baptiste is serving up. Half of the group is leaning forward, hanging on his every word. As Baptiste moves from side to side, I can literally see them puffing up, swollen with entitlement as the pitch and volume of his voice rises and falls. It's "Triumph of the Will" in a more intimate setting.

"Gentlemen, I am one of the world's leading Master Sommeliers. That means I have an exceptional palate capable of tasting and identifying the aromas, flavors, and notes in every varietal across the globe. I can and have tasted what an overwhelming majority of the world cannot because I have spent years studying how things feel in my mouth. How they lay across my tongue. How two flavors can be combined to create a unique sensation yet unexperienced. And now, gentlemen, I am sharing that expertise with you."

My gut burns every time Baptiste refers to these assholes as gentlemen. At best, they are criminals and at worst, the vilest of pedophiles. But I have to admit, he has them right where he wants them.

"You have each been chosen to experience what only a tiny fraction of the quarter percent will ever even dream about. Tastes so exotic, you simply will not find them anywhere else in the world. Jessica is giving each of you tonight's menu, and I encourage you to spend a few minutes deciding which indulgence you prefer. Some of tonight's offerings are silky smooth on the palate. Others aromatic, bursting with the flavor of juicy berries and a lingering sweetness. Some of you may prefer something simple, but well-balanced, while others will be drawn to something full-bodied with a robust finish. There is no right and wrong. Only personal preference. Choose yours and when you are ready, Elle will come by and accept your payments. Tonight's vintages range from $8,000 to $25,000. If you have any questions, I will be at the bar. This is your moment gentlemen. Enjoy it! "

Because I'm near the end, I'm one of the last to receive a menu and by the time I get mine, most of the other guys are already heading to the bar, peppering Baptiste with questions and from the forced smile on his face, inane conversation. I look down at the menu and am immediately dumbfounded by its contents. It's not the smoking gun I was anticipating. It's just a menu. A wine list with 15 bottles listed from vineyards across the globe. There's an Adrenaline Pinot from a vineyard in Sydney. A Chardonnay from a village in Chiang Mai. A full-bodied Cab from somewhere near Capetown.

I turn the menu over thinking the back must have additional details but there's nothing. It's blank. I look over at Baptiste surrounded by those not off picking cigars out of the humidor and then back to the menu. Am I so blind to this guy and who I believe he is that I've convinced myself he's the man who took my sister 20 years ago? With every fiber of my being, I know I'm not wrong. The voice. The hair. The jaw. It's him. But there is nothing on this menu that screams young girls, trafficking, or anything illegal.

While Baptiste is engaged at the bar, I get up and wander the perimeter of the club, looking for other rooms or some suggestion this is somehow like the club below Sunset. But it's not. There are no video screens. No aquarium windows. No carnal dancefloors or seating areas. It's just a small men's club with a world-class wine list. From across the room, I scan the back of the bar for doors or openings. I walk in and check the back of the humidor. There's nothing. This space is what it is and nothing more.

Exiting the cigar room, I pause, considering what I should do. I could join the rest of the group at the bar, but I don't have a good handle on what's going on. If I knew more, I could thread the needle even with the others sitting around and get more information. But I'm still flying blind. There's no guarantee I will find this guy again, but this is also not the venue to pepper him with questions. Not until I know more.

It kills me, but very quietly I tuck the menu inside my shirt and slip out the door. I know in my bones this guy is an evil fucking criminal and even if I don't yet understand how he's doing what he's doing, I know it's going on. I know there is something I'm missing. And when I figure out what it is, I'll come back. It won't just be another meeting I have with Baptiste. It will be reckoning.

28

Back at home, I hit the door more amped up than when I walked out of Lucifer. I'm too close to this and not in any way that's helpful. I need to breathe, and I need to change my perspective to figure out what it is I'm missing. It's there. I'm just not seeing it.

I change into my sweats and a T-shirt so old the P in "Semper Fi" has almost faded away. But it's comfortable and I'm gonna be up for a while. I pour three fingers of whiskey into a rocks glass and light the fireplace. I know I've looked at the menus a dozen times, but I pull them out again and set them out on the coffee table. They're the only physical evidence I have if you can even call them evidence at this point.

Again, I sit the wine lists side by side in the order I got them – Violetear, Anna's, Calliope, Marvelous, and now Lucifer. I start to pick up the menu from Las Vegas but switch to the last two menus from Dallas and L.A. that came from the private Friday night events. If there's something to find, it will most likely show itself in some difference between the last two menus and the first three.

I pick up the wine menu from Marvelous and scan the options from top to bottom. At the top of the menu just under the masthead, Baptiste has written a personal note to his guests.

"Welcome to Marvelous! It is our privilege to serve you. We are committed to providing an exceptional experience you will remember for the rest of your life. We have thousands of tantalizing options to choose from so there is always something new and delicious for you to try. For tonight, we have personally chosen these temptations to satisfy your palate. Enjoy!"

Under his note, there's a list of the wines to choose from. The arrogant prick has even listed numbers after each listing to scoreboard us again on how many different wines he offers. I read each listing carefully trying to let them sink in.

Cabernet Sauvignon

LA MAISON (816) Nairobi, Kenya, 2007 – Dark, full-bodied, robust $2,600/bottle

MALLARD ESTATES (227) Bend, Oregon, 2009 – Earthy, a bit lighter $3,400/bottle

BLUE SPRINGS (1635) – Provence, France, 2003 – Feisty, bold flavor $2,175/bottle

Pinot Noir

HOMESTEAD (73) Yadkin Valley, North Carolina, 2008 – Sweet and rich $2,300/bottle

BRIAR HILLS (1011) Sonoma, California, 2007 – Light on the tongue $1,950/bottle

FIELDSTONE (21) Krasnodar, Russia, 2011 – Bright, First vintage $9,500/bottle

Merlot

ELK'S RANCH (467) Fredericksburg, Texas, 2002 – Strong, nice bite $2,100/bottle

NINE HALLS (2390) Munich, Germany, 2007 – Velvety, full-bodied $2,950/bottle

SEAMUS (9) Dublin, Ireland, 2009 – Fruity, notes of lavender
          $4,100/bottle

Chardonnay

THE PASTORAL (833) Napa, California, 2004 – Complex, creamy $1,900/bottle

CROOKED TREE (127) Willamette Valley, Oregon, 2009 – Surprisingly elegant $3,500/bottle

CHATEAU AZUL (336) Barcelona, Spain, 2010 – First vintage, light vanilla $9,000/bottle

Pinot Grigio

SHADOW CREEK (1620) Alto Adige, Italy, 2006 – Sassy, exceptional finish $2,650/bottle

PEREGRIN TRAIL (18) San Antonio, Texas, 2005 – Fresh notes of apple $2,400/bottle

SMOKE (527) Adelaide, Australia, 2010 – Refreshing, clean, light $5,250/bottle

I trade the Marvelous menu for the one from Lucifer to see if there is something I recognize. All I find is more of the same including a similar note at the top.

"Welcome to Lucifer! It is our privilege to serve you. We specialize in exceptional experiences with memories that last a lifetime. Our Master Sommelier has spent a lifetime collecting special flavors and vintages you will not find anywhere else. Tonight, we have personally chosen these temptations to satisfy your palate. Enjoy! We look forward to serving you."

Again, under his note, there are 15 wine listings to choose from, each numbered from the collection. They are different from the wines listed in Dallas, but not that different.

Cabernet Sauvignon

MANSION HILLS (345) Cape Town, South Africa, 2003 – Full-bodied, tart $2,450/bottle

MI AMOR (694) Santiago, Chile, 2013 – Fresh, first vintage $8,900/bottle

PROVENÇALE (2) South of France, 2006 – Complex, dazzling flavor $5,750/bottle

Pinot Noir

BLACK PALMS (418) Jasper, Georgia, 2004 – Simple, light on the tongue $3,200/bottle

ADRENALINE (908) Sydney, Australia, 2005 – Full flavor, heavy accents $4,150/bottle

HUSKY RUN (1334) Snake River Valley, Oregon, 2008 –
Dark, cherry notes $5,375/bottle

Merlot

ANDALUCIA (14) Barcelona, Spain, 2002 – Spicy, aggressive
bite $3,600/ bottle

OCEANVIEW (2116) Charleston, South Carolina, 2009 –
Sweet, quiet finish $7,200/bottle

TYRIAN (345) Canberra, Australia, 2007 – Medium-bodied,
velvety $5,850/bottle

Chardonnay

MARSEILLES (1787) Burgundy, France, 2006 – Rich, notes
of pear $3,100/bottle

HIGH CANYON (1734) Chiang Mai, Thailand, 2001 –
Smooth, sensual notes $2,900/bottle

PAINTED SUNSET (1601) Tucson, Arizona, 2008 – Creamy
and nutty $4,350/bottle

Pino Grigio

ROOFTOP (706) Kinshasa, Congo, 2010 – First Vintage,
smooth $8,750/bottle

GARDEN PARK (102) Watertown, New York, 2003 – Sweet,
light $3,150/bottle

SWEET VINE (1441) Napa, California, 2004 – Dazzling, fantastic finish $4,000/bottle

Since I left early tonight, I have no idea how this circle jerk actually works practically. I guess everyone chooses the bottle they want and then all sit around getting crocked talking about how great it is to be rich. By the end, you know some of these assholes are going for seconds or thirds.

I pick up the menus from Anna's and Calliope and look back and forth between them and the menus from Marvelous and Lucifer. I'm not shocked they're a bit different. The first two are regular menus from the bars while the second two are from exclusive events. But other than the exorbitant prices on the event menus, nothing seems out of the ordinary to me. I don't recognize any of the wineries on the last two, but at these price points I wouldn't. These are not the circles I run in.

At Anna's and Calliope, the wine listings are all high-end and expensive, but not out of line with any other fine restaurant. There's a balanced mix of wine types with domestic wines just beating out the number of international brands. And the vintages are all 2019 to 2022 in keeping with their moderately high prices.

I count the choices on the menus from Marvelous and Lucifer and see the international wines slightly outnumber the domestics. The vintages are also older and more expensive. No surprise there. Their ages naturally make them more exclusive which raises the prices. I look at the antes again trying not to choke on the thought of spending $3,500 on a bottle of wine, or for that matter, anything I would only enjoy for a few hours.

Oh my God.

What did Rachel say to me in our last conversation, sitting right here? "Men expect a lot when they're paying $3,500 for something personal Jake." I grab the menus and scan the prices on the Marvelous menu and then the ones from Lucifer. Son of a bitch. It's been right in front of me the entire time, but I didn't see it. Rachel was right. Men expect a lot when they're paying $3,500 for something. But they expect a hell of a lot more when they're spending $9,000. For a bottle of fine wine, that means the older the better. For the vilest of predators, it's the opposite.

I suddenly remember the video screens with the auctions at the Hummingbird sex club on Sunset. The bids were the highest for the women who were the youngest. It's the same on the menus from Marvelous and Lucifer. On the regular wine lists from Vegas, DC, and Atlanta, the pricing is perfectly in line with the age of the vintage. The older the vintage, the more expensive the price. But on the last two invitation-only menus, the younger the wine, the more expensive the price. And $8,000, $8,900, $9,500 for a first vintage? Wine gets better with age, not worse. Baptiste isn't selling bottles. He's selling bodies.

My stomach flips with that realization, knowing I'm right. I can feel the bile rising in my throat when I look again at the listings. These menus aren't describing wines. They're teasing the girls Baptiste is selling. Where they're from. What they look like. And especially their ages. All you have to do is subtract the year, 2024, from the vintage.

Nairobi, Kenya, 2007 – Dark, full-bodied, robust

Provence, France, 2003 – Feisty, bold flavor

Sonoma, California 2007 – Medium, light on the tongue

Alto Adige, Italy, 2006 – Sassy, exceptional finish

Snake River Valley, Oregon, 2008 – Dark, cherry notes

Charleston, South Carolina, 2009 – Sweet, quiet finish

Kinshasa, Congo, 2010 – First Vintage, smooth

The girl from Congo is 14. Jesus, help her.

I read through the descriptions on the Lucifer menu and the pricing follows. I had done the math in my head when it was wine, but if he's selling girls at these prices, Baptiste is easily clearing $50,000 a week at each location. That's $1.2 million a month on the backs of girls as young as 10. But where? That's a lot of movement. A lot of coordination and there were no back rooms at Lucifer. The invite-only events must be just for the transactions. Smart. If cops or the FBI blow in, all he's done is gouge some poor suckers on overpriced wine. He claims caveat emptor and buys the next round. He has to be connecting the girls and the Johns off site somewhere.

I look back at the Marvelous menu to see if there's something else I missed but I don't notice anything. I switch to the Lucifer menu from the L.A. restaurant and looking at the wineries, two of the names jump out to me immediately only I don't know them as wineries. I know them as hotels. High Canyon is a resort hotel up in the Hollywood Hills and Oceanview is a chichi boutique hotel in Santa Monica right down the street from me. Quick searches for a High Canyon Winery in Thailand and an Oceanview Winery in Charleston as they are listed on the menu confirm they don't exist. Same goes for Mallard Estates in Oregon, Chateau Azul in Barcelona, and Smoke in Adelaide. Google has never heard of them.

Laying the Lucifer menu on the table next to my computer, I start typing in the names of the wineries listed with "hotel in Los Angeles" added after each one. Each query turns up a luxury high-rise, resort, or bungalow in the greater Los Angeles area.

"I got you motherfucker!" I howl jumping up and punching the air in front of me.

I look down at my computer screen and watch the slideshow for the Highland Canyon Resort and Spa cycle through images of their penthouse suites, massage service, rooftop pool, and breakfast in bed. I throw back the two fingers of whiskey in my glass and hold it in my mouth, savoring the flavor before the smooth heat slides down my throat. I'm so close.

I check my watch. 3:12am. Too late to confront Baptiste tonight but tomorrow, I'll go back and see if he's still at Lucifer. Worst case, I'll confront him a week from now, but it won't take that long. Evil's not that patient and neither am I.

I consider going to bed, but I'm so juiced there's no way I'll get to sleep. I put on my shoes and run down Idaho toward the beach. The Pacific has a dark serenity when the rest of the world is sleeping, but tonight there is a slight reprieve. There's a full moon shining through the sea air and across the breaking waves casting a muted glow on the beach. Even with a slight breeze, the air feels heavy, like it does in my dream. It's harder to breathe, but the weight will burn off by the time the sun rises. When it does, I will be one step closer to Catherine. One day closer to ending this nightmare for both of us. The only thing standing in my way is the man who set it all in motion. I know who he is now and in due time, I will introduce myself properly. For now, it's enough to just feel a glimmer of hope. I've run in the shadows long enough. I turn toward the moon and for the first time in a decade, I start running toward the light.

29

Around 7pm the next night, I pull up to Lucifer and make my way to the door feeling far more confident than I felt passing over this threshold 24 hours ago. That and another $300 to the maître d' gets me a seat in the bar. He probably would have taken two, but I don't feel like dicking around. I know there's no private party tonight, but I'm hoping Baptiste may still make an appearance.

I grab a two-top in the corner of the bar where I can see everyone coming and going. It's surreal thinking about last night and what was going on in the space two floors beneath where I'm sitting now. I can only imagine that's where Baptiste spends his time when he's actually here. I could try to make my way back down there, but that's not the play. At least not right now.

I pick up the menu sitting on the table and flip it to the side with the wine options. It's designed just like the other bar menus from Anna's, Calliope, and Violetear. Super pricey, but recognizable brands with pricing that matches the ages of the vintages. It's the complete antithesis of the menu I was given downstairs.

Looking up, I see the devil in the blue dress from last night making her way to my table, only tonight she's wearing a red, strapless mini and her hair is pulled up. I can see her perfect smile and warm eyes shining from across the room. I wonder if she recognizes me.

"Mr. Hardy, welcome back to Lucifer," she says, answering my question with a quiet, smoldering voice. "We missed you late last night. We were concerned perhaps you hadn't enjoyed your stay with us. I'm certainly happy to see you've come back."

"I, uh… it's a little embarrassing," I dance. "Last night, when we got downstairs, I had this panicked realization I had forgotten to put my credit card back in my wallet. I didn't have enough cash to cover what I was considering, and I didn't want it to be some big thing, so I just slipped out. I hope I didn't offend anyone."

"Not at all," she says, leaning forward and laying her hand on mine. "I'm excited to see you again." Her hand is warm, and her breath is sweet. The devil indeed. "What can I bring you?"

"How about a glass of the Winchester Cab?" I smile.

"Mmm, one of my favorites. I'll be right back."

Smiling, she pulls her palm across the top of my hand letting her fingernails gently rake across my skin and walks away from me without any sense of urgency whatsoever. A warm current moves through me. It's shocking that men ever became apex predators. We're so fucking basic.

A few minutes later, the siren in the red dress returns with my wine and a mixed bowl of warm pistachios, macadamias, and cashews. She waits with raised eyebrows and an expectant smile to make sure I'm pleased with the wine. It's delicious and I tell her so.

"Is someone joining you?" she asks, looking at me as though she hopes the answer is no.

"No," I answer with a slight turn of my head. "Just me tonight."

"Would you like some company?" she asks seemingly filled with optimism. Her question surprises me as I assume she's working the bar and has other customers to care for. How I would have loved getting this question from this woman sitting at Paddy's. At very least, a conversation with her might get me one step closer to Baptiste.

"Of course," I smile, standing and pulling out the chair beside me. "I'm always up for great company."

"Wonderful," she says, and then turns and walks away. Before I can sit, Baptiste emerges from the back of the house, striding my way, pulling the cuffs down from inside his jacket. This is not what I expected but I'm also sure that was fully orchestrated. I've spent the better part of two decades planning what I would say to this prick when I met him again face to face but now that the moment is here, I have no idea what to say. Fortunately, he speaks to me first.

"Mr. Hardy," Baptiste says warmly, extending his hand to me. "Welcome back." I put my hand in his and he grips it firmly. The last time I felt his hand it was tossing me across a room. "I'm so pleased to see you've returned to Lucifer." The seeming irony of what he's just said almost makes me smile.

"Thank you," I answer. "I hope no offense was taken by my leaving last night. A miscalculation on my part that has since been remedied."

"No apology necessary," Baptiste answers in his deep, resonant voice. "I understand things happen and on occasion, I am happy to make concessions to take care of our guests. Since you deprived me of the pleasure of getting to know you better last night, please, tell me about yourself, Jake."

"Not much to tell really. I live here in L.A. Work in finance. Served in Afghanistan."

"A soldier," Baptiste starts.

"A Marine," I correct him.

"Ah yes, a Marine. I remember you guys are very particular about that. Thank you for your service."

"You don't have to thank me. I got paid," I answer a bit more callously than I should. I take a large mouthful of wine, watching to see how Baptiste responds to my attitude. He doesn't.

"Working the markets. I find finance to be a fascinating profession. Long hours, I imagine. Lot of pressure."

"It has its moments," I answer. "It's like anything else. You work with some great people and then there are the raving assholes you'd just as soon shoot."

"Sounds exactly like my business," Baptiste laughs. "So, tell me Jake, being in the finance business, what brought you to Lucifer? How did you find us? I'm always interested in where our investments are working and where they're not. Sometimes, I feel like I'd be better off driving down the 405 and just throwing hundred dollar bills out the window with business cards stapled to them."

"That would certainly be a different approach," I answer. Baptiste smiles and signals to the woman in red to bring him a glass of wine. I'm trying to get a bead on how much Baptiste knows about me, but it's hard to tell. There's no way he recognizes the 12-year-old me and unless he's way more connected than I think, he won't find any information from before I changed my name. My persona is tight and won't return anything that would help him make any connection to Catherine or my father. What I don't know is whether Rachel has told him anything about me. At this point, I still don't know whose side she's really on. I'm willing to bet that nobody from Marvelous would have tipped him off about my questions in Dallas, but it's just that. A bet. Still, I'm willing to roll the dice a bit to see how exposed I am, if at all.

"So, how did I find you? It was a referral actually. I was just in Dallas on business and had a drink at Marvelous." I watch Baptiste's eyes for some twinkle of recognition, or some signal that dots are connecting in his brain, but I see neither. Just the pleasure that someone at one of his other restaurants thought to recommend this one.

"That's fantastic," he says raising his glass and clinking it against mine. "So, what did you think of Marvelous?"

"The location is fantastic," I answer, trying to park my disgust for Baptiste and warm to the conversation. "Right at the top of the hotel? I just had a few glasses of wine after a big pitch we had. I would love to have had dinner, but we couldn't get into the restaurant."

"Yes, we're very popular," he answers a bit smugly.

"Dallas was very nice, but frankly, I like this location better."

"I'm a bit partial to this one myself," he says leaning in as though there's someone nearby whose feelings he might hurt. "You know we have seven restaurants in the group now. We're open in Las Vegas, Atlanta, Miami, Washington, Dallas, and now here and in Houston. You'll have to visit us if you're ever in any of those other cities."

I'm not about to tell him I've been to all but the one in Houston. It's possible he's snowing me completely, but I don't think news of any of my former visits has preceded me. To Baptiste, I'm just another customer and that's exactly what I want him to think.

"I will definitely visit those when I'm in town," I say. "I don't suppose you have a special pass that would get me a table for dinner?"

Baptiste narrows his eyes and smiles at me. He reaches into the breast pocket of his jacket and pulls out a small, silver box. He opens it and pulls out an embossed, linen business card with his name on it. He puts it on the table in front of me and taps it with his index finger.

"You give this to any of my restaurants and they will get you in for dinner without any question."

"Thank you," I say, picking up the card and looking at it more closely. It's like the one I got from the kid in DC, but nicer. "I'll have to make plans to travel east."

"Or just come back to Lucifer," Baptiste answers, his expression becoming a bit more serious. "What it is you're looking for, Jake? What do you want? What do you… need? You work hard. You bust your ass for everyone else and for what? When was the last time you felt the love? The appreciation? When was the last time you felt some goddamn respect, Jake? Huh? What I said to you last night wasn't a performance. It's the truth. We are the titans. The creators. The music makers. Without men like you and me, the whole world stops spinning."

Baptiste raises the wine to his lips and finishes what's left in his glass. He leans into the table, and I lean in to meet him. "Men like us don't expect the world to give us anything Jake," he says with an intense hush. "All we ask is that when we take what's ours, everyone else just stays seated and shuts the fuck up." There is a cold fire in Baptiste's eyes that immediately shifts my perception of him. He's not just in this for the money. He honestly believes what he's saying.

He's smart enough to not outwardly condone trafficking and non-consent, but there's no doubt in my mind the pathological predator sitting across from me believes he deserves to enjoy all the world's pleasures, at his command.

"I ask you again, Jake. What are you looking for?"

Fine. You want to dance motherfucker? Let's dance.

"I want to enjoy something I've never tasted before," I say.

"Well, you're in luck because that's what we serve here. Tell me more about what you like. Do you have a preference for domestic or international'?"

"No. Either is fine."

"Would you prefer something full-bodied, or a bit lighter?"

"Full-bodied for sure, and maybe on the sweeter side, but nothing that will give me a headache in the morning."

"Of course. How about vintage? We have everything from a 30-year-old Spanish port to a crisp 2014 Pinot from Africa."

I consider ordering the Pinot to try and save the youngest little girl, but as tragic as it sounds, this is bigger than just her. If I can take down Baptiste, I could potentially save her and everyone else in his control. Including my sister.

"For the sake of this first taste, let's say a full-bodied International with a vintage from sometime in the early 2000s. The more aged the better. I don't care what year. Surprise me. If I like what you serve, I'll be back."

"Outstanding. I like your open, adventurous spirit Jake. I have a lovely 2003 High Canyon Pinot Noir from Thailand. Dark, full-bodied with great legs and a long finish."

"Sounds perfect," I answer, trying to stroke Baptiste's ego.

"I think you will particularly enjoy this," he says writing something on one of the cocktail napkins on the table. "And if not, come back and we will find something more to your liking." Baptiste rises and hands me the napkin, once again extending his hand to me. "Jake, I look forward to seeing you again and wish you an extremely pleasant evening. If you'll wait right here, Jessica will bring over your tab shortly."

I can feel my heart racing and the sweat rolling down my back. Baptiste has no idea who I am, and I am in. He whispers something in Jessica's ear and disappears into the back. Sitting down, I look down at the napkin and it says, "Jasmine, Highland Canyon, No. 1734, 8pm." Looks like I was right about the hotel connection. I do wonder about the others who don't know or haven't put the pieces together. I suppose that's what the approaching woman in the red dress is for.

"If you have any questions, I'll be more than happy to answer them," she says.

"I'm good," I say confident that I cracked the code correctly.

"Fantastic," she smiles. "If I can have your credit card I will be happy to take care of this for you." I look at the bill and it's $2,900. I hand her my credit card and she taps it against the small tablet she's holding. It beeps and just like that, I've committed a crime even though, theoretically, all I've purchased is a bottle of wine.

"It was wonderful to see you again Mr. Hardy," Jessica says handing me my card. "I do hope we'll have the privilege of serving you again soon."

I check my watch and see it's a few minutes after 7pm. With Saturday night traffic, it should take about 40 minutes to get from Lucifer to the Highland Canyon Resort and Spa. I swallow the last of the Winchester Cab in my glass and head toward my date in the Hollywood Hills.

I have no idea what I'll do or say to her when I actually get there.

30

Coming out of Santa Monica, there's a wreck on the 10 and red lights as far as I can see. I've only got a 20 minute buffer before I'm late and after last night, I don't want to look like a flake. Then again, Baptiste has my money already and if I burn half an hour of my time stuck in traffic, that's not his problem.

Now that the pieces are starting to come together, my thoughts turn to how we put this guy away. I have to admit, on paper, the scheme construction is smart. Johns buy an expensive bottle of wine in location A. They go to location B where they meet a woman, have a few drinks, and end up going to her room. No money is exchanged. Just a hookup. It's a scenario that happens in every bar in America every night. And with the exception of the girls who look 15, nobody would think anything of it. Baptiste is smart enough to not have his women dress in any way that would draw the wrong kind of attention. They're more likely to be dressed like Jessica than one of the girls in Big Alice's camp up on Sunset.

Even if I'm 100 percent right about what I know, it will take a forensic accountant months to unravel all the payments and the money trail. Seeing how measured and intentional Baptiste has been with every detail, there is zero chance everything's not heavily encrypted with every cent possible flowing to an offshore account. God knows how much he's made off these girls in 20 years.

About 10 till eight, I finally get to the exit at La Brea and turn north toward Hollywood. Even if I hit every light all the way up

Highland, I'll never make it on time. But I'll be close. The concert at the Hollywood Bowl started early so at least there's no traffic where Highland and Cahuenga come together by the front gate. I lower my window as I roll past the entrance and a cool breeze blows in carrying hints of whatever the LA Phil is playing tonight. Something classical.

I take Cahuenga up into the hills toward Mulholland and in the distance ahead of me, I notice a glow of alternating red and blue lights. This time of night on a Saturday, I'm putting my money on a DUI stop but it seems like a lot of lights for one drunk. The lights look to be straight in front of me a couple hundred yards ahead. But as the road curves to the right, my perspective shifts and I realize the lights are actually up on the hill to the left. They're flashing in front of the Highland Canyon Resort and Spa. Baptiste.

My immediate thought is the son of a bitch tried to set me up and that being late might be a blessing in disguise. Maybe he does know who I am. If Baptiste has cops in his pocket, he could easily have called in a favor to raid my room. But the closer I get, I realize that's paranoia talking. That's not what this is at all. Another police car with its red and blues flashing zips around me and up into the drive in front of the Highland Canyon. I pull in after it and park in one of the open spaces near the road.

Even before I get out of the car, I can hear the sounds of panic echoing across the parking lot. There are now three LAPD cars with lights flashing, and officers moving in every direction trying to get a handle on whatever has just happened. As I walk toward the hotel entrance past the massive fountain in the front turnaround, I see the reason for the anxiety. A woman's naked, broken body is spread over the hood and shattered windshield of a black SUV parked by the valet entrance. She is twisted in a way that could only have come from a jump. The officer nearest to her is screaming for a sheet or a blanket to cover her up. A younger cop rushes into the front door of the hotel, yelling for housekeeping.

By the nature of the activity, it's clear to me, this has just happened. It's a shocking scene, even for those who have seen it before. Most of the cops are turned away, most likely waiting for the coroner. Maybe that's why no one sees me or says anything to me when I move closer to the body. I learned early on if you just act like you belong and know what you're doing, people rarely stop you. Even if someone asks, just the reach for my wallet should suffice before they waive me off.

There's no way of telling whether this woman was aiming for the SUV when she jumped, but she hit it flush, her hips crashing through the front window and her shoulders and head cratering the center of the hood. There are clearly a number of bone fractures, but it's not the breaks that stop me. It's the excessive bruising and cuts on her torso and face. Someone beat the Hell out of this woman before she jumped. It must have been brutal for her to think jumping might seem like a better option. Or was she pushed? Is this just supposed to look like she jumped? If so, there's a predator in this hotel washing blood off his hands right now.

"You know this girl?" a grizzled EMT asks walking up behind me.

"No," I answer. "I just got here to check in and found the chaos. Pretty horrific."

"It's a damn shame. Heard the guy at the front desk say her name was Jasmine. I just hope the poor kid was loaded when she jumped so she didn't feel much," he says shaking his head.

"She felt enough," I say, almost to myself. "Look at her." And I do.

There are streaks of blood coming from long gashes down her legs and knees as though she crawled through broken glass. Her hips and buttocks are dark purple, covered with a mosaic of bruising. Her left flank is completely black and collapsed like someone smashed her ribcage with a crowbar. The fall certainly could have caused that. But by the way she's positioned on the car, I wouldn't bet on it. There are deep red scrapes across her breasts as though someone was trying to grab her or hold her in place, and there are blue bruises on both sides of her throat where she was clearly choked. But the most heartbreaking, and enraging thing about her, is what this animal did to her face. The bones in one of her eye sockets appear to be completely shattered. The other eye is almost completely swollen shut. Her lips and nose seem twice their size and on one of her cheeks, there is a tight grouping of bloody, uniform circles from what must have been the top of a ring. Even through the bruising and the swelling, I can tell this woman was beautiful. I cannot imagine what could have caused this kind of rage. I can only hope the police are scouring the resort top to bottom to find the guy who did this to her.

"Word is she jumped from the 24th floor," the EMT says lighting a cigarette and looking up. "They found blood on the balcony floor and on the ledge up there. There's also a guy in the suite missing the back of his head. Single shot from a nine mil. Rumor is he's a cop. Maybe the pressure finally got to him."

"Or maybe she couldn't take anymore," I answer, looking at the woman in front of me.

"Could be," he says. "If the son of a bitch did that? Good for her."

"Agreed," I answer. "Just a little late."

Behind us, the front doors to the hotel slide open and the young cop who ran in looking for housekeeping finally reemerges with a sheet to cover the body. As he rushes over to give this poor girl some final bit of dignity, I move to the other side of the SUV to get out of the way. When I do, I see the back of her neck for the first time. Her hair is swept over and trapped under her head leaving her neck bare and open to the night air. The young cop raises the sheet skyward with a crack, and as it's floating down over the body, I notice a swath of color just below the girl's hairline. It's a small, blue, and scarlet tattoo. Just like the one I saw on Rachel's neck in my bedroom.

It's a hummingbird with wings unfurled.

31

I'm not entirely sure why, but I stay until the coroner comes and takes the shattered young woman away sometime close to midnight. Only when he and his assistant try to pick her up do I realize the extent of her broken bones. They try to move her body respectfully, but no matter where they try to pick her up, her body shifts. They finally just wrap the sheet under her and carry her quickly to the waiting coroner's van.

Though there is chatter for hours from the cops, the EMTs, the staff, and even curious guests who have gathered around the yellow caution tape keeping them from getting too close, no one seems to know much about who she is. When the hotel owner comes out to see how long the flashing lights will be parked in his driveway, driving away guests, he dares a quick glance at the SUV and just shakes his head. He says she was always very nice. He clearly recognized her as a regular guest.

I don't know anything more about Jasmine, except she was the girl Baptiste had chosen for me from the menu at Lucifer. Her tattoo alone tells she was one of his. More than once during the time I've been standing here, I check my pocket for the name and room number Baptiste wrote on the napkin he gave me. "Jasmine. No.1734." Nowhere close to the 24th floor, but clearly, that's where her earlier date had been.

It strikes me that Baptiste may have no idea about what's happened here and considering Jasmine was one of his, it won't be good. The attention, the exposure, and the loss of revenue will no doubt infuriate him. I wonder if there is a way I can spin this to my advantage. Part of being good undercover is finding ways to get closer to your mark in ways that seem natural and unforced. Baptiste sent me to this hotel an hour ago. Calling and letting him know what's happened is the mark of an ally looking out for his best interest, not some random John. As much as it sickens me, getting closer to Baptiste could be my ticket to finding my sister.

Back in the quiet of my car, I pull Baptiste's business card out of my wallet and call the number under his name. Four times, the ring from his cell phone buzzes through the speakers in my car before tripping over to his voicemail. I hang up and call again. News like this is something that needs to be discussed, not left in a voice message. But that won't be the case tonight. After my third failed attempt to get Baptiste on the phone, I hang on when the phone rolls to voicemail. Knowing how careful he is with everything else, I'm mindful that the message I leave should be equally measured.

"Mr. Baptiste, this is Jake Hardy," I start. "We met earlier this evening. I'm calling with some urgent information I thought you might want to know. Upon reaching the destination you and I discussed previously, I came upon a tragic scene where a woman had jumped from the 24th floor. I believe she might be an acquaintance of yours and I thought you might like to know. I have remained on site and both the authorities and coroner have now departed. At some point, someone mentioned her name, but no one seemed to know any more than that. If you'd like to discuss this further, feel free to call me back at your convenience."

At this point, I see no reason to light Baptiste up with the rumor about a dead cop. If that's the truth and he's as connected as I think he is, the news will find him soon enough. For 10 or 15 minutes, I sit in the driveway waiting for the Master Sommelier to call me back, but my cell never rings. By now, someone will be sliding Jasmine's naked, broken body into a cold, steel vault at the morgue. It will stay there for a month. When no one claims her body, it will be cremated and kept at the county coroner's office for three years. If she's still unclaimed at that time, she'll be buried in a mass, unmarked grave. The final indignity for a woman whose entire life was likely measured by one abuse after another.

For the rest of the night and the entire next day, I wait for Baptiste's call, but it never comes. At first, the silence makes me anxious. Now it's just pissing me off. I can't stop thinking about the hummingbird tattoo on the back of Jasmine's neck, or the fact that Rachel had one exactly like it. And what is it with these birds? The names of the restaurants, all hummingbirds. The password at the sex club on Sunset – hummingbird. This afternoon, trying desperately to do something productive, I go back through my case files and pulling up the pictures from the Houston shipyard, I realize there's a goddamn hummingbird on the side of the shipping container carrying the girls we saved. I don't know what this guy's fascination is with hummingbirds, but the information is all connected.

I found Jasmine late Saturday night, and by Tuesday, my restlessness and impatience have finally gotten the best of me. It's not even noon, but I drive over to Lucifer hoping to find Baptiste and to see what I can find out. At the very least, I can feign my anger at paying a fortune for some night to remember and then driving up to a nightmare scenario and a hotel crawling with cops. Theoretically, as a customer scorned, the power dynamic should shift in my favor. But we're not talking about cold soup or a hair in my sandwich. I have no idea how Baptiste will respond to this. He could pull some "caveat emptor" shit and tell me to fuck off.

Pulling up to the restaurant, I'm not surprised to see the lot empty and the lights off with six hours left until dinner starts. But I wasn't expecting to find the sign taped inside the front window.

"Closed for Renovation!" the sign says in big, block type with a smaller message underneath. "To our dear patrons, three nights ago, Lucifer experienced a damaging kitchen fire that while small, has left us unable to prepare our menu to the high levels that we demand, and you expect. To make the necessary repairs to our kitchen, we will be closed for the near future with the hope of being open again for the holidays. Our profound apologies, and eternal thanks for your support of Lucifer. We look forward to serving you again soon."

Right. A fire, three nights ago. The same night one of Baptiste's girls presumably jumped or got thrown off a 24th floor balcony. Closing the restaurant is total cover but I'm not sure of what. Does Baptiste need to shut things down until whatever investigation into Jasmine's death is concluded? Has somebody at the L.A.P.D made the connection? Doubtful. Maybe he's just being super careful. Whatever it is, I was close and now I'm not. The irony. I've been grinding for months trying to burn this asshole to the ground, and it's a fake fire that takes me out.

32

This morning, I hit the wall. I haven't felt this way since my second tour in Afghanistan, but I recognize the feeling. It's an overwhelming sense of futility and hopelessness. The drone of a failed mission. It's a mindset I frankly don't have time for but as much as I wish for the contrary, I am not in control of when or how hard it hits me.

The first time I felt like this was after my mother died. Even at nine, I found myself the rock for my sister through Mom's cancer diagnosis, her decline, the funeral, and then navigating life after the one person who ever really loved us was gone. Life after my mother was more survival than living. The hatred and arguments that flew back and forth between my father and my grandparents was too much for Catherine and when we turned into collateral damage, I was her refuge. Over time, her anxiety mounted until I could see the panic attacks coming even before the shaking and the sobbing started. Sometimes just putting my arms around her could stop them. More often than not, it was just solace until she could breathe again.

One morning a few months after my mother died, I remember waking up and my whole body hurt. My arms and legs felt like they were full of concrete, and it was painful to move. My brain was in a fog and my will to do anything other than hurt was gone. I fought through that feeling for weeks, never daring to mention it to anyone. My father would have laughed or just called me a pussy and told me to man up. My sister would have understood, but I wasn't about to add my issues to hers. I simply soldiered on, shoving the pain further and further down until I could no longer feel it. It was a lesson I learned well.

The next time I noticed that heavy feeling of paralysis was three years later when Catherine told me our father had been abusing her almost nightly. In that moment, it wasn't pain I felt but hatred. Where my feelings of grief had been cold and heavy, Catherine's confession ignited my insides into a volcanic fury. I'm still not sure how I navigated that at 12. It was a bitter vitriol I choked down any time I was in Miller Clark's presence. I felt it every day until he splattered his brains against the living room wall, and every second after. My father settled his gambling debt with my sister's soul. That's not something that fades over time.

The feelings of hopelessness and abandonment came and went over the next seven years. A lot of misplaced anger. The kinds of bad choices and stupid decisions you would expect from a teenage boy with no love or direction. When I joined the Marines at 19 and had drill sergeants up my ass 24/7 trying to make me into the man my father said I'd never become, I finally learned to funnel my anger and defiance into an undeniable resolve. For the first time, I believed in who I could become. I believed I could become the man who would search the earth to find what had been taken from him, enduring whatever pain or discomfort that required.

For a long time, I thought the weight of loneliness and loss had finally left me. But that was the blindness of a kid in a new uniform. When bad intel walked us into our first ambush in Afghanistan, the truth and an IED exploded my naïve hope, killing four of our new brothers and putting Jonny and me in the hospital for two months. There's nothing hopelessness loves more than someone who can't get out of bed, with just their thoughts to pass what feels like endless time. Physical injuries I could deal with. Those I knew would heal.

The spiritual casualties never really did. For all its imprecision, war is an exacting, relentless crucible for mental anguish. It was only after I got out that I realized it wasn't the only evil that could be described that way.

At Homeland, there's an unspoken notion that you always remember your firsts. The first kid you save. And the first one you don't. For me, they didn't come in that order.

Addison Jackson was the first case I was ever assigned at Homeland. A 14-year-old girl from Tupelo, Mississippi who had gone missing from a Halloween street party. Her father Theo ran a local tire shop, and her mother Henny was the receptionist and pastor's assistant at Mount Calvary in the town next to Tupelo. Smart and athletic, Addie made straight As with an occasional B, and was the center on the Middle School basketball team. She was tall, more than a foot taller than some of the other girls on the team and had developed early. For 14, she was a big kid. Beautiful, well past the awkward teenager phase. Addie Jackson could easily pass for 17 when she wanted to and sadly, there weren't many things Addie wanted more than to be 17. When you're a teenage girl with three hours by yourself every afternoon after school, practice and homework are not your only thoughts.

For her birthday in August, Addison's parents had finally caved and given her a smart phone under the auspices of security. Since she was walking home from school every day and would be going out with her friends more, they reasoned, with a phone, she would always have the ability to call if she needed them, or just needed to communicate during the day.

At first, Addie's parents closely monitored her phone every night per their agreement with her. With the gift came accountability and Addison was happy to make that trade. She knew that like all parents, hers would eventually tire of the ritual and just trust that she was doing what she promised them she would. Besides, she was smart enough to do a Google search for how to cover your tracks, wipe a search history, and make everything look normal.

The first time Addie met Paul Langston online it was just after her 14th birthday. Addie had buried the chat app her friends told her about in a folder called "School" on her phone and when she wasn't at practice or finishing homework, she was texting with the senior point guard from Lee County's biggest high school who had chatted her up. Addie had been floored when she saw Paul's image appear on her phone along with a friend request from "Baller24." She couldn't accept it fast enough. He didn't have time for calls, but texting was cool. It might have been magical if, in truth, Paul Langston ever really existed.

Over the course of the Fall, Addie and "Paul" chatted after practice, late at night before bed, and occasionally before school, but that was harder with her parents floating nearby. They talked about how tough it was to balance school and sports. The weight of expectation, both as athletes and students whose parents had high expectations. Paul told Addie he would be the starting point guard his senior season and if that went well, he might have a shot at playing for a D1 school. He didn't have time for social media. He was going hard at practice and hustling his ass off. The rest was God's will.

By October, Addison found herself falling hard for Paul Langston. She knew he must be 17 or 18 because Paul said he was a senior, but he had never asked about her age or where she actually went to school. Like most people, she figured he just assumed she was older than she was. But after a lot of thought, Addie decided she needed to be honest with Paul. For a week, she agonized over when and how to tell him, but finally one night, she just did.

"BTW, how old are you?" she texted Paul.

"18. Why?" he answered back.

"How old do you think I am?" she clicks, holding her breath.

"DK. 17? 18?"

"I'm 14."

There. She'd said it. She waited and she waited for Paul's response, but nothing came. The screen was still. She knew it. Paul didn't know her age and now she was never going to hear from him again. She thought they called it ghosting. Addie hated crying, but she felt her eyes starting to well up. But then her phone lit up and a response was finally coming.

"You're perfect," is all it said. Paul Langston, all-everything basketball player, senior, love of her life said she was perfect. His response just made her love him that much more. For Addison Jackson, that text sealed the deal. She had no way of knowing it, but it also sealed her fate.

The next day, Paul suggested they finally meet in person. There was a Halloween street party in downtown Tupelo the Saturday night before Halloween. They could meet there and since they'd be wearing masks, no one else would know it was them. Paul said he would be in a ghost mask and wearing a red basketball jersey with 24 on the front. Addison said she didn't have a mask but would figure something out.

The night of the party, Addison Jackson told her parents she was going to spend the night at her friend Maddie's house. Addie and

Maddie had been friends since they could walk so her parents never thought twice when she kissed them both, jumped on her bike and pedaled off down the street with her backpack over both shoulders.

Two weeks later, a sanitation crew found Addie Jackson in a dumpster behind a café in Hamilton, Alabama, 45 miles east of Tupelo. She was dressed in a ripped white T-shirt and had a purple ring around her throat where she'd been choked to death. It was impossible to know how many times she had been violated, or whether the killer left his semen while he was killing her or after. Knowing the sick twists I dealt with, I bet I knew.

When the locals ran the semen sample, they got a DNA hit on some 42-year-old redneck meth dealer from Marion County, Alabama named Walker Bryan who had priors for drug possession and indecent activity with someone underage. He was also wanted in connection to two other homicides that matched Addie Jackson to a T. There was suspicion Bryan and his buddies had been passing these girls around before killing them, but the locals hadn't been able to nail him. Now with three bodies across two states, it was time to call in some bigger guns.

Within 36 hours, we had Walker Bryan in custody and chained to a heavy metal table in the interrogation room. Walking through the door, I reminded myself of the concept, "innocent until proven guilty," but I'd seen the pictures of Addison Jackson's bruised, bloated, naked body and I'll be damned if Walker Bryan was ever gonna see the outside of a prison again. When we searched his doublewide, we found Addie's backpack and her phone. We also recovered Bryan's iPad and when we compared it to Addie's phone, the entire conversation between her and Bryan posing at Paul Langston was still there.

My boss started the interrogation while I stood in the back of the room watching. After 30 minutes of unanswered questions and smug indifference, my boss got up and walked out of the room slamming the door behind him. Understanding this was strictly theater, I pulled up a chair and held my stare on Walker Bryan until he turned and looked at me.

"Fuck you want from me B.I.?" he said too stupid to even understand who we were.

"I'm not with the F.B.I. Mr. Bryan. I'm with the Department of Homeland Security."

"Homeland?" he exclaimed sitting back with eyes open wide. "I ain't some fuckin' beaner or raghead. What the Hell Homeland want with me?"

"Why do you think we're here?" I asked.

"I'm guessing it's over that girl they say I kilt."

"Did you?"

"Did I what?"

"Did you kill her? After you kidnapped her and beat her. Did you rape her? Try to whore her out to the rest of your hillbilly buddies?"

"Hey, slow your roll Homeland," Bryan blurted back at me through a mouth of broken and missing teeth. "I didn't do shit. You don't understand how it is."

"No?" I answered, "enlighten me. I want to understand what this all must have been like for you Mr. Bryan, after you kidnapped that poor girl. Maybe she didn't listen. Maybe you were nice to her, and the little bitch just didn't appreciate what you were doing for her. Cold truth? Women don't appreciate men like us."

It was all I could do to hold down the bile and sour vomit rising from my stomach behind the words that were coming out of my mouth. I didn't believe a word I was saying but if it got this asshole to spill it was worth fighting through the exercise. Bryan looked at me sizing me up and shifted in his seat.

"You got no idea what that girl was like," he started. I don't know if it was my delivery, or the effects of his mounting withdrawal that turned him, but his shoulders slumped, and he looked me in the eye as though we were now kindred spirits. Twenty seconds ago, we were at an impasse. Now he was talking to me like we were at some high school reunion, sharing a bottle of whiskey.

"How is Paul Langston involved in this?" I asked him. At that point, we were still unsure of who Langston was. We could find no record of him.

For what felt like an eternity, Bryan danced around his sad, pathetic life. Shitty parents. He couldn't read. In and out of jail. Losing his family. Dealing meth. But then, almost an hour in, he finally came to the truth.

"There ain't no Paul Langston, you dumb shit. I made that boy up. Fished that bitch right on the computer," he said almost proudly. "I pretended to be some stud basketball player. Took me four months. I was gonna turn that girl out and pretty as she was, I woulda made a mint."

"So, what happened?" I asked.

"She lied to me!" he yelled defiantly, as though Addison Jackson owed him something. I must have looked confused because he leaned in as if I was in need of clarification. "The girl had braces. Not in her picture. In real life. Ain't nobody gonna stick their glory in a mouth full of metal. You'd pull your junk out all cut up and shit." He paused and looked away before mumbling under his breath. "Don't matter. Ain't nothing you got gonna stick."

"Mr. Bryan, I've got all I need to keep you inside a 10 by 10 concrete block 23 hours a day for the rest of your sad, pathetic life."

"Oh, you think so?" he laughed. "Where you from smart guy? Somewhere up north? I'll be outta here by this time Thursday. This is Alabama, boy. Ain't nobody give a shit about some black girl. I ain't goin' nowhere but back home and you can take that to the bank!" And with that, he sat back, crossing his arms with the biggest shit-eating grin I've ever seen. "I just took what I was entitled to."

Walker Bryan should be thankful to this day there was a table between us. In a flash, I exploded out of my seat, kicking my chair into the door behind me with a loud crack. I stretched across the table grabbing Bryan by the front of his stained wife beater and ripped the collar straight down to the arm.

"This isn't 1962 you fucking cracker. You don't even know how dumb you are. First, you were too stupid to wear a condom when you raped that girl, so we've got your DNA dead to fucking rights. Plus, it matches the skin cells we found underneath her fingernails where she tried to fight you off. Second, you picked a girl who was 14 which makes this case statutory, even in Mississippi. The best part that guarantees you're gonna get the needle – and not the kind you love so much – is that you took a girl from Mississippi and killed her in Alabama. That combined with the other two dead girls we just matched your DNA to makes this Federal, motherfucker." I was seething and as I leaned in so close I could smell his rancid breath, I watched every ounce of life and arrogance drain from his gaunt, pock-marked face. Walker Bryan was dumb as a pine stump, but the boy knew the word Federal. "You're going to Death Row monkeyfuck, if I have to drive you there myself."

I never heard the door open behind me, but I could feel the force of my boss's hand pulling me back by the shoulder. I was good. Walker Bryan was gonna die in prison, and I helped put him there. In the moment, I was elated. But then I remembered the circumstances that got us here. Three dead girls and the parents who had to bury them. Bryan was only one of the thousands of predators we were chasing, but you had to start with one.

There have been countless girls who have haunted me at night over the years, but with the exception of Catherine, none visit me more often than Addie Jackson.

Thankfully there are hundreds we save. Thousands globally. But every time I find dead girls who have been raped and abused too many times to count, or those for whom death would be a welcome release, I have to fight to keep my own grief at bay. I have little doubt the stress of this job will kill me prematurely. It's a hard job. But because of the life I've led, I'm hard too and will keep fighting as long as I can. There are far bigger priorities than me. I ache all over this morning and today I will let myself feel it. All of it. I will drink it down. But tomorrow, I will push the pain away and reengage.

The Lucifer closure and the fact that now a week after my call, Baptiste has never answered, tells me he is in the wind and nowhere near L.A. The second Jasmine landed on that SUV, I'm betting this town got really hot, really fast for him and I'm convinced the sommelier has disappeared back to one of his other restaurants or if he really thinks he's in deep, to somewhere without extradition to the United States.

I haven't talked to Jonny to fill him in on everything I know so I'm not sure what the Department actually knows about Baptiste. At very least, I now know what he looks like and what he sounds like. I also know who this guy is and how long he's been hip deep in trafficking young girls. Even 20 years later, I know he will remember my sister and taking her from me. I just have to hope he didn't sell her to some other scumbag years ago. Either way, I'm coming Catherine.

Please, just hang on.

33

I've worked with a number of good informants during my years in L.A. and I'm still in contact with most of the ones who haven't died or disappeared. I've always found CIs to be an interesting breed, constantly straddling the line between the criminal world and the straight and narrow. At their core, I believe most of my informants have good souls that have been tarnished by addiction and abuse. There's no other explanation for why someone would trade help and stability for living on the street and trusting that, even high, they can work criminals who would just as easily have them beaten or killed as squashing a rat under a steel-toed boot.

After my second tumbler of coffee, my first text is to Angelo Roselli, listed as "Anger" in my contacts. Angelo is unabashedly connected, but his family takes no part in running women, so we've never had a reason to get sideways. For some gangsters, there's an invisible moral line that runs between guns and drugs and humans. Angelo's family has been on the contraband side of the ledger in L.A. for four generations. And for four generations they have understood the benefit of being generous with information about those running women and kids. The concept of Omerta is not lost on the family. But the thought of children being abused is so morally repugnant to them, a whisper-campaign to hold that abomination in check was long ago justified.

"Anger, it's J. Need to talk," is all I text him. It's all it takes. "The place in 30," comes the response a few minutes later. I put on my shoes, stretch my calves, and take off in an easy run toward the beach. Angelo has always liked meeting at the shoreline. The air is thick and while we can hear each other, the sounds of the wind and the waves make it hard to record anything. I would never burn him like that, but I understand the apprehension. Assuming anything is the kind of carelessness that gets you 20 to life or killed.

I haven't seen Angelo in about a year, but I recognize the large silver sedan that pulls into the lot next to the beach. Anger's driver gets out from behind the wheel and when he opens the door to the back seat, I don't recognize the man stepping out. I feel the hairs on the back of my neck stand up as I consider why he would send someone new to meet me. Angelo Roselli is in his early 60s and built like a Rottweiler. Anger is five foot seven, about 270 on a good day. The guy heading in my direction looks more like Andy Garcia on the Mediterranean Diet. I've never seen Angelo not dressed in a dark suit and with his black hair slicked back and the guy walking toward me is wearing a Cuban dress shirt and shorts with his silver hair blowing in the breeze. It's only when he's ten feet away that I see it is Angelo, but in a whole new body.

"Look at you," I say smiling at my contact. "You lost a whole person since I saw you!"

"Looks good, huh?" he laughs, throwing his arms around me in a familiar bearhug. It's never lost on me this man has the strength to snap my spine if he ever chose to. "Intermittent fasting. Goddamn life changer."

"That's it?" I ask him.

"Eh. Maybe a few less sausages, some more miles on the treadmill. But yeah. I eat from 11 to 7. Fruits, veggies, and lean meats. Over the course of 11 months… 78 pounds gone."

"You look fantastic," I say looking him up and down. "You've got to feel better."

"Fucking like I'm 22," he smirks.

I grab Anger's shoulder and smile, sincerely proud of him and honestly, a little envious of his love life. To some, it would seem morally gray for a Federal agent to consider someone in the Family a friend, but on more than one occasion, Angelo Roselli has gone out of his way to get me information that saved my life. I don't live in a black and white world and neither does he. I think that is a shared understanding we will always have, even though we often exist in the opposite fringes of gray. He's always treated me more like a son than an agent and I'm thankful for it.

"It's good to see you Jake," Angelo says turning and walking north up the beach. "What's going on?"

"Have you ever heard of a man named Jean-Michel Baptiste? He also refers to himself as 'the Sommelier.' He runs a restaurant in the hills called 'Lucifer.' Michelin-quality food. Super expensive wine."

"The name's not ringing any bells. He running girls too?"

"If I'm right, on one of the biggest scales I've ever seen. Through restaurant fronts in at least six states."

I spend the next 10 minutes sharing what I know with Anger. All about the restaurants, the wine menus, my dinner at Lucifer and then finding Jasmine, broken on the hood of the SUV at Highland Canyon. I also tell him about Rachel and the hummingbird tattoos. Over the course of my story, I can see Angelo's face shifting from comprehension to gangster mode. He has no tolerance for abusing women, and especially the sexual assault of children no matter who they are. I don't know anyone who can shift from Teddy Bear to

Grizzly faster than Angelo. He's listed as "Anger" in my phone for a reason.

"He sounds like an evil guy, Jake."

"He is, but there's something else." I purse my lips and swallow hard. "Angelo, Baptiste is the man who took my sister."

"He took Catherine? Way back? *Marone*." At this point, nothing much floors Angelo Roselli but I can tell this does. I can literally see the anger and stress moving from his head to the fists he's balling up. And then without hesitation, Anger grabs my arm and looks me dead in the eye. "Is this something we need to deal with?" We. To think he would take the risk to put Baptiste down for my benefit tells me everything I need to know. But now is not the time, nor do I want to be in debt to Angelo as close as we are.

"The offer means the world, but right now I'm just trying to find him. I think the dead girl paired with a dead cop put Baptiste in the wind and I just need to find him. But quietly."

"Understood. Let me check around, see what I can find out," Angelo says. He grabs my forearm and gives it a little tug. "Be careful Jake. If this cocksucker's fronting what you think he is, he'll smoke you the second he knows who you are without one goddamn about who you work for. And the world needs you Jake." He smacks my cheek with the pads of his fingers to make sure he has my full attention. "Your sister needs you." Angelo smiles at me, pops me again on the cheek, and walks back across the sand toward his driver who is already moving to open the back door of his Mercedes.

By the time Angelo pulls out of the lot, the sun is cresting over the Pacific. Another time, this would be a perfect window for a run down to the pier and back. But not today.

Halfway back to my house, it occurs to me who my next call should go to. Probably who my first call should have been to. I haven't spoken with Charlotte Kimbrough in two years, but there's no one in L.A. who knows more about high-dollar escorts than she does. Charlotte has been Hollywood's best unspoken secret for the past 30 years. If anyone is running girls for $3,500 a night, Charlotte Kimbrough will know about it. For all I know, we may already be secret comrades in arms waging war against a common enemy.

When I get back to the house, I decide to jump in the shower before calling Charlotte and for some reason my thoughts jump to Rachel. This woman who drops in and out of my life at will. I know Baptiste is the one who took my sister, but Rachel is still the closest connection I have to her. That's assuming I trust what Rachel told me the last time she was here. My heart wants to believe she knows where my sister is, but my head keeps shouting that I'm getting played. It doesn't matter. If Baptiste is in the ether, I'm betting Rachel is too.

I throw on some clothes and move to the den to call Charlotte. I look at my watch and see it's just after 1pm which means she's most likely having lunch at the Devereaux. Way before cell phones existed, anyone who needed to find Charlotte Kimbrough knew the first place to look was the back left table in the dining room at the Devereaux Hotel on La Cienega. There was a time before online ads and dating apps when Charlotte was as much of an institution in L.A. as the boutique hotel itself. That was before my time, but I've heard the stories.

Deciding this is a conversation I would rather have face to face, I jump in the car and take the 10 east toward Hollywood. It's a bit presumptuous to just show up at the hotel, especially as long as it's been since I saw Charlotte, but if she's there, I don't think she'll be offended. She'll be flattered. If there's anything that woman loves more than men on a string, it's being the center of attention.

Walking in the front door of the Devereaux, it smells like a hotel whose time has passed. Not bad. Just old. Like an elderly woman wearing gardenia perfume that's no longer made and screams 1947.

I tell the hostess my name, slip her a $20 and ask if she would please check to see if I could have a few minutes of Ms. Kimbrough's time. I watch her walk away toward the table in the back and while I can't see Charlotte, I can see the swirl of smoke rising from the long, thin cigarette she's inevitably smoking. Either lunch is over, or she's sending the kitchen a signal she's tired of waiting. On her way back, the hostess waves me over, smiling. I thank her as we pass.

"Well, well…" she starts, a warm recognition in her sultry voice. It's like I'm listening to Lauren Bacall. "My little Blue Jay has finally come back to the nest. How are you sweetheart? I've missed you. Sit," she orders.

From almost the first time I met her, Charlotte has lovingly referred to me as Blue Jay. At first I was offended since Blue Jays are assholes. But when she told me the Jay was for my first initial and the Blue was because I always seemed so sad, I understood. I suppose in her line of work, keen intuition becomes a superpower. That, and I'm sure it's always been standard operating procedure for her to avoid real names as much as possible.

"I've missed you too," I answer back. It's been two years but even at her age, Charlotte Kimbrough is still stunning. She has to be almost 70 but I swear, she doesn't age. She's dressed in a silver silk shell that matches her hair, and a beautiful lavender blazer with a pin on the lapel of a golden magnolia with a large pearl in the center.

"How are you Charlotte?" I ask sitting down.

"Other than the fact that the world has gone and lost its goddamn mind… not bad," she answers. "I've come to the realization that most people in this town don't worry much about me anymore and that's not a bad thing."

Like with Angelo Roselli, being friendly with L.A.'s most prominent madame for decades may seem like a serious conflict of interest with what I do, and to a certain extent, it is. But having talked extensively with Charlotte and her girls over the years, I know three things to be true: 1. Not one of the women who work for Charlotte has ever been coerced into doing what they do. 2. Every one of her girls is over the age of 21. And 3. They are all vigilant about looking out for underage girls being trafficked or exploited and when they see someone in trouble, they tell Charlotte and I'm the first person she calls. Is that dancing with the Devil? Absolutely. Is it hypocritical? Maybe. The line between trafficking and prostitution is a razor's edge, and a sharp one at that. I wish I could fix it all, but long ago, I realized I had to choose one side of that knife or the other. I made the decision to try and save those who have been groomed, coerced, and forced to sell themselves against their will, especially the ones who are underage. It was in that pursuit that I told Charlotte about Catherine when we first met five or six years ago.

"How are you? Have any luck finding your sister?" She clearly hasn't forgotten.

"No," I answer her, "but I have a few leads that I'm following up on and I was hoping I could ask you about them."

"Sure darlin', you know I'll do whatever I can to help you."

"I appreciate that. Thank you for letting me just drop in on you"

"Sure baby. I'm not doing anything I shouldn't," she says through a smoky laugh. "Just a few old friends having a chat."

"Does the name Rachel Meredith ring any bells for you?" I ask Charlotte.

"No, I don't think I've ever heard that name before. Pretty. But no," she says taking a long drag on her cigarette.

"Ever heard of an underground sex club called 'Hummingbird' up on Sunset?"

"I haven't, but it sounds like I need to," she answers tilting her head back and blowing a lazy billow of smoke up into the air. "I'm familiar with most of the adult clubs in L.A. but ever since polyamory and consensual cuckolding became the 'fetishes du jour,' more and more of these swing clubs seem to be popping up."

"Hummingbird is that to the Nth degree. Imagine all the beautiful people you know, packed into the hottest club you know, overlayed with a Roman orgy, a voyeuristic human zoo, and a live auction selling women and girls as young as 14 to the highest bidders."

"There is nothing good about that," Charlotte says, a defiant tone in her voice. "I know there is certainly a cohort in this town with a taste for that kind of thing. Always has been. But they're not anyone I would entertain in any way."

"I understand," I tell her. "I wasn't suggesting you'd ever be part of that. I mention Hummingbird to ask you this… Have you ever met or heard of a man named Jean-Michel Baptiste? He also goes by the moniker 'the Sommelier.' Tall. White hair. Fancies himself as some sophisticate committed to giving rich men all they deserve."

Charlotte starts to twist in her seat, then purses her lips and looks at the wall. I know few people as confident and present as Charlotte Kimbrough and because of that, her long silence on the other end of the table is deafening. The blood has also drained from her face, and I swear to God, there's a chill in this booth.

"I know Jean-Michel," she says finally. "I only met that frigid bastard a few times, but I know him. He's serious evil Blue Jay. As dark as they come."

"Tell me," I say leaning in.

"I first met Baptiste about 12 years ago, but back then he wasn't the faux dandy he pretends to be now. When I met him, he already had girls in tow, but he wasn't much better than a college educated pimp. He was smart enough not to abuse his girls physically, but even then, I could tell he was a sadist emotionally. A lot of the pimps I knew controlled their girls by beating them when they got out of line without the first worry about bruises, cuts, or broken bones. Honestly, I think some of them had clients who got off on girls who were all beat up. That was a whole different side of the business from where I played. I dealt with studio execs looking for a nooner, or actors looking for some discretion. I provided an outlet for elegance and attention. Baptiste was servicing the savage side of sex.

"The first time I met him I was at the Pompano, killing time over a martini before a date later that night. In walks this handsome man with that deep voice and when he made a beeline straight for me, I was naturally intrigued. He bought a round and we talked and laughed about the basic bullshit you discuss on any first date. But then, the conversation turned, fairly quickly. It became clear to me that he knew who I was before he ever walked into the bar, and that he was way more interested in what I knew than who I was. What was the L.A. market like for sex work? How did my clients find me? How much did I charge? How did I keep the cops at arm's length? When I realized what Baptiste was really after, I shut him down pretty quick. For all I knew, he was undercover, or something worse, so I cut him off. I'll never forget the instant transformation that occurred in his face. Baptiste had been charming up to that point. But the second I shut him down, his back stiffened, all warmth dropped out of his face, and there was a smoldering resentment that I could see behind his eyes. He did not like a woman dictating anything to him and he wasn't about to abide it. I remember he got up, threw a $10 bill on the bar to cover his drink, and moved close enough to whisper in my ear. He called me a slag or a whore or something like that and threatened that I'd do well to stay out of his way. He said, and I quote, 'unless I needed a sound fucking, he would hate to destroy an L.A. legend.' He walked away and I didn't see him again for nine years."

My stomach turns with every story like this I hear about Baptiste. Not just because he's an evil fuck and I know there are girls in every kind of pain imaginable because of him. I'm sick because I know Catherine is one of them and has been for 20 years.

"The last time I crossed paths with Baptiste was in 2019," Charlotte continues, lighting another cigarette. "One of his girls, a South American named Alexandra, about 19 years old, had somehow broken away from him and met one of my girls who told her about me. I invited Alex to lunch, and she came and sat right where you're sitting and explained her situation to me. Pretty girl. Beautiful really. And cultured. We didn't get into her childhood, but you could tell before things went off the rails, she'd been raised right. I thought she would fit in well with the clients we serve, and I really liked her."

Charlotte looks up, taking a long drag. When she blows out the smoke, it's more like a massive, remorseful exhale.

"When I asked Alex who she had worked for before and the name Baptiste tumbled out of her mouth, I almost said no. That sounded like trouble remembering his warning to me at the Pompano. But you know me. Fuck Jean-Michel Baptiste. I wasn't about to let some man bully me, so I welcomed Alex with open arms.

"When Baptiste heard one of his girls was gone, and especially working for me, he completely lost it. He called me a dozen times and when I refused to answer, this is the message he left me."

Charlotte picks up her smartphone and pushes a few buttons on the face. She increases the volume and extends her arm over the center of the table, handing me her phone. I put it my ear, and after a few seconds, I hear Baptiste's chilling bass.

"I tried to warn you. But like the dumb cunt you are, you didn't listen. You took what doesn't belong to you. Even worse, you took something that belongs to me. You willingly sowed the wind you stupid bitch. Now, you get to reap the whirlwind."

Charlotte takes another drag on her cigarette that's so long I worry she'll burn through the filter. Her eyes look up to the ceiling as though she's searching for something, and she finally exhales stubbing what's left of her cigarette out on the salad plate in front of her.

"Three days after he left that message, a couple having a picnic on the beach found Alexandra's hand sticking out of a shallow, sandy grave behind a sand dune. After they dug her out, the ME said with the amount of internal hemorrhaging and blood lost from sexual trauma, it was hard to pinpoint what killed her. What truly haunts me is he couldn't confirm Alex was dead when they buried her in the sand. That motherfucker beat her, let multiple men rape her for hours, and then buried her alive, so broken, she couldn't breathe. That's who you're dealing with Blue Jay. Do I know Jean-Michel Baptiste? I wish to God I could say I didn't. You mentioned Catherine. Please tell me Baptiste doesn't have anything to do with her."

I wish I could.

34

My visit with Charlotte does nothing to help me sleep easier and neither does the fact that I'm still out of sleeping pills. No matter what I do, or how many fingers of whiskey I drink before bed, it's nearly 3:30am when I finally fall asleep. That's what makes it so painful when the ring of my cell phone shatters the silence at 6:00am. I look at the screen through one half-opened lid and see "Jon James" on the readout. I grab the phone and roll onto my back, rubbing my eyes.

"This is early even for you Bear," I choke out, my voice scratchy and not yet lubricated. "What's going on?"

"What the fuck are you doing Jake?" I know I'm not really awake, but I'm taken aback by the parental edge in Jon's voice. "Last night I got a very interesting, unexpected call from our good friend Angelo Roselli." Shit. Anger called Jonny. That explains the tone. "So, let me ask you again, Jake, what in God's name are you doing chasing Baptiste? Do I really need to remind you that you're suspended?" Jonny's pissed and I can hear it in his voice.

"Jon, listen…"

"And before you give me some ridiculous excuse or bullshit story," he interrupts, "remember who you're talking to."

I sit up, now very much awake and resisting the urge to ask my best friend who the fuck he thinks he is. I know he's trying to look out for me, but he doesn't understand what I know and how close I am to finding Catherine. If he did, his tone would be a lot different.

"What did Angelo tell you?" I ask, immediately realizing how defensive that sounds. "I don't want to waste your time rehashing what you already know."

"He told me everything Jake. At least whatever you told him. About Baptiste, about the girls he's running and the restaurants, about your little soiree at the Hollywood sex club, and at the risk of continuing to bury the goddamn Lede, he told me Baptiste is the man who took Catherine when you were a kid. Is that true?"

"Yes. That's true," I answer.

"Jesus Jake. Why didn't you call me?" The pointed frustration and anger in Jonny's voice has shifted to hurt, and it's well earned. No one in the world has heard more about Catherine or nursed me through more misery navigating that part of my life than Jon has. He should have been my first call and it's a miss I'll have to fight to make good.

"I'm sorry Jonny. Things are moving fast, but I should have called you. I only realized who Baptiste was about a week ago, but I'm telling you, there's no doubt in my mind he's the one who took my sister."

"OK, we'll come back to how you're pulling this shit off without a gun and a badge, but for now, tell me where we are." Again, with the we. It would do me well to remember I'm never as alone as I think I am. "Where is Baptiste now?"

"I wish I knew. He disappeared a week ago. One of his girls fed a service revolver to a cop who beat her until she was unrecognizable. Then she took a swan dive off the 24th floor balcony.

I went to Baptiste's restaurant three days later and there was a closed sign on the front door. I called him but he hasn't called me back."

"You called him? How did you get his number? Wait…. have you met Baptiste?"

"I did. A few nights before the girl jumped off her balcony."

"Please tell me those events are unrelated."

"They are," I assure him. "More or less."

"What do you mean, more or less?"

"Baptiste sent me to meet the girl who jumped, but she died before I got there. When I saw her, she had a hummingbird tattoo at the base of her neck. It's all connected Bear. I'm telling you, this guy runs deep. The trafficking. The restaurants. The private events. I haven't put every piece in place but I'm really close to understanding exactly how the whole thing's being run. I cracked a major part of it, but there's still a lot to figure out. I'd tell you to move on him, but we can't fuck this up. Not now. If this guy disappears forever, I will never get another shot at finding my sister."

Jon's silence tells me he's trying to process everything I've just thrown at him.

"There's nothing in the file about the restaurants, or the private parties," Jon says. "Since our Houston bust, Homeland has built a decent profile for the type of figure we suspect is behind the shipping container busts and a few others, but we haven't connected the dots with Baptiste. From what you're telling me, I'd bet money we're looking for the same guy."

"I know we are Jon. This motherfucker drips arrogance. Baptiste is so sure he's untouchable, there is ZERO chance he doesn't make a mistake. We just have to be close by when he does."

"Any word from Rachel?"

"Nothing. I haven't heard a word from her since she tased me the night I kept her from killing Baptiste."

"Since she WHAT?" Jonny's reaction tells me I need to stop talking or do a better job remembering what I have and haven't told him. "She tried to kill him? And then she fucking tased you?"

"I'm alright. We got into an argument after we left the 'soiree at the sex club' as you referred to it, and when she told me she had actually seen Catherine, I let my guard down."

"Wait, Rachel has seen Catherine? She's alive? You know she's alive?" I can hear the hope in Jonny's voice, and then, complete understanding. "No wonder you're losing your mind."

At once, I realize this too was information I should have called to share with Jon, but that it's also intel that will frame for him why I haven't been completely forthcoming. Jon Joseph would run through fire to save my sister and have my back. In the years we served together, there were countless times he put my safety ahead of his. I didn't want to send him chasing shadows until I knew I was right. But it's time to once again put my life in his hands. If there is any human on the planet who won't fail me, it's Jon.

"I'm really sorry Jon. I should have told you all of this, but now you know everything I know." Jon doesn't speak, but I sense it's because the gravity of what I'm saying is finally hitting him. "Catherine is alive Jon and I'm closer to finding her than I have been since the day I lost her. If I can find Baptiste, or Rachel, they will lead me to her. I know it."

"What do you need from me?"

"Honestly, check and balance. I promise you, from here on in, I will update you the second I know anything new. Just help me make sure I'm seeing the field clearly and let me know if I'm catching any heat on your end."

"As far as I can tell, the brass still thinks you're at home pissed off about your suspension. What do you have, seven weeks left?"

"Six and a half," I correct him. What I'm doing is a risk. But I'm so close to finding Catherine.

"You should be good. Had Roselli not called me, you'd be completely under the RADAR."

"Yeah, I need to have a little chat with him about what 'between you and me' means."

"I think I'd let that go. Angelo's just worried about you going off on this guy and getting yourself killed. For some reason, Angelo has a soft spot for you my friend. Which, trust me, is WAY better than the alternative."

"Believe me, if Catherine wasn't part of the calculus, I'd be more than happy to turn Baptiste's head into a pink mist without a second thought. But as long as this guy knows where my sister is, I assure you, I will keep him alive."

"I trust you," Jonny says. "You said you cracked some code on how he's running the girls. You want to tell me about the part of this you have figured out?"

"Sure," I answer him. "Go get a pen and a big cup of coffee and I'll call you back in five."

"Roger that. I love you brother."

"Love you too buddy. Go get your coffee. You are not going to believe this shit."

35

I finish the call with Jon and make the mistake of laying my head back on my pillow and shutting my eyes. The soft support under my head and the ceiling fan moving the cool air over me is all it takes for me to crash. Three hours of sleep will catch up with you in a hurry if you're not paying attention. Unfortunately, it's when I'm most tired that the nightmares come. This time, it's not the dream of women chained in the ocean that descends but the rabbits in the wood.

As the sun makes its final descent behind the tree line ahead of me, I find myself walking through a field of heavy grass. A gentle breeze blows the dried blades against me and every few feet, I hear the crack of a dead limb snapping under the weight of my steps. Behind me and to each side, yellow fields stretch as far as I can see. By the look of the thinning grasses and the crisp bite of the temperature, it's Fall or maybe the beginning of Winter. I can feel the temperature dropping with the sun now out of sight and I'm wishing I was wearing a thick sweater or a jacket. I'm dressed in the same T-shirt, shorts, and running shoes I would wear for a run down the beach and I'm painfully aware I am ill-prepared for the place to which I'm being drawn.

Thirty yards ahead of me lies the edge of a dense wood full of hundred-foot pine trees and spreading oaks. For the first fifty feet, solitary shafts of light shine down through the canopy illuminating the soft floor of the woods. But as the pines give way to the oaks, there is very little light and an ever-thickening darkness that both attracts and terrifies me. From where I stand I can't see how deep the blackness goes, but intuitively, it feels like it goes on forever.

Twenty feet from the trees, the high grasses taper off revealing a soft brown rise of pine straw. To my left, a small warren of rabbits has gathered to munch on the pinecones that have dropped for the winter from the trees ahead. I look to my right and realize there are a dozen more rabbits sitting, hopping around, and rubbing their ears. Some bright white, some brown, some black. Not the least bit skittish. I take a few steps in their direction and crouch down, extending my hand. I hold still and one of the white rabbits hops over beside me and sits while I pet its body and stroke its ears. The rabbit purrs, much like a cat, letting me know it's content, but then slowly, she hops away and disappears into the trees.

As I stand, I notice there are now hundreds of rabbits to my left and right and that many of them are also moving toward the tree line as if drawn, unaware of what waits for them in the dark. I follow the rabbits into the woods and immediately feel the temperature drop. There's a distinct, uncomfortable chill in the shadows that only gets more acute the deeper I go. No more than a dozen steps in, I look back to the field from where I came, and the light seems dimmer and further away than it should. I'm struck by a fear that I'm about to be consumed by darkness with no orientation for how to navigate my way out. I look back to the wooded interior to gain some bearing, relying on my senses of sight, hearing, and even smell to dictate where I should move.

With just enough light to move through and not into the trees, I make my way deeper and deeper into the wood. Slowly, my eyes adjust to the darkness. I can no longer see the rabbits around me, but I can sense their motion aided by the sound of them hopping through the clusters of dried leaves at the base of the trees I'm moving around. I hear them all around. And then I don't.

From what sounds like an echo carried on the wind, the lonely cry of a large wolf floats past me followed by another and another. The pack is calling to each other. They cry again and again, closer, and closer each time. I step back toward the field, but the wolves seem to follow as quickly as I can move. I consider climbing for protection, but second guess being trapped and having to try the patience of a pack of hungry wolves. Instead, I reach down and grab a branch the size of an oar and anchor myself against the side of an oak that must stand four feet wide. I stand and wait.

Twenty yards to my right, a painful scream pierces the darkness. It's not the wolves. It's one of the rabbits. Mercifully, the wolf must have killed it quickly because after the initial shriek, there's just silence. But then the next scream comes. And the next. And the next. And the next.

Over the course of what feels like an hour, I stand and cower as rabbit after rabbit is annihilated by wolves. Each anguished shriek is a high-pitched scream that could only come from an animal weighing five pounds. But then gradually, one by one, the sounds suddenly drop in pitch until they sound as though they are coming from a rabbit the size of a deer. The thought hits me the cries are almost human-like. It's then that I hear, "Help me," from deep in the dark. Convinced I'm just hearing things, I dismiss it. Until I hear it again. "Help me. Please!" From three words, 100 feet away, there's no way I could know the voice belongs to Catherine. And yet, I'm sure of it.

"Catherine?" I scream, moving toward the sound of the voice.

"Jake?" she screams back, a pained sound of relief in her voice. "Help me!"

I drop the heavy branch I'm holding and take off on a sprint into the darkness. My eyes have adjusted enough to make out the trees, but I still can't see anything with definition. I bounce off tree after tree, praying I'm running in the right direction.

"Catherine?" I yell, needing her voice to guide me.

"I'm here. I'm hurt. Hurry!" she screams back, her voice seemingly right in front of me.

Twenty yards ahead between two massive trees, I see a shock of moonlight shining through the canopy, illuminating what looks like a giant clearing. I run toward the light until I feel it surround me. I stop in the middle of a large, circular break in the trees. A moderate covering of dark green moss that looks soft enough to sleep on covers the ground. Looking up, I see open sky and hundreds of stars bright enough not to drown in the moonlight. Slowly, I turn in a circle looking at the trees framing the circle. This should be a tranquil temple in the woods. In my dream, it's a killing field.

The round clearing runs fifty feet in every direction and suddenly, no matter where I look, there's a wolf standing at the edge of the circle. Feeding. Black wolves, brown wolves, grey wolves, all devouring the bodies in front of them, their snouts and teeth red with blood. I pray they are eating the rabbits I heard crying earlier, but they're not. Each wolf is standing over the body of a different young woman. Some completely annihilated and mercifully dead. Some still whimpering and suffering. The wolves eye me proudly, confident I am no real threat. Even with an AK, I'm not sure I could kill them all before they converged on me.

Turning forward, I look to the tree line at the front of the circle. A wolf twice as big as the others with snow white hair stands over the top of a young white woman lying on the ground, bleeding but still breathing. The wolf locks eyes with me and lets out a sharp howl that shatters the silence. Without breaking eye contact with me, he lowers his paw to the abdomen of the woman in front of him and scrapes his claws, deep across her stomach drawing blood. The pain stirs the woman from her shock, and she turns her head toward me, opening her eyes. They are ice blue.

"Catherine," I whisper. I feel anger and adrenaline rising through me and I start toward the white wolf. But the second I do, the other wolves around the circle quickly close ranks around me, their heads lowered, their teeth bared. In that moment, I realize I'm too far away from the white wolf to do anything before the pack tears me to shreds. He knows it too.

With deafening abandon, the white wolf howls again and starts barking rhythmically as though initiating some kind of chant. The others join, some barking, some growling. With each sound, the wolves get louder and louder until the white wolf throws his head back and roars into the moonlight. I look at Catherine. A tear swells in the corner of her eye and rolls down her cheek as she raises her right arm. She puts her hand to her heart and closes her eyes. The white wolf opens his jaws and with one final scream thrusts his head toward Catherine's throat.

The sound of the attack and the sight of blood dripping from the white wolf's muzzle is more than I can take. I turn and retch, vomiting until there is nothing left in me. I drop to my knees, completely broken by my failure. It's then that I hear the demonic laugh. Not of a wolf, but Baptiste standing over my sister, laughing, his face covered in blood.

That's the image I wake up to. I know it's a nightmare. But that doesn't mean it's not real.

The nightmare leaves me angry and with a pounding headache. I pop four Ibuprofen and take a hot shower until I feel the pain starting to ease away. I stand under the warm spray for another ten minutes and then turn off the water. Only then do I hear my cell ringing from my bedroom. I throw a towel around my middle and drip my way from the bathroom to the edge of my bed. I pick up my phone and a jolt races through me. The devil is calling.

"Baptiste?" I question into the phone. My dream has left me with no niceties and very little civility where this wolf is concerned.

"Mr. Hardy?" he answers somewhat warmly. "I'm sorry it's taken me so long to return your call." The greatest oversight there's ever been is assuming evil isn't smart, calculating, and polite. "I'm sure you can appreciate the last week has been a bit hectic and… complicated."

Half of me wants to tell this fuck where he can go. Thankfully, the other half remembers the mission and that there's a higher calling here than the momentary rush of exploding into the phone.

"I would imagine," I answer, taking a deep breath to calm down. "What happened?"

"I would like to tell you, but I'd prefer to tell you in person. Your experience was most unfortunate, and I assure you, this is not how I do business. I have a resolution that I think you will find very intriguing. Are you available for a quick meet at say, 2 o'clock?"

"I can make that work," I say, giving him nothing.

"Fine. Are you familiar with the beach in Santa Monica?"

"I am."

"Good. I will meet you in front of that blue diner with the palm tree on the wall. I believe it's called The Kitchen. Thank you Jake."

"Sounds…" I start, but Baptiste is gone before I can finish answering. Here we go.

The Kitchen has been a fixture in Santa Monica since the '40s. Anyone who's anyone in the history of Hollywood has eaten here at three in the afternoon or four in the morning for what's easily some of the best comfort food in the country. I've landed here after many a long run and unlike most things in L.A., The Kitchen actually makes good on the legend.

Not sure where this might go, I decide to drive the half mile to the beach in case I need my car for something. I park just up the beach from the diner and take the winding sidewalk weaving between the palms. I arrive at 1:45 for our two o'clock meet and find Baptiste sitting on the metal bench in front of the restaurant. He's dressed in cream slacks, a billowy linen shirt, and a large straw hat as though he's readying for a trip to Panama. Dark sunglasses shade his eyes, but when he senses me walking toward the bench, he takes off his glasses, hangs them over the front of his shirt, and stands to greet me.

"Thank you for meeting me, Jake," Baptiste says extending his hand. Now in front of him again, I'm reminded just how tall this man is, how broad, and how massive his hands are. I squeeze his hand because I have to and force a smile. "I hope this location wasn't too inconvenient."

"It's fine," I answer. For the last few hours, I've been considering how to play this and I'm convinced that strength is the best way to go at him. Baptiste is an apex predator and at his core, strength is the only thing he understands. I drop his hand, look the man in the eye, and start the dance. "You want to tell me what the fuck happened at Highland Canyon?"

"Sure," Baptiste answers with a slight cock of his head. "Walk with me."

Just like Angelo had done a few days earlier, Baptiste starts off across the sand toward the ocean to give our conversation the privacy it requires.

"Let me say again to you how much I regret the experience you had at the Highland Canyon, especially it being your first taste with us. Had I known what was happening, I assure you, I would have directed you to someplace different. I will say, I appreciated your call."

"I just had a feeling she might be one of yours and if so, you might want to know."

"You were correct on both counts. Jasmine was an exceptional woman. What happened to her was unfortunate."

"Unfortunate?" I question. "It was criminal."

"However sad, the poor girl jumped to her death. I'm not sure I see the crime in that."

"Did you see any pictures of her," I ask, trying not to completely explode.

"I did not. As we were not technically family, I have no access to the crime photos. Besides, the poor bitch left my primary police contact in the room she jumped from with the back of his skull blown out. So, no. I did not see her."

"Well, I did," I say stopping and turning to Baptiste. "And that 'poor bitch,' had been beaten within an inch of her life. Her body was almost black from the bruising and her face was so swollen, she almost didn't look real. Whoever your police buddy was, he tortured that girl. If she's the one who shot him, it was because she was fighting for her life."

"I suppose the real question is what you believe that life is worth," Baptiste answers. "Do you honestly believe the life of a whore is equivalent to that of a police captain?"

"From your tone I'm guessing you don't," I say.

"No, I do not," he answers stoically looking out over the Pacific. Baptiste pauses, taking a long, deep breath and squares around, looking me in the eye. "Jake, God made man in His own image. Man, and man alone. Women… were an afterthought. Taken from a rib and crafted into something with one purpose – to be pleasing to men. To be caregivers and to breed. Too many men, and certainly too many women, have forgotten that. We've gotten weak, Jake. Where are the men who embraced manifest destiny, the ones who built this country from nothing with their bare hands? The strong, virile, unrelenting swinging dicks who saw what they wanted and took it! Carnegie. Rockefeller. Vanderbilt. Sinatra. I'm talking about the fucking titans Jake. If Jack Kennedy was president today, he'd have pussy hand-delivered to the White House lobby five nights a week without giving the first fuck about who saw it arrive. Women are the most glorious, delicious, satisfying things that have ever been created and never more so than when they know their place. Women were made to be givers, Jake. We, are the takers."

The smile on Baptiste's face and the fire glowing behind his eyes tell me he's just warming up. This is my opportunity to dig deep and see what I can get out of him. Any fears I had that he knew who I was, or what I do, are gone. I'm just another high-dollar revenue stream for this delusional prick. Another prospective soldier in his growing army of entitled males who think using and abusing women and young girls isn't just an indulgence but their God-given right. It's unbelievable that Baptiste believes the putrid shit pouring out of his mouth, but he does. The greatest pleasure I ever have will be burning this motherfucker to the ground.

"You've got, what… six restaurants with the private parties now?" I ask him.

"Seven," he corrects me. "We just opened in Houston, and we have plans to open a dozen more in the next two years." Jesus. If Baptiste scales at that rate, he'll be pulling in four or five million a month and that buys a lot of girls overseas.

"That's impressive," I say praising him. "Awful lot of um… vintages… to keep track of."

"Jake, the greatest joy for any Master Sommelier isn't drinking the wine. It's building the wine cellar and sharing that passion with others who appreciate the exclusivity and value of the curation. I am building the most exclusive collection the world has ever seen and within five years, it will also be the most coveted. You are meeting me at the perfect moment in history Jake. Eventually, this enterprise will only cater to an elite membership who will have the world's most beautiful and attentive women at their fingers any time they want them. For a modest annual contribution, you'll be able to choose whatever race, nationality, body type, eye color, hair color, fetish, and personality type you want, and they will show up when and where you want them within 24 hours."

"That's visionary," I say stroking his ego even more. "And what would said membership run?"

"To start, five million dollars per year," he says, his chest expanding.

"Five million dollars? To fuck on command? That is certainly exclusive."

"We don't all have your bone structure, Jake," Baptiste answers with a fake, self-deprecating smile. "With your build, I'm sure your cock is equally impressive."

"It gets the job done," I answer curtly.

"I'm sure it does," he says. "Enough about your endowment. Let's discuss why I asked you to meet me. As I said before, I regret the circumstances of our last transaction, and I would like to set things right with you. To that end, I would like to propose two options. First, I would be more than happy to arrange a new tasting with the vintage of your choosing taking care of any reasonable cost differential."

"That's very nice," I answer.

"But," Baptiste continues moving closer, "if you would prefer, I am planning an evening that is beyond exclusive, and I would like to offer you a seat at the table. For those accepted, the ask is $200,000. But to show you my degree of contrition and brotherhood, I am inviting you to join me for half of that."

"$100,000. That's gotta be one spectacular woman."

"It isn't one. It's five. All in the course of a single night. I cannot give you all of the details right now, but I'm confident this is an experience even you have not enjoyed. I don't need your answer today, but as you can imagine, there will be a long list of men who would love to take your place. Take the day to think about it and I will call you tomorrow for your answer. If you choose to stick with option one, that is fine with me. But believe me, option two will be the most satisfying, decadent night of your life."

It takes everything in me, but I reach out my hand. "I appreciate the generous offer," I say as he puts his hand in mine. "I will consider them both and look forward to giving you an answer tomorrow."

"I like you Jake," Baptiste says patting my shoulder with his other massive hand. "You sir are my kind of gentleman. Au Revoir." And with that, Baptiste pulls his sunglasses from his shirt, turns, and walks back toward the diner. I watch him as he strides through the sand, fighting to retain every detail of what he revealed to me about his plans. I wouldn't say I underestimated Baptiste, but he is far more calculating and meticulous than any other trafficker I've encountered. An exclusive society of men willing to pay five million dollars a year to satisfy every warped proclivity that controls them. There is a special circle of Hell for men like Jean-Michel Baptiste and watching him walk away, I already know the fastest way to send him there is to accept his offer. I just have to put my hands on $100,000.

36

For the first time in months, I sleep peacefully through the night without the aid of sleeping pills or the coming of nightmares.

Yesterday, when I got home from meeting Baptiste at the beach, I called my financial advisor to discuss where and how quickly I might be able to access $100,000. I gave her some story about wanting to do some renovation to the house and taking an extended vacation. Thanks to my Mother's trust, the house has been paid for since I bought it and with the market growth around Santa Monica, the value has only gone up. My advisor assured me a loan for a hundred grand won't be a problem and that I should be able to access it within a couple of weeks. I can only hope Baptiste's night of sin isn't sooner than that. It's not a small financial risk. Even if I nail this guy, there's no guarantee I'll ever see this money again. But if it gets me closer to my sister, it's worth the risk. I know my mother would agree.

Thinking of her, I pull a small photo album from the shelf by my bed and open it. There, in a plastic sleeve on the front page, is a picture of Julia Grace. It's faded and only a square Kodak snapshot, but it's the best picture of my mother I have. She is sitting on the porch at my grandparents' house in a cotton sundress. Her hair is pulled back into a ponytail and she's holding a cocktail, laughing. By any era's definition, my mother was a stunning woman. And even after all these years, her brilliant blue eyes still jump from her image. I miss her. I'm not sure I'll ever move past the bitterness of having her taken away so early and everything we missed, losing her so soon. How incredibly different our lives would be had she not died when she did. Yet another long, angry conversation I intend to have with God someday.

At 2pm, my cell phone rings with the call from Baptiste. Last night, I couldn't stop thinking about what he said to me, challenging masculinity and the very nature of what it means to be male and female. I have been playing the conversation I intend to have with him over and over in my head since mid-day yesterday and now, my moment of truth has arrived. I have come to realize that among traffickers, Baptiste is a whale, and I'm about to set the hook.

I press answer. "Jean-Michel."

"Hello Jake," he says warmly. "How are you?"

"Enlightened," I start.

"Enlightened?" he answers, his voice thick with intrigue. "Do tell."

"I'll be honest with you," I tell him. "In the moment, yesterday, I wasn't sure what to make of our conversation. But last night, I spent more than a few hours with a very nice bottle of Scotch thinking about what you said to me. About women and about men. You're right, we have gotten soft. We're afraid. We're fucking afraid. Toxic masculinity. Me Too. You want to buy a woman a drink? You've got to get a goddamn consent form signed and notarized first. You, my friend, are dead on. Men have been castrated and it's time for those of us who can, to grab the mantle and reestablish God's natural order."

"I'm glad to hear we are on the same page, Jake. As for the end of our conversation yesterday, I take it you're in for the second option?" Baptiste asks.

"You're goddamn right I'm in. Just tell me where to send the payment and when to show up."

"Outstanding!" he answers almost laughing. "I am beyond excited that you will be joining us. Ten years from now, we will look back and see this was the precipice of history, Jake. A new beginning unlike anything you or I have ever experienced."

"I'm in," I say again. "What's the plan?"

"Are you familiar with New Orleans?"

"I know it well. It's one of my favorite cities in the world."

"Splendid. If you know New Orleans, then I'm sure you know that in about six weeks' time, a certain football game is being played there along with all the peripheral celebration it entails. Clearly I will be there with a full menu of my associates, and I have scheduled our engagement for the night after the game. Here's what I can tell you now – as a part of your itinerary, you will meet my private jet at LAX the day before the game and fly nonstop to New Orleans. When you land, my car will pick you up and take you to a 5-star luxury hotel where I have booked a suite for you. For the two days prior to our engagement, feel free to enjoy the Empire of Sin at your leisure. As you know there are plenty of distractions for men like us but don't get too tuckered out. You will want as much energy as you can muster the night after the game. The morning of, I will call you and tell you when and where to meet the car for transportation to the night of your life. I could certainly tell you more, but I don't want to ruin the surprise. How does that sound?"

"It sounds like you've got this dialed in," I say.

"You have no idea," Baptiste answers with a serpentine swagger. "This is the kind of night men don't even dare to dream about."

"What about payment?" I ask.

"You remember Jessica from Lucifer? She will meet you at the hangar at LAX to receive payment before you board the jet for New Orleans. Jess will have means for encrypted electronic transfer to make your payment easy and secure. If, for some reason, you choose not to attend or are unable to complete the transaction at that time, then our agreement will be broken, and our relationship finished. I take great care to respect those I do business with and only require the same respect in return."

"With all respect," I challenge him, "that level of trust works both ways. I'll be there. But $100,000 is a lot of money and if you fuck me in any way, I assure you, there will be consequences."

"Of course," Baptiste says smoothly. "But I assure you Jake, it will not be me fucking you but five of the most exquisite women you've ever laid eyes on. Rest up. I look forward to seeing you in New Orleans." The screen turns black, but still not as dark as the hatred boiling inside me.

I will meet Baptiste again in a little more than a month's time. Still a week shy of the end of my suspension. I'd feel better going into this fully reinstated in case things go south and there are uncomfortable questions to answer, but my situation is what it is. As promised, I call Jon and fill him in on the last two days with Baptiste and the trip to New Orleans. As I would expect, he quickly shifts into tactical strategy.

"Where is this night of debauchery supposed to take place," Jon asks. "One of the hotels?"

"I don't know," I tell him. "I won't know until the morning of."

"Seems like a lot of movement for a busy hotel. He could be renting one of those Greek Revival houses on Jackson or Philip. More than enough rooms. Just hide in plain sight."

"I don't think this guy is hiding from anything, Jon. He has this simmering arrogance that underlies everything he says, but I'm telling you, Baptiste is more controlled and calculating than any of the traffickers we've chased before. It's like he's three steps ahead of everyone else and he knows it. Getting caught is not even on his periphery."

"And that's when he'll make a mistake. What did you say this little party is costing you?"

"$100,000. Apparently, the normal ante is twice that but he's cutting me a break because of the incident with the jumper."

"A hundred grand's a lot, Jake. You mortgage the house?"

"They think I'm redoing the kitchen and celebrating my anniversary in the Maldives."

"What anniversary?"

"Exactly," I laugh.

"We'll get it back brother. It might take a while, but when we catch this son of a bitch and freeze his assets, we'll get your money."

"I'm alright. If I can get close enough to Baptiste to get the truth about Catherine, the money won't matter."

"It always matters," Bear answers. "But I hear you. The good news is DHS will already be in New Orleans looking for girls being trafficked in for the game. I'll be somewhere up on Canal or down near the waterfront."

"I appreciate it Jon, but it's still a week before the end of my sentence. I can't involve you in this without giving away that I'm playing outside the lines."

"I'm not talking about storming the gate, brother. Just letting you know I'm nearby if you get in a pinch and need the cavalry."

"Thanks man. Baptiste is a bad guy, but I don't think he's ready for open warfare in the middle of Magazine Street. He's more the type to slither out the back door. But I appreciate the backup Jon. Always."

Jon Joseph has been my salvation more times than I care to count. There's nothing I would love more than heading into this fight with him beside me. But there are some things in life you just have to do alone and for me, this is one of them. Like two rams with giant horns, the collision with my sister's abductor has been coming since I was 12 years old. For most of my life, I was sure the day of retribution would never come, but at last, it has. One month from now, the unspoken history between Jean-Michel Baptiste and myself with explode in a blaze of wrath he has no idea is coming. He is completely unaware of the conflagration about to consume him. But that doesn't change a thing. Somewhere in the bowels of a city built upon generations of lust, power, and prostitution, Baptiste will finally answer for his sins. Hell will rain. And only one of us will walk away alive.

37

I've had a month to prepare for my trip to New Orleans, but the morning of, I'm still packing the leather duffel sitting on the end of my bed. I'll only be gone for three days so clothes aren't really an issue. The question is whether Baptiste is paranoid enough to have muscle checking my carry-on at the hangar. Preparation being the prerequisite of valor, I take my 9mm from the wooden box on my dresser, snap it into a holster, and tuck it into the compartment beneath the bottom of the bag. Since I'm not flying commercial, I don't have to declare it and if I drive up to a waiting party at the airport, I can always pull it and hide it under the seat of my car.

The private hangars at LAX are only nine miles from my house, but it still takes almost an hour to get there. In his call to me a week ago, Baptiste said the flight plan called for wheels up at 11am and not to be late. I pull into a parking space next to the hangar at 10.20, not about to take any chances or cause any last-minute problems. Not seeing anyone extra, I get out of my car and walk into the massive aviation barn. The floors and walls are immaculate, and even the air smells clean. Inside sits a brand new, elite Twinjet aircraft. The sleek body is pearl white, with a blue-gray nose and tail highlighted by navy accents that make the plane look even faster. Walking to the back, I get a complete view of the tail, a green and purple hummingbird painted in the center.

"Mr. Hardy," Jessica calls from behind me. I turn and find the beautiful woman who first greeted me at Lucifer a little more than five weeks ago. She is dressed in an ivory shell, a richly tailored jacket, and a skirt that hugs her hips the same way the electric blue dress did the night I met her. With her left hand, she brushes a strand of auburn hair away from her face while extending her right hand in my direction.

"Hello Jess," I answer, taking her hand. "It's good to see you again."

"And you," she smiles. "Are you excited about your trip to New Orleans?"

"Very much," I say. "Are we expecting anyone else?"

"No. Just you and the crew. Flying time is three hours and forty-five minutes and there appears to be nothing but smooth air between here and there. I do hope you will find the accommodations on the jet to your liking."

"I'm sure they're fantastic," I smile at her. "My understanding was that I should handle my financial obligation for the trip with you."

"Yes sir. If you have the routing numbers for the transfer, I'll be happy to take care of that for you so you can board and have some time to relax before takeoff."

I hand Jessica a folded piece of paper worth more than I make in a year and say a silent prayer that one day the $100,000 will find its way back to me. She thanks me and walks into a small office at the side of the hangar. I shift the leather duffel on my shoulder and stare out the doors of the hangar at the other jets taking off from distant runways. Over the next 24 hours, more than a few of those planes will be heading to the same location I am to take part in the biggest sporting weekend of the year. I can't help but wonder what else those passengers will be taking part in during their trips to New Orleans.

Everyone knows the marketing phrase, "what happens in Vegas, stays in Vegas." It's Sin City's warped permission slip giving Vegas tourists some magical license to ignore any sense of morality. We expect that in Vegas. But the same thing happens in big cities across the country at every major sporting event, convention, music festival, and corporate retreat.

Jessica's "Mr. Hardy" startles me from my thoughts and from the tone of her voice, I perceive something may be off. But as I turn toward her voice, I see her smiling as she closes the distance between us. "You are all set," she says, again reaching for my hand and this time, grasping my hand with both of hers. "I sincerely hope this weekend brings you all the happiness you are searching for." Her warmth and sincerity make me question whether she truly understands the man and the enterprise she's working for. I suppose it's possible that she doesn't know all the details, but after the night at Lucifer, I find that highly unlikely. In truth, I decide this woman is just really good at what she does.

"It was lovely to see you again," she finishes, releasing my hand. "You may board when ready."

I take one last look out the hangar doors and walk up the stairs into Baptiste's jet. For all I know, he knows exactly who I am and we're not flying to New Orleans at all. At the top of the stairs, I'm greeted by name by the two pilots sitting in the cockpit. Men in their 30s who look strong, fit, and not the least bit consumed by suicidal tendencies to crash this plane into the Pacific. Or worse, to pitch me out the door from 27,000 feet. When you work undercover, part of the job is balancing paranoia with reality to make smart decisions that don't also restrict the mission. Possible that Baptiste is completely in the know and just wanted my money before taking me out? Anything is possible. But I'm still betting I'm good.

The normal seating capacity of the jet is 12, but Baptiste has configured this plane for eight. There are two seats – one on each side of the plane – with their backs to the cockpit. Two sets back-to-back in the center, and a final set with their backs to the tail. Each supple, gray leather seat is larger than a normal first class seat with a footrest that rises and falls on command. I walk to the back of the plane past the galley and put my bag in a small closet across from the lavatory. There's also a third door between the closet and lav, presumably for additional storage.

I walk back toward the front and settle into one of the seats facing the pilots. The first mate has closed the outer door to the plane as well as the cockpit door and I can feel the engines coming to life. Out the window, I see Jessica still standing attentively. Moments from now she will report to her boss that I am onboard and headed east.

From behind me, I hear the door in the back open and a stunning, lithe, 20-something Asian woman walks up the aisle and crouches down beside me, putting her hand on my forearm. Her black hair is pulled up and pinned on top of her head with the same heavy needles Rachel wore at the club on Sunset. This woman's skin is flawless, her small mouth smiling warmly. Her deep brown, almond-shaped eyes are the kind you could get lost in.

"Hello Mr. Hardy. My name is Mei-Ling. I am here to serve at your pleasure. If there is anything I can do to make your flight to New Orleans more enjoyable, please, let me know."

"Thank you, Mei-Ling."

"Would you like a drink before takeoff?"

"I would. Scotch if you have it," I say.

"Of course. I have this 24-year," she says holding up a $400 bottle of Scotch. "Would that be to your liking?"

"I think I can make do," I say.

"Wonderful," she answers smiling. "Welcome aboard."

By the time we're nearing Texas, I've killed more than half the bottle. It turns out $400 Scotch is pretty fucking good. Looking out the window, I watch the Southwest disappear behind us, remembering just how vast our country really is. So much space. So many places to hide. Hunting traffickers in Monaco or Vatican City would be easy. The United States is almost four million square miles.

My mind wanders back to Baptiste and the evening he's promised. I have no idea how many people are involved, where it will be, or what kind of security he'll have in tow. I'll have no backup, most likely no firearm, and no definitive plan going in. This is the literal definition of flying blind. But I'm ready. After six years in the Raiders and Special Ops, I'm no longer scared of improvisation. It's not my first choice, but I'm still here.

I'm staring down at the cold peaks of the Franklin Mountains north of El Paso when Mei-Ling comes back to offer me another three fingers of Scotch.

"I'm good," I say, cutting myself off. "Thank you Mei-Ling."

"Of course," she says walking behind me to secure the bottle back in the galley. I turn back to the window but immediately feel Mei-Ling return on my right. I look up and see her pulling the needles from her hair. She tosses her head and black tresses fall to her shoulders by each of her cheeks. She tosses the needles in the seat behind her and kneels down in front of me.

"We have about an hour and a half left in our trip," she says placing her hands on my knees and looking up at me. "Is there anything more I can do to make your trip more enjoyable?"

Knowing the kind of trip I'm taking, Mei-Ling's advance shouldn't surprise me. Baptiste is pulling out all the stops to deliver this ultimate fantasy he's selling. Even with half a bottle of Scotch in me, I can't help but stir looking at the gorgeous woman at my feet. When she reaches up and slowly runs her hand across my lap, I'm tempted to run this out and play through my cover. If Baptiste was on the plane, I might have to. But he's not. And when Mei-Ling grasps my zipper and slides it down, I gently take her hand and move it away.

"It's ok," she smiles up at me. "I'm here for you. No extra charge." She reaches again, trying to slide her hand through my zipper, but I catch her arm with one hand while raising my zipper with the other.

"Thank you Mei-Ling," I say as warmly as I can. "But not now." She suddenly looks frightened, and it occurs to me there may be some ramification for her for not pleasing me. She doesn't know me and doesn't know what story I might choose to tell Baptiste about the flight. Her entire existence is predicated on making men happy, whatever that takes. Anything short of that is failure and a threat.

"Come here Mei-Ling," I say pulling her to her feet and gesturing for her to sit on the seat opposite mine. "Please don't be offended. You are beautiful and any man would be lucky to spend 10 minutes with you. I'm just waiting until I get to New Orleans."

"Of course," she says, trying not to tremble. "I am here for whatever you would like. But if you don't want me…" she stops. "I just want you to be happy."

She wants me to be happy. As it does so often in the field, my heart aches for this woman and the whipped puppy she is. Men like Baptiste leverage every physical, mental, and emotional angle they can to control the women and girls they run. Mei-Ling is putting on a brave face, but I can still see the worry in her eyes. There's a part of me that wants to break cover, explain who I am and how I can rescue Mei-Ling from all of this, but I can't. Her discomfort over the unknown will pass and after I rave to Baptiste about the incredible things she could do, she might even get praised.

"Thank you Mei-Ling," I say reaching over and patting her hand. She leans down and takes my hand. She turns it and gently kisses my palm.

"If you change your mind, I'm right back there." She smiles and walks to the back of the plane.

An hour later, we touch down at Louis Armstrong Airport and taxi to a small terminal on the southern edge of the airfield. Mei-Ling brings my bag from the closet and bows as she wishes me an enjoyable stay in New Orleans. Once the pilot disengages the lock, he opens the door and we're hit with a strong blast of arctic air. While the city of palm trees and movie sets is still primarily in the 50s, February has brought winter to New Orleans with unexpectedly low temperatures in the 30s during the day and mid to low 20s at night. It's flat out cold here, but at least it's dry.

I walk down the stairs and find a black SUV waiting 15 feet away. A large, swarthy man with a heavy beard comes around from the driver's side and opens my door as the back hatch of the SUV rises. "Welcome to New Orleans Mr. Hardy," he says. "Let me take your bag for you." The big man throws my bag in the cargo area and presses the button to close the back. I start to get into the car, but a, "one moment sir," stops me. I turn and square myself to the driver.

He's six five if he's an inch and probably 300 pounds. I'm guessing Arabic from my time in Afghanistan, but he could just as easily be South American.

"Arms out please," he says to me. I have nothing to hide so I extend my arms to the side. "Nothing personal, sir," he says as he pats me down. "Standard security… for your safety." For my safety. Right. Finding nothing, he gives me two quick taps on the shoulder and gestures to the backseat. "Alright, let's go." I wonder if he'll check my bag at some point, but for now, he's not interested.

The driver jumps on I-10 for what he says is a quick 20 minute trip to the hotel. This time of day, traffic is light from the airport all the way into the French Quarter. It amazes me that less than four hours ago, I was 2,000 miles away on the other end of this same road.

We exit I-10 at Poydras and make two quick turns onto St. Charles, and Royal, coming to a stop in front of what has to be one of the crown jewels of old New Orleans hotels. Stepping out of the car, I can hear Bourbon Street two blocks to my left and smell the Mississippi River three streets to my right. A white and red awning with the hotel's name and crest stretches across the front entrance of the hotel. The outer façade is ornate, a creamy exterior accented by flower boxes and wrought iron railings.

I grab my bag and move to the front desk for check in. Baptiste has booked me into the Plantation Suite, one of the largest and grandest suites in the hotel. Apparently, a number of southern icons have stayed there from Twain to Faulkner.

Walking to the elevator, I pass the doors to the bar and see it's already beyond capacity. Even if I wanted to get soaked on the heavy pours New Orleans is famous for, it will be hours before there's an open seat. In this town, it's no great surprise to see a bar full at one in the afternoon, but with the game here in two days, there will be a million more people than normal in New Orleans, all trying to push their way into the French Quarter. What is already a circus normally will be all NOPD can handle.

I take the elevator to the top floor and find the Hemingway Suite at the end of the hall. I open the door and am met by a quiet undercurrent of Dixieland jazz coming from somewhere by the fireplace. There's a faint smell of Magnolias coming from a large candle burning in the bathroom and on the bar, I find a chilled bottle of champagne and a platter of fat, red strawberries, dunked in various chocolates and coated with nuts and candies. Beside them, there's a note from Baptiste.

"It begins," is all it says.

38

I crack open the bottle of champagne and fall back onto the sofa in the den. I set my glass down and pick up a book about the history of New Orleans sitting on the coffee table. Apparently, for a 20 year stretch, from 1897 to 1917, if you wanted to buy sex in New Orleans, you had to visit a sequestered 38-block red-light district between North Robertson, Iberville, Basin, and St. Louis. The area was called Storyville, named for the alderman who penned the legislation creating it. There was even a guide called "the blue book" that allowed clients to choose their favorite prostitutes from women who were black, white, Jewish, French, or Octoroon.

Even for those opposed to it, sex for hire seemed a moral contradiction. The Storyville ordinance passed by the New Orleans City Council in 1897 didn't try to abolish prostitution. Only to control it. And just for good measure, they put the new red-light district right by the train station to make it easy for those coming and going. Hop on, get off, be back in the office by three. Home by six.

The "houses" ran the gamut from shotgun shacks to the opulent mansions lining Basin Street. Those with 50 cents for a toss went to one end of the street. Those with five or even ten dollars frequented the other. It was only World War I and the threat of having the Navy troops stationed in New Orleans distracted by Storyville that closed it. In 1917, prostitution was officially made illegal in New Orleans.

For years, the Storyville jazz bars and nightclubs endured, as did prostitution, but only in the shadows. Then in 1940, most of Storyville was leveled to make room for New Deal housing projects. For some, it was a symbolic cleansing of moral decay. That's the tragic hypocrisy of the outrage regarding the buying and selling of human beings. For too many, if they can't see it, it doesn't exist.

The next morning as I'm running through what was Storyville and now the historic Faubourg Tremé neighborhood of New Orleans, it's clear to me very little of the former neighborhood has survived. It's said Tremé is the oldest black neighborhood in the United States. I can only imagine what stories these old Storyville streets could tell. It's 6:30 in the morning, but already you can smell the soul food cooking at Willie Lou's. If I was at the end of my run and not the beginning, I might just have to stop. But not today.

The temperature in New Orleans is 27 degrees and dropping. It must have rained during the night because thick icicles hang from the bottom of every wrought iron railing overlooking the French Quarter. Everything is covered in a thin sheen of ice that gives the city a reflective quality, bringing it to life every time light bounces off a building, tree, or sidewalk. The fact that city trucks came through this morning to salt the streets is the only reason I can even run.

The game is still more than 10 hours away, but already New Orleans is stirring. If there was ever an occasion for steady day drinking, this is the day and place to do it. On what seems to be our national day of excess, the same goes for other vices. For years there have been rumors that thousands of prostitutes flock to whatever city is holding a given sports championship. For a lot of reasons, that can't be proven. But empirically, I believe it's somewhat true. Walking down the street yesterday, walking through hotels, I know they're here. I see them. For those buying and selling pleasure, this town is low hanging fruit.

As I make the turn onto Canal and head toward the river, I see no fewer than six hotels and suddenly wonder whether Baptiste is sleeping inside one of them. Is it possible Catherine's here as well? I could be running beneath her window right now and neither of us would know it. I also wonder if Rachel is here. If she was truthful about working for Baptiste, I'm betting she is. I still need to thank her for the scar she left on my neck the last time I saw her. Between her and Baptiste, I'm running out of room for bitterness and anger. It will take everything I have to control myself tomorrow night and not blow whatever progress I've made getting closer to the devil. Vengeance will have its time and place. Tomorrow is about getting to the truth.

I head down Chartres Street, running parallel to the Mississippi until I get to Jackson Square. The park and its manicured gardens are quiet, the giant statue of Andrew Jackson keeping watch over the French Quarter. Starting to feel the cold, I exit the park to run back toward the hotel, but I feel something pulling me in the opposite direction. I'm flooded by an overwhelming feeling that there's something I need to see here. I look to my right and across the park, I see the towering spires of the St. Louis Cathedral rising into the air. I'm not being pulled. I'm being called.

Walking toward the church, I know I'm resigned to see tomorrow through no matter how it goes. To me it's no different than going into battle knowing I may have to take a life to protect those around me or lose mine in the process. In my head, I made peace with that a long time ago, but I'd be lying if I didn't admit my soul is restless. Only God knows what fate awaits me tomorrow, but I've done this long enough to know bad things happen and that there are no guarantees. Looking at the church, I could just walk away, go have my breakfast, and let things unfold as they may. But running away has never solved anything. I pull open the church's heavy wooden door and walk into a tall, vaulted entry toward the entrance to the sanctuary. It's time to make my peace with God.

39

While the outer façade and trinity of spires rising above the St. Louis Cathedral are impressive, they pale in comparison to the inner sanctum. The seat of the Roman Catholic Archdiocese of New Orleans, the sanctuary inside the Cathedral-Basilica of Saint Louis, King of France, is the model of an exquisite European cathedral, undoubtedly due to the French history that flows through New Orleans like the Mississippi. The ornate vaulted ceiling down the center of the church is covered in vivid murals as detailed and beautiful as anything in Rome. Tall stained glass windows and sculpted stations of the cross line the walls leading to the altar and the transept. At the back of the church, a marble cherub larger than I am holds an enormous font of Holy Water. I dip my fingers in the water and genuflect making the sign of the Cross. This early in the morning, the church is dim with just the light of candles and the barely rising sunlight starting to come through the colored windows to light the room. A subtle glow from somewhere below the altar illuminates the golden depiction of the Ascension above.

I walk to the front of the church and light candles for my mother and Catherine. Like the times I've gone to St. Matthew's in L.A., the scent of incense triggers memories of going to church with my mother and sister when we were kids. If I close my eyes, I can still see our tiny Catholic church in Sea Island and feel the buzz I felt in my nose the first time the priest walked by with a thurible filled with Frankincense and cinnamon, swinging it in our direction. I didn't realize it then sitting between my mother and Catherine, but my life would never be happier than that. My mother loved me. God loved me, and the promise of a good life was all in front of us.

God and I have had a tenuous relationship since then. We had many angry conversations in the black of night in Afghanistan, admittedly one-sided, and they certainly haven't stopped. I know God exists. I also know He has no obligation to answer anything I ask even if I do have more questions than any good Catholic is supposed to have. Still, there have been more than a few occasions when a burning bush would have been nice.

I close my eyes and pray over the candles before settling into the center of the front pew. The sanctuary is enormous, and yet this morning, it's completely quiet. Above me, the Ascended Christ is flanked by a pair of aqua, purple and orange stained glass windows. A light wash of jewel tones push up toward the Latin words on the wall above Him. *Ego Sum Via Veritas Et Vita.* I am the way and the truth and the life.

Lowering my gaze to the altar, I see an old black priest walk out from the right side of the transept. He has dark skin, tightly cropped white hair, and walks slightly hunched over as though he's carrying the weight of everyone in this parish. Whispering to himself, he makes his way across the altar and down the steps toward where I'm sitting. He jumps when he looks up and realizes there's someone sitting in the pews.

"Sorry Father," I say standing up. "I didn't mean to startle you."

"No apology necessary," he answers, putting his hand to his heart and continuing over to me. "One never needs to apologize for visiting God's house. I'm just old, that's all." He extends his hand, and I shake it. "Father Elijah Fontenot." I can't help but smile at his warm baritone voice and the accent that leaves no doubt he's from here.

"Jake Hardy. Pleasure to meet you Father."

"You as well. You know you're a little early for Mass, Jake. The first service isn't until nine."

"I was out running and just decided to come in for a minute," I answer him.

"Must be ordained. That outside door is supposed to be locked. I was just going out to open it up." Not exactly a burning bush, I thought, but it's a start. "How do you like our little church here?"

"I don't know about little," I say. "But it's beautiful. How old is it?"

"That depends," he answers. "There have been three churches on this site over the years. The first church was built in 1718 after the founding of New Orleans, but this cathedral has been here since 1789. It's the oldest cathedral in continuous use in the country along with a chapel out in Monterey."

"California? That's where I live," I say.

"My condolences," he answers with a gravelly laugh. "So, what can I do for you Jake? Did you come in to just look at the church, or is there something I can help you with?

"I don't want to bother you," I answer.

"Jake, the door is open, and Mass isn't for two hours. Tell me how I can help." I look at Father Elijah's face and his eyes lock with mine in the kind of connection that only happens when two people look directly into each other's eyes, not simply staring in each other's direction. "Tell me. What's troubling you son?" Father Fontenot gestures to the pew and we sit down, facing each other.

"Do you believe in evil, Father?" I ask.

"Most assuredly," he answers, without hesitation. "But evil is not the nameless, faceless entity most people fear. It's not some wicked phantasm seeking out good to destroy it. Evil is what bubbles up from inside each of us when we consider right and wrong and choose the latter. Free will is a gift from God. When we choose the wrong path, it causes suffering. And when that happens, it is we who are to blame for that evil, not God."

"And you believe God will hold us accountable for that."

"I believe the only way to the Father is through the Son and that those who choose a different path shouldn't be surprised when they reach a different destination. What's really troubling you, Jake?"

"In the next 24 hours, I will come face to face with the vilest evil you can imagine, and my job will be holding that evil accountable."

"Holding evil accountable is God's job, son," the priest responds gently.

"In Heaven, yes," I answer, "but on earth, Father, that responsibility falls to people like me."

"According to who?"

"The Department of Homeland Security and the United States government."

The old Black priest looks at me skeptically, folding his arms, but then purses his lips and leans back toward me. "Tell me."

"I track and eliminate human traffickers, Father. Truly evil men who kidnap young girls from all over the country, all over the world, and sell them to every kind of predator you can imagine. I know evil, Father. I've seen it. And I can tell you, fighting it feels hopeless. Every time I eliminate one threat, half a dozen more take their place. There are so many girls, Father. So many women suffering, waiting for us to find them while their souls are slowly being ripped apart piece by piece. You were called to be a priest? I was called to find these women and girls and punish those who abuse them. But what good am I if I can't save them? Surely God would ordain a mission like that."

"You are an instrument of God, Jake. There is no doubt in my mind you are doing God's work on earth, and He will give you the strength you require. I know it's not always on our time frame, but you will be delivered and so will the women and girls you are searching for. Are you familiar with the story about the Valley of Dry Bones from the Old Testament prophet Ezekiel?"

"I'm not," I answer.

"By chapter 37 of his book, Ezekiel is feeling a bit less than – kinda like you – and God takes him out to a valley full of dry bones. God asks Ezekiel if he believes the bones can become people again. The prophet looks at God and basically says, 'Why are you asking me? You'd know better than I would.' God tells Ezekiel to speak to the bones saying, 'O dry bones, listen to the words of God, for the Lord God says, 'See! I am going to make you live and breathe again! I will replace the flesh and muscles on you and cover you with skin. I will put breath into you, and you shall live and know I am the Lord.' Ezekiel does what God asks and suddenly, a massive rattling sound sweeps over the valley. The bones come together and as promised, muscle and flesh form over the bones followed by skin.

The bodies become fully human again, and yet, they are without life. They are breathless. God tells Ezekiel to call to the wind to fill the bodies with breath again, to fill them with His Spirit. Ezekiel obeys, calling to the four winds and in verse 10 it says, 'the bodies began breathing; they lived and stood up—a great army.'"

I'm not sure why, but I feel my eyes starting to well up. Father Elijah sees it and puts his hand on my shoulder, closing his grasp. "You are living in a valley of dry bones, Jake. Surrounded by the lost and the forgotten, but you, son, are the breath of life they are waiting for. Through you, God is breathing new life into these broken souls and raising up a renewed army of women rescued by a love a thousand times greater than the evil trying to destroy them. You have to believe that and not be afraid. That's where your strength will come from. Son, every time you confront evil, God is with you. That I know."

"And when I come face to face with the Devil himself?"

"You lean on Ephesians. 'Put on the whole armor of God, that you may be able to stand against the schemes of the Devil.' You planning on meeting up with Satan sometime soon?"

"When I was 12, a man… a trafficker took my sister from me. I've been searching for him for a decade and tomorrow, I will meet this man face to face. He is evil incarnate, Father. As dark as it comes. And now that I've found him, if my sister is still alive, I will do whatever it takes to get her back. If she's not, then perhaps I am simply God's vengeance on the wicked."

Father Elijah gives my shoulder one last squeeze and sits back knowing he's said everything he can say. We stand and he puts his arms around me, hugging me tightly.

"God bless you, Jake," he speaks softly between us. "With all my heart, I hope you find your sister. Go in peace, now, and always."

Taking one last look at the altar, I make my way back past the stations of the cross and out to the street to finish my run back to the hotel. Over the three mile stretch, I replay my conversation with Father Elijah and his final wish for peace. Even if I shouldn't be, I'm completely at peace about tomorrow and whatever may happen in my confrontation with Baptiste. There is one last thing I have to do in that regard. As soon as I get back to my room, I grab my cell and call Jon Joseph's number.

"Hey buddy, you OK?" he asks as soon as he picks up.

"I'm good. Just had a little chat with the priest at the St. Louis Cathedral by the river."

"Never hurts to ask for forgiveness before the sinning starts. Any word on tomorrow?"

"Not yet," I answer. "Supposed to get a call sometime tomorrow morning. Listen, Jon, I'm calling because I need a favor."

"Anything," he answers quickly. "You know that."

"Actually, it's not so much a favor as a promise. I really don't know how this is going to go tomorrow night with Baptiste. As much as I know, there's still a lot I don't, from the unknown location, to his protection, to whether he's armed. He's easily one or two steps ahead of me. There are just a lot of unknowns. You know me, and you know I'll fight like Hell, but if things go south…"

"Fuck that noise," Jon interrupts. "With your training, you'll take this guy."

"You don't know that. I hope that's true, and I know you do, but you said it yourself. Baptiste is an evil fuck with the world to lose and if I'm outgunned, or he realizes who I am, my situation could turn in a hurry."

"And if that happens, you pull back and live to fight another day."

"If Baptiste knows where Catherine is, you know I won't do that."

"First rule of combat Jake, make sure everyone comes home."

"That's the promise I need Bear. If something happens to me, you have to promise me you'll find Catherine and bring her home."

"That goes without saying, brother. If something goes wrong tomorrow, you have my word, I will find your sister."

"Thanks Jon," I answer him.

"Right after I kill the motherfucker who took you out."

This morning, Father Elijah spent an hour trying to convince me that in my constant battle with evil, God is and has always been right beside me. It occurs to me now, Jon Joseph has been my burning bush all along.

40

I wake up to rain and hail battering the sliding door that leads from my hotel bedroom out to the balcony. The temperature has risen out of the 20s, but looking out my window, the city still looks cold and wet. New Orleans is one of my favorite cities in the world, but more so when it's neither frigid nor pushing 100 degrees with matching humidity. Looking out over the French Quarter toward the Mississippi, I wonder if this time tomorrow, New Orleans will still be one of my favorite cities, or forever the burial place of my hope and pain.

Just before eleven, my cell rings and it's Jessica, Baptiste's associate from Lucifer and the hangar at LAX.

"Good morning Jessica," I say with a smile. This woman is so lovely, I want to like her. But then I remember she's joined at the hip with evil.

"Hello Jake. How's New Orleans?" she asks.

"It's great. Rainy."

"I hope the hotel is to your liking."

"It's very nice, thank you," I answer.

"I'm calling to give you the details about your extraordinary evening tonight. At 3pm, the driver who took you from the airport to the French Quarter will pick you up outside the hotel. No need to bring your bag. We will return you to the hotel tomorrow afternoon.

Once the driver picks you up, he will drive you to the marina at Grand Isle. At 5:30pm, you will board a boat that will take you to your destination. Please do not be late for your 3 o'clock pick up and once you arrive in Grand Isle, do not deviate from your instructions. Go straight to the dock and one of our associates will be waiting for you. Do you have any questions?"

I have a shit ton of questions, but nothing I care to divulge to Jess.

"I'm good," I say.

"I can only imagine," Jessica answers, an air of seduction in her voice. "Goodbye Mr. Hardy."

As soon as the call drops, I Google "Grand Isle." It's a barrier island two hours south of New Orleans that opens to the Gulf of Mexico. It's also inhabited. My gut tells me Baptiste has a secluded house on the island for tonight's festivities. It's far away from prying eyes and the island offers a quick getaway by sea if needed. It also keeps the girls isolated. Smart. But if the house is on the island, why would a boat be picking me up at the marina?

I expand the map of the island and see there are a dozen other barrier islands nearby. We could be going to any of them. Just because they're not overrun by tourists doesn't mean there aren't houses hiding the vilest of evil, lest we forget Little St. James Island and the atrocities there. Even with Google Earth, it's impossible to see what may or may not be out there. I'll have to wait until tonight to discover the truth as Baptiste intends.

I dial Jonny's number and get his voicemail. He said he was covering another case down here, so I'm not surprised he doesn't answer. I consider calling him back later, but I don't know what his schedule is or if I'll have the chance once the wheels are in motion.

On the click, I leave him a short message. "The party starts at five on Grand Isle. Thanks for keeping your promise. Love you brother." If that's the last time he hears my voice, he'll hear the two things that really matter.

After my call to Jon, I plug my phone in to charge and try to breathe. I'm like a caged tiger, pacing the room, my head a hurricane of choices both tactical and emotional. The rain has picked up even more from this morning and the temperature is hovering just above freezing. I can see icicles still stubbornly anchored to the iron balconies along Royal, and the pea-sized hail that hit my window this morning is still gathered by the rail outside the door. I down a bottle of water and look at the clock. Three hours until pickup.

By two o'clock I'm dressed and ready. I've considered taking and not taking my gun half a dozen times, but with the number of handoffs Jessica described this morning, there's a zero percent chance Baptiste won't have people patting me down. Two days ago, the driver at the airport didn't let me get in the car before checking me for a weapon. I double check the bottom of my bag to make sure the 9mm is still safe and it is. If God smiles, I'll be back to pick it up tomorrow. If not, I can only hope Jonny gets here before Baptiste's people do.

From across the room, I notice a subtle glow in the drapes hanging in front of the balcony door. I walk to the window and see the rain has finally stopped and a shaft of sunlight has found its way through the clouds. Pressing my hand to the glass, I can feel it's still frigid outside, but at least there's light. It's a momentary sense of calm that's quickly shattered by the sound of my cell ringing across the room. I move to pick up my phone and immediately, I feel the breath knocked out of me. The caller display says Rachel Meredith. I push answer and put the phone to my ear.

"Jake?" she asks with an anxious tone in her voice. "Are you there?"

"I am," is all I say, trying not to explode into a sea of questions and expletives.

"Listen, you can hate me later. Right now, I need you to hear me, and I need you to stay calm. I don't have much time and I need you to listen. I'm with Catherine."

"Bullshit you're with my sister. Why should I even…"

"Jake! Shut the fuck up. I don't have time to explain everything but there's something I need you to get your head around in the next few hours. When you reach your destination, I will be there and so will your sister. Do you hear what I'm saying? You will see Catherine tonight Jake. I'm telling you this because it's going to be a shock and it's going to be emotional. If you lose your shit, or come roaring in like some goddamn cowboy, you will not survive it and I'm not sure we will either. Do you understand me? Jake?"

"I hear you," I answer, collapsing onto a chair by the door.

"I know I'm the last person you think you can trust, but I've got you, Jake. Your sister, too. I promise, I've got you." She pauses, but I don't say anything in response. I'm not sure what to say. "Jake," Rachel says quietly, "I've had you all along. Breathe. I'll see you tonight." Click.

The phone call guts me. The last woman in the world I want to trust just promised to deliver my sister to me in a few hours. The last time I trusted Rachel she dropped me with 50,000 volts. Now, I'm supposed to blindly believe she's telling me the truth? It's beyond possible that she's setting me up. For all I know, she knows my sister's been dead for years and she's already told Baptiste who I am. What did she just say? "Listen to me." I should have listened when she stood in my house and told me she got close to me to find out what I knew about Baptiste. This entire party tonight could be one massive charade. Baptiste gets my hundred grand. They take out the agent who can fuck up their plans and the world still spins. There's only one woman in the world with the knowledge to play me and it's Rachel Meredith. I don't trust her.

But tonight, I have no choice.

41

At three on the nose, the black SUV pulls in front of the hotel and the driver from the airport gets out to greet me. To avoid a scene, he comes around the car and hugs me like we're old friends, checking my waistband, then quickly patting me down. He ushers me into the back seat and roars away from the curb like we're already late.

It's 108 miles from New Orleans to Grand Isle, but it takes us 20 minutes just to get out of the city. The heavy rain has stopped, but the sky is still spitting enough that the wipers never stop. The metronomic back and forth is both hypnotic and annoying and I'm thankful when they finally rest. The world passing outside the window looks drab and gray, as though the whole of southern Louisiana is depressed and taking a day off.

Around Golden Meadow, the land starts giving way to water with more and more of the ocean coming into view. It's an illusion, but as the marshes get bigger, the road ahead seems to narrow. On the left, a squadron of pelicans glides past, riding the cool air and occasionally diving for fish. I love this part of the country. The salty air. Small communities built by blue collar hands buoyed to the smell of the ocean and fish and shrimp not yet caught. Genuine, salt of the earth people who love God, country, and family in that order. They're a far cry from the men I'm about to meet who paid $200,000 for a night of pseudo-consensual rape.

As we reach Grand Isle, what little sunlight there was disappears behind a thick bank of dark clouds. We turn left and drive east across the island until we reach the entrance to the Grand Isle Marina.

Opening the door, I'm immediately hit with the chill in the air. The driver doesn't bother getting out of the car. He simply points and grunts toward the two large men in black standing at the head of the boardwalk that leads to the dock. We're here almost 20 minutes before the 5:30 departure, but I see no reason to postpone the inevitable. I shut the door and move toward the men in black, wondering if this was how it once felt to walk the plank.

The boardwalk is a straight shot to where the boat is tied off to a heavy mooring a couple hundred feet away. In the summertime, there would be a symphony of insects, frogs, and birds adding a soundtrack to my walk. But tonight, there's just an eerie silence with only the distant sounds of breaking waves in the background.

When I reach the two men, I discover my driver wasn't even close to being the least cordial of those in Baptiste's employ. Each of the thugs waiting for me are at least six feet two and outweigh me 20 to 30 pounds. The look on their faces is one of annoyed indifference and while I'm not sure what they think I might do, if they even sniffed a threat, I know they wouldn't hesitate to go for the pistols they have holstered to their hips.

"You Hardy?" asks the one with the beard. When I nod, he pulls my arms out to the side. Normally, I'd make some smartass comment about buying me dinner first, but this is not the time nor the place to fuck things up being a smartass.

"You carrying?" his partner asks while the bearded wonder pats me down.

"I'm not," I answer. I hold still as the big man's hands run over my shoulders, down my back and chest, around my waist, down the outside and up the inside of my legs, ending with a subtle pat against my zipper for good measure.

"He's good," he says clearing me to drop my arms. "The boat is at the end of the dock. Find a seat." The accent sounds Russian, but it could be from anywhere in the Baltics. My walk down the boardwalk is nothing short of eerie. It just feels like none of us should be here. The water is almost still, as though weighed down by the cold, as is the 45-foot flybridge yacht floating at the end of the dock. Stepping onto the boat, I look around me one last time, but with night quickly approaching, there's nothing to see.

I walk through the door of the main cabin and see four other men already seated, cocktails in their hands. I immediately recognize the tall Scandinavian from my first trip to Lucifer. He's wearing the same cashmere half-zip he had on that night. He nods with a subtle smirk I imagine he passes off as a smile. Next to him sits a large man with a heavy beard who looks like a thousand guys I saw in Iraq and Afghanistan. His gaze is intense, and I can tell he has no interest in making eye contact with me or anyone else. Across the room from them sits a fit, older man in his 60s who's in better shape than most agents I know. The only thing that betrays his age at all are the tortoise-shell trifocals he wears. When I enter the room, he's listening politely to the guy next to him, some 40-something salesprick talking way too loud for the room he's in. When he hears me enter, he turns, still jawing to the old man next to him, yet immediately dovetailing into some conversation with me.

"What do you say, chief?" he asks. I hate him on sight.

Before I can answer, the guys from the boardwalk crowd in behind me and move up to the bridge as the motor roars to life in the darkness. I grab the arm of an open captain's seat and sit as the boat moves off from the dock and picks up speed. I'm already in no frame of mind to talk to these assholes and assuming our trip to whatever nearby island will only be a matter of minutes, I swivel my chair and look out the window beside me. Only it's not a few minutes.

Half an hour after leaving the dock, we are surrounded by darkness and cutting through the waves with the engines maxed. It's not lost on any of us that we would have reached any island close to Grand Isle long ago. We are heading into open water. But why? It's certainly possible that Baptiste took our money and is having us driven out 30 or 40 miles to be shot in the head, weighted down, and dumped so no one will ever find us. But I don't think that's it. He's too keen on repeat customers and though it sounds ridiculous, that would be rude. We're definitely heading somewhere. And after just under an hour at sea, that somewhere materializes from the frigid murk ahead.

At first, all I can see is a small, static grouping of lights on the horizon. But the closer we get, the more the lights spread out end to end and top to bottom. In the darkness, it's hard to tell what we're approaching. But as more and more lights appear, the dots connect. When I realize the true origin of the lights, I move through the door to the back of the boat for an unhindered and truly spectacular view of the 400-foot yacht coming into view. When our captain breaks to the port side to dock at the back of the behemoth we're approaching, I can see there are five stories illuminated with golden light and a large helipad at the top of the bow. A subtle cerulean glow lights the name "Phaethornis" in two-foot letters on the back of the ship and in a single moment, it becomes clear to me my worst concerns about the scope of Baptiste's operation are woefully inadequate.

I'm not just chasing a whale. I'm Ahab.

42

Back at Grand Isle, even in near darkness, the 45-foot yacht we boarded in the marina felt impressive. It's dwarfed by the floating fortress we're docking to now. The stern stretches nearly 70-feet across with dual staircases rising from a lower deck big enough to hold 100 people. Though first out to take a look on our approach, I am the last to set foot on the "Phaethornis." It's even more stunning up close. The brass railings. The custom curvature of the structure. The heavy wooden decks alone are laid in a tight herringbone pattern that must have taken weeks to finish. Under our feet, in the center of the bottom deck, there's a 12-foot inlaid mosaic of a teal-throated hummingbird I imagine took equally as long.

Looking up, I see Baptiste standing in between the staircases on the deck above us with his arms outstretched, wearing a tailored blue suit and an evil smile. "Gentleman," comes the distinctive, booming call from our host. "Welcome to Phaethornis and the greatest night of your lives. Please, come."

One by one, we ascend the lighted staircase and when we've all reached Baptiste, he leads us up a second staircase, through a large foyer, and into a towering, two-story dining room that can only be described as opulent. The floor and the six columns framing the 25 by 40 foot room are all made from ivory-colored Italian marble. Each wall is adorned with vibrant, abstract art and in the center of the room, there's an enormous hand-carved wooden table that could easily seat 20 with gold edging and reliefs of hummingbirds.

Beyond the table at the far end of the room, two matching staircases curve up to the next level from each side.

"Have a seat," Baptiste says from the head of the table. "I know you are eager to start your evening."

The five of us gather around the end of the table closest to the staircases. I grab a seat on the right with the Scandinavian in the half-zip who sits between Baptiste and me. The table is fully set for 12 though I don't get the impression we'll be eating. Drinking will be another story. Across from me, there is a massive bar built into the wall with shelf upon shelf of the world's most exclusive liquors and a refrigerated section holding 100 bottles of fine wine.

"Tonight, my friends, is about pleasure. Your… unbridled pleasure. It's about scratching itches. Satisfying urges. Becoming the men you were made to be and taking what's yours. You are what we used to call conquistadors. You are strong, you are brave, and by God, you are entitled. In a moment, you will meet those entitlements and you will finally understand what I've been telling you, that tonight will be like nothing you've ever experienced. Tonight, we indulge in the finest the world has to offer on every level. We will eat. We will drink. And we will fuck!" Baptiste bellows with his arms raised and his face shaking with intensity. A cheer erupts from around the table as a wave of nausea moves through me. I force a smile, raising my fist.

"For more than 20 years I have traveled the globe in search of the finest vintages that could be found. Most I bought. Some I took. But tonight, I am sharing the absolute crème de la crème with you. What they can do with their bodies and mouths is the stuff of dreams. And gentlemen, every dream you've ever had is about to come true."

Baptiste turns his back to us and shifts his gaze to the top of the staircases. He raises his arms as if asking for a hug, and with some overmodulated press in his voice, he becomes the MC to the world's most horrific beauty pageant.

"From Odessa, Ukraine, meet Natalia." A truly gorgeous, athletically built woman walks to the top of the left staircase. Her blonde hair is pulled back revealing a long neckline and a beautiful, pale face. With the exception of the pendant necklace around her neck, she is naked. She's smiling, but anyone remotely attuned to truth can see it's forced. As she starts to walk down the stairs, it's apparent from the sway of her body that she's real. There is nothing artificial about her. Nothing manufactured. Baptiste has taken what was truly pure and beautiful and conserved it, all while simultaneously destroying it from the inside out. At the bottom of the stairs, Natalia makes her way to Baptiste, kisses him cradling the back of his head with her hand, and then moves to the right of him, standing a few feet in front of where the Scandinavian and I are sitting. Smiling like a proud father, Baptiste turns back to the top of the stairs.

"From Monterey, Mexico, meet Sofia," he says triumphantly. A sun-kissed woman, equally stunning as the first, moves to the top of the right staircase. Her black hair is pulled up and she too is adorned in a necklace and no more. She's of medium height, fit, busty, and short through the middle. She's absolutely beautiful and Baptiste is right, the stuff of dreams. Her skin is flawless with a skin tone that could be Mexican, Italian, Spanish, or Greek. As she moves down the stairs, she exudes a confident air that screams "you may buy me, but you'll never own me." Passing in front of us, I can see the hummingbird tattoo at the back of her hairline. Looking over at Natalia, I can see she too has the mark of the sommelier. Sofia kisses Baptiste gently and moves to his left.

"Next, meet Zuri from Lagos, Nigeria." The dark brown woman who walks to the top of the left staircase looks as though she could have been sculpted. Her face is an oval shape with large eyes, taut cheeks, an elegant nose, and supple lips perfectly framed by the curve of her chin. Her hair is cut tightly to her head and her long neck would give poets pause. Even from here, I can see she too has the hummingbird tattoo. I can see it because Baptiste has rendered it in white ink. She's thinner and more muscular than the first two women, but in demeanor, a contradiction of strength and resignation. She moves down the stairs with the grace of a queen, kisses Baptiste like the others and takes her place in front of me beside Natalia.

I'm suddenly conscious that my heart is beating faster, and I can feel beads of sweat dripping between my shoulder blades. Baptiste has introduced three women which only leaves two more. I don't know if I'm more anxious about Catherine being here or not being here, but given the choice, I'd certainly choose the former. The two thugs from the boat are somewhere outside, but other than them, I haven't seen anyone to deal with except Baptiste. With his ego, he probably captains this ship himself but even if there is a true captain, I don't see him taking a bullet for a guy like Baptiste. My first order is finding a way to immobilize the two assholes who patted me down. Then I can deal with Baptiste. My mind drifts from Baptiste to his guards to my sister, but a familiar name snaps me back to attention.

"From Los Angeles, California, this… is Rachel." As soon as Rachel reaches the top of the right staircase, I can see her looking down, scanning the table looking for me. We lock eyes and in my gut, I question whether I'm looking at an adversary or an ally. She smiles, but that does nothing to settle me. I've fallen for that smile twice before. Though I can vividly remember Rachel from her night in my bedroom, it's strange to see her standing naked at the top of the stairs. I know that body. I've explored every inch of it. But here, it almost seems foreign, as though the change in context somehow makes her not real. It's safer to feel that. And yet with every step Rachel takes down the staircase, I feel my heart race and my breath catch. I want to believe in her. Tonight, I have to. When Rachel kisses Baptiste, my stomach turns. I can only imagine how it makes her feel. She takes her place next to Sofia and looks at me, pleading with her eyes for me to keep my shit together. Rachel knows what's coming next.

"Gentlemen, I promised you every inch of five extraordinary women and five you shall have. From Sea Island, Georgia, feast your eyes on the exquisite… Catherine." I have waited 20 years for this moment. I have seen my sister repeatedly in my dreams, but it all pales to seeing her walk to the top of the stairs. The last time I saw Catherine, she was 12. A small, skinny kid kicking and screaming for her brother to save her. The Catherine at the top of the left staircase is a jaw dropping, statuesque woman. Breathtaking, all grown up, and still with the piercing blue eyes seared into my memory. Like the others, Catherine's chestnut hair is pulled up revealing the hummingbird at the bottom of her hairline. Looking at all five women, I realize having them all wear their hair up is intentional. Baptiste wants us to see the hummingbirds. Just another reminder that these women belong to him. He owns them. We're just renting them for a few hours.

When Catherine starts walking down the stairs, part of me wants to run to her and cover her nakedness, while another part wants to explode out of my chair and break Baptiste's neck where he stands. When she reaches the bottom step just 10 feet away, my eyes suddenly well up. I say a silent prayer for the patience and restraint to see this through. But when Catherine kisses Baptiste and moves beside him, it's all I can do to choke down the hatred and anxiety threatening to drop me on the spot.

"Tears, Jake?" Baptiste barks, pulling me out of my head. "I like a man who can appreciate true beauty. And I think you'll agree, the women in front of you now are as beautiful as God ever created. There's not a man in the world who wouldn't give anything to savor one of these goddesses for an hour," he chides, raising the volume and pace of his voice. "But tonight, you shall enter the gates of paradise not once, not twice, but five separate times. Five uniquely sensual experiences that will nurture your soul and fan the inferno inside you that the rest of the world is trying so desperately to snuff out. You are Alpha males! It's time to fucking act like it."

Stealing glances around me, I watch the others consume Baptiste's misogynistic bullshit as fast as he can dish it out. It's just like the night by the fire in the club under Lucifer, only now, there are five gorgeous, naked women standing three feet in front of them. If any of them started frothing at the mouth, it wouldn't be surprising.

"Rachel, would you please do us the honor of pouring the wine?" Dropping back behind Baptiste, Rachel moves to the massive bar on the wall across from me. There are four bottles of Cabernet already open on the countertop beside a round, crystal decanter with a tapered swan's neck throat. One by one, Rachel pours the wine into the vessel slowly letting it breathe.

"To toast our evening properly, I have chosen an exceptional, 2013 robust Italian red that will literally dance on your tongue. Chocolate, plum, violet… these are just the first of the many flavors you will enjoy before the sun rises tomorrow."

As Baptiste holds court, I look over at Rachel pouring the wine. She's pouring with her left hand and without looking at me, very subtly bounces her right with a flat palm signaling me to stay calm. To anyone else, it appears she's merely counterbalancing. But I understand her gesture. She knows this is killing me, but she also knows I have to trust her. When the fourth bottle is poured, Rachel picks up the decanter and brings it to the table where she fills the large wine goblets in front of each of us including Baptiste.

"To enhance your pleasure, I have placed bowls of some familiar friends on the table in front of you," he says. "You will also find them in each of your bedrooms. Just to be clear, the diamond pills are Sildenafil, the ovals are Ecstasy, and the bowl of white powder was a personal gift from Pablo Escobar. You will find no finer cocaine anywhere on the planet. I invite you to enjoy these things to your heart's content. Just don't overdo it. There are no refunds for any failure to perform," he notes with a laugh.

When Rachel has finished filling our glasses with $2,500 wine, Baptiste reaches for his goblet, but then hesitates, looking instead at the Cocaine sitting on the end of the table. He's eyeing the bowl like an addict who's been sober for a decade and suddenly finds himself face to face with his chemical nemesis. Slowly, and almost lovingly, Baptiste dips two fingers into his wine glass and swirls them around the liquid inside. He watches the wine spinning in his glass, transfixed, and once his fingers are good and wet, he pulls them out of the wine and rolls them in the bowl of Cocaine. Holding up his coated fingers, he looks at each of us and smiles. I'm not sure if I expect him to put them in his nose, or his mouth, but he does neither. Instead, he turns to Catherine and puts his fingers between her legs.

I'm not sure how long I blacked out for, but it couldn't have been long. The rage and anxiety flooding through me when I saw

Catherine gasp short circuited any sense of reality. Inside my head, I can hear my heart thundering. I can hear the in and out bellows of my labored breathing. The only clear thought in my head is to kill the man in front of me and to make it as slow and painful as possible. My instinct is to strike now while his back is turned. But looking left, I realize the men in black from the boat have joined the party and are flanking us on both sides of the room. I'm quick, but even I can't outrun bullets coming from two different directions. I take a deep breath and pinch my side hoping the pain will shock me back into reality. When I look up, Baptiste has his glass raised and is giving some long elaborate toast. In my head, his voice is low and muffled like he's deep in a tunnel. But then in one quick swoosh, his voice returns to full volume.

"To the night of your lives," is all I hear him say.

43

The naked women standing in front of us are trying to smile and make eye contact with each of us. No doubt Baptiste has coached them to try and make some connection. We are not, after all, some regular Johns. Each of the men around this table paid $200,000 for the privilege of tonight's experience and I'm sure each of the women were instructed to make sure we get our money's worth. Not that the girls will see any of it. If they're spectacular, Baptiste might give them a crack on the ass and a night off at his discretion.

More than once, Catherine has locked eyes with me with a forced smile, but as soon as she does, she quickly shifts her gaze to one of the others. She clearly doesn't recognize me, which breaks my heart. But I can't blame her. For Catherine's protection, I'm betting Rachel hasn't said a word about me. She's endured what I'm sure is a brutal 20 years with Baptiste and at this point, I imagine to her, one man pretty well looks like any other.

"So, here's how tonight is going to work," Baptiste starts after downing half his glass of wine. "Each of you will select one of the eight bedrooms on this level for your own. You may choose any bedroom on board except the Master upstairs. Once you choose a room, feel free to relax, take a shower, pop a pill, change into or out of any clothing you'd like. At 9 o'clock, each of you will be joined by one of these exceptional lovers for 90 minutes. You will not know which one is coming until they arrive, but remember, you will all be given time with each of them. After the first hour and a half, the girls will leave to freshen up for their next date and I encourage you to do the same. The second date will commence at 11pm, followed by the other three at 1am, 3am, and 5am. Under no circumstances are you to leave any outward physical marks on any of these bodies, but other than that, they are here to please you however you choose."

While we take in the rules of the game, Baptiste downs the rest of his wine and fills his glass again from the decanter. He takes another long pull and sets his glass back on the end of the table.

"Now before I release you to your rooms, I do have one little surprise for you. It's a bit unexpected, but something I think at least a few of you may find enticing. Sacha," he says turning to the tallest man in black, "the appetizer please."

Baptiste's thug disappears into the space behind the staircases and reemerges dragging a young girl by her arm. She is dressed in a pink nightgown and wearing a red sleep mask over her eyes. Her blonde hair falls past her shoulders and is vibrating with the shake in the little girl's body. Looking at her and from the pitch of her squeal when the man yanks her forward, I'm betting she can't be much older than 16. The second Natalia hears the girl's cry, she turns to her and an involuntary "Nyet!" escapes her lips. She spins her head the other way locking eyes with Baptiste, entreating him for mercy. He returns her gaze with a mix of schadenfreude and revenge. As Natalia's eyes fill with tears, she faces back to the front mumbling "Nyet. Nyet. Nyet." to herself over and over again. My intuition from hunting hundreds of trackers tells me the little girl is her sister, or at the very least, someone she knows. Either way, part of this is about punishing Natalia in some way. For what, only God and Baptiste know.

"Gentlemen, meet Mila. A delicious 2009 vintage from a small Black Sea village outside Odessa." 2009. Jesus, she's 15. "She is pure. She is untouched. And tonight, the bidding for her virginity starts at $250,000."

The Scandinavian beside me doesn't flinch and neither do I, but across the table three hands immediately fly into the air. I'm reminded there are still pathological circles in the world where admitting you prefer young girls isn't something to be feared. I look across the table and make a mental note to remember what these sick fucks look like so I can find them and put them down after this is all over.

"Do I hear $300,000?" Baptiste barks.

"$300,000," the fucking chatty Cathy salesman says bowing out his chest.

"$350,000" counters the older man, again, raising his arm high.

"$350…" Baptiste starts until the heavy set Middle Eastern man cuts him off cold.

"One million dollars," he says slamming his hand against the table. He glares at the two men who were bidding against him and appropriately, they shrink like scrotums in icy water. He picks up his glass of red wine and kills the entire goblet at once.

"SOLD!" Baptiste screams refilling the man's glass with the rich Italian burgundy from the decanter.

It's all I can do not to vomit on the table. I reach for my wine to wash away my disgust, but then leave the glass on the table. I need all my wits about me tonight and wine isn't going to help that. Baptiste is probably offended that I haven't yet tasted his $2,500 aperitif, but right now, I could give a fuck. That vile motherfucker just auctioned off a 15-year-old girl's virginity for a million dollars and I was right here to see it. Now, I just have to pray I can disarm the two goons and get back before the Afghan across from me tries to collect on his winning bid.

While Baptiste moves to shake hands with the man who just paid a mint to destroy a little girl's life, Rachel dutifully picks up the decanter and refills the rest of the goblets. When all the wine from the four bottles is gone, she puts the decanter back on the table and hands Baptiste his glass. He smiles and immediately raises it high.

"Gentlemen, a toast… to our friend Nasir… the first member of the Hummingbird Elite." In a rite of sick solidarity, each man raises his glass and downs the wine inside. I raise my glass feigning participation but put it back on the table without consuming a drop. If Baptiste notices, he doesn't say anything. He's busy celebrating the cool million he just made. This is part of the secret society he was talking about when we met on the beach in Santa Monica with an even darker twist. Hummingbird Elite. HE. Even the acronym for the name is misogynistic.

"If you'd like something else to drink, help yourself," Baptiste offers gesturing to the bar. "Otherwise, choose your bedroom and prepare for paradise."

As we push away from the table, I see Baptiste give Natalia a hateful glance and say something to her I can't hear. Wilting, she takes Mila's arm and leads the little girl down the hallway behind the staircases toward the bedrooms. Sofia, Zuri, Catherine, and Rachel follow.

Unconcerned about choosing the first bedroom, Nasir moves to the bar and fills a rocks glass with an aged Japanese whiskey while he continues talking with Baptiste. The Scandinavian also makes his way to the bar grabbing two glasses and a frosted bottle of vodka out of the freezer. I make a beeline for the closest bedroom I can find. I need central access. With what I have to do, I don't want to be trapped in a bedroom at the far end of the hall.

I open the door to the first bedroom and find a luxurious suite nicer than any hotel room I've ever seen. The room is dominated by a king-size bed set in a massive wooden frame and a curved wall of floor to ceiling windows overlooking the ocean. A large antique dresser anchors the wall just inside the door and on the far side of the bedroom between the bed and the bathroom lies a large sitting area with two contemporary chairs and a table. Under different circumstances, I would be thrilled to spend a lazy day and night in this room. But not tonight.

My heart is still hammering from earlier and I take long, deep breaths to calm myself. It would be easy to get consumed by what's in front of me, thinking about the consequences should I fail. But that isn't my mindset. Failure isn't an option. It never has been. The first thing I have to do is immobilize Baptiste's thugs, preferably without getting shot. Once they're out of the way, I will deal with Baptiste. Save the little girl. Save Catherine. Save everyone.

Putting my ear to the bedroom door, I listen for any movement in the hall but it's quiet. I put my head against the door and close my eyes, game filming one last time how to handle the two guys in black. I did enough stealthy recon in Afghanistan to know I can pull this off. All it takes is everything going right.

With one last heavy breath, I twist the knob and pull open my door. Rachel Meredith is standing there waiting. Naked, and laser focused.

44

Before I can react, Rachel pushes me back into the suite and shuts the door behind her.

"Nice job holding it together back there," she says turning to lock the door. "I can't begin to imagine how hard it was seeing Catherine next to Baptiste and not exploding when he pulled the little stunt with his fingers." If Rachel is trying to calm me down, her words are failing. Her hand on my chest is not. With what looks like genuine love in her eyes, she rubs her palm against my heart and taps my chest. "We're going to make it Jake, but you have to listen to me." I pause, the anxiety swelling inside me, and then nod.

"In about 15 minutes, these guys should be dead to the world. This afternoon when Jean-Michel sent me to set up the bar, I put 45 crushed up Diazepam in the bottom of the decanter."

"That's a month and a half worth of sleeping pills," I mutter starting to see a glimmer of light.

"All courtesy of you. I grabbed the two bottles in your bathroom before I left the night of the party. I've held on to them since, knowing this moment would come. I tried to subtly signal you not to drink the toasts, but thankfully you were already abstaining. Unfortunately, Baptiste's two scumbags weren't drinking so they're still alert and very much armed. I'm sure they have weapons stashed around the ship."

"You let me worry about yin and yang. You go make sure the Valium is working and try to find Mila. It's not too late to save that little girl."

"I will," Rachel says patting my chest. "You be careful. We're too close for you to go and get yourself killed. I just saw Sascha and Alexei heading toward the lower deck to smoke. You take care of those two fucks, and we're good." She's right. We are so close. I look deep into Rachel's eyes with a feeling of profound thanks. She grips the front of my shirt and pulls me into a kiss that lingers longer than it should. "You're welcome," she says. "Now go."

Opening the door, I look down the hall and see it's clear all the way to the grand dining room. I hurry through the corridor and pause to take a quick look at the top of the stairs. Baptiste may be drugged, but I'm sure he has a firearm nearby and even if he's half aware, if he sees me heading outside he could fuck this up royally. When I see the room is empty, I move quickly along the wall and out toward the rear deck. Rachel was right. Sascha and Alexei are standing on the bottom deck with their backs turned to me, smoking and jabbering in Russian.

Taking advantage of their position, I move in the opposite direction toward the front of the ship searching frantically along the outer deck for anything I can use as a weapon. I pass a number of utility and supply closets, one filled with two dozen life preservers, and another with a sign that says "Fishing" on the door. I'm almost to the staircase by the Helipad when I stop and move back to the Fishing closet. Seeing the area for the helicopter reminded me exactly what kind of ship we were on. People on 400-foot yachts, don't throw a line with a bobber off the back to see what bites. They hunt. Sharks. Grouper. Marlin. Large fish that require serious firepower. I open the door to the "fishing closet" and my intuition is immediately rewarded. There, hanging on the wall, are half a dozen spear guns and a quiver of extra spears. I grab two of the spear guns and the extra bag of barbs and retreat toward the Russians at the back of Phaethornis.

When I can see the back of the ship again, I notice there's only one man standing at the rail. It must be the man Rachel described as Alexei. The man who pulled the little girl into the dining room for Baptiste's sadistic auction was taller and thicker than the man I see. I don't know how far Sascha has moved away from his comrade, but it can't be that far. I have to make this as quick and quiet as possible.

I don't remember the last time I was thankful for all the night missions in Afghanistan, but I am tonight. Stealth is a learned skill, and it certainly helps to have the sound cover from the ocean. Staying low, I creep along the edge of the outer rail until I'm at the top of the stairs where Baptiste greeted us earlier. Alexei is standing on the lower deck just beyond the right staircase on the other side of the teal mosaic of the Phaethornis hummingbird. He's lit another cigarette and seems mesmerized by the ebb and flow of the waves moving past the ship. I watch him for almost a minute and realize he's no longer checking the spaces around him. He's forgotten the one cardinal rule of a protection detail and that's "never lose your concentration." His gaze is fixed out into the ocean. His hands are gripping the rail in front of him. His gun is in the holster on his right hip. Once he sees me coming, it will take him less than four seconds to grab his gun, turn and fire. That means I have to get this done in three.

I consider moving back through the dining room to the other side of the yacht to get behind where Alexei is standing, but if Sascha is on that side and it becomes two on one, this will be over before it starts. It has to be now.

At the bottom of the left staircase, I check the spear gun in my right hand to make sure the safety is off and then do the same with the one slung over my shoulder. They're both good to go. I look up and, as if on cue, Alexei turns his head to look at something off to his right. From a low crouch, I sprint toward the big Russian like a starving panther, the spear gun raised and ready to fire. When he finally notices the blur of motion approaching quickly from his left, he turns to me, reaching for his pistol, but he's too late. It turns out two seconds is all I needed. When I pull the trigger of the spear gun, I'm no more than three feet away from Alexei's head. The spear hits him in the throat, center cut, and drops him like a bag of rocks. Through a moderate gurgle, his body jerks a few times and then he's still. I turn him over and pull the heavy pistol from the holster on his hip. It's standard Russian military issue. I pop the clip and see the mag is full. One down.

I have no idea where Sascha is or whether he heard me take out his friend, but when a bullet whizzes past my head I have my answer to both questions. Sascha is on the second deck behind me, running toward the rail. Reflexively, I raise Alexei's gun over my head and blindly fire back toward Sascha's position while I'm running to dive behind a heavy oak table anchored to the deck. The table will give me plenty of cover, but from where Sascha is positioned above me, I'm pinned down. I'm not sure what kind of shot he is when he's not trying to run and shoot at the same time, but with any proficiency, it wouldn't be hard to pick me off should I try to run around the edge of the table.

"You have nowhere to go," he says in his deep, heavy Russian accent. He fires the pistol, and a bullet digs into the deck to my left. "Throw out my brother's pistol and come out and maybe you live." Two more shots ring out, chewing up the deck to my right. He has no intention of letting me live and if that really was his brother I killed, bad just got worse.

Hoping to get lucky, I lift the pistol over the crown of the table and blindly fire two shots toward the second deck. I pause, shifting my angle and direction, and fire two more.

"Not even close you Mudak," Sascha laughs. "You fucking Americans are so arrogant. You think you can just shoot without looking and the bullet will magically find its target. Well, I have news for you my friend, not this time. I have patience of Job, superior position, and 100 times more bullets than you. Come out and we ask Mr. Baptiste what to do with you."

No way Baptiste lets this guy shoot me. My lifetime value to him as a customer is far too high. But I know as well as Sascha does, the second I lift my head up, he'll shoot me. I could run. To the left, it's 15 feet from the table to the space under the upper deck, but I'd be running right into the big Russian's line of sight. If I go right across the hummingbird mosaic, it's probably 25 feet to cover, but more room to change direction. Either way, for a trained marksman, the shots aren't that tough, even hitting a moving target. The fact that both men carry military pistols makes me think they aren't run of the mill hired guns. Whether they are or aren't, I can't take the chance. Not with Catherine as close as a bedroom upstairs.

I still have both spear guns and the extra spears, but they pose the same issue as the pistol. I can't hit what I can't see.

"OK, for last time, throw down the gun and walk toward me with hands in the air."

When I don't respond, a volley of bullets flies over the top of my head, bouncing off the brass railing at the edge of the yacht with a loud clang.

"I'm done fucking with you!" he bellows from the upper deck. There's a long pause and then a stinging spray of bullets chews into the table and the decking on both sides of me. I don't know where he got it, but I can tell by the sound and stream, Sascha is now firing a machine gun. As some of the new shots tear through the railing, I realize the water is just six feet away. I consider my chances of diving off the back and somehow finding another way back on board without getting shot. Possible I live, but not likely that I save my sister. This time of year, hypothermia is real and even if I could get to the boat we took to get here, take it back to Grand Isle, and call in backup, by the time we found this yacht again, Baptiste and the girls would be gone.

Fuck. This cannot be how this ends. I run every scenario in my head and come to the conclusion I have one shot, literally. When he stops shooting or I hear him moving toward me, I'll have one chance to stand and fire. One or two seconds to find my target and hit it. I cradle my left hand under the barrel of the pistol and put my finger across the trigger with my right. I take a deep breath and whisper a promise to my sister I fully intend to keep. In truth, it's a prayer. This is in God's hands now.

As it often did in Afghanistan, my world shifts into slow motion. When I hear Sacha start screaming his final directive at me, something guttural in Russian, I rise from behind the table and take a bead on where he's standing. When he sees me, he pulls the automatic back to his shoulder and closes an eye preparing to fire. He never gets off a shot.

As I squeeze the trigger and feel the gun kick in my hand, the left half of Sascha's head disappears in a cloud of blood and bone. My adrenalin firing, I hit him twice more in the chest before he drops to the ground. I'm relieved, but my immediate thought is one of confusion. There's no way my first shot hit him in the head and even if it did, the angle wouldn't have had that reaction. A shot like that could only have come from beside me.

I look over my right shoulder and see the smaller yacht we took from Grand Isle still docked at the back of the Phaethornis. It sits in the shadow of the five decks rising above it, with only the front half of the bow enjoying a sliver of moonlight. But now, there's a second, smaller speed boat floating beside it. I drop the pistol to my side and lift a prayer of thanks. That's when Jon Joseph walks out of the shadows holding his rifle that was once again my salvation.

With a shake of my head and tears in my eyes, I move to the edge of the Phaethornis and grip Jonny's hand to help pull him to the ship. Even before he lands, I can hear him laughing. We embrace like we have after so many harrowing moments together, gripping each other in profound thanks.

"I put a tracker on your phone when we were in Houston in case I ever needed to find you. I hope you don't mind."

"I'll live," I answer, squeezing Bear even harder.

"Catherine," he says pulling back from me with a cautious hope in his eyes.

"She's here Jon. I saw her," I say, choking on my words.

Jon looks to the sky with a massive exhale, then back at me. "Go get her brother," he says grabbing the side of my face. "I'll take care of these assholes."

I hand Jonny the spear gun still slung over my shoulder and sprint up the stairs to find Baptiste, hoping Rachel's plan to knock him out with the Diazepam is working. No matter how much he had to drink, Baptiste is a big man, and drugs don't always react the way you hope they will. It doesn't matter. After what I just endured, I will handle anything he throws at me.

When I get to the dining room, it's still quiet and empty. I move past the table and take the stairs two at a time moving to the third level and the Master Suite where I'm betting Baptiste has gone. Unlike the second level that houses eight suites, the entire third level is comprised of the Master Suite on one side and a massive owner's living area with a den, home theater, gym, and library on the other. Listening at the bedroom door, I can hear Baptiste talking but I can't make out anything he's saying. If he's not praying, he should be.

Quietly turning the handle, I push open the door and see Baptiste sprawled out on the bed across the room. By the way he lifts his head when he hears the door, I can tell the drugs have started to kick in. He seems groggy, but he immediately recognizes me. Baptiste starts to smile. But when he fully registers the look on my face and the veins popping out on my forehead, his smile turns to arrogant defiance. Jean-Michel Baptiste still has no idea who I really am. But he had to know one day, retribution would finally come calling.

That day is today.

45

The second Baptiste sees the look on my face, he pushes up off the bed and moves to where I'm standing. The dark smile on his face masks whatever he's really thinking, but I'm sure he can tell I'm not here for extra towels.

"What's with the look, Jake?" he asks moving toward me on more solid legs than I would have expected. "Something wrong downstairs?"

"There's no end to what's wrong downstairs you sadistic motherfucker."

I could have played this a number of ways. But after two decades trying to find this man, tonight, my special forces training as an apex predator will be my blunt instrument of choice. Rage and adrenaline my fuel.

"You still don't recognize me, do you?" I ask him.

"Should I?" he answers. "I mean, other than the man who paid me $100,000 to live out some Alpha Male fantasy?"

If I had any question whether Baptiste would crater when finally confronted, now I know. He knows the balance has shifted and he's choosing aggression. I shouldn't be surprised that when evil is cornered, it comes out with teeth bared and claws at the ready.

"Twenty years ago, you took my sister from me and ripped my fucking life apart. Tonight, it's time to pay for your sins Baptiste."

"Jake," he says with sinister dismissal, "you have clearly mistaken me for someone else. I don't know your sister and up until a month ago, you and I had never met. I'm truly sorry if something unfortunate happened to you, I am. But I assure you, I played no part in it. Perhaps," he says leaning into my face, "you should talk with that sot father of yours. Oh wait," he says pausing, "He's dead."

My fist is balled before Baptiste finishes his sentence. I don't know if he was triggered by 20 years, the mention of a sister, or if he's been playing me all along, but there are no longer any mysteries. There are zero pretenses. Jean-Michel Baptiste knows exactly who I am, which means he understands what I'm here for.

I throw a punch toward his chin, but Baptiste takes a step back and catches my fist in his hand stopping it cold. "As for my sins," he says pushing my fist back toward me, "unless you are Jesus Christ in the flesh, I don't answer to you."

"I assure you," I say grabbing the front of Baptiste's shirt, "before the sun rises, you will."

With as much force as I can muster, I drive my knee up between Baptiste's legs and smash his cheek with a vicious left cross. He grunts, and grabs for my neck but misses, losing his balance and crashing to the floor. Before he can react, I drop onto his chest pinning his arms under my knees. With Baptiste on his back, any explosive action is limited and I'm heavy enough and strong enough to keep him from bucking me off. The man I've chased for 20 years is immobilized and defenseless. Yeah? Fuck him. I can see Baptiste's eyes fluttering, trying to make sense of what's happening to him. The drug is starting to kick in and he roars as reality sets in.

"I should kill you right here," I say feeling the years of hatred and rage coming to the surface.

"Yeah? Well go ahead. Kill me. I'm sure your sister will be very proud."

With a roar, I drive my fist into the side of Baptiste's jaw with every measure of strength I have. Immediately, blood starts to pool in his mouth.

"If you really are going to kill me, there's something you should know first," he says, fighting to focus his eyes on mine. He lifts his head and whispers, "Catherine… your sister…" He pauses and smiles. I lean in, suddenly panicked that I'm too late. Oh God!

"What did you do?" I bellow. His smile turns to a deep, rumbling laugh that builds from his chest. Roaring in pain, I hit him again, and again, and again and he's out. Alive, but unconscious. I sprint to the door and down the staircase to the second level. I skip the door to my bedroom and open the second. Sophia is there standing over the Scandinavian unconscious on the bed. I move to the third bedroom and find Zuri with a panicked look on her face. The older man lies naked and unresponsive at her feet.

Rachel meets me coming out of the fourth bedroom and hugs me, thankful to see I'm alive.

"Where is Baptiste?" she asks.

"Upstairs, unconscious. Where is Catherine?"

"Not in there," pointing to the bedroom she's exiting. "Natalia and Mila are in there, both safe. I told them to lock the door and not open it for anyone but me."

"I've got to find my sister. I think Baptiste…"

"Go!" Rachel orders. "I'll deal with Baptiste."

I open doors to two empty suites and then push through the door to the last bedroom. My heart drops. It's empty. I step inside and there's no one on the bed. No one on the floor. Every horrible scenario courses through my head. That motherfucker killed Catherine and threw her in the ocean. I'm about to go race through the rest of the ship looking when I hear the faint sound of crying. I stop and turn my head. It's coming from the bathroom. I move around the bed to the entrance to the bathroom and find the chatty salesdick from before dead on the tile. My sister is standing over him crying and splattered in blood. Looking at me wide-eyed, her ice blue eyes ignite my soul.

"We were in the shower, and then his eyes closed, and then he just fell through the glass," she says a bit panicked. Worried, I'm sure, there will be hell to pay from any man looking to blame her. "I think he cut his neck."

There's a thick shard of jagged glass sticking out of his neck right next to his carotid artery. The guy bled out in a matter of minutes.

I step into the bathroom, grab one of the large towels folded on the counter and hand it to Catherine. She takes it timidly, as though there might be some punishment for accepting it. There is no joy in her face. No relief. In her mind, I've simply come to take the dead man's place. I look into her eyes and put my palms together in front of my chest. Now a foot away from her, I realize in a moment how exceptionally beautiful my sister is and all that I've missed with her gone. A sob catches in my throat as I try to smile.

"I never stopped looking for you," I say, trying not to lose my composure.

"Me?" she asks confused. "Do I know you?"

"Catherine, it's Jake," I say.

"Jake… Have we met before?" she questions, gently shaking her head back and forth.

"Catherine," I say reaching out my hand. "It's me… It's Jake."

Nervously, her eyes dart right and left, trying to make sense of what I'm saying to her. But then her head snaps and she locks eyes with me. Light fills her as I see the recognition dawn in her eyes. She explodes across the two feet between us and throws her arms around my neck, squeezing me as tightly as she can. "Oh God," is all she says as I wrap my arms around her and hold her. "Oh God!" I feel her move in my embrace as heaving breaths and racking sobs start to consume her. But I'm not letting go. I won't ever let go again. I too start to cry, but not for me. As hard as this has been for me, it was always a thousand times worse for her.

"How did you find me?" she asks pulling back to look at my face.

"It's a very, very long story and I will tell you all of it. But right now, there's one more thing we have to take care of to make sure all of this is over."

I take off my shirt and give it to Catherine to wear. I tell her what I have to do up in the Master bedroom and without blinking, she sprints out of the suite heading for the stairs.

When we reach the hallway outside the Master, I'm struck by the frigid temperature. Entering the suite, I understand why it's so cold. Rachel has opened the French doors that lead out to the balcony from the bedroom and with the outside temperature still in the high 20s, the cold night air has made its way in and through the entire third level. It's wet and heavy like it was in the French Quarter, with the same drifts of icicles hanging from the balconies above. Looking at the bed, I understand the want for the cold.

Rachel has moved Baptiste to the bed, and has him lying naked on his stomach, his arms and legs tethered tightly to the four posts of the King-size bed. She is tightening the last of the straps and clearly wants him alert for whatever she has planned. A responsible Homeland agent in good standing would stop this immediately and place Baptiste in custody. It's a good thing I'm suspended and not technically here at all.

Rachel beams when she sees me come through the door with Catherine. She, as much as anyone, knows what finding her means to me.

"I had you," she says, as my heart swells.

With the cold blowing in, Jean-Michel starts to stir on the bed. When he comes to enough to realize his situation, he tries to violently pull at the straps, but they are taut and secure. He's not going anywhere but Hell.

I move to the top of the bed toward Baptiste's head while Rachel circles behind me to the foot. For the first time, I see she has another leather strap in her hand. From this position, Baptiste can't see a thing without breaking his neck, giving Rachel complete control. But he can hear her, and he can feel.

With a loud scream, Rachel pulls back the leather strap and cracks Baptiste over the ass with it so hard his skin immediately starts to turn red. The second strike draws blood.

"Unstrap me you worthless cunt," Baptiste screams at Rachel.

"You know, I don't think so," she answers. "This… Master Sommelier… is your penance for a lifetime of destruction. A stinging moment of pain for every "vintage" you've sold and ruined. This is for the girls from Thailand," she screams strapping him again. "This is for the girls from Mexico." Blow. "And Russia." Blow. "And Germany." Blow. "And Kenya. And Vietnam. And the U.S. And China. And the Caribbean." For every stripe she's delivered, Rachel has been standing on the side, across the bed from where Catherine and I are standing. But now, she moves to the back of the bed directly behind Baptiste. "This… is for every place you took little girls away from their families and shattered their souls, selling them piece by piece, for your own power and greed."

I know what Rachel is about to do before she does it and reflexively, my stomach turns. With Baptiste pulled spread eagle to the four posts, his heavy scrotum has no cover and when Rachel doubles the strap, raises it over her head, and drives it down between his legs. I can only imagine the excruciating pain that shoots through his groin, stomach, and chest like nothing he's ever felt before.

As Baptiste screams out and then starts to whimper, Rachel throws the strap to the side and walks toward the balcony. Her final strike at Baptiste was brutal and watching her move toward the doors, I imagine she's finally sated and needs to catch her breath. I couldn't be more wrong.

I look at Catherine and she's seething. Twenty years of hate and anger is also bubbling up inside of her and it strikes me now that it may be her turn for retribution.

A loud crack pulls my attention to the balcony doors as Rachel strides back into the bedroom. In her hands, she's cradling a thick icicle at least two feet long with a sharp point on one end and the tapered girth of a steel pipe on the other.

"What are you gonna do with that?" I ask her, worried she's about to stab Baptiste in the eye with it.

"Just have a little fun," she answers coldly.

"What's she doing?" Baptiste asks, turning his head to my side of the bed. From the panic in his eyes, I know he isn't going to like the answer, whatever it is.

I look to the foot of the bed just in time to see Rachel slide three inches of the icicle up Baptiste's ass. If she didn't have his full attention before, she has it now. He starts to whimper again and finally calls out her name. But the second he says, "Rachel…," she pushes in another inch.

"Come on baby," she taunts him. "Doesn't that feel good?"

When she pushes the icicle in another inch, it's clear by Baptist's reaction that the pointed end is starting to cause him some real pain. If I had to guess, it's starting to push through his prostate.

"That's enough! That's enough!" he screams. "Rachel, please…"

"I'll decide when it's enough," she screams at him, "and when I want your fucking input, I'll ask for it!" As he cries out, she gives the icicle another slow push and moves to the head of the bed across from me. "Look at me!" she barks, grabbing him by his white hair.

Baptiste turns his head and does his best to look at her, his teeth chattering. Between the frigid air blowing across his naked body and the icicle up his ass, he's starting to shiver. Rachel grabs his chin and yanks it to the side.

"Before we leave you to die a slow, painful death, there is one thing I want to know from you," she says, leaning into his face. "What is the fucking fascination with hummingbirds?"

I can't see Baptiste's eyes from where I'm standing, but I imagine they are as surprised by the question as I am. Then again, I'm not the one who had a hummingbird forcibly tattooed on my neck.

"I respect them," he says mustering what little arrogant energy he has left. "They're beautiful and they're resilient. They defy the laws of nature. They can flap their wings more than 80 times per second. And yet when they need to, hummingbirds can induce a state of torpor, a suspended animation to reserve energy. They can appear cold, lifeless, and unresponsive to the touch, even dead. But when it's critical, when their survival is at stake, they come alive. Their vibrant, beautiful bodies spring to life and against all odds, they survive." With a final twist of his head, Baptiste finds Rachel's eyes and utters the last words he'll ever say. "Hummingbirds are the closest thing in nature I ever found to you girls."

Rachel and I are so locked into what Baptiste has been saying, neither of us notice Catherine move to the foot of the bed. Two decades of sexual assault are shaking my sister like a steam vessel with no valve and no ode to the wonders of the hummingbird is going to relieve it. Catherine's fists are balled into stones by her sides, and her eyes are fixed on the thick cylinder of ice sticking out the back of her tormentor. Her persecutor. Her kidnapper. Her rapist, and torturer. I was wrong when I told Baptiste he would answer to me before tomorrow's sunrise. Tonight, he answers to my sister.

Quietly, I extend my hand over Baptiste's head and reach for Rachel Meredith. This woman who saved me. Smiling, she gives me her hand, lacing her fingers in mine. We turn back toward Catherine, and with a ferocious roar Jon will later say he heard on the front deck, my sister raises her foot and drives the remaining 16 inches of the icicle deep into Baptiste's bowels. His momentary shriek of pain before the deafening silence tells us she hit her mark.

Catherine looks at me and starts to sob, her bright blue eyes fully reflecting the realization that her enslavement is finally over. She collapses into my arms, and I hold her tightly. I lay my head against hers and like so many nights before, I close my eyes and give in to the darkness. This nightmare tried to destroy us. But squeezing my sister, I open my eyes and look into hers. Those icy blue beacons that pulled me through the dark so many times. We smile through the tears. This time when I open my eyes it's different.

Catherine is real.

Catherine is here.

Catherine is safe.

46

Moments later, Jon runs into the bedroom with his pistol drawn. I could see the instant relief on his face to find the three of us – and just the three of us – alive. When he burst through the door, Catherine was still wrapped tightly in my arms.

"Jon Joseph," I say pulling back and smiling at him, "This is Catherine."

"I've waited a long time to meet you," he says, beaming at my sister. "We have a lot to talk about," he adds, bouncing his head in my direction. "Your brother is a piece of work."

Catherine smiles and hugs me again.

For the next two hours, we retrace our steps, removing any evidence that I was ever on the Phaethornis. By sunrise, there will be a plausible explanation for the rest.

The truth is that, after our cleanup, Jonny directed Rachel, Catherine, and myself into the speedboat he had taken to find me and shepherded Sofia, Zuri, Natalia, and Mila into the small yacht that brought me here. Side by side, we cut through the night, riding a streak of moonlight toward land, and re-dock the boats at the Grand Isle Marina. This early in the morning, there is no one else around and quickly and quietly, the eight of us scurry through the mist, down the boardwalk and into Jonny's SUV for the drive back to New Orleans.

Not a lot is said on the 90 minute trip north. Just a lot of breathing, crying, and silent relief from the girls that the help they feared would never come, finally arrived.

Around 4:20am, Jon pulls up in front of the hotel so I can get my clothes and my gun from the room upstairs. I push the button for the elevator and immediately realize I don't have the patience to wait. I sprint up the stairs to my room and when I walk in and turn on a light, the faint smell of Magnolia still lingers in the air as though nothing has changed. But it has. Everything has.

I walk to the window facing the French Quarter and look out over the large bend in the Mississippi. I put my hand against the cold glass and from somewhere deep inside me, a deluge of tears comes. For the first time since I was a kid, I let myself feel the weight. The anguish. The responsibility. And then… the joy. My world, my forever future has changed, and I am grateful.

Grabbing my duffel from the closet, I take my holster out of the fake bottom of the bag and put it on. I snap my pistol into place. Baptiste might have been the biggest snake in the garden, but he's not the only one.

When I get downstairs, Jonny is waiting for me next to the car. I've never appreciated him more than I do right now, and I can see in his eyes, the feeling is mutual.

"Man, I'm so happy for you," he says handing me the keys. "Take care of the girls and be safe. Not sure how I'll explain why the SUV I checked out from Homeland here ended up in Los Angeles, but you have 28 hours to figure out my story."

"Maybe you just figured you'd had enough, and it was time to go home," I say.

"Maybe," he says throwing his arms around me. "You did it brother."

"We did it," I answer.

"Semper Fi motherfucker."

I squeeze him tight and get into the driver's seat of the SUV. Rachel has taken the passenger seat beside me. Looking into the back seat, I see the other women have fallen asleep. Even curled up in a car, it will be some of the best sleep they've had in years. I pull away from the curb and follow the signs to I-10. It's 1,900 miles from New Orleans to Santa Monica and if I get on it, tomorrow night we'll be having dinner on the beach.

Sometime shortly before 7am, Jon Joseph places a call to the New Orleans office of the Department of Homeland Security to report a tip he'd received during the night about a massive yacht 40 miles off the coast of Louisiana, rumored to be involved in trafficking young women.

According to the report Jon would file later in the day, at approximately 4:30 am, on a routine patrol just off the coast of Grand Isle, he encountered a small cruiser flying an upside down American flag indicating extreme distress. Onboard, he found five women and a teenage girl who claimed to have escaped a group of men trafficking them on a massive yacht called the Phaethornis. One of the women rescued indicated she worked for an undercover operation of the DOJ committed to rescuing and protecting sex trafficked women and girls. She showed Joseph her credentials and assured him she had medical resources in New Orleans where the others could be examined and cared for out of the public eye. There, they would be protected from anyone in the traffickers' network who might seek to silence them or do them harm. Once docked at Grand

Isle, Joseph released the girls into the woman's care to facilitate immediate medical help, with assurance from the woman that she would keep him briefed.

When the Homeland team, led by agent Joseph, located the Phaethornis four hours later, all they found was a dead man on the second level lying in a pool of shattered glass, three men in other bedrooms in deep sleep and barely alive from what would later be determined to be near toxic levels of Diazepam, and another tall male with white hair, deceased in the Master bedroom. With the exception of some bruising on his ankles and wrists, and some welts on his buttocks, the white-haired man showed no outward signs of trauma or injury. Curiously, the sheets beneath him were bloody and wet, but forensics would turn up no additional fingerprints, or hair samples other than those of the deceased.

Thanks to the helipad on the ship, the three sedated men were helicoptered from the Phaethornis to the primary hospital in New Orleans. When the Diazepam finally wore off, none of them could remember, or were willing to admit, how they got on the ship or why they would have been there. After an extensive background check that revealed no criminal records among them, they were released with the promise to call Homeland if they remember anything later that might be useful. They would not.

As for the deceased man with white hair, a fingerprint check through INTERPOL revealed his identity as Henri Allard, a French National wanted for questioning in at least six countries on the suspicion of human trafficking and criminal activity. Another four months of deep financial forensics will show Allard has been operating globally, but acutely in the United States, under the alias of Jean-Michel Baptiste, a major trafficker who managed to fly under the RADAR for nearly two decades, but whom Homeland has been tracking earnestly since a rescue in Houston by Joseph and his partner, Jake Hardy, almost three months ago. As the Phaethornis was seized as part of a criminal operation, it is now the official property of the Department of Homeland Security. It would make a hell of a party barge for the department Christmas party. But that's not how government rolls. Six months from now, accounting will quietly sell the yacht to a wealthy Emirati in Dubai for $237.6 million. All in all, a nice, unexpected surprise.

. . .

About 45 minutes outside New Orleans, Rachel reaches over and grabs my hand.

"Thank you," she says quietly, "for coming to get us." She pauses. "And I'm sorry. I really am."

"For what?" I ask her.

"For our last night in L.A. For not trusting you more. After the scene at the club and in the elevator, I was really worried that if Baptiste saw us together, he'd know something was up and he'd kill me. I also wasn't sure where Catherine was until the setup on the yacht. Once that was planned, I knew where she'd be and when. It was lucky you ended up with one of the invitations, but I would have let you know the details just the same. I knew you'd never stop looking for her and I knew the only way I'd ever get you back was to deliver Catherine to you."

"Get me back?" I question her. "I don't think I'm up for getting played again."

"I never played you," she says, almost hurt.

"Rachel," I almost laugh. "The first night I met you at Paddy's you lied to me. The second night, you slept with me and then disappeared with my case notes. The third night – after I saved you from killing your boss by the way – you tased me. You tased a Federal officer!... Oh, and then stole two months' worth of prescribed medication."

"All true. But you got your sister back, so I figure that makes us even."

"We will never be even," I say looking at her with an expression of gratitude and affection. "What you did to bring Catherine back to me, and at your own risk? I can never repay you for that Rachel. But what you can be sure of," I say squeezing her hand, "is that I'll spend the rest of my life trying."

Rachel smiles at me, expelling the breath she'd been holding. Unbuckling her seatbelt, she leans across the console and kisses the pink scar under my right ear where she tased me. Feeling her lips on that patch of skin again sends an electric jolt all the way through me. I couldn't deny the chemistry with this woman if I wanted to, and right now, I don't want to. Rachel kisses me again and moves back to her seat. She buckles in and takes my hand, pulling it across the space between us. She presses it to her heart. Then she turns her head toward the window, lays her head against the seat, and falls asleep.

47

It's been two weeks since the rescue on the Phaethornis and I'm still physically and emotionally exhausted. So much so, that I completely forgot my suspension ends today.

After our rescue mission in Houston and the ordeal with Baptiste which included seizing a $238 million asset, Jon Joseph finally received the long overdue promotion he deserves. Today he starts as the new director of the DHS office in Los Angeles which officially makes him my boss. His first action is calling to personally let me know my suspension is over and that I can pick up my gun and badge. I set a meeting with him for 4pm today. Close enough to Happy Hour to crack open the bottle of 18-Year Scotch I bought him for his promotion. Before we hang up, Jonny tells me we caught a new case he wants to discuss with me.

A month ago, a team of guerrillas stormed a middle school in Colombia and kidnapped 27 girls at gunpoint. The girls still haven't been found. Initial intel suggested the group intended to traffic the girls to the U.S. sometime in the next 30 days through Miami, Charleston, or Baltimore. Now it looks like they might be trying to bring them in through the southern border near San Diego. Jon wants me to take point on the operation two days from now. Sensing my apprehension, he says we can discuss it at four.

I head toward the kitchen to get some coffee and notice the door to Catherine's bedroom is cracked. I nudge it open and stand watching her sleep. She is curled around a large pillow with another one under her head and a third cradled in her arms. Now I know how parents of newborns feel. Watching their children sleep for hours, just to confirm they're still breathing. The first night we arrived back in Los Angeles from New Orleans, Catherine slept for 17 hours. I know, because I didn't sleep at all. I just sat and watched her breathe. Praying. How freeing and relaxing it must feel to know you're safe and nothing can hurt you?

My sister hasn't shared much with me about her years with Baptiste and I'm not sure she ever will. Truthfully, I don't care if she ever does. I'll find her an excellent therapist for all that. Knowing she's safe and he's dead is enough for me. We've spent most of the last two weeks talking, and laughing, and just getting to know each other again. We still have two entire lifetimes to cover.

After so many years under Baptiste's thumb, Catherine loves that we live so close to the water. Every day, she makes the short walk from our house to the beach and spends hours sitting on the sand and walking by the ocean. It's all I can do to let her out of my sight, but I know I have to. The same pull of freedom I feel from the Pacific is soothing her soul and I'm thankful for it.

As for me, for a couple of days after New Orleans I considered letting Jon keep my badge and finding something else to do with my life. Chasing human traffickers is a brutal job and now that Catherine is found, I could certainly find something less taxing and less dangerous to do. I recovered my sister. I've checked that box. But then I think about all the other Catherines in the world. The Milas. The Rachels. The Natalias. The Sophias. The Zuris. The Addie Jacksons. As hard as my job may be, they're the ones suffering. They're the ones being sold. Being raped. They need someone fighting to bring them home and why not me? Why not now? We don't even know how many Catherines are out there. But as long as there's one, that's enough.

As Father Elijah said to me the morning before the rescue, I cannot let myself be dismayed by the vast and overwhelming valley of dry bones that surrounds me. There are millions of women and girls around the world surviving on little more than the hope that someone like us will hold their tormentors accountable. The truth is, we didn't rescue the women from Baptiste. We only recovered them. Now, the hard journey of rebuilding their lives begins. Our job is to give as many of the trafficked as possible the chance to live again. Yes, that means guys like Jonny, and I have to live with the darkness. But where there is shadow, there is also light. One day, the women we free from the Hell they're living in will feel that light again. They will feel safe. And when they do, they will rise up like Ezekiel says, newly filled with the breath of God. They will thrive again, and they will live. How could I not fight to make that possible?

"Hey," Catherine calls to me, sitting up in bed. "What time is it?"

"About 9:45," I answer checking my watch. "How'd you sleep?"

"Better," she says. "Not so restless."

"Good," I smile. "You hungry?"

"Starving. You know anywhere that serves good pancakes?"

"There's a diner with the best pancakes in L.A. if you don't mind a quick walk to the beach. Belgian with Chocolate chips."

"Pancakes on the beach? Yes!" she says bouncing out of bed to change her clothes. Catherine reaches for the T-shirt hanging on her closet door, but then stops, runs to me and throws her arms around my neck.

"I love you Jake," she whispers, squeezing me tight. "Thank you for never giving up on me."

"I love you too Cath," I answer pressing my cheek to hers. "Thank you for hanging on."

I imagine the warmth radiating through both of us must be what happiness feels like. Neither of us harbor any illusions that life is suddenly perfect. Catherine endured one of the most harrowing things a human can experience, and it will take time to rebuild her life and her spirit. I don't know what that revival will look like, but

I will be here for it every step of the way. I will continue silencing evil, and I will love my sister.

I'm here for the fight. For as long as it takes.

ACKNOWLEDGMENTS

First, to everyone who took the time to read Hummingbird, thank you for taking this journey with me.

I've wanted to be a writer since I was six. For the last 30 years, that took the form of a career in the advertising and marketing world. Publishing *Hummingbird* is the fulfillment of a lifelong dream to write and publish my first novel and I sincerely hope you enjoyed it. I've already started on the second book, and I hope you will join me for that story as well.

Acknowledgements are largely about thanking the people who helped make a book happen. For me, that begins with my friend Susan Coppedge who kindly wrote the quote on the back of this book and was the first to read it once it was finished. Susan is a former Federal prosecutor and served as our country's first U.S. Ambassador-at-Large for the Office to Monitor and Combat Trafficking in Persons under President Obama. Four years ago, I asked Susan to lunch to tell her about my idea for a story with human trafficking as a backdrop. Her encouragement at that lunch, and in the years since, helped me believe this was a story worth telling.

For the beautiful look of *Hummingbird*, I have to thank my gifted friend and creative director partner Tina Tackett who took my words and crafted them into the book you hold in your hands. Thank you for your artistry and book design, but mostly for your lifelong friendship.

I'm incredibly thankful for all the friends who read early versions of *Hummingbird* and offered smart, insightful edits that made the story better. Kimberly Smith, Liz Burkhart, Mike Sullivan, Brian and Nadine Roberts, Chris Sears, Amber Tuggle, Jim Koonce, and Susan Coppedge, thank you for all your wonderful suggestions and support.

It's no secret navigating the publishing world is a daunting task for first time authors. Profound thanks to literary agent Kayla Bramante with Storyteller Talent Agency. Her encouragement and insights about how to market a new book and make it into something far more than a vanity project have been invaluable.

I know it's a writer's job to always know what to say, but there are no adequate words to thank my family – my incredible wife Ginger and our children Matt and Caroline. When I doubted whether I could ever get this done, they never did. I love you three more than I can say. You are what makes this all worthwhile.

And finally to my mother, Sue Tuggle, who has been, and will forever be, my biggest fan – it's real Mom! Now you can tell everyone.

ABOUT THE AUTHOR

MICHAEL TUGGLE has enjoyed more than 30 years as a professional writer in advertising and marketing. He is a proud graduate of Washington & Lee University and the University of Georgia. Michael's screenplay "Opening Night" was an Official Selection at the 2017 Beverly Hills Film Festival. HUMMINGBIRD is his first novel.